More Praise for THE WIDOW NASH

"With *The Widow Nash*, Jamie Harrison breathes fresh life into a fascinating period of American history. Indeed, the past has not passed. An adventurous, ambitious, inventive novel by a writer to relish." —Colum McCann, winner of the National Book Award for *Let the Great World Spin*

"This deliciously ambitious novel delivers one memorable character after another. None is more magnetic than the 'Widow Nash' herself, a fabulous heroine and irresistible travel companion. Jamie Harrison is a clever, gifted writer, and this shining book is flat-out terrific." —Carl Hiaasen, *New York Times* bestselling author of *Razor Girl*

"With Technicolor, vibrant prose, Jamie Harrison's novel *The Widow Nash* re-invents the Western from a feminist perspective; from the first page, the fierce Dulcy brings the reader into her unforgettable world. A novel as wildly original and memorable as the West itself." —Karen E. Bender, author of *Refund*, a finalist for the National Book Award

"If an Edith Wharton heroine had decided to ditch the bustles and the propriety and simply lit out for a fresh start in the Territories, she might have called herself the Widow Nash. Jamie Harrison has turned her formidable talents to breathing life into just such a creature, with astonishing results. Not only do we get a pitch-perfect evocation of a prior time, but a subtle reworking of America's great central myth— and its inheritor, Dulcy Remfrey, is so well rendered as to make you forget you're reading about any particular era at all. That's the mark of greatness." —Malcolm Brooks, author of *Painted Horses*

"From the profoundly generous and encyclopedic mind of Jamie Harrison comes a compelling novel of reinvention and the seismic sacrifices we make for difficult family. Every page contains a new historical and emotional discovery. Harrison is a true original, and she gives us a father-daughter love story for the ages." —Sheri Holman, author of the *New York Times* bestseller *The Dress Lodger*

"Debut novelist Harrison paints a lovely and memorable portrait of a desperate woman's flight to a new life . . . Harrison's lead is a strong and clever woman who is easy to admire, while the rest of the heroes, villains, and ambiguous sorts are as vividly drawn as the raw and terrible scenery of Montana. Readers will treasure Harrison's rich characterization and sharp turns of phrase."

—*Publishers Weekly* (starred and boxed review)

"When Walton dies before anyone can figure out what's happened to Victor's money, Dulcy decides that her only option is to disappear. Thus, Dulcy Remfrey turns herself into the young widow Mrs. Nash. This baroque setup is nicely balanced by Harrison's prose; the narrative voice here is restrained, with just a hint of quiet irony. And there's the fact that, as fantastical as the scenario might seem, Walton Remfrey is an entirely believable Gilded Age figure . . . Thoughtful, richly written historical fiction."

—*Kirkus Reviews*

"Harrison . . . writes atmospheric historical fiction featuring both drama and bizarrely entertaining humor. There are Whartonesque touches in the demarcations of society . . . A subtler comedy of errors among a quirky cast of characters."

—*Booklist*

"Readers prizing action above all may appreciate this Western saga by the daughter of author Jim Harrison."

—*Library Journal*

"I love this [book]; it's so good."

—Liberty Hardy,
Book Riot's All the Books! podcast

"With loads of drama (murder! theft!) and an empowering message, this guy is pretty unputdownable."

—*PureWow*

"Richly descriptive, *The Widow Nash* is the luminous story of a woman suspended between two worlds, one promising, the other catastrophic."

—*BookPage*

"I loved *The Widow Nash*. It was one of those books that, when I read the first page, I could barely put it down to do anything else."

—Nancy Pearl, librarian and author of the *Book Lust* series

THE WIDOW NASH

A NOVEL

• JAMIE HARRISON •

COUNTERPOINT
BERKELEY, CALIFORNIA

Paperback ISBN: 978-1-64009-036-1

The Library of Congress has cataloged the hardcover edition as follows:
Names: Harrison, Jamie, 1960– author
Title: The widow Nash : a novel / Jamie Harrison
Description: Berkeley : Counterpoint, 2017
Identifiers: LCCN 2017004027 | ISBN 9781619029286 (hardcover)
Subjects: | BISAC: FICTION / Literary
Classification: LCC PS3558.A6712 W53 2017 | DDC 813/.54—dc23
LC record available at https://lccn.loc.gov/2017004027

Cover design by Michael Fusco-Straub | mpluse.net
Book design by Elyse Strongin, Neuwirth & Associates

COUNTERPOINT
2560 Ninth Street, Suite 318
Berkeley, CA 94710
www.counterpointpress.com

Printed in the United States of America
Distributed by Publishers Group West

1 3 5 7 9 10 8 6 4 2

In memory of my parents, who were nothing like anyone in this novel, and for John Fryer, a very fine storyteller

CONTENTS

THE WIDOW NASH

Cordelia Blake had spent the beginning of the end of her first life, an All Souls' Day, wandering through the new east galleries at the Metropolitan, studying marble running girls and naked men with weapons, squinting at vases and sarcophagi and gold boxes that had once served as coffins. Upstairs, a millennia later, the girls and angry men were made of oil and watercolor, framed between the play of light on hanging game and wine glasses and lemon peels, sharp and beautiful; beyond every scene of human pursuit, and through the windows of the still lives, almost all the paintings had moving water and idealized ruins, smashed down by time or war or—possibly— earthquakes.

Which made Miss Blake laugh.

—Lewis Braudel, The Lady Vanishes, 1908

CHAPTER 1

ALMOST ALL SOULS' DAY

•

People paid attention when they arrived because Carrie was beautiful and Dulcy had jilted a rich man. Dulcy hadn't been to the city since, and once she had a glass in her hand, she found she enjoyed the spiky, expectant whispers, the open curiosity. They wore black dresses and masks, because they were in mourning for Martha, but most of the other women were pretending to be Marie Antoinette or Cinderella, and the dust from their powdered hair dropped like dandruff. Dulcy studied the men, skimming over the earnest costumes—kings and knights—for odder types like headhunters, sheiks, and Vikings, but as she often did, she found she liked the idea of people more than the reality. An insurance man at her elbow put aside his bullfighter's cape and cap and began talking about oysters— their different shapes, their increasing rarity—and for a little while his obsession, his sliver of strangeness, was interesting. But he didn't bear long study; he dissolved like a bad mint.

"I met your father once, at my club," he said. "A genius, but such a character. A little all over the place. I gather you are always in the process of traveling."

The insurance man came from a good family, with bundles of money, but his eyes were evasive, and she could see him work through his memory, try to suss out stories of the lost engagement. As he thought, he pursed his lips and moved them in and out.

All around them, Carrie's friends were playing divination games, courtship games: people were supposed to drip candle wax in finger bowls, blow out lines of candles and count the years they'd stay unwed, throw peels over a shoulder and guess what letter they formed, and bob for apples. There was no one in this room Dulcy felt like bobbing for, and probably no one who wanted to bob for her, but she allowed herself to be herded toward a dangling, tarnished hand mirror, to look behind her reflection for the man she would marry. For Carrie, who'd left a trail of peels every Halloween since she was three, the man in the mirror was peach-faced, hovering Alfred Lorrimer, who seemed to expand with wine and her attention that night, not so much opening like a flower as swelling like a sponge.

Dulcy stood obediently in line and opened her eyes on cue: she saw her face and a black curtain, and felt a train move below them, not a sound but a shudder. "Of course it was black," Carrie hissed in her ear, pointing to the drapery that faced the mirror. "I want you to have fun. Can't you just do that for a bit?"

A line of handsome, placid-faced men in silly costumes, waiting to be picked, found this amusing. "All right," said Dulcy, finishing a second glass. "How do you say *yes* in Halloween?"

"As if it were a language?" asked one man.

"As if it were a language," she said. The whole strange city vibrating around her, and here she was in a puddle of normal.

"We give up," they said.

"*Oui*," she said. "And *ja*."

"*Hohoho*," said the bullfighter. And: "Let me fetch another glass for you." When he headed off, as Dulcy slid toward the door, she could hear Carrie pipe away: her sister had spent years with their difficult father, months at the farm in Westfield helping their dying grandmother, but she was so happy to see people again, happy to be social. In the front hall, Dulcy put her finger to her lips when she asked a maid for her coat.

Outside, she walked away from the line of waiting hansoms, heading south down Fifth Avenue and Broadway. The champagne had done wonderful things for her brain, now that she was alone. In Madison Square she stopped at a cart for a cheesy Greek pastry and skipped on, giddy, wiping oily fingers on a churchyard's brick wall. Past the half-lit triangle of the Fuller Building, she turned east at the Rivoli Hotel and waved to the doorman, who was loading a collection of large people into a carriage. A moment later, she heard footsteps and turned to find the doorman hurrying up behind her. "A telephone call," he said. "We just sent someone to the apartment to find you."

In the Rivoli lobby the German at the front desk pointed to the telephone, and she tried to think through her panic as she reached for the receiver. If someone was dead, a telegram arrived. Telephones meant someone was still dying—an aunt upstate in Westfield—and there was a point to haste.

But it was Henning Falk, calling from Seattle, and Dulcy's champagne mood evaporated while the operator finished introductions. "Walton's dead," she blurted out. "His ship went down. You're calling to say he's drowned."

The man at the desk flinched.

"No, no," said Henning. "I met your father this morning at the docks. But things are missing."

She hadn't spoken to Henning in almost three years, and never before on the telephone, but he sounded so much like himself— perhaps the voice was a little tighter, maybe there was less of a Swedish lilt at the end of each sentence—it took her a moment to find a new way to worry. "Missing. Documents?"

"Well, yes, those too, but the money," said Henning. "We need your help; you need to come."

Dulcy's face was hot from alcohol and her bolt through the city, and she wiped a last flake of pastry crust from her coat. Jabbering people floated around the lobby, and a little man who looked like death was sneezing ten feet away, each seizure driving him deeper into the soft upholstery of an armchair. This "we" meant Victor

Maslingen, her father's business partner and her former fiancé: a royal summons. "You know that's not possible. I'm sure Walton's simply spent it."

"Nobody could spend that much. Your father is not well."

"Not well in what way?" There were so many possibilities.

"He's lost his mind," said Henning. "What little remained. He is having problems with his memory, problems with logic. He is balmy. Barmy."

"Put him on the train. I can meet him halfway and take him home."

"No, Dulce. He's weak and he's feverish and he unbuttoned in the cab and fiddled himself. And it's all of the money, entirely, every drop gone. Victor is very upset."

Every drop, fiddled. She felt Henning pick his way around a second language and an audience. At least six people in the hotel lobby could hear her end of the conversation; only the operator, who kept clearing his throat, could hear Henning's. She wondered if Henning was standing in Victor's library, if some of the static crackle was Victor, holding his breath, actually worried enough to have Henning beg her to come to Seattle.

"I don't want Victor near me. I don't want to have to talk to him or see him every day."

"He won't touch you," said Henning. "He doesn't want to see you, either. Please, Dulcy."

Everything pleasant was over, again. A door slammed a continent away, Victor leaving the room.

AUTUMN (SEPTEMBER 21 TO DECEMBER 20)

September 27, 1290, Chihli, China, 100,000 dead.

October 18, 1356, Basel, 1,000.

October 20, 1687, Lima, 5,000. A wave followed.

October 21, 1868, Hayward, California, 30.

October 27, 1891, Nobi, Japan, 7,273.

October 28, 1707, Hōei, Japan, 5,000.

November 1, 1755, Lisbon, 80,000.

November 11, 1855, Edo, 5,000.

November 16, 1570, Ferrara, 200.

November 18, 1727, Tabriz, Iran, 80,000.

November 24, 847, Damascus, 70,000.

November 25, 1667, Shemakha, Caucasia, 80,000.

December 16, 1811, New Madrid, Missouri. (Damage to St. Louis.)

December 16, 1857, Naples, 11,000.

December 16, 1902, Andijon, Uzbekistan, 4,700.

December ?, 856, Corinth, 45,000.

—from Walton Remfrey's red notebook

CHAPTER 2

THE RED BOOK OF DISASTER

•

Walton Joseph Remfrey, engineer, earthquake enthusiast, and sufferer of tertiary syphilis, had been born in the Cornish seaside village of Perranuthnoe in 1842. His father died when he was two, before his brother, Christopher, was even born, and when their mother, Catherine, died four years later, they were sent to the workhouse in Redruth.

At fifteen, when Walton gained an engineering apprenticeship in a copper mine on the Beara Peninsula in Ireland, he first scribbled into a plain leather notebook:

12 February 1858—
The roar was like a monster's breath, a dragon exhalation: red, yellow, then following darkness. Timbers came down like spears, through a boy's head, a boy's back, a rock fall landing with a sucking sound. I ran.

The notebook was a gift from an Allihies miner's widow, who'd plucked Walton from the novice pack and slept with him. Five boys died next to him in the mine that day, and forty-six years later, while he was sick in Seattle, he would scribble down variations of what had happened without knowing if they were memories or dreams. Dulcy wasn't sure if it made a difference: mining deaths were repetitive, and dreams were repetitive, and what did it matter, what was true or imagined? A big dark hole in the earth, and people dropped inside and disappeared. Walton had earned his nightmares.

Still, he'd enjoyed life:

8 August 1867—
I'm leaving, I said. Show me some mercy, show me your sweetness, and I'll make it happy with mine.
 No, no, no, says Ellen.
 It's my birthday soon, I said. I might die on that ocean and never know. Let me touch you—you have fevers, you might not last, you need to know, too. And, well, isn't this wonderful?
 It is, she said. Most other things are worth forgetting.

Walton had worked just as hard for his syphilis as he had for his dreams, but even before his illness, he tried to keep topics separate. Sullying the body was all good fun, but his mind deserved a system. He worked his way up and purchased two new journals, black and dull red. He scribbled an introductory limerick about a maid in his rooming house into the black one (*There once was a woman from Norway, who'd happily kneel in doorways*). By the time he was twenty-five and had saved enough to leave the Beara mines, he had separate notebooks for his travels, his scientific theories, his favorite poetry. The first brown leather notebook became a record of his financial life, while the red had the right look for disaster. He traveled with scissors and glue, pens and ink and blotting paper, trimming and pasting down newspaper accounts of tragedy, pornographic cartoons, stock prices. When he was older, he put most of these journals aside for weeks at a time—he was a busy man, not a dilettante—but the black, the red, and the brown averaged an entry a day for most of his life.

• • •

When Walton's last ship from Africa (Cape Town to Wellington to Honolulu to Seattle) docked on the morning of October 30, 1904, Henning Falk found him perched on a trunk on the docks, clutching his satchel of notebooks. He was singing—

> *Columbo went to the queen of Spain and made a proposition,*
> *But what she wanted most to do was fuck in the prone*
>> *position.*
> *The queen of Spain then said to him she'd give him ships and*
>> *cargo,*
> *He said, "I'll kiss your royal ass if I don't bring back Chicago."*
> *He knew the world was round-o. The queenly cunt he'd*
>> *pound-o.*
> *That fornicating, royal-mating son-of-a-bitch, Columbo.*

Henning was no sissy, but as the lyrics rolled out, and people veered away from them, he stuffed Walton into Victor's maroon Daimler. Walton hated automobiles, and the horror of the vehicle broke the melody in his head. He began to talk about the fact that it was almost the anniversary of the All Saints' Day disaster in Lisbon: a great wave after the shock, thousands crushed as they prayed in swaying stone churches. "And now here we find ourselves, old friends together in another port city prone to shaking."

Henning asked about Walton's other luggage, the proceeds from the sale of three mines; Walton said he thought he'd thrown the money overboard as an offering to the gods of seasickness, and that the thing to do, now that he could smell rocks and a city, was to have a razzle-dazzle, and find a woman or two.

• • •

Back in the other world, Walton's daughter left New York on her third train across America. Dulcy's full name was Leda Cordelia Dulcinea Remfrey, but no one but distant relatives and teachers had ever called her Leda. Her hair was thick and brown, and her eyes were large and brown. She had a long face and nearsighted eyes, a figure that was generous without being lewd, and nervous movements. She was twenty-four years old with good posture but the shadow of a limp from breaking her leg as a young child. She seemed patient to people who didn't know her well, but she had a bad temper and a habit of saying cruel, articulate things she later regretted. She was flawed in other ways, but she loved her sister and friends and aunts and even her older brothers, though at a distance. Her mother, Philomela, had died when she was ten, and she'd spent much of her life since then traveling with her father. She'd only missed this last trip to Africa to spend the summer in Westfield, New York, watching her grandmother Martha die. She loved her father, and she was happy enough to see him again alive, but she did not want to see her former fiancé, Victor.

When Dulcy, still trimmed in black, reached Seattle on November 5, 1904, Henning Falk met her, too. It was raining, and he was wet despite an umbrella, the city and harbor and man all shining like metal. Henning never looked quite human, anyway: when he smiled he was golden and angelic, but at rest he was so sharp-angled and preoccupied—long, slanted gray-blue eyes, high cheekbones, and hooked nose—that people moved out of his way on the crowded sidewalk here, just as they had in New York.

With Dulcy, he was usually lighthearted, almost silly; he was only a year older. He hummed, used the wrong slang, talked about a play he'd just seen, offered her a cigarette. Victor would never notice, he said; Victor had stuffed the apartment with spruce boughs to ward off the smell of Walton's many medicines. But though Henning didn't explain the crux of the issue as blatantly as he'd described what Walton had been doing in the auto, by the time she arrived at Victor's apartment in the Butler Hotel, she understood that at least one million dollars—the entirety of the profit from the African mines Walton had just sold on Victor's behalf—really was missing. Walton had arrived with a letter from the mines' new owners, hoping they would do business again, but there'd been no other hint of the profit, gold or cash or bankers' notes or documents.

This explained why Victor, who hadn't spoken to Dulcy in three years, was willing to see her: he was virtually ruined. "Drained dry, tapped out," said Henning. "Mightily buggered. He paces and he boxes and he watches your father, waiting for him to remember."

Dulcy didn't pretend to mind Victor's pain. "And what does my father do?"

Henning smiled and looked away. "He tells stories about earth shocks."

It was early morning, and an army of bowler-clad men moved around the cab, a school of fish in a port city, under a sky clotted with gulls. "What does the doctor say?"

"That it's in his brain; I wanted to say well it's always been there, hasn't it? This is just the last stage, true?" A wagon of seltzer bottles dawdled in front of them, and he pressed on the horn. "Victor's angry, but he isn't drinking. He is awake all night. They should both go to clinics. Different clinics." He flicked his cigarette onto the wet cobbles. "The point is all the goddamn notebooks. You must see what might be new, what he might have written down before he forgot everything." He slowed the Daimler for a trolley, and a covey of office girls, pressed together under a glass awning, surged forward into the rain. Henning watched until the last had boarded. He met Dulcy's eyes and smiled. "He doesn't let me out often."

· · ·

And what would cousin Henning do, if he could get out? Different things than Victor Maslingen, honey-blond coward, rich, pretty, tortured brat. They seemed only to share the same color hair and a great-grandfather, a Swedish fisherman who'd married a Danish fisherman's daughter and started a minor herring and cod empire (not really a minor thing at all, in the Baltic). One son kept fishing, but the other bought a bigger boat to ship his catch, and by mid-century Victor's branch of the family had a fleet of ten. They ran barricades during the American Civil War, while Henning's side raised chickens and taught school. Victor's father invested another rich bride's dowry in Pacific Northwest shipping and timber. Henning's father, a middling playwright, drank himself to death. By the time Henning got into trouble, and his cousin took him in, the whole notion of family equality was long gone, but they had settled into roles: Victor dealt with bankers and ideas and dinner conversations; Henning was pure and pragmatic, a weapon, the man for direct action and dirty work: newspapers, unions, bribes, and beatings. He was tall and wide-shouldered but moved quickly. Dulcy had often turned to see him leave a room she hadn't realized he'd entered.

Victor had used his inheritance to buy hotels and newspapers, but had wanted a faster profit, and it came with an introduction to Walton Remfrey, engineer, fixer, inventor of machines aimed at safety—engines and portable braces and magnometers, gas masks and heat suits and probes, hoists and bolts and engine designs— with a royal pedigree. Walton had been trained by Michael Loam, inventor of the man engine, a hoist to bring men up from a mile-deep ore. Loam, in turn, had been trained at Wheal Abraham by Arthur Woolf, who perfected the Cornish steam engine. And Woolf had been trained by Joseph Bramah, who invented the world's first hydraulic press, Queen Victoria's favorite water closets, an unpickable lock, a bank-note printer, and a beer-making engine. Walton had access to an army of engineers who knew what not-quite-depleted mines should be bought and how and when they should be refurbished and reopened: copper in Butte and Keweenaw and Arizona, silver in Idaho, everything imaginable in southern Africa, where he'd managed to stay in the game despite the expulsion of other Uitlanders—English and Cornish outlanders—during the Second Boer War. He'd been in and out of the Cape Colony, Natal, and Transvaal for years, gathering options, keeping an eye out for the next big territory, and in late 1900 he swapped Boer partners for British and helped Victor buy three flawed copper mines. In September of 1904, before he climbed aboard the boat to Seattle, he had sold these mines, now gold mines, for a hundredfold profit.

Victor, his office papered in African maps, would never see the scene of this triumph. He would not get on a boat, and did not even tolerate trains well. He disliked being off-balance, and forays into wine and sex and emotion rattled him badly. He had no direct knowledge of Africa at all, and now that Walton had returned empty-handed and empty-headed, the whole adventure might as well have been a dream. The money was gone.

Despite Henning's explanation, Dulcy still found it hard, arriving at the Butler Hotel—not grand by New York standards, but at least marbled—to feel that there wasn't a small vault of gold left. Victor owned the whole hotel, and lived in the top two floors, just as he had at the Hotel Braeburn in New York. Henning would tell Victor she needed to rest from the train ride, but she went to her father instead and startled him out of a nap.

Walton began talking immediately: no greeting, no surprise at seeing her. In his dream, he'd been in the mountains, in some Ottoman area, and a kaftaned nurse had given him a bed on the ledge of a cliff, ideal for the view of the rock strata looming above and a canyon below. But one of his legs kept dragging him closer to the edge when he dozed off, and finally he woke in midair. "I felt like a bird with wet feathers," he said. "There was nothing to be done but fall."

A crane trapped in a greenhouse, soggy and white, all sharp angles and flopping plumage. He was flushed and his long hair was damp and tangled; he'd lost twenty pounds since she'd seen him in July. Someone had stuffed him into a high-necked, long-sleeved nightshirt and given him red wool socks. Except for the ceiling-high French windows, the room was similarly padded: cushioned carpets, velvet walls, a tapestry that showed dancers who had very short noses and legs. Victor had packed the room with palms, as if he thought he could coax Walton into an African memory. Maybe Victor thought Johannesburg was a jungle.

She read through the doctor's notes and found no obvious slide: he didn't have fresh sores, his vision was fine, and much of his confusion could possibly be put down to overmedication, rather than end-stage tabes dorsalis. He'd never looked like someone with syphilis: he was a good-looking man, outwardly austere, a cultured figure with a solid sense of humor, tall and lean with a strong, bony face. He dressed well and spoke well and no one meeting him guessed he was sick, let alone that he'd been raised in a workhouse. Under the bespoke suits he tracked the progress of potential sores with pens, drawing circles and stars and arrows around potential gummas, the necrotic holes many tertiary syphilitics developed. His lesions came and went, but they rarely left a scar and almost never appeared on visible skin, his face or neck or hands. He kept a chart in the last pages of his medical notebook listing rumored victims and the men (and women) he'd met at the world's clinics, with notes on the duration of what he called their *benign suffering*, and at every clinic, worn down by language—chancres, preputial edema, indolent buboes—he'd peer through doors at the other, hidden patients, his imagination wrestling with the horror of dissolving eyes, food falling through an open cheek. Some people survived for decades without the events he dreaded: a dropped nose or penis or mind.

Dulcy read the spines of the books on his table—mythology, minerals, medicines—while he told her about the ship home, a new plan to buy diamond mines in Namaqualand, the injustice of being kept captive as he recovered. The cold air from the open window cut through the violet and aspidistra fug, and while she listened she arranged the talismans he always carried: a soft chunk of native copper, one small root of silver, an acorn of gold. He began to wind up: If he could not walk down a sidewalk, was he truly alive? Where did they think he would go, an old unsteady man? Why were his nurses ancient and ugly? He hissed—in a whisper like a magpie call—that everyone was trying to take his money and his medication, and that he'd appreciate Dulcy locating both. His medicine chest had been replaced by a bottle of Bromo-Seltzer and a bellpull. He wanted a new doctor, and he wanted his potions back.

The chest had been taken away when he'd been found trying to jam several substances up his nose. "Henning says you took too much of everything. They're afraid you'll kill yourself."

"I should think it would be a relief." His eyes fogged. "I had forgotten that you and Victor had reached an agreement."

"We haven't," she said. "I've come to see you." She gave him a sip of water, but he kept his eyes on the window and a roof across James Street, where a young workman hurried to patch some tar before the rain fell again. Clouds scudded behind the building, which had a glassed turret and an open door. It looked like a fine place to hide, but she doubted the workman would be allowed inside for long. He'd stacked lumber next to the tar bucket, and she wondered if the person in the turret would have a roof garden.

"My bad moments are due to the state of my stomach. The bilge they give me—raw cabbage and rolls with wheat like quartz shards. Fetch that journal, the one on top."

He pointed to a gaudy turquoise silk-covered notebook at the end of the bed. "A new one?" she asked, before she took in a dozen jewel-toned journals nearby. "You're starting fresh?"

"No," he said. "The same old. I spruced them up a bit. This one's for dreams; I seem to spend half my time having them now. I found a talented Hindu binder in Cape Town."

"Why this color?" she asked.

"Daydreaming. Looking at the sky."

Not Seattle's sky. The air above the workman across the street was a resolute battleship gray. Walton, man of science, had never cared about the sleeping world before. He smelled boozy, but maybe the spruce boughs in the hall had ruined her nose. She was surprised that Victor, who was terrified by illness, would knowingly have Walton under the same roof.

But: the money. She flipped the new book open and stared down at someone else's writing, a baby's jiggery lines. "Oh, Dad."

"What? I had such visions on this last ship, beautiful things. A woman appeared to me—semi-classical, you know—and as she came closer all the fog or fabric fell away entirely." He smiled, locked on other skin even though his own looked as if it would crack over his cheekbones. "She was soothing."

Inside, he still believed he was beautiful and adept, fast and smart and smooth. Dulcy started to drizzle, tears rolling down her face. "What the hell is wrong with you, Dulce?"

"You can barely hold a pen. You must have brain lesions."

"Spare me, please. I'm only a bit punky, and if your fiancé could find a real doctor in this fogbank town, there'd be no problem at all. If he can't, I'm off."

"He's not my fiancé." This was how things would fall apart, if Walton kept it up.

"Well, I'm sure that's news to him." But he looked away, a retreat. Walton was arrogant, but he wasn't Victor; he hadn't spent life on an untouchable plateau. So much hung on keeping both altitude (though Walton still used the word as a synonym for drunkenness) and a certain dose of self-deprecation, even in a nightshirt, even with a tremor that could thresh wheat. She watched him seesaw, searching for a safe change of tangent. "I would appreciate some meaningful medicines, darling. You'll set these people straight. I have a snake in my gut."

"No," said Dulcy. "You don't."

"A snake on fire, running up my throat to my brain. Go fetch a real bottle."

One snake would lead to another—he could talk about nearly stepping on a rattlesnake in a Nevada silver mine for hours. She stalled by turning pages: the newest entry was a description of a childhood dream, about being small and trapped. At the end of *underground, you can hear the rocks scrape and talk*, Walton had scratched out *and talk* and replaced it with *and swell and growl*.

"Is your silly sister cavorting in the city?"

Dulcy nodded. Swanning, dancing, running a finger too far up timid Alfred's sleeve. And why not? The workman across the street moved with economy and grace. She liked his curly hair, and wished she were in the turret, though it made her queasy when the man walked near the edge. She was no good at heights.

• • •

An hour later, Dulcy walked into Victor's murky feudal study, an acre of Canadian rain forest smashed into four hundred pompous square feet. Her face was calm and scrubbed, and she wore a flattering moss-green dress that went well with the paneling, but her mind seethed. She didn't want to be here; she didn't want to be anywhere.

Henning gestured to a chair. It took her a moment to make out Victor in the gloom at the far end of the room, showing a kingly profile, backlit by the window she had to face. He nodded but did not come to greet her, and she sat down, rattled and queasy, and pretended to look around. This study was almost identical to the one she remembered from his Manhattan apartment, but maps of Africa had replaced logging regions in the Pacific Northwest, and everything that could be thrown—lamps, chairs, ashtrays—was metal or wood. No porcelain.

He said nothing. He looked well, though her examination was sidelong. He seemed a little thicker, not plump but plush; his frame was still graceful at thirty-five, though he'd never been boyish. He'd shaved his moustache and looked a little less like a catalogue illustration. He had glass-green eyes, smooth skin, even features. His voice was steady and low, his movements careful and contained, his mind a system of angry crevasses.

He thought things to death, one reason why he hadn't greeted her: she needed to crawl through all three acts of the revenge drama he'd been writing in his mind before he'd deign to see her as human again. She was here only because of money; she was here because she was the keeper of Walton's unreliable mind. They'd stacked all the bright notebooks on the table next to her chair, and somewhere above her head she heard a muffled phonograph play soothing violin music for the man himself, who was being bathed by two matronly nurses. Twice Dulcy thought she heard Walton's cane hit the tile in time with the music.

Henning lifted the black notebook from the top of the stack and handed it to her with a glass of red wine. Tea leaves, or maybe a bowl of entrails: she was the oracle who'd be executed if she failed to divine a story. "We've looked through each book," said Henning. "And we can find nothing helpful."

She wanted the wine, but she opened the black journal. New shiny silk outside, the same musky interior. The first pages, the only part she'd ever seen, were in Cornish, and presumably gave an explicit account of every moment young Walton had spent touching a woman's skin. Her brothers had filched it one afternoon when Dulcy was about ten, shrieking with joy while they worked out words like *bronn* and *pedryn* and *kussynnow*, *lust* and *seks* and *plesour*. "Say that we saw this, and we'll drop you in a hole," they said. Her mother had just died, but theirs had been gone for years.

When he sailed to America, Walton had left his Cornish evasions behind and recorded women's names and dates. Failing names, he'd provided short descriptions:

Beryl, red top and bottom, plump. Bisbee, 2 April 1877, morning.

Mrs. Jas. Merton, Lafayette at Sixth Street, 13 November 1891. A horrible laugh.

A Circassian! Every hair braided! Constantinople, 7 and 8 August 1899.

Dulcy turned pages and determined a method: if Walton slept with someone more than a few times, an asterisk next to the name led to a separate page of hash marks and insights. Jane, his future first wife (*some progress; a conversation about alternative methods given her aversions*), was the ninth woman to earn this honor.

Across the room Victor shifted his feet and picked his nose. Sometimes, when he was nervous, he was capable of forgetting himself. Dulcy took a sip and turned pages. Philomela, Walton's second wife, Dulcy's mother:

So pliable, so reactive.

Dulcy had never been sheltered, but she didn't want to know everything Walton's memory had to offer. She flipped ahead and a *carte de visite* of a naked woman with a limber leg fell on the floor.

Henning stretched out his own long leg, capped with a good boot, and dragged the card closer. He placed it facedown on a side table. She turned to the last entries.

Ayama, so very tall, Cape Town, last days of August.

Edina Branstetter (Brandsdotter?), brunette, so ill, 2 October, near lifeboats.

So, so, so. Dulcy wasn't sure if Walton had meant that he wasn't well, or Edina wasn't well; if Edina had been well to begin with, she might not be for long. Only one of these women had given Walton syphilis, but he'd been criminally generous in giving it back to the world.

"Did you know?" Victor finally spoke, but he hadn't budged from the far side of the room.

"Know what?" asked Dulcy, eying the pile, wondering what was missing.

"That he was sick again."

There was no *again*; Walton had been sick for twenty years. Victor had always been good at avoiding unpleasantness, and Walton certainly hadn't volunteered the truth when they'd first bought the mines, or when he'd introduced his daughter to his new business partner. After the engagement, when business in Africa was going full bore and Dulcy finally understood Victor's ignorance, she'd watched his face flatten as she told him his partner was syphilitic: he shook his head and walked out of the room, and she never brought it up again.

"He said he was a special case. He seemed so well, and his mind seemed so clear. Is it possible someone reinfected him deliberately? To bring me down?"

"There are no special cases," said Dulcy. "And this has nothing to do with you."

"This has a great deal to do with me."

Well, she thought. Don't tell Walton that he isn't the center of his own universe. She started to speak, but he held up a hand: silence.

Dulcy's face burned, and she could feel Henning study the floor. "We must cure him."

"Victor, there's no cure. It kills everyone."

"Nonsense," he said. "Your father has mentioned a half-dozen new therapies."

Dulcy, with the evidence of Walton's optimism sitting politely on her lap, looked directly at Victor for the first time. His face was still perfect, but his eyes jumped around the room. The part of Victor that checked and double-checked most situations had always veered away from thinking sanely about Walton's disease. She could imagine her father's monologue: all he needed was another month of electrical magic wands or radioactive hypodermics in an Italian or German clinic. All he needed was another batch of nurses.

Dulcy put the black book down and tried to speak without rage, derision, or drama: Walton's brain had been invaded, and it might finish dying slowly or overnight. There was nothing anyone could tell her about the disease that she hadn't heard from forty doctors at twenty clinics in a dozen countries, and if and when there was a new therapy, it would be too late for Walton. He might remember what he'd done with the money, and he might not.

"No," said Victor. "You're wrong."

"I don't understand how this money could simply have been lost," said Dulcy. "If it was a check, never cashed—"

Another wave of the hand, but Victor's voice had a hint of a whistle. "Didn't he write you? Why didn't you go on this trip? Perhaps there's a code in this book," he said. "This particular one, filled with numbers. You would know, wouldn't you?"

He pointed to the black book. He only thought that because he couldn't comprehend the notebook's topic. Henning, who plainly could, stretched again in his chair.

"My grandmother was ill," said Dulcy. "He sent one message in three months." *Thieves everywhere, but I've outwitted them, and have found a safe way in strange winds. Curries everywhere, too—I've begun to like them! Seattle by the end of October, New York on the ides of November.* Even for Walton, who was fond of words like *ides*, this had been theatrical. She'd read the telegram on the porch steps in Westfield, bees zipping through the apple trees in the sticky September heat. Martha had died a week earlier, and Carrie was crying upstairs. Dulcy had tucked the message in her apron and gone back to planting bulbs—she was happy to hear he'd been eating, but she had no patience for imaginary thieves.

Now she opened her bag and held the telegram out to Victor. He didn't move—Henning had to bring it to him. The handsome cheek twitched while he read, and the brain on the far side of the dainty ear churned through a variety of unacceptable thoughts; she knew he was suffering. "I don't understand," he said.

"I'm sure he hid the money. He loves to hide things, even in the best of times."

A commotion overhead, and the nurses' voices piped. Henning reached for the notebooks. "We need to replace them before he returns to his room," he said. "Or he'll be upset."

Dulcy finished her wine. "I think you're missing his accounts book," she said. "It used to be plain brown leather. It might help; I'll give a look."

● ● ●

Since 1867, Walton had traveled thousands of miles each year. Once he established himself financially—and once he fell ill—each grand tour had four legs, four purposes: the acquisition and tending of mines, research into an earthquake (preferably recent and deadly), pleasure, and bodily recovery from task number three. Mining and earthquakes determined the itinerary, though the order might vary, and pleasure was possible anywhere, but a clinic was inevitably the last stop.

Why Victor needed Dulcy, beyond the fact her father was crazy: she had been his companion on half of these trips since she was fifteen, and she knew he'd hidden treasure everywhere, because she had been the keeper of most of the keys. She had six in a jewelry pouch for different bank boxes across this country, and she knew where others were hidden in the Manhattan apartment. Some of this urge to hide money came from his workhouse days, and some was a matter of control: he didn't want his sons, Dulcy's half-brothers, both beginning bankers who'd already been given plenty, to tell him what to do.

Victor knew about the trips, but not the tendency to hide; he thought he needed her simply because the Cornish stuck together. Henning had tried telegramming the men Walton worked with in Africa and had learned nothing. Walton's greatest asset had been this birthright: he'd given Victor a whole network of men who knew what rock was profitable, promising, played out. Those men wouldn't talk to a civilian, but they would talk to Walton's daughter. People bitched about the Irish and tribalism, but they had no idea of how far it went with other Celts. Cornishmen were so white and so Protestant and sober, so competent and buttoned-down, that Good People in the States, who assumed they were actually English, never doubted them. The Cornish mining captains all had good educations, careful accents, well-built suits. They asked no favors, and kept their voices down, and no one recognized that they had successfully achieved one form of world domination.

On the other hand, Walton and his oldest friend, Robert Woolcock, had been particularly successful because they chose their tribal moments carefully in Africa. When most Uitlanders—either English or Cornish—were expelled in 1899, Walton learned to selectively shed his English accent and flaunt German bank accounts. Woolcock, with a Boer wife and a Swahili mistress, stayed in southern Africa throughout the war, funneling Victor's American money into devalued mines. By the time the war wound down to guerilla attacks, and other Uitlanders flooded back into the Rand, they'd purchased the right mines. Walton and Victor stuck to the partnership despite the broken engagement and made a fantastic, now missing, profit.

Dulcy usually knew so much about what Walton owned and leased that her dawning sense of ignorance about this last trip was hard to accept. He'd had no chance to stash a cent since he reached

Seattle. Henning had vetted the nurses, and had his four brothers follow them on off-hours. He'd brought the brothers over from Sweden one by one, dotting them throughout the Northwest, all doing small chores for Victor while they studied trades—tailor, printer, carpenter, detective. Now, in Victor's time of need, they were in Seattle. The morning after she arrived, she watched all five Falks from her window, fascinated enough to get close to the pane. From this distance, she couldn't tell the difference between the men until they began to move, and Henning's wolfy lope gave him away.

On her first night, while Walton slept, she brought all of the notebooks she could find into her bedroom. She'd been given a room with a connecting door, presumably so she could spy, but it only meant she had to listen to him talk in his sleep. She'd heard him through dozens of thinner-walled hotels, but now there was no one to seduce, no one to amuse but himself, and his mutter was unnerving: *Deafness. Daftness. Daphne's dapper Dan.*

Each book had thick new boards and quilted spines, but even the original endpapers had been saved, still covered with a blurred mess of old addresses, some erased and some simply crossed out. Hotels and houses, different lives in different inks and ages, scrawled on trains, on boats, in clinic beds. On each creamy new inner board, Walton had glued down a fragment of the original covers and written a fresh title and date above: *Theories of Science, by myself and others, belonging to Walton Remfrey, October 22, 1904, Transvaal.* His subjects had stayed the same, but all the titles were newly phrased— *My Understanding of Seismic and Volcanic Events, My Family & Life, My Financial Affairs, Advances in Medicine, Travels Around the Globe, Correspondences, Anomalies of the World, Green Things* (this was really Dulcy's book; she'd thought she'd lost it but he'd had it rebound in a silk leaf pattern), and *Adventures* (the short pithy title of the black book)—and all but Dulcy's were signed with his signature and date and "Transvaal." Only four of the ten had fresh entries—the black book, earthquakes (*Sichuan, August 30, 400 dead*), medicine (*I fear I am become a leper*) and travel (*I must never board another of this company's ships*). No fresh code, no account numbers, riddles, names. She had no idea what towns he'd seen on that last trip, and now, given the inscriptions, she wondered if an incident or a fever or a night of drinking had been enough to tip him into idiocy.

Henning had shown her the bill for the rebinding, and the work had cost a fortune, old penny notebooks dressed up for ten and twenty pounds apiece: more evidence of brain rot. Walton had stuck with his old color schemes: the notebook about anomalies, originally a faded blue peacock paper, was now rich lazuli silk; the family book was innocent peach velvet. Dulcy couldn't remember why theories were garnet or miscellaneous facts and statistics were dark jade, but if Walton thought of illness and pain and medication, he'd reach for dark yellow, the color of bad urine. Green, surrendered years earlier to Dulcy, was meant for gardening. If he wanted to make a comment on travel, he'd find the gray of oceans. If he wanted to enter information about a recent earthquake, he'd think of red blood soaking into the shaken ground, and the new fabric brought the notion home with appropriate vibrancy. Love poems were rosy pink, but sex was black.

It all made sense, to Walton; it would never make sense to Victor.

• • •

Where's your money book?" she asked the next morning. He'd been served invalid's oatmeal with chunks of canned peach and knobs of butter and brown sugar, presumably to fatten him back to health.

"With me, always. I didn't have that one touched."

She could see it now, half under his pillow. "Could I see it?"

"No, dear. You'll give it to Victor." He slid it inside his robe and combed out his hair with his fingers. "He's a murderous neurotic. It's unfortunate that he still loves you."

"I would not, and he does not. He needs to know where you put the money from the mines. Then we can get on the train and be done with him."

"He longs for someone who knows him. He longs to not have to explain. I do, too. I don't know what you're going on about, moneywise."

But she thought he did—the side of his mouth curled in a smile, and his mood was fine and cocksure. He stabbed out the chunks of fruit and left the mash. "Do you remember where the money is or not, Dad?"

He drained his tea and looked down at his shaking hand; by now she understood he shook most of the time and had noticed his strange, choppy walk. "What money?"

She waited. "Don't give me that sort of look," said Walton. He tried for glib, but his eyes were flustered. "Why do you keep asking? I remember that it's safe. It will all come clear when I stop feeling so spavined. And, Dulce?"

"What?"

"If he must see the account books, take out the pages with the Western accounts. He has nothing to do with them, and you might need them someday."

• • •

That afternoon, when the nurses dragged Walton down the hall for another bath—cleanliness, godliness, Victor believed in living underwater—she slid the brown money book out from under the pillow. She sliced out the two pages that listed accounts in Seattle, Denver, and Butte and tucked them into her underwear drawer next to the bag of keys Walton had always had her keep. She brought the notebook down to Victor's study.

This was the only journal which had grown thinner rather than fatter: when Walton updated his accounts, he ripped out most old notes, and so only fifty or so pages of onionskin were left, though the little silk folder pocket sewn into the inside cover was stuffed full of receipts, and though he had, for some reason, decided to keep drafts of seven different wills. The first will left everything (not much) to his first wife, Jane; after she died in childbirth, he'd left his small fortune to Philomela; in 1895 he'd left everything to Dulcy's older brothers—Jane's sons—Walter and Winston; in 1898, it had all gone to his mother-in-law Martha (*who hates me but has good sense*). In

1900, *all my worldly possessions to my daughters, who at least enjoy life*; in 1902, angry with everyone, he instructed that any survivors of his era in the Cornish orphanage should split the estate. And in October of 1904, on his way back from Africa, he left a little to all his children, with Victor overseeing the consequent mess.

None of these theories of life were signed, and Dulcy was surprised he'd saved them. For a memoirist, he had an aversion to reflection. Most pages were refreshed yearly:

1904—WHAT I POSSESS

Tab 1: Storage, listed by nation and city.

Tab 2: Bank boxes and accounts, same.

Tab 3: Properties: Westfield and Manhattan; Chile page 10, Butte page 12, Bisbee page 13, Pachuca page 14.

Tab 4: Properties sold, and profit noted: Redruth, Blue Hill, Lone Pine, Hailey, Douglas & Bisbee, Calumet, Butte.

Tab 5: The Transvaal.

Tab 6: Stray items (bonds, art, furniture of value, scientific instruments, horses).

Under Tab 5, Walton's last note was dated September 12: *Sale pending Verre Bros.*

Pend away, thought Dulcy, watching Victor flip through the translucent pages. Today he acted as if there were nothing out of the ordinary, as if they were all at ease with each other. "This is all copper money, from the New Levant in Namaqualand, and this is from that small investment near Cape Town. None of it has to do with the Swanneck, the Berthe, or the Black Dog. And how would he have made a deposit anywhere, if he hasn't left this building?"

Henning copied the accounts, and Dulcy ran the book back to Walton's room—happy splashing sounds coming from the bathroom—before they sat down to lunch in the long dining room.

Victor, talking to a point near the salt, announced that he didn't know how to proceed.

"Perhaps someone should speak to the binder," said Dulcy. "He must have spent a good deal of time with the man."

Victor dabbed at his mouth. "Would he really chat with an Indian?"

Victor's cocoon was absolute, but Walton would have talked to a Martian, if a Martian could bind a book or cut a suit or whisper about a vein of ore. Henning elaborated: they had wired Walton's hotel, his engineers, his doctor, but they needed to be circumspect, and could finally only ask if payment had been satisfactory, if all was well. Could she perhaps wire her father's partner, Mr. Woolcock, and suggest that Walton was ill but improving, a little confused? No one could know the full disaster.

Walton and Robert Woolcock had been friends since the workhouse, which meant that Woolcock had known everything there was to know about Walton since approximately 1846. Dulcy ground pepper onto her chowder and decided not to puncture the impression that this worked in one direction: Woolcock likely knew everything about Victor, from his physical aversions to his poor understanding of smelting. "I'd say Dad was ill on his return, and I wanted to make sure there were no loose ends, and that I asked in greatest confidence."

"As if you were not telling us?" asked Henning. He sat across the table from her, watching a sleet storm bash the grand windows.

"Yes."

"But will you tell us?" asked Victor. He'd finished his glass of wine and stared pointedly at the bottle on the sideboard, but Henning ignored him. Now he looked at Dulcy directly, a small but ugly flare of self-pity and old longing.

"Yes," she said.

"Please pass the pepper," said Henning calmly.

"He tried to get into his trousers this morning," said Dulcy. "If I were you, I would freeze any joint accounts. But let him walk a bit, or he'll just keep trying to run."

"I suppose he was the one who taught you how," said Victor, reaching for the wine bottle.

• • •

That night, as Walton watched her glue the two account pages back into the brown book—he insisted it be remade, though she had copied the information and tucked it into the brocade jewelry bag—they listened to Victor hurl things in his office, and heard Henning talk him down. A half hour later, they heard the elevator.

"They're out to find a girl," said Walton. "He's soused enough to try that now. They could have had me along."

Dulcy tossed the brown book in his lap.

"I'm sorry," said Walton. "I'm sorry I said that, and I'm sorry you ever met him."

Too late, but he couldn't have known, and apologies were rare. She kissed him good night, went into her room, and locked the door to the hall.

• • •

Years earlier, after Walton had introduced them, Victor would sit near her without quite touching, and this containment made her head reel. It seemed like a promise, and of course it was one. When they walked, he would touch her elbow and no more; when they sat together at parties, he was always two inches away, heat instead of touch. He was so handsome, so smart, so painfully shy: she daydreamed a revolution, a revelation, a man reborn, but that had been before the clarity of their first physical encounter.

In 1901, Henning had only been in the country for two years—he was slender, young, and silent, more of a servant than a cousin—but as he circled in the background, he was already vigilant for something Dulcy hadn't quite understood. She was a veteran of Walton's world, and she knew Victor loved her, could tell that he desired her, but whatever difficulty he had—not entirely mysterious, as she watched his ramrod parents across crowded Manhattan ballrooms—so much of him was considerate, and literate, that she didn't pause to worry. Dulcy was fond of saving people, and the sense that Victor was somehow suffering within his phenomenally handsome skin, and the idea that she might change his life by allowing him even a small loss of control, was powerfully tempting.

In early November of 1901, they set a wedding date for the following spring—sealed with a peck against her hair—and started into the fall season of dinners and dances. She was a horrible dancer; he steered her with glancing fingers. But just before Thanksgiving, after people opened cases of champagne at a city mansion, and Victor, who never drank, had several glasses, he argued with some Princeton friends about who had enlisted, and who hadn't, in the Spanish war three years earlier. Victor had his hands up to box, but another man simply swung a bottle. He missed, and Victor was on him.

Dulcy hadn't really comprehended what followed; she'd only wanted it to stop. A few weeks later, as she sailed to London with Walton, he pointed out that "murderous rage," in a sentence, was a very dry thing, and the sound and vision of it was quite wet.

After the men were pulled apart, Dulcy tried to calm Victor down in a side room, forced him to let her touch him for the sake of sponging blood off his face and his hair, and suddenly he was on her, saying he *loved loved loved* her, rubbing his face against hers as if he thought he were kissing her, ripping her skirt up, forcing himself inside her, with a hand against her mouth. She wasn't sure if it was to hide her voice or hide her face. Minutes later he wept, he apologized, he was unable to look at her, clearly revolted by the naked, sticky, panting moment. He said that she had to understand that everything would be different when they married; now that they'd done this, everything would be easier, and sweet. He'd never been so happy in his life; he'd never been able to do this thing before.

She said she had to clean herself, but instead she walked out the door without her coat. In the morning, lying in bed in the crowded top floor of the 19th Street house, she thought it through with mounting nausea and found no intellectual way around the problem. Was this something that happened to other people, all the time? She didn't think so, but how did she even start the conversation with city friends, people she saw twice a year? On the other hand, it was a simple decision: she didn't want to marry someone who was insane, who was violent, and who would apparently never want to make love in the way she assumed people made love. She felt sympathy for his ruined mind, but it was coupled with a profound aversion, and fear.

She wrote a letter saying that she released him from his promise and hoped that he would have a good life. They had misled each other. She slid the emerald engagement ring in the envelope and had one of the Germans from the corner hotel take it up to Victor at the Braeburn. She packed for Westfield while Carrie raged at her: Carrie thought Victor was wonderful, and wonderfully well connected. She was finally of the age when she could go to dances, and Dulcy was ruining her life. Dulcy showed her the bruises on her neck but didn't elaborate.

Over the course of the day, a series of pleading notes and apologies arrived by messenger, and then a clichéd screed: he would spit on her grave; he would treasure the knowledge of her regret and loneliness. *You cannot live without me*, he wrote.

I can, thought Dulcy. That's the point.

That evening he sent Henning. This was their first real conversation: Henning said that Victor would like her to know that he would never do anything "like that" again, that by having "accepted" him, she had cured him.

"Cured?"

Henning writhed in the chair, without visible movement. She waited until he finally looked at her directly. "Do you think I should change my mind?" asked Dulcy.

"No," he said, reaching for his hat. He seemed relieved by the question. "He'll only ever touch you when he's angry or drunk."

She went back to the farm. Martha, not understanding Dulcy's reasons, was smug—she hadn't liked Victor, and Dulcy now found this reassuring rather than maddening. Carrie passed on rumors from the city, sometimes out of kindness, and sometimes out of spite: people said Dulcy was a cold fish; that she'd had affairs during her travels with her father and fretted that Victor would discover the truth; that she'd been worried about all the normal things marriage entailed (this last was especially amusing). There had to be an explanation: all that money, and good looks. They didn't usually go together. Why ever had Dulcy let that one go?

But as stories of Victor's unraveling had begun to float up to Westfield—fights, some eruption at a whorehouse—any notion that she was in the wrong was lost to growing panic. Dulcy and Walton were due to leave for London and Portugal and Africa, a trip they'd planned as a last hurrah before the wedding was canceled. Now Dulcy slipped into the city a day early, and saw a doctor a friend had recommended, and understood she wasn't free of Victor, after all. She told Walton—who'd had the sense to not tell Victor about Dulcy's presence, or the trip—they'd have to delay, but Walton reacted to the news of her condition by telegramming a London doctor and booking them onto an even earlier ship. They were gone by nightfall.

• • •

In Seattle, three years later, Dulcy was careful with her telegram, and Woolcock wired back immediately—

> Dulce, all grand—hell of a turnaround, fine deal made, hope the Lord is happy, ask the Da when he'll voyage next? Keeping mine eyes on happy places Huns and Sows haven't noticed yet.

"Sows?" asked Victor.

"The English," said Dulcy.

Henning looked amused, in a shuttered way. "Would he say more if you pretended to be your father?" asked Victor.

"I won't," she said.

"Mr. Woolcock wouldn't feel the need to explain to Walton," said Henning.

She'd be half in love with Henning, if he didn't terrify her. She wrote again to Robert Woolcock:

> DA ILL NOW BETTER SOON PLEASE ADVISE ON NEW PROPERTIES AND REMAINING OPEN ACCOUNTS.

In the long hours before the reply, Dulcy imagined the wizened engineer studying the slip of paper.

> ACCOUNTS HERE? HOW ILL? WHAT DID HE LEAVE? WILL ADVISE ON NEW PROSPECTS.

It was her turn to stare at a piece of paper. When she took Walton his lunch that day, she tidied his room, piled books by topic and color, and rattled on about wanting to be organized so they could leave soon. Did he have keys for a bank box or hotel box in Cape Town or Johannesburg, keys for her to keep from the last trip? Any bit of information she should pass on to Robert if Walton had some sad turn of health?

"Why would I keep a box in a tottery country like that, dear?" asked Walton. "And Robert knows to tell you everything."

For the next round of wires, Dulcy was given permission to be circumspect but honest about the degree of Walton's illness and the missing funds, and Woolcock sounded authentically frayed, even in telegramese:

> I CANNOT BELIEVE. I WILL BE DISCREET. WILL HE RECOVER?

Dulcy didn't know. That night she once again heard Victor in the gym, drumming on the punching bag while Henning talked through the rage, soothing, singsong, matter-of-fact. When they stopped, she listened to all the usual noises—drunks, wagons, ships' horns; Seattle was a small city, but still a city—and sorted through the receipts in the brown book, peering down through the glasses she had too much vanity to wear in public.

She came up with nothing. Walton had docked in Cape Town on September 5 and checked in to the Mount Nelson Hotel. The next day, while Martha was beginning to die back in Westfield, he'd set up an account at Bank of Africa and given the bookbinder fifty pounds. This was mind-boggling: Dulcy wondered if the notebooks had gotten wet on the trip over, or if some blow to the head had driven Walton into this extravagance. He'd picked up the tab for a table of six that night at the Mount Nelson—Woolcock would have made the trip south from the Transvaal to meet him—and the next day he'd consulted a doctor she remembered too well, and then headed north to the mines, a two-day journey.

There was nothing about meeting the buyers on September 12, nothing about a transfer of nine hundred thousand pounds. A good hotel in Johannesburg and another doctor there, and then a train ticket south again, and two nights back in Cape Town. And then, after all this activity, nothing but receipts for a train to Port Elizabeth and stubs from that beach town—laundry, an Indian meal, whiskey, a pharmacist's tab for a stomach fizz, morphine, and mercury. She looked in the black book and all the others, but there was no entry for any of those days, because all the notebooks but the brown were at the binder's. He'd rendered himself mute—how had he possibly spent his time if he wasn't recording his time?

A week later, he was back at the Mount Nelson. She imagined him wandering through Africa's spring in the linen suits she'd found crumpled in his trunk, his mind filled with silk samples and women rather than mines. On September 27 he paid the Cape Town bookbinder one hundred pounds, and on September 28 he boarded his first ship home. There was nothing in the notebook to show if he'd left for even a moment when the ship docked in Australia or Hawaii.

Ides, wind, brain rot. He hadn't lost anything important before, not even a pair of eyeglasses, but here they were.

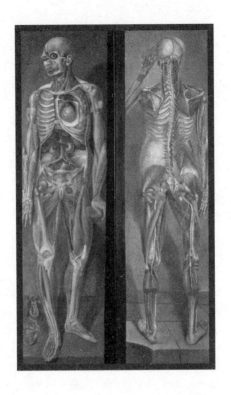

Even when you are positive that a person has syphilis, it is not always best to say so . . . Indeed, in practising medicine, you will see and understand many sins and blemishes of which you must appear oblivious.

—Daniel W. Cathell, 1882

CHAPTER 3

THE DEEP YELLOW BOOK OF CURES

•

Walton may have told Victor that he'd been cured by a fever treatment in Italy, but he knew better, whether or not he'd speak the truth out loud. Syphilis killed everyone, fast, slow, showily, invisibly. It had killed Dulcy's twin brother and sister soon after birth, and it had killed her mother Philomela a few years later. The yellow book was filled with happy theories—written with a flourish, in a large hand—that Walton later covered with crabbed rage, big black hindsight *X*s, and brutal details: *cock oozes, chancre on tongue, the lump on my ass cheek tells their lie.* He'd attempted lymph and blood inoculation, fever treatment, platinum, tellurium, vanadium, gold, every purgative in current use. He read historical accounts of the guaiacum cure and had Woolcock buy a lignum vitae plantation in Nicaragua near the harbor of Bluefields, where they'd first landed to cross the Isthmus in 1867.

Walton had either been lucky for twenty years or his energetic search for new treatment had been at least partially successful. He had recovered from palsies, bouts of mercury poisoning (ointments were the recognized treatment, but he'd tried older methods of inhaling or injecting; mercury always worked, after a fashion, but it deafened him, damaged his kidneys, and ulcerated his mouth), and a considerable amount of what was known as "excitability." He had yet to experience a stroke, blackened teeth, blindness, meningitis, or—until now—memory loss. Unlike William Lobb (a fellow Cornishman), Calamity Jane, Oscar Wilde, Paul Gauguin, Randolph Churchill, or the thousands of other men and women who died from syphilis each year, he was still alive.

But the symptoms of tabes dorsalis—spinal neurosyphilis, wasting, and paralysis—had begun. Before, whenever Walton fretted about numbness while traveling, they would abandon a disappointing earthquake (or an earthquake that disappointed Walton's theories) for a *progressive clinic staffed by intelligent men*. In Zurich, Berlin, Madrid, Walton was always reassured that there had been no measurable change. Dulcy would remind him that the numbness in his hand might have been caused by a binge of rant-writing to geology journals, or that the tingling in his foot had first appeared after a slide down half an Ottoman mountain, but a doctor was always more convincing with the same explanation. But now movement gave Walton away: some atrophy of the nervous system gave him a herky-jerky walk, so that he misjudged distance and slapped his feet down, and he had a strange way of moving his jaw when he was thinking.

In Seattle, Victor, a Princeton man, sought out Ivy League talent. The doctor was elegant but spent more time talking to Victor than to Walton. After her father left the room, Dulcy, on the far side of the room—she always took the far wall with Victor—watched as the doctor laughed—*ho, ho, ho*—patted Victor's arm, and brought up a promising new treatment involving cobra venom.

Victor jerked his arm away. "My father's tried that," Dulcy said. "I would like a realistic appraisal of his condition."

The physician shrugged and looked for his hat. "He's dying."

The next doctor to visit the hotel apartment was a frayed mess from Philadelphia, a Swarthmore man who insisted on talking to the patient directly, and he very tentatively suggested that Walton was doomed. He had gray sponges of hair above each ear, and nothing on top.

"Fool," said Walton. "Find someone who knows their business, Henning."

The doctor's smelly bag made her think of an English expatriate who'd tended to Walton in Greece. That doctor had just come from the amputation of a tumorous foot, a souvenir he'd forgotten by the time he'd asked Dulcy to reach into his bag for a set of calipers. Her first feeling had been surprise, even a little wonder and humor, but the ragged filaments of tendon had done her in, and before she could budge she'd vomited into the bag.

"Serves you right," Walton had said to the doctor.

Dulcy had knelt in the mess, focusing woozily on her lunch of greens and orzo, and threw up again: shreds of lamb and dark red bits of hot pepper. "Miserable girl," the doctor had said. Walton had slapped him.

This new doctor, who staggered whenever he turned his head and steamed with the afternoon rain, wasn't capable of giving an insult. "Mr. Remfrey, have your hands always shaken like that?"

"Of course not."

"If your daughter wouldn't mind leaving the room, it would be helpful to examine other areas."

"Fuck yourself," said Walton. "I am intact and unsored."

The doctor, showing a bit of spine, marched over to the open French window and latched it.

"Well, what shall we do?" asked Dulcy.

"Morphine," said the doctor. "With a regular emetic."

"Your mother was an inbred whore," said Walton, ratcheting himself out of bed to reopen the window. "Heal thyself, cretin."

Walton worried about his eye falling out, but he had no notion that his brain was losing control of his limbs. He stalked up and down the halls of Victor's apartment like a marionette. Dulcy made his nurses take him outside, and though he moved along with some of his old pace, the foot slap continued. "But I'm dead if I don't walk," he said. "I need the air."

Victor insisted on interviewing staff personally, probably with an eye for spies, and chose a dimpled redhead for a nighttime nurse. "This won't do, will it?" asked Henning, his eyes sad.

"No," said Dulcy.

Henning hired the next applicant, a stout Bavarian with bottlebrush hair. She carried her own metallic thermometer, and Walton, without his glasses, went into a frenzy: the giant woman would put the giant needle in his cock, kill it for good.

Not such a bad idea, dozens of women too late. He moved quickly; she rarely had a chance to warn them.

• • •

Long, dark, still days, such large windows and so little light. Dulcy had Walton's bed moved closer so he could watch gulls and pelicans, and once he claimed a falcon brought a fish to the sill. No one believed him. People hid in corners of the apartment. They were all very quiet—Victor had a problem with noises. He liked some voices, notably Dulcy's and Henning's, but as Walton's grew weak and hoarse, it grated despite the English accent. Victor had told Dulcy that he'd never liked his mother's voice, even when he was a baby, and maybe he hadn't liked to be touched, even then. Some of his fitness mania had to do with his pleasure in not having clothes against his skin; on the other hand, he couldn't bear people seeing that skin. He liked soft, light fabrics, which worked well with his Byronic profile. It was all very misleading.

Their truce continued, careful indifference. Victor and Henning disappeared most evenings, and Henning shrugged when she asked where they went: banquets, the opera, dinners with nervous investors for new hotels. Victor inevitably sent Henning back up the elevator for things he might have forgotten, a neuroticism she'd once found charming. She learned to wait to make the run to the kitchen or to search through the papers on Victor's desk, where she found doubt and rage, half-written letters to creditors and debtors and unions and commands to Henning:

Tell them I'll use them for ink if they threaten a stoppage.

Tell Monty we'll find him, wherever he goes.

And:

Tell the doctor to give us some hope, or I'll break the old fool's cra-
nium myself and dig my money out.

Victor's aversion to laying a hand on another human was now
reassuring. She wondered how far Henning's duties went. His only
free nights came when Victor visited his new fiancée, whose existence
had dripped out over the course of the week. The girl's name was
Verity; her father, predictably, owned a dozen Western newspapers.
Walton, in a stage whisper: "He's found someone perfectly
unhaveable. She looks like a tall goat, a thin stoat, a human moat."

His language had become obsessive, unaware. If he said "putting
on the dog" in the morning, someone later would be lying doggo,
being dogged, suffering through dog days, and (eventually) acting
dodgy, which then led to Dickens and daggers and digging. It took
a night's sleep to break into a new letter of the alphabet. She couldn't
imagine that he'd really met the fiancée; Victor wouldn't have
allowed that to happen.

Victor's chef, a tiny, dun-colored man named Emil from
Strasbourg, liked to put capers in every dish and sent a menu of
dinner options to the captives each afternoon. Walton always
requested the same few things and ate little of what arrived. After
the first week, once Dulcy heard the chef's tiny lurching footsteps
move above her bedroom in his attic quarters, wine bottles clinking
gently, she went to the kitchen and made Walton the things he truly
liked, despite the enthusiasm for greens and lean meats he claimed
when he spoke to doctors—potpies and veloutés and puddings,
nothing fresher than parsley or an apple. She snuck a glass of wine
from any bottle Emil hadn't emptied.

On a pretty night after days of rain, when Victor had stayed home
with a head cold and she could hear him droning at Walton in the
library, she grabbed an open bottle and climbed out the window
onto the fire escape where she'd seen Emil smoke. The steps hung
only a story over the hotel's central roof, not as scary as the full drop.

She pushed the bottle out, and then a glass, climbed up on a chair and crawled out, and turned to see Henning perched a few feet away, smoking a cigarette.

"Get another glass," he said.

• • •

According to Walton, when Henning had left Sweden at seventeen, he'd been about to start his second year of university, with the intention of teaching literature like his parents. But his brother-in-law beat his pregnant sister, and when she miscarried and nearly bled to death, Henning set out to find him, then took the ferry from Malmö to Copenhagen before anyone fished the brother-in-law's body out of the harbor. He sailed on to Hamburg, then to Galveston, where he sent a telegram to his cousin. He'd worked for Victor ever since, moving up from an errand boy to an emissary and negotiator, working in his spare time and investing some of his own money in the growing number of film studios in Queens.

By the time he had to abruptly board a ship again late in 1901, this time to England after Victor had responded poorly to his broken engagement with Dulcy, Henning had begun to wonder at the point of returning. Victor had been drinking heavily, which always made him a little looser, a little likelier to act directly, and had started a fight at a friend's wedding party that continued at the bars in the Village. The next morning a dead rich boy was found frozen into winter mud in an alley off of Bleecker Street, and Henning was perceived to have the least to lose as an inquiry began. Victor's parents put him on a merchant ship to Southampton with a chunk of blood money in his pocket; Victor offered more if Henning found Dulcy in London and reported back.

In London, Henning did find Dulcy, and followed her long enough to understand what had happened, though he did not telegram Victor for weeks. He walked around the city, thought things through, and ended up buying himself a job at Clarendon

Studios. He held the cameras for *Alice in Wonderland*, and he even did well writing the scripts, because his very direct English had a good pithy ring. He read—he still read—all the hours of the day he wasn't working or sleeping around—and decided that he'd been born to record beauty: Shakespeare, fables, history. He didn't want to film a stage—why limit yourself if you didn't have to? Why not film *The Tempest* on a beach, or *A Midsummer Night's Dream* in a forest; why not give the words of the whole play underneath, while the image spooled out? If Henning could keep up, even with an immigrant's English, surely the average *schtuck* could manage.

"Schmuck," said Dulcy, as Henning explained all of this to her on a bench at the British Museum and promised that he wouldn't tell Victor about the pregnancy.

"I worry he'll kill you," he said. "If he knows, he'll kill you."

Victor also left New York in the wake of the fight, and he took the train west. He bought the Butler in Seattle, and when the Maslingen family deemed it safe for Henning to return to this fresh coast, the balance had changed between the two young men. Henning had a key for every lock in the apartment and the padlock on the wine cellar, the combination for the safe, the numbers for all bank accounts. Henning had said no to selling his stake in the London film company to help Victor through the African mess. He had planned to use his 5 percent of the African profit to begin filming plays in London in April.

"Does this ruin things for you, too?" Dulcy asked now, out on the balcony in Seattle.

"I'll be all right," he said. "I'm patient."

Henning liked to scribble down all of Walton's mythic memories, and twice during their stay in Seattle, he set up a camera and showed them some English films: *How to Stop a Motor Car, Alice, The Mistletoe Bough*. Walton wanted to watch them over and over, the projector overheating. On other nights, Dulcy and Walton would play rummy or cribbage, though he had trouble holding cards or pegs, and sometimes she set up a skittles game, though he couldn't pull his own top. Sometimes she read to him, and sometimes she gave him extra medicine and hid in her room. Sometimes he was himself, wandering from topic to topic: a plan to move to Veracruz to grow coffee, a consideration of his ultimate vindication by the Royal Society. When she got him to talk about the last few months in Africa, he seemed more or less coherent, but if she surprised him with a question about the money, he'd flinch, a little shard to the brain, and then they'd wade through confusion.

Did he want to see Carrie? she asked. Let her dance, said Walton. The Boys? Let them bank. "Carrie eventually," he said. "I can do without a lecture from my sons."

Eventually was an admission, which might help in the end, but he veered away. "Let's have a game: If you were a bird, which?" He'd never cared a thing for birds, but Henning had given him an illustrated Swedish guide, all the colors cheerier than nature, and the names broke him out of that morning's echo chamber: bats, battery, butter, bitter.

"A nuthatch," said Dulcy. The only bird that tended to eat upside down.

"*Sanglarka* or *notvacka*!" He was delighted. "Carrie, all tall and pink, would be a flamingo, or better yet a roseate spoonbill, but there's no good translation, naturally. *Skedstork. Spoonbillen.*"

He rattled on: owl was *uggla*, crow was *kraka*, bluebird was *bla-sangare*, curlew was *spov*. Gull was *gratrut*, which sent him spinning off to Gertrude, and Shakespeare. He summoned Henning for a copy of the plays and, dithering over which to read first, flipped the volume open to *The Merchant of Venice*. Dulcy, who was curled in the chair by the window and had fallen into her own fascination with Swedish bird names, knew the volume would be too heavy for Walton to hold, but Henning was so transparently happy she said nothing.

"It's an ugly play," said Henning. "And not fair. Have *The Tempest* or *Much Ado*."

"Ah, but it's the way our world works," said Walton. "Cunning, dunning, haunting, hunting, Henning, lending, lemming."

Henning sounded the last word out, and his face burned.

"I'm sorry," said Walton, suddenly sane. "My mind goes at its own pace. Please accept my apologies. You will outthink us all by the end. Tell Dulcy the word for hawk."

"*Falk*," said Henning.

• • •

Two weeks after Dulcy arrived, Walton demanded a dressing gown, insisted that they all dine together, and took Henning's seat at the end of the table facing Victor. He lifted an empty wineglass with an arched eyebrow. The staff hustled; Dulcy began to daydream of her own disappearance and tried not to watch her father talk and eat at the same time. Walton's newest topic was the Rift Valley, which would surely be the site of the next great hard-rock rush after Namaqualand. They should buy now, before the *fucking Germans* figured out the *fucking truth*. Victor, who hated swearing, chose his battles. "I have nothing left," he said. "You have lost my money."

"Don't fret," said Walton. "Your money is in New York, practically speaking. I had it wired."

"To which bank?" asked Victor.

"The bank you told me to use." Walton dabbed his mouth, lurched upright, and left the room.

Dulcy started to follow, but Henning stopped her: he'd hired an agency to search for a wire, but so much money traveled into and out of the Rand that the task had proved impossible.

"If he kept the profit as cash or a check," said Victor, "if he did not deposit it in some forgotten bank, it may have been taken from him on his way home. He talked of diamonds, but we can find no evidence he changed out the money. While I recognize his love of the symbolic, gold is hardly portable. He said something about a friend, a man named Penlawy who advised him, but our detectives haven't managed to find him. Have you met this man?"

Dulcy stared down at Emil's spongy fish. "Penlawy?"

"Yes. Charles, I think."

"Penlawy was his childhood friend. He was sliced in half by a rock fall when Dad was a boy. A fall of quartz, before he even went to Ireland."

She watched Victor's mind go dark. In the corner, Henning hummed. It sounded like a lullaby, and she tried to imagine his mother, singing to her little boy. "He'd have said if it was stolen," said Dulcy. "He's never shied away from assigning blame before."

Later, after Emil had tottered off to bed, she gave Walton a whiskey and made potatoes poached in cream, with a little sharp cheese. He ate like an ardent man for the first time since she'd arrived, and when he'd wiped the plate, he said, "Ah, well, I found out that someone from the bank had contacted wreckers, and they would have been lying in wait. I changed my plans."

"Lying in wait where?" If he had wreckers on his mind, land wreckers rather than the people in his childhood who'd raided foundering ships, he was back in Cornwall.

"Jeppestown," he said. "A man named Brahn oversees these grabs, and he kills."

She telegrammed Robert Woolcock again and learned that he'd heard of a highwayman named Brahn, but when Brahn was found, he didn't have a fortune, and when he was beaten, he didn't produce an answer.

The next day, Walton said, "The Hindu had seen everything in terms of hiding and thieving money. Wonderful stories."

The Hindu was the bookbinder named Iyer; he and Walton had become friends over the course of the expensive rebinding of the notebooks. Dulcy said she imagined Iyer must have plenty of his own money to hide, given his fees; she said the journals looked like pillows at an Indian wedding, gaudy wrapped gifts.

"You must be back to loving Mr. Maslingen's subtle high-society style," Walton said.

Vague to vicious in seconds. He complained of shooting pains in his eyes, and the next day the doctor visited and whispered that the right eye was bulging. Dulcy sent Carrie a telegram:

AFRAID YOU NEED TO COME. DAD QUITE ILL. DON'T
TELL BOYS YET.

And Carrie wrote back:

AFTER CHRISTMAS. VERY BUSY, IN FACT ENGAGED! I
DON'T BELIEVE A THING ABOUT HIM.

That night, while Dulcy lay in a bathtub, the room shuddered, the
bathwater moved in a new direction, and the buildings across the
street swayed. She watched the window glass move and thought
about what might happen next: she'd fall, more or less intact and
still wet, through the six floors below her, crushing the innocent
beneath her cast iron, cushioned by water and bubbles and the
fact that right now, feeling the ground throb, she felt a great indifference. People who cared the most were struck down in a dispro-
portionate ratio; death would only happen to her when she no longer
wanted it to.

When everything stopped moving, she slid down into the water
so that only her face and knees showed. Even underwater, she
could hear Walton howl in happiness through the wall. An hour
later, when she went to say good night, his bed was empty. Henning
found him at midnight at a tavern near the station, a ticket to
Sacramento and a suitcase in hand, four whiskeys into his escape.
Walton had never been much of a drinker, and he was sick on the
way back to the hotel, ruining Victor's car. He told Dulcy he'd been
on his way to Lone Pine, to relocate a successful mine, and when
he managed speech over the next few days, he said many other
things: that he had sold the African mines, that he hadn't, that
he'd been paid, that the buyers had refused to pay him, that there
were no mines to sell, that he had been in Chile, not Africa, that
his head hurt terribly, that someone should tell his mother he'd be
home soon.

• • •

Woolcock's account of tracking Walton through Africa arrived in seventeen numbered telegrams. Number fifteen was missing, which put Victor into spasms of paranoia; he and Henning had been off courting money when it arrived, and Dulcy was in the habit of checking his desk. It had alluded to her illness in Africa three years earlier, and it was nothing Victor needed to know. She burned it while she sat on the fire escape, smoking another cigarette.

The sale of the mines had been scheduled for September 12. Walton had asked the purchasers to draw up a single bank check, without percentiles to the partners (80 percent to Victor, 15 to Walton, 5 to Henning), and said he'd carry the check to Johannesburg himself. On September 10, he delayed the transfer of ownership by requesting gold and an escort in lieu of paper; such a request wasn't out of the ordinary in post-war southern Africa. He had asked Woolcock about who would be safe to hire but insisted that he not worry about coming for the transfer.

Now, Woolcock learned that the Bengalis he'd suggested as escorts had never heard from Walton, and people allied with the new owners said that Walton had arrived with five black men and left with gold. Nothing more, nothing less, everyone in a fine mood. The staff at the Mount Nelson said Walton had arrived alone on the evening of September 16. He seemed tired and carried a satchel. No one at the stations in Johannesburg or Cape Town had seen an escort of blacks, or heavy freight.

Dulcy had a fantasy: They would put her on a boat. Having proved herself with Woolcock, she would sail off, find the money, save the day, and disappear. Over the next few days, while telegrams darted back and forth and Victor roared directly at Walton about bankruptcy, humiliation, ruin for the first time, this fantasy—of running away being a useful thing, instead of a convenient act of cowardice—took hold, and during longer daytime walks Dulcy headed up Second Avenue for useful travel items, and up an even greater hill on Pike for the sake of character improvement and fitness.

On a windy day after the delivery of telegram seventeen, she turned to catch a section of a newspaper that had just blown from her hands and thought she saw Henning. Looking like Henning was not an average thing. She waved, but the man disappeared.

The next day, she left a bookstore (a new Baedeker for Sicily, Tunis, and Corfu) shadowed by the same sort of man, but this version of Henning had red hair. She walked on to the post office with letters for Carrie, her aunts, and Walton's brother, Christopher, who was the Methodist minister of Pachuca, near Mexico City. When her follower didn't have the sense or nerve to come in with her, she left by the side door, shedding him and trying to leave behind a crushing but nonsensical disappointment at the idea that Victor and Henning did not trust her. She should be flattered: they thought her capable of running away, maybe even of stealing a million dollars.

When she reached the apartment and the hall to the bedrooms, she saw Henning come through the door to the servants' stair. He slept at the other end, the guard dog near Victor's bedroom, but he was straightening his shirt, and when he saw her he looked away.

"You're a busy man," said Dulcy. "It's good that you have brothers to help with chores. What are their names, again?"

Henning met her eye as he fixed his tie, and behind him, in the stairwell, she heard a maid's footsteps. "Carl, Martin, Ansel, and Lennart. I believe you saw Martin."

"Where do you think I'm going to run away to?"

"Anywhere, I suppose," said Henning. "But he'll keep you here until the money's found or your father is dead. Make the best of this."

"Send me to find the money, then," she said. "I can't bear this."

He walked away without answering her.

Dulcy spent the next three days walking miles, losing her Swedish tails behind produce stands, in the museum, and—cruelly—on the ladies' underthings floor of the Bon Marché. The bone from her childhood break still hurt sometimes, but she embraced this bitterness, too. On the fourth day, Henning drove two of his brothers down to the harbor for a reversed version of Walton's travels—Seattle to San Francisco to Hawaii to Melbourne to Cape Town. She wanted to snap out a Walton quote—*They couldn't wade through hummingbird shit in boots*—but she ran out into the rain for one more walk, and when she returned, she stayed in her room or in Walton's, and listened to Victor walking the hall.

A few days after the Falk brothers departed, Walton announced that the proceeds from the sale of the mines would arrive with a man named John Viram Singh, on a packet ship called the *Silver Moon*, in the form of a check from the Bank of Cape Town, a different branch than the one he'd first remembered. He should have told them earlier. He had forgotten.

No such ship was scheduled into Seattle, but a *Silver Star* was due into San Francisco in five days, carrying a passenger named V. Singh. Dulcy, sensing misdirection and envisioning the debarkation of an elderly Sikh cloth or curry merchant, grew queasy when Victor reacted with elation. Henning decided to go to San Francisco himself, and Victor insisted that they go to the station together. At the platform, though she knew Henning was watching her, she studied the times for the eastbound Empire Builder. He did not look worried—Henning looked however he liked—but he leaned down and whispered, "Don't hook it, Dulcy."

"No one says that anymore," said Dulcy.

"Your father does," said Henning.

• • •

It rained; with Henning gone, Dulcy again stayed in her room or in Walton's unless she knew Victor had left the building. They'd gone two days without having to see each other when there was a knock on her door.

"Let's go out," Victor said. "We should have a conversation."

"I'd rather not," said Dulcy.

"I'd rather we did," said Victor.

One of Henning's remaining brothers drove the car to the feeble new botanic gardens. It wasn't raining for the first time in days, and as they walked, not talking, Dulcy peered at plant labels.

"I'm engaged again, you know," said Victor, finally.

"I had heard. I'm happy for you."

"No, you're not," said Victor, smiling. "But I can live with that. I can't imagine being happy for you with another man."

A covey of older women fluttered by, eyes on Dulcy, who preferred to let that sentiment slide away. During their engagement, Victor had planned gardens for her: a greenhouse on the roof of his Manhattan hotel, walled gardens at the Hudson Valley house. He had never shown an affinity for live items, either flora or fauna, but he'd understood this about her. Now she tried for something like a normal conversation. "Does your fiancée like to garden?"

"I haven't heard her mention it."

"What does she like to do?"

He frowned. "Now you're worrying me. Perhaps I'm better off without her. She isn't curious, or experienced; she doesn't understand the world."

Dulcy turned back to the waiting car. "I believe he's lost the money," she said. "There's no point in keeping us here."

He kicked a stone off the path. "There's no point in letting you go, either."

They returned to find that Henning had met a Mr. Singh, who did in fact carry a package for Walton, but it was a last rebound notebook, rose-pink poetry. Dulcy burst into tears—it was a bad habit, but an honest one—and retreated to a balcony off the sitting room. If she went to her room, she'd hear Walton warbling "Skip to My Lou" or a stunningly filthy sea chantey, and if she ran to the fire escape, she'd hear Victor beating his own mind to death in the gymnasium. Henning joined her a few minutes later, and they smoked in silence while he studied the women at a party on a balcony below them, guests of the hotel proper. Dulcy watched his face and thought of fishing birds, crows on fences, cats on rodents.

And in the morning, Victor introduced a new plan: since nothing stirred Walton's memory in the apartment, perhaps they should get him out and about. If he were given the "illusion of freedom," of fun and play, would he rediscover his mind?

Victor was flushed, and Dulcy didn't immediately understand. "I suppose he'd love the theater," she said. "And we could use some games here. A dart board, or billiards."

"I do not enjoy billiards," said Victor.

This meant that he wasn't good at them—if he wasn't good at something, he couldn't enjoy it. Dulcy thought she'd enjoy being bad at many things, if she could only try. "You're good at Ping-Pong. And if you dislike it, you wouldn't have to play. You'd just have to buy the table."

"And watch you play, with Henning."

Henning was pulling on his coat, taking time over his scarf. She almost said yes, and then she took in Victor's face. The nurse was yammering about rain and inappropriate shoes. "I had a trip to the outside world in mind," said Victor, "though I fret about the dangers. He's not well."

"I'll keep him alive," said Henning. "I'll keep everyone alive."

He had the nerve to look at her, though she knew it took an effort. "You're taking him to a *woman?*" she asked. "What about the poor woman?"

Victor gave a fake laugh. "I'll find the right person," said Henning.

Dulcy had a pen in her hand and thought of throwing it like a dart; her interior monologue was pure mining Cornish. Henning, prowling the misty streets—he might be stuck here with maids six days a week, but there was no question that he fucked himself silly in the off-hours.

"Everyone will be safe," he said. He looked happy, and young, a little wide-eyed, wild to be out of the building. If she could have painted a human state, she'd have called this *Vigor*. He was going to make his Grecian marble physique move in a variety of warm, soft directions, after he handed over a giddy Walton to a hag with a dozen gold coins. "But I agree about the games," he said. "Something pleasant in these dark months."

"Go away," said Dulcy.

• • •

Happiness, safety: she thought through the range of definitions as the men set out for Chinatown, Walton with his head high in a dove-gray coat. But he responded to his outing by sleeping for twenty-four hours, and when he woke he told Victor he hadn't been to Africa for ten years, and that something was growing in his stomach. A new doctor was summoned, a cold, calm Presbyterian, an advocate of the Graham school. Decades of hydro- and electrotherapy had left Walton underwhelmed by such approaches, and he was fractious from the beginning. In the absence of female comfort, he believed in opium, alcohol, and mercury. Dr. Dagglesby believed in bran and cold surfaces and—weirdly—large quantities of shellfish. He asked Walton to take some steps ("note the tabetic gait"), looked at his hands and feet, ears and eyes, and asked him to stand naked and perform certain exercises. Walton said that he would attempt these after a quick trip to the toilet, but once inside he locked the door.

"Mr. Remfrey does not have long," said Dr. Dagglesby.

"Please keep your voice down. Please think of something to help," said Victor. "We would like him to be as relaxed as possible. Peace of mind may help his memory."

"Where would he store that memory, might I ask?" said Dagglesby. "His brain has shrunk to the weight of a web."

They all knew Walton had been able to hear this through the door. Later, when she heard him pace on the other side of her wall, she left him to it and turned out her light, and later still, when she woke to the sound of a woman laughing, she rolled over, trying not to think of Henning. Another resonant croak brought her into the next bedroom, where she found a heavy woman, a bouncing billow of flesh, seesawing on top of Walton's frail body.

They gaped at Dulcy. "The floral flouncing floozy flummoxed me," said Walton.

Dulcy slammed the adjoining door, slammed her own door, and ran out in the hall and slammed Victor's library door so hard that the pretty bronze knob came loose and bounced away, which brought enough relief to allow her to head to her room to pack a valise. She took the servants' stairs and was just short of the hotel mezzanine when she faced Henning, who'd taken the elevator all the way down and run up. "No," he said. "You can't leave him."

Which it, she wondered. Run away with me, then. But she let Henning take the valise, and she walked back up the stairs, knowing he was just inches behind. They opened the door to a wail: Victor, bellowing for help, because Walton was having a seizure.

Victor stayed pressed into a far corner while Dulcy held Walton's foaming head on her lap and Henning tried to buffer his jerking body. But by the time Dagglesby reached them, Walton was peaceful and smiling. "I'd appreciate it," he said, "if you could manage to make these episodes stop. They're quite embarrassing."

"They'll stop," said Dagglesby. "You're on your way. You've put this off a good long time, but there's no getting around it."

"What on earth are you talking about?" said Walton.

Dagglesby had a dark, cropped beard, and his face had gone brick red. "Well, you're dying. The thing's winnowing through your cerebellum. Have you heard me at all? What did you think would happen, twenty years in? Tell your children you love them. Write letters."

"Devil," said Walton. He gestured Henning to help him up, and he propped himself on the teak changing bench and said, "I am reminded of the words the great painter Turner directed to his physician: please go downstairs, have a sherry, and then look at me again."

Dulcy picked herself up off the floor. Walton, who'd never been good with punch lines, had managed to remember the quote, but not what had happened after the sherry.

"I don't drink," said the doctor. "And you've been dead on your feet for years. Try to meet the end with some relief."

At four a.m., Dulcy opened her eyes. Victor was sitting in a chair by her bed with his head in his hands. She shut her eyes again and pretended to sleep. When she heard him leave, she locked the door, though she knew she'd done this before; he had a key. Now she wedged the chair he'd been sitting in under the knob. She stared at

the door into Walton's room, but it was hinged out, and there was no
way to block it. She doubted it mattered: Victor had never entered
Walton's bedroom, and she thought he never would.

• • •

Walton said the seizure was a mild thing, a *shit burlesque*. He wrote
a succinct note.

> *Dear Dr. Dagglesby:*
>   *Your suggestions for my treatment are ludicrous and outdated.*
> *Finer doctors on several continents have elaborated on the flaws in*
> *these techniques. Your comments that I have reached a "nadir," and*
> *that this is my "final struggle," are equally misplaced. I feel quite well,*
> *and believe my recent troubles might be put down to the effort of a*
> *Pacific voyage and adulterated medication. That having been said, I*
> *appreciate your brevity, and your personal bravery in making these*
> *statements to my face.*
>
>

W. Remfrey
(as dictated to my daughter, Miss Leda Remfrey)
>

Walton managed outrage in the letter, but once he'd finished
dictating, he curled onto his side and shut his eyes. "Would you like
to talk, Dad?"

"No, dear. I would rather not even think."

Dulcy left him alone. It was a strange, warm day. Victor was in the
gymnasium again—*tadoom, tadoom, tadoom*, a tribal drum from the
world's least primal human. Henning would be with him, trying to
talk his employer through the end of things; she'd heard some of it
at breakfast. If Victor sold the newspaper, and one of the hotels, they
might slide through.

"I don't want to sell," said Victor. He'd acted as if nothing had
happened the night before, but she knew he was no sleepwalker. He
stirred spoon after spoon of sugar into his oatmeal. "I want to buy. I
want to crack his skull open and pull the memory free."

Henning poured fresh coffee into Dulcy's cup. She watched the liquid, not his face.

"You and I will go out tonight, Hen," said Victor.

They wouldn't bother following her through the city that day. Dulcy wrapped up and took the staff stairs all the way down. Fluttering leaves, seabirds, blue sky: she stopped at the pharmacy and a newsagent, studied shoes in a shop window, and eventually found herself in a pier restaurant with fish and chips and a beer, postponing a first effort at a telegram with a three-day-old *New York Times*. And there was Carrie, far down a society column:

> Mr. and Mrs. Philip Lorrimer of Philadelphia announce the engagement of their son, Alfred, to Miss Clarissa Remfrey of Westfield, New York. A wedding is planned for summer, after Miss Remfrey's period of mourning for her late grandmother, Mrs. Elam Bliss (née Martha Wooster).

Wise of her not to bother asking for Walton's approval. Carrie loved this world, even though she was only attached by Martha's threadbare family. Dulcy's telegram would ruin all of this.

> C—MUST COME. NO CHOICE. YOU NEEDN'T STAY TILL THE END.

Dulcy scratched this out. She needed to take a firmer line.

> C—NO CHANCE OF IMPROVEMENT. YOU MUST COME NOW.

She ordered a second beer and read items she never bothered with: business pages, household tips, politics, sporting columns. James Jeffries was considering retirement. Victor had taken Dulcy to a Jeffries bout during the last summer of their engagement; Jeffries had won against a New Zealander named Fitzsimmons while Dulcy held her fingers over her eyes, chugging champagne and queasy with the subtext: Victor had killed a boy, Stinson Vanderzee, in a boxing match at Princeton, and she couldn't imagine why he'd want to see this. Vanderzee had officially died of nephritis six months later, but he'd been simpleminded after the fight, and everyone knew he'd drunk himself to death out of despair and befuddlement. But Victor watched the Jeffries fight like a child watches fireworks, and every day in Seattle he either pounded the big bag or the chauffeur. This was one task Henning, who coached from the side, flatly refused. "Have you ever practiced with him?" she'd asked once.

"I used to. I began to dislike it." Henning was good at letting a world float away, without explanation.

Victor had no spots, no visible scars or unbalanced physical feature. During the Jeffries bout, he boasted that he'd never bled during a boxing match, which made her skin shimmy. A few minutes later, she managed, "But what about the boy?"

"Oh, Vanderzee never bled," said Victor. "He barely bruised. Who knows what really happened."

The problem of Victor, besides everything else: he wanted; he didn't want. She tried again to remember how it might have been that she'd found him interesting, before the world had swiveled and stopped giving him what he wanted, before he killed another boy, before he sent his proxy to London after Dulcy, out of longing but primed for revenge. He had looks, and money, and what she had assumed was just an edge of the strange. She had enjoyed the way other women watched him, and she'd liked the fact that he paid such close attention to her without descending into sappiness or obvious, ardent manipulation. He was observant about politics and finance and things that didn't include emotion. He read books, and when they'd talked about history and culture and countries, she only gradually realized he'd never see any of them, that he truly hated travel. He thought this would be no problem for Dulcy, who'd tired of tagging after her father around the globe.

"But I love to travel," said Dulcy. "I simply don't want to travel with him anymore. I don't want to have to take care of someone. I don't want to have to worry."

"Well, then, I'll do it," said Victor. "I will do anything for you."

Victor believed in other types of activity: sit-ups, push-ups, pull-ups. He was a good tennis player, but any sport had to be planned out, nothing impromptu, variables limited. He would swim, but in a pool, not an ocean; he would walk, but not happily in tall grass. And he would box, wearing gloves: boxing had begun as therapy gone wrong. Touching another body, even in a game, was a struggle. He had wild urges and crawling skin; no one had worn his surfaces down. He needed a cocoon to muffle the world, and she guessed that he believed knowing her well would make key parts of life—her body, for instance—approachable. If his mother had been locked in a bin before he turned one, things might have been different, but Dulcy thought he'd been born this way. He could dust a kiss on her hair, touch her through cloth, but any moment of real contact was a little like a stabbing, an act of will, body over mind.

She'd caught Victor reading romantic novels as how-to manuals, with palpable disbelief. There was always a tension between what he wanted and what he knew was expected. Above his desk, he'd pinned a handwritten quote from Lafcadio Hearn:

Everyone has an inner life of his own, which no other eye can see, and the great secrets of which are never revealed, although occasionally when we create something beautiful, we betray a faint glimpse of it—sudden and brief, as of a door opening and shutting in the night.

"Very private," said Dulcy to her friends. She'd liked his intelligence and his obsessiveness and his looks, and it wasn't as if she knew if the novels were right, anyway.

• • •

On Thanksgiving, Emil drank and turned the turkey to leather. The potatoes had raw bits, the scalloped oysters were dotted with shell and sand, and the pumpkin pie was stringy and vegetal. Victor sent word to fire him, but a maid said that Emil had found out that morning that his brother was dying, crushed in a logging accident.

Walton wondered if the falling tree had been a sequoia, and had perhaps been weakened by an earthquake. Could Emil afford a hearse, would Hearst write this up, was it all hearsay?

Henning walked up to the market and returned with fresh Olympias and spot prawns. Dulcy found butter, and a wizened lemon, but there was no bread in the kitchen, no greens, no fruit. They all drank too much, even Victor, who headed into his office to have a fuddled, screaming telephone call with his parents in New York before he set off to charm his fiancée Verity and her family at dinner. Dulcy and Henning heard parts of the conversation while they leaned out the window, sharing another cigarette in the sleet.

"Have you seen some of the crabs in the market?" asked Henning. "Three feet across, still moving. Sea spiders; nothing like this at home."

She shivered. Cigarettes made her feel terrible after the first puff or two. Walton had tried to tell her once that some of Henning's side of the family had been wreckers who lured ships to the shoals, salvaged the cargo, and stripped passengers' bodies of belongings.

"And flat fish as big as Walton's fattest nurse, with larger eyes."

He'd bought some herring, too, and they waited until Victor slammed off, then found another bottle of wine and tiptoed around the kitchen. She dusted the herring with flour and fried them and dressed them with raisins and sweet vinaigrette, as if they were sardines. Pickled herring by way of Sicily, she told Henning, who ate twice as much as she did while they drank brandy. They were playing gin at the kitchen table, dirty plates pushed to one side, when Victor returned, complaining of the alien smell.

"I didn't expect you to be here to be bothered," said Dulcy. "I'll rinse the plates when I'm done with this hand. Why was your dinner so short?"

"I do not enjoy those people," said Victor. He picked up Henning's empty plate and smashed it on the floor.

Dulcy fled to her room and turned her key in the door, wedged the chair, and then knelt next to it, listening, listing. The room spun from too much brandy, and she finally gave up the fight for balance and lay flat on her back on the carpet, listening to the footsteps in the hall. Pace, pace: she admired the dangling crystals of the light fixture above her, the novel nature of the bulb and its soft, yellow, fascinating glow—where had Victor gotten such a thing? She turned and watched the shadow of his steps pause near the doorsill.

A second set of footsteps approached, Henning trying to fix the problem. "I know what I want," said Victor.

Well, no, thought Dulcy. No you don't, not at all, no matter how often you say it.

The key turned, a push against the chair. "You're a fucking fool," said Henning. "Go to sleep."

WINTER (DECEMBER 21 TO MARCH 20)

December 22, 856, Persia, 200,000 dead.

December 23 and 24, 1854, Honshu, 10,000.

December 25, 1899, Palm Springs, 6.

December 28, 893, Dvin, Armenia, 30,000.

January 1, 1837, Galilee, 7,000.

January 11, 1693, Catania, 60,000.

January 14 and 16, and February 2, 1703, Apennines, 10,000. A southern progression!

January 19, 749, The Levant. Complete destruction.

January 23, 1556, Shansi, China, 800,000.

January 25, 1348, Friuli, 10,000. Plague followed.

January 26, 1531, Lisbon, 30,000.

January 28, 1872, Shemakha, Caucasia (see 1667 and 1902). Large toll.

February 2, 1428, Catalonia, 10,000.

February 4, 1169, Sicily, 15,000.

February 4, 1797, Quito, 40,000. Humboldt's notes.

February 4 to 7, and March 1 and March 28, 1783, Calabria, 50,000. I can discern no directional pattern.

February 16, 1810, Crete, 2,000. Accompanied by a wave.

February 20, 1835, Concepción, 50. See CD's notes.

February 28, 1780, Persia, 200,000.

March 3, 1901, Parkfield, California, ?

—from Walton Remfrey's red notebook

CHAPTER 4

WINDOWS

•

Walton was fond of round numbers. When a news account of a disaster cited "thousands," he entered *10,000* in the red notebook, the thickest of the dozen. When dates were unclear, he invariably chose those with the most resonance, the anniversary of another earthquake or a moment that coincided with an eruption a thousand miles away. He tended to include small earthquakes in Europe and North America, while an event in Asia or South America needed hundreds of fatalities to earn an entry. If he could find no fatalities in a Western quake, he still put a question mark: no one could be sure that a miner somewhere hadn't had a rock drop on his head, or that a fisherman hadn't been swallowed by a wave.

The list was organized by season, rather than by area or by year, because after his first earthquake in 1868, Walton had become convinced that events were likelier in times of flux—fall and spring—than solstices. By 1872 he'd decided that it was all about the moon, all a matter of magnetism: ocean tides were echoed under the crust in magma. Even when he'd realized there was no pattern in historical accounts, he continued to maintain that events like the Corinth quake near the winter solstice of 856 were an anomaly, and he remained in love with nature's machines of destruction. He traveled to earthquake and volcano sites searching for variables— vulcanism, tides, storms on the sun, orbits of other planets, fermenting rocks—and he believed that a code would make itself clear someday. The earth knew what it was doing, and shivered in concert, with a goal in mind.

By the end, he believed:

- that earthquakes and vulcanism were all of one piece;
- that gravity and tides informed the movement of magma;
- that certain elements akin to uranium, as yet largely unidentified, actually fermented, and acted, under the considerable pressure of the earth's mantle and lower crust, not unlike soda when it came in contact with vinegar. This led to subsets:
  a. the notion that magnetism and vulcanism happened because of a chemical reaction, or
  b. the notion that it happened because the inside of the earth was alive with microscopic organisms.

He also believed:

- that some minerals had been created by these tiny microorganisms in caves underground, and
- that some minerals had been created by impacts and fires from meteorites and comets, and

➤ that other minerals had been carried into older rocks as microscopic seeds by water, which cracked open these rocks, allowing these seeds to fill these cracks and mature as veins, and

➤ that the earth had once been upside down (or was currently upside down, and had once been right side up), and

➤ that amber and tiger's eye and lapis and opals and turquoise came from ancient drowned crustaceans and forests, still remembered in myth.

Someone's myth. Walton had listened to the nurses who'd pummeled and plunged him in Europe and Asia and Africa: these were the stories Henning patiently transcribed, thinking that someday he could make them visible. A woman in Danzig had told Walton of an amber forest under the Baltic, surrounding a drowned castle; a woman in Syria told of the sap of blue roses melting into lapis; a woman in Ceylon spoke of shimmering tigers transformed to wood. "It would be convenient if I could believe in gods and the whole load," said Walton. "But I can't, and so I'll pick and choose, if you don't mind."

"I don't mind," said Dulcy. One of the only things that could make their existence worse would be Walton finding God. Once, in London, he'd parked her at the British Library, and after hours reading current geologic journals, she'd realized they had nothing in common with her father's version of events. It was a daunting moment—they were in this together. "The minerals in water aren't alive, Dad," she said.

"They are," he said. "Pure science. But for the stories—I can't believe the bit about opals and fossil teeth anymore. I've seen the veins—simply not so. Perhaps ground shell, washed down crevasses in some great flood. But we forget old fables at our peril."

He wouldn't forget anything, and he liked his nightmares. Every Cornish bugaboo from childhood, every phantasm glimpsed in the ocean, every dead body was given its own place, its own rosary bead. He'd grown up in the dark, underground. Dulcy, having been down in mines only a handful of times when she was a child, believed in forgetting, but she couldn't begrudge him any mumbo jumbo, because the sense of the old world waiting at the end of the tunnel or bottom of a shaft had been overwhelming, a given. She'd heard the hot, wet walls gnash their teeth. Everything that had gone before had come here to hide; everything that might be alive could rise up from these places again.

Therefore, when Walton began having child-sized nightmares about sexually rampant witches and goblins coming to take him home, such screaming fits that Victor decamped for a different hotel one night, Dulcy sent another ultimatum to Carrie, and she wired her brothers as well. She did not show the response—bring him to New York—to Walton; any slight chance she could bundle him on a train would evaporate if he heard that tone. But when a letter arrived from his brother, Christopher, Walton read it off and on all day long.

I have been thinking of a visit in the spring, given that neither of us is spring-like. Dulcinea was kind enough to let me know that you have been to Africa again, and your mother-in-law has gone to heaven (or some other strange afterlife with rich food and good manners) or hell; I hope you are sobbing yourself to sleep on her behalf, and I hope you are well, but I doubt both.

We have had a shooting star this last week which seemed to land at the entrance of an old mine filled with buried dead men: even I felt some excitement. Some melted rock and burned trees on the ground, as if it exploded just before impact.

Jane has gone to visit our Marcia in Veracruz, where she has been delivered of a boy. They intend to move to New York, and I am melancholic, but that will give us two reasons to visit.

With love from the small boy

"Why visit now?" asked Walton. "Do you suppose he's ill?"

She sometimes forgot how selective his mind had become. He reached for the gray notebook. "I'm happy he's bringing his lazy ass north, but I'd thought perhaps we'll visit him instead. I'll even sit in his silly church for one of his rants. Remember how lovely that route is, Galveston or the Keys to Veracruz and then up the mountains?"

Walton loved Christopher, despite seeing no point in God. That night when Dulcy brought his medicine, he talked about how fragile his brother had been as a motherless little boy (as if Walton, three years older, had been above all that) and how given to visions, but how brave. Once they ran away from the workhouse with Woolcock and a few other boys and hid in an old tin mine on the outskirts of Redruth, diggings so old—Roman, at least—that they reached the tunnel through a crack under a churchyard wall. Christopher was only five, but he was the best and fastest at finding food or water or wood to burn—he would slide into the rector's house for bread, into the church for water from the font; he would light bits of wood and walk down into the old mine to see the things from stories, and once he came back with an amber bead that looked like a dog's head. One of the older boys had tried to take it, and Christopher had bitten the boy's hand. The next morning, they were plucked out of their cave and returned to the workhouse, and a week later the older boy's arm was amputated for infection.

Dulcy imagined Christopher, a good Christian, had felt guilt. "Not a moment of it," said Walton. "Even when the boy died. He'd tried to crush Chris's little head. Bitten, a bitter pill, but the boy was a rabbit, then rabid. Rapidly." He laughed, surprised at himself. "Chris has the bead still. Do you remember the thing dangling in his kitchen window?"

He turned his head to his own windows now, a wall of Puget Sound sleet. He had a fever again. Dream, memory: she found more retellings in the notebooks, stories about men being steamed to death, a man engine rising on a cable like a flaming bird cage, a note from Walton's uncle describing, as requested, the manner of Walton and Christopher's father's death, when Christopher was not yet born: badly, burning underground. Finally, next to a clipping about a boy's death from blood poisoning, she found a story from a Penzance paper, about six small boys who'd run from the workhouse, hidden in an abandoned mine, and nearly died before the elder found a way out.

Nothing was ever quite the way he told it.

• • •

A week later, on December 10, Clarissa Mabena Galatea Remfrey arrived in Seattle. Carrie was tall, blond, and twenty-two, customarily cheerful and beautiful and soulful; she aimed to please, and she often took the unhappiest person at a party to one side. Other people saw pure empathy, but Dulcy recognized curiosity, and some of Walton's love of disaster and despair.

But now she was in a state of tamped-down rage over her ruined holiday season, the delay in her engagement planning, a problem she had yet to confess. One meeting with Walton, who maundered on about thousand-year-old Persian earthquakes, put her facedown on a bed. "If he's going to die anyway, I wish he'd get it done with, and we could go home, and I could reason things out with Alfred."

"What do you need to reason about?"

"I'd like to shorten the engagement. I'd like a winter wedding."

So many things made Dulcy angry. "Why on earth would you rush into a bad idea?"

And Carrie told her. The whole notion that watery, soothing Alfred could impregnate someone in advance of Episcopalian marital bondage was so stunning—Alfred wielding his tremulous nib, Carrie actually willing to touch it—that Dulcy (who'd never told her sister anything about what had happened with Victor) laughed in disbelief, and Carrie, her father's daughter, promptly locked herself into the bathroom.

Dulcy talked through the door until Carrie emerged and took her through every bad option. The truth might stun Alfred, too, though as a physician Dulcy hoped he understood cause and effect. He clearly lacked much talent for observation. During a week in

Westfield that July, Alfred hadn't seemed to recognize the nature of Walton's illness, despite his future father-in-law's shaking hands and metallic whiff.

But Carrie said she loved him. He wasn't caustic or strange or ill. She couldn't bear Walton (or Dulcy, probably) for more than a few days, and she couldn't live with her aunts in Westfield, and she couldn't endure her tight-laced sisters-in-law in the city. She hoped Alfred didn't mind that this had happened. She said she wouldn't consider ending the pregnancy because she was afraid of pain.

Dulcy wasn't sure how the pain qualification would play out when Carrie found herself in labor for a full-term baby. Maybe she couldn't remember their balloon-shaped screaming mother or the dead twins, but Dulcy did, and she could not imagine Carrie undergoing any of it. Everything about her sister was beautifully attenuated— fine-boned arms and high cheekbones and a dancer's neck. Dulcy was four inches shorter and three years older. She was nice looking, but when she and Carrie were together, she was invisible. The same blood that made Walton look like a walking stick made Carrie look like a queen, while Dulcy was left with Walton's coloring and the padded but quick frame of Martha.

Carrie's presence made the apartment a little happier. Victor treated her to monologues on business and society, which gave Henning a little time away, and Walton talked her into endless gin games. Even the news (not shared with Victor or Henning) that Carrie was pregnant didn't dent the mood—Walton stared at the ceiling for a few moments and then said, "Who am I to judge?" Emil the cook was still away mopping up his dead brother's affairs, and Dulcy had real fun for a few days—sweet moist clams, crabs that rippled across the floor at Carrie's ankles, beautiful smoked mackerel, the prettiest salmon she'd ever seen in her life. Walton and Victor both had trouble with the shape of things, and for them she made quenelles and soufflés and polite lumps bathed in cream, suspended in chowder, or fried crisp.

Oysters, caviar, abalone, Dungeness. "Dear," said Walton. "You'll give yourself gout."

On nights when Henning and Victor were off banqueting, or threatening partners, or making peace with and promises to investors and Verity, she and Carrie would wait until the floor was quiet, the bottlebrush nurse and Walton both snoring, and pad down the dark hallway to the kitchen. Dulcy would make Carrie beautiful piles of food, and Carrie would eat all of it, and talk about how much she'd loved Martha, about how she wouldn't know what to do with a baby without Martha.

"Don't be a fretful mess," said Dulcy, because she wanted to cry. "You'll be a fine mother."

"Not like Mama?"

"Not like Mama."

"She was only a mess because Dad made her sick. It's difficult not to hate him sometimes," said Carrie, after a moment. She slathered chutney on her melted cheese. "I'll be a grand bully like Martha, and Alfred will be a wonderful father."

Martha would have eaten Alfred in a single glance, with a cream sauce, and forced Carrie to look for a better mate. Martha had disdain for "mental wrecks," even her invalid daughter, and especially the neurotic engineer who'd married and killed Philomela. On her dressing table, she kept a silver-framed photo of a brother who had died in the Civil War. The photograph of the brother who'd fought in the same war and died ten years later of drink was kept in a drawer.

"We could go live somewhere else," said Dulcy. "We could run away."

"No, I want Alfred," said Carrie. "You'll see. He's a fine man." She'd popped out of her mood, and she read aloud from the *Herald* about a cotillion, rolling names like Orme and Stuyvesant. Parrots as party favors, a truffle-laden menu. She tried for ridicule, reading with long, fey syllables, but she would miss this life terribly. Carrie had brought along the dress she'd ordered for the season, but she knew the waist wouldn't fit for long.

They heard the elevator churn, and they put down their plates. Dulcy pushed the light button and they sat in the dark, listening to the opening elevator door and Victor, drunk and in mid-rant: the Portland people should understand the situation had changed. Their precious exposition would have to find new moneybags, and Henning should retrieve his cash—

"There's no point," said Henning. "Perhaps if I leave it with them, I'll have some profit."

His Swedish accent came out when he drank, an up-and-down pattern to a sentence, ending at something close to a question. "And that ass from the Washington Hotel," said Victor. "How dare he not trust me? Arrogant little Mick. I want you to throw him off a dock."

"No," said Henning. "It won't do you any good." He walked away, the long, thumping stride.

Dulcy thought she could still hear Victor breathing, hear rage, but this was impossible: the hall was carpeted, life muffled and smothered. Carrie, frozen in her chair, stared up at the glow of the skylight with wider eyes, and when the door at the end of the hall finally clicked shut, she said, "Where is the money?"

"I don't know."

"You know everything about Dad."

"Never. No one does."

"Maybe you are well away from him." But she didn't mean Walton.

• • •

Walton was dreamy and sluggish for a few days after Carrie's arrival, and then he dropped into a higher fever and had a series of seizures. He muttered about mines, but he called them Wheal Charlotte and Tolvadden and Wheal Neptune, Cornish mines from his childhood. He asked for music, and Henning found a violinist, but the man did not know any Vivaldi and was banished after an hour. Vivaldi had been born during an earthquake in Venice, or so Walton had been told during a stay in a clinic in Trieste. Walton was peeved that Victor couldn't hire Fritz Kreisler to play for him.

• • •

Henning roamed Seattle and returned with a cellist. They had peace, each in a different pocket of the sitting room, scribbling: Dulcy writing her aunts in Westfield to say that they should prepare a room for Walton, Victor writing his creditors, Henning taking notes on a Danish play, Carrie agonizing through a draft of a letter to Alfred about his impending fatherhood. They all scratched paper, but Walton, king of the notebooks, simply listened to the cello propped in a wing chair in the winter sunlight, tears rolling out of his closed eyes.

Dulcy's heart surged, a stab of panic: you can know a situation won't end well, and survive a slow, downward drip, but the moment, for whatever reason, was a jolt—Walton looked dead, and looked like he knew it. But everyone else was oblivious, buried in private miseries or daydreams. Carrie snuffled and balled up a sheet and began another draft. Victor had a finger stuffed in his ear. Henning hummed again, out of tune.

Henning didn't know he'd always only be Victor's attack dog, thought Dulcy. And a new thought: Walton didn't know that Victor was only trying to keep him alive for the money.

• • •

At Christmas, Walton gave them poems he'd copied onto pretty paper.

To Carrie:
> *I will leave all and come and make the hymns of you,*
> *None has understood you, but I understand you,*
> *None has done justice to you, you have not done justice to*
> *   yourself,*
> *None but has found you imperfect, I only find no imperfection*
> *   in you.*

To Victor:
> *Thou seest all things, thou wilt see my grave;*
> *Thou wilt renew thy beauty morn by morn,*
> *I earth in earth forget these empty courts,*
> *And thee returning on thy silver wheels.*

To Henning:
> *I know how men in exile feed on dreams.*

To Dulcy:
> *Full fathom five thy father lies;*
> *Of his bones are coral made;*
> *Those are pearls that were his eyes:*
> *Nothing of him that doth fade,*
> *But doth suffer a sea change*
> *Into something rich and strange.*

A little bit of everything: Merry Christmas. Fifty years with a fountain pen, reams of blotting paper, but he might have liked his handwriting better than the poetry. Walton had always been self-referential, but this was sharper stuff than he usually enjoyed, and none of it came from the rose-pink journal or the stacks of Bullfinch and the Brothers Grimm on the bedside table. How could he still remember Shakespeare and not a fortune?

They were all in the sitting room again, trapped together with their cards, while Walton, having spread this wisdom, flipped the pages of an illustrated copy of Aesop. Dulcy jumped when Victor whispered, just a foot away, "Why is he reading books of fables?"

Except for Victor, who had turned to brandy, they were all reading fables. "Because he thinks his dreams are turning into fables."

"Maleficent, malaprop, melon, mellow, melodious," said Walton.

"What does that mean?" asked Victor. When he spent more than a few seconds listening to Walton now, his face beaded with sweat.

"Paddle, saddle, straddle, fiddle-faddle."

Victor gripped his head. Dulcy headed for her room and woke an hour later to the sound of Victor and Walton howling at each other, Walton having evidently crept into the library for another volume. When the voices stopped, she stayed where she was, weighed down by wine and the notion that she could sleep through a murder, and woke again to someone lying down on the bed: Victor, on top of the covers, stiff and staring at the ceiling. He'd come through Walton's bedroom.

"Let me stay, just like this. Let me stay. I won't touch you. Don't laugh that I even say that."

Let me let me let me; the idea that she'd laugh about any of it. They lay without moving for an hour before he left, and in the morning she found Henning in the kitchen. He had new locks placed on both doors. Victor spent the day in his room, claiming a headache.

A few nights later, Victor went to dinner and the opera with Verity and friends. He drank too much, and Verity chided him in front of the others. Victor said nothing but drained another bottle. When she commented, he broke his glass against the edge of the table; when one of their dinner partners remonstrated him, he beat the man bloody, and when others stepped in, he left Henning to deal with the mess.

It was the end of the engagement. Victor began to jump rope instead of box, and he talked about going to plays, going to movies, going to concerts. At meals, he droned on about mineral prices and lumber prices, things that he only half understood. He'd had a better grip on newspapers, his main topic in the past, but now he would talk without pausing about everything that came through his mind—about his day, his past. He had no sense of sarcasm, or much humor at all. It made for dense, maddening conversations, heavy like bad bread, cream soup without salt. Carrie was willing to listen to him—they gossiped about New Yorkers—and Dulcy escaped to Walton, who wanted to hear Melville, *The Tempest*, and *The Golden Bough*, with little blasts of silliness from Edgar Nash and Wilde. She guessed his vision was failing.

One night they all (not Walton, left with a nominally female nurse) went to dinner and a play, and seeing people who might be sane, all out enjoying their lives, pushed Dulcy into a thrum of longing. She felt as if she were in the middle of a dream where she couldn't run. All these lives; all these men who weren't Victor. A tall man leaning against a doorway, a man with a red angry beard and dark blue eyes who stroked a woman's arm. Anyone, almost: the world was hysterical with possibility, women she might have been, men she might love. Tall, short, smiling, strange—she studied them with a sliver of revulsion, a shiver of pleasure.

In the car after dinner, Victor touched her elbow, a pinch on the bone. "I am comfortable with you again," he said.

Bully for you, thought Dulcy, pushing against the door. But the giddiness lasted: back at the Butler he brought out brandy and bowed when he handed Walton a glass. "To your health," he toasted, and he refilled their glasses.

"To business," said Walton, all sunshiny. "And travel. When will we leave to meet Christopher?"

Victor turned slowly to Dulcy. "Leaving?"

"His brother will be in New York in the spring."

"No."

"The spring. Months away."

He threw his brandy glass past her head. Dulcy turned to see it hit the wall, then made herself stare at his blank, flushed face while she finished her own glass. Walton looked more like a bird than ever, swiveling his neck to take in the room.

"That won't do," said Henning.

"She knew that would upset me," said Victor. "She said it deliberately."

"She said it because she'd like to believe the world will go back to normal."

Victor left the room, and Carrie laughed. "Love blooms eternal."

But Henning, stitches still in his forehead from mopping up the end of one more Victor engagement, was less sanguine. Out on the fire escape, bundled up with the remnants of the brandy and cigarettes, he told her she should take Walton east. Victor might protest, but if she asked when he was sober, he would be forced to allow it. "You need to be away from here," he said. "You see how he looks at you again."

That night she heard a key in Walton's door, and she could feel Victor's confusion. A moment later, the same sound in the hall, and then one great blow against the door before he walked away.

• • •

At New Year's dinner, Walton toasted Victor and Dulcy as if they were engaged—*to your love, to your multiplication, you can pick up the mine proceeds when you reach Manhattan for your honeymoon*— then turned to Carrie and proclaimed, "I know they are still in league against me. I know they meet at night and suck and fuck and plot. She forgets that he's a murderer."

Carrie blinked virginal eyes. Victor headed off to smash things in his office. Dulcy finished her wine and watched Henning tap Walton's hand. "Don't be such an ass, old man. We want to be able to miss you when you finally die."

On Twelfth Night, Dulcy baked a king cake, and Walton, who got the slice with the bean, was the Lord of Misrule. Carrie, aptly, found the pea. Walton seemed to enjoy himself, then became enraged: this bean and pea thing was English, he said. Dulcy should have included a thimble and a ring and a sixpence. She wanted to forget that she was Cornish.

He made less and less sense. His right eye began to cloud, and his left hand turned into a claw. One ear suppurated, and a front tooth was going gray. His muscles twitched, and his voice was hoarse from a mercury overdose. He moaned, babbled, lectured Dulcy on the hotel they should use in Constantinople. He knocked over inkwells and refused to try modern pens. He went back to dabbing ink in patterns on his skin, stars circling imagined sores; never a good sign. "They're trying to find their way out," he said. "Perhaps if I dig a bit." He discussed Carrie's rushed wedding logically and fired off sane instructions to the Boys about some property in Michigan. But on the topic of what had happened to the proceeds of the Berthe or

Black Dog or Swanneck mines, he made no sense: he had or hadn't sold them, they had or hadn't existed. There had been a fire, a collapse; Victor had owned diamond mines, not gold mines, and diamond mines were difficult to sell. He'd deposited the money in Durban; he'd hidden it in his pants. Had they checked his pockets?

Whatever end-stage syphilitic unraveling was happening in his brain and spine, the changes came faster. He'd had X-rays the previous spring—crackling green light, what smelled like cooked meat—which had miraculously shown pristine bones, but she knew he had passed a point. He cried out, his fingernails digging into the bedding or their arms, and even Carrie took to reading to him in between bouts of morning sickness. No one could take pain forever, and he wanted more and more morphine, too much morphine, but who was anyone to judge. Dulcy hoped it would end with a vessel in his brain, a kink and an explosion rather than slow rot or a tumor or an utter loss of mind. She didn't want him to worry, and he didn't: on any given day, Walton might be found looking for his clothes, "looking for a ramble."

"You're very weak."

"I'm not a zoo animal."

A circus animal, then. He was in the sense that he was putting on a show, but she didn't say this, and she didn't remind him that he was dying. Walton had made it clear he didn't want to know the truth, and she went along. She didn't tell him to do anything anymore— take walks, eat apples, take medicines other than morphine, stop trying to touch his nurses. She was a bad daughter, but the definition of *good* was faulty.

Walton noticed, and it seemed to worry him. "You haven't been carping at me lately."

"You haven't done anything carpable."

"I'd as soon embrace my weak points. To what end would I change?"

Well, this one, thought Dulcy. His thoughts, these days, only enlarged for his own soul, and sometimes he claimed he wasn't ill at all—it was all a mistake, a momentary lull. He said he was embarking on his third life, another wife, no strife. Back to the idea of Mexico; perhaps he'd seek out a fine woman he'd once known in Christopher's town.

• • •

But then: He called out in the night, and after a bolt of fear that Victor was involved, she hurried to unlock the door. Walton was hysterical, wild, curled up like a little boy; he'd had a dream, and all he could say for a bit was *no no no*. He said he was hot, and she put a wet cloth on his head, but his skin was icy. Dulcy brought tea, and then whiskey, and an hour later Walton managed to tell his dream:

His mother had sent a light to find him underground, where he slept; he had followed a glass candle upward for miles. She wanted him to find a lost horse, and he'd started out, but he was so tired, his feet so sore, that he'd decided to fly. He'd circled over the peninsula—he remembered seeing Penzance, and he remembered swooping closer to see glittery-eyed dolphins in the water. But no horse, and the rain began to fall, and it made his plumage wet—he was really a bird by now, again, as in the dream when Dulcy had first arrived—and he began to plummet toward the waves, diving like a seabird with his mouth open, feeling himself dying as he plunged past seahorses and sharks and octopi, swallowing the world—*the unwarped primal world*—toward a mountain which split his breast.

"And you woke up?"

"And I died," he said. "And that wasn't so hard, but then I understood I wouldn't see my mother again. It was as if it was sixty years ago."

Tears ran down his face again, and she dabbed with a handkerchief. "Tell me what's happening to my eye," he said. "Tell me what you see."

He watched her intently, and she didn't react. "I think it could be some sort of rash, perhaps from all this seafood. Perhaps just a sty."

"Are you sure?"

"No," she said. "But I think that's the likeliest thing." Her hands were shaking: his eyelid was about to open up.

"Bring me a mirror?"

"No," said Dulcy.

"Well," he said. "*Vanitas*. Everything means something, dear."

· · ·

Dr. Dagglesby's wiry assistant showed up panting with a prescription and a note the next morning, delaying an appointment—the doctor was busy saving a life, a *worthy* life. The nurse had sent word that she was sick. It was that kind of day.

"Worthy," said Victor, flushing.

"No one wanted to see the man, anyway," said Dulcy.

She wasn't sure if Walton had slept. When he was wheeled into the dining room for breakfast—Henning had found a wheelchair for Walton that had a large tray, and he managed to balance his eggs and two notebooks (black and turquoise) without spilling—he told them it was the 212th anniversary of the destruction of Catania, sixty thousand dead so long ago; he'd been hearing old voices every time he shut his eyes. *Old* was the sound of the day, as in *sold*, *mold*, *told*, and *gold*, which was why Victor delayed a meeting at the newspaper. But Walton worked his way to *rolled*, and *cajoled*, and *retold*, and then told Henning stories about the notable card games of his life, so many of which had happened during earthquakes.

"You played always," said Henning. "Are you trying to say earthquakes happened because of the game?"

Victor, transparently hungover, was sipping tomato juice.

"Everything happens for a reason," said Walton, smiling.

"You lost my money for a reason?" asked Victor.

"Your money is safe."

Victor drained his glass and stood and walked over to Walton's wheelchair. Dulcy started to rise and Henning was halfway there when Victor bent with his face a few inches from Walton's and screamed, "*Where is the fucking money, old man?*"

Henning moved past him, twirled Walton's wheelchair, and pushed him out of the room. "I will kill you if you touch him," said Dulcy.

"I might welcome that," said Victor.

She ran down the hall after Henning, and they helped Walton into the bathroom, and then into bed. Henning said he'd get Victor to the newspaper; the meeting would be long and would give him time to calm down.

"Such an unhappy human," said Walton. "Henning, you must never forget that you are the better man."

"Are you sure?" asked Henning, at the door. He pointed to the lock, and Dulcy nodded.

"I am."

Walton slept, and Dulcy waited for the sound of the elevator. When it came she went to the window and watched until she saw the cousins emerge and climb into the maroon Daimler. Walton's voice startled her.

"It's no good. I can't remember, but he won't give up until it's over."

"We'll just have to find it then." She straightened his stack of notebooks, bird books, mythology. The garnet journal was on top, and she opened it to read a calm but lunatic entry about transformation and memory, germs and gems and genies and gender and gentleness. "Sooner or later, they'll find the bank you used. Your writing is steadier."

"So it goes," he said. "I'd like us to be on a train next week. You must get some things for me while they're away."

"I don't want to leave you alone."

"I'll call Carrie if I need anything. You must go to the library to find books of sea mammals and fish. I would like to identify the things I saw in my dream. And I would like another bottle of morphine."

"Didn't someone go to the druggist yesterday?"

"Bottlebrush spilled it all. I need more. My head is full of forks. You think I'm at peace when I sleep, but I'm not."

"Is this a new pain?" His skin was gray, and it caved in around his mouth and the bridge of his nose. She touched his hand and it was cold; she touched his icy foot and he didn't even notice and wave her away.

"When my eyes are shut, I'm in a bad place, Dulce. I'm underground, and I need to be out in the air. Buy some train tickets, San Francisco or Santa Barbara. Get us some champagne, too. I haven't had champagne for the longest time."

"All right. Don't think about the underground."

He wanted to sit by the window; Dulcy got Carrie, grumbling, to help get him into the rolling chair. Walton was still teasing his younger daughter about learning to be motherly as Dulcy pulled on a coat and a knit cap and stuffed banknotes into her pocket. She kissed his forehead and started for the door. "Dulce."

"What?"

"When this is over, you must leave this place, and you must never see this man again."

Carrie rolled her eyes. Dulcy took the stairs—she'd push herself into a mood that matched the weather instead of life. As she walked up Second Avenue in the cold, fresh air toward the pharmacy, she thought of ways that they could leave despite Walton's condition, places to go in California or the Southwest. Henning would help now; they all understood there was no choice.

The druggist handed over the morphine with an intense look, eyebrows arching left to right and back again. "The lady with the wiry hair fetched two for him yesterday," he said. "Keep an eye on the breathing."

"He says she spilled it," said Dulcy.

He rolled his eyes. "I'm surprised he can even talk."

Every other errand was about ginning up some happiness: the florist's for something bright, the library so that Walton could identify his dream animals, the markets for veal and shellfish, cheese and vegetables for the next few meals, all to be charged to Victor and delivered. She needed three or four days to make Walton strong enough for a train; she needed to talk to the doctor about ways to keep him alive long enough to die in a better place.

And then, some disquiet, thinking of the doctor, thinking of medicine: she'd never seen Walton take more than a spoon of morphine at a time, and Bottlebrush wasn't the spilling type, or an addict. Maybe she sold it to someone, or maybe Walton wanted to give it to someone, or maybe he'd just wanted her out of the apartment.

She thought all this while standing in the wine and tobacco store, looking for the right bottle of champagne. He never drank champagne. She'd stopped listening to the clerk, who made a clucky sound of annoyance as she turned for the door.

Dulcy reached the sidewalk, skin crawling, and broke into a trot. She was only a block away when she looked up and saw Walton in the open window. She began to run, morphine bottle bobbing in her coat pocket, and saw him step forward and fall, a small and strange and fragile figure. He dropped slowly, nightshirt twisting, arms and legs outstretched. In the very long moment while he was still in the air, sprinting the way she had when she was a little girl, she must have believed she could catch him.

She reached him a moment after he hit the ground, before anyone else came close, and she crouched next to him on the sidewalk. His lips opened and his eyes shifted from cloud to cloud, moving to keep the light while people craned in to watch him die. Blood spread under his head, and a butcher-shop smell floated through the air. She didn't believe that what he felt was pain, but Walton couldn't speak, for the first time in her memory, and as people surrounded them and jabbered and blocked his view, she leaned down and whispered things in his bleeding ear: that she loved him, that all pain would be over, that he'd been a great man, a poet, a scientist, a wonder. She pulled his shirt down to his legs and tried to shield his face from the crowd's view with her body, but people kept bending low, shadows around her head while she watched Walton's skin stop moving. When she turned, there was a shape just above them, blocking the dim sun: a dark-haired man was holding his bowler hat out to give them privacy from the crowd, his back to them as he thrashed the onlookers: What in the fuck are you looking at here? Go to the roof, if you'd like a view. Piss off and let her love.

• • •

She persuaded the police to bring him to the apartment instead of to the morgue: poor confused old man, look at the open window, he'd been Mr. Maslingen's guest. Someone had gone to find Mr. Maslingen now; someone else had told Carrie, because Dulcy heard screams from above, and she left Walton while the police waited for the stretcher.

Upstairs, Dulcy wrapped Carrie into bed and headed for Walton's room. The bedclothes were tossed to one side, and the tall French windows were still open; two drained morphine bottles lay on the carpet. She did not look out and down. He'd always left a note before, when he'd run away in any sense, and she found it in a scrawl on blotting paper under his specimens, the gold, copper, and silver lumps: *That's that. I can't bear the wait. My love to all.*

She scooped up his notebooks and papers, carried them to her room, and came back for his briefcase. She felt through the drawers and his shoes, checked under the pillow and the bed. She couldn't find the plain leather book of accounts, and she tried not to imagine it flying away while Walton smashed into the street. Her windows were open, too, and between the racket of passing trolleys Victor's frantic foghorn voice floated upward and began to dig away at her brain.

Dulcy lay facedown on her own bed. She should go back down and sit with Walton—she'd left him alone for so much of the time in Seattle, and now she was doing it again. She was horrible, and she wept, tears pooling on the pillow. When she floundered for a handkerchief on her bedside table, it took her a moment to focus on Walton's eyeglasses, folded on top of the brown money book, curved from being worn against his bony chest.

• • •

The police lowered Walton onto his bed, and Victor wept with his hands over his face until a maid arrived with a bowl of warm water and soap and Henning pulled him down the hall. Carrie helped at first, then sat stunned and sick while Dulcy stripped away what was left of the nightshirt and the strange bandages, draping a towel over each section of skin while she dabbed away at blood and the magic pen markings. Though his face was unbroken, the rest of his body felt like it was stuffed with loose gravel. Dulcy stopped trying to clean the body when she realized that his ribs had forced their way through the skin of his back.

Two hours later, she took the side stairs all the way down to the service entrance. She slid past the stain and hooked north until she reached the Gold Building, and she looked for Schaub on the elevator list. This Schaub was a cousin of Walton's New York banker, and when she sat down across from him, she showed him the next-to-the-last note in the leather book:

> D—*close the special accounts with Schaub. He may take revenge. Do as the notebooks say.*

Walton had listed accounts at four banks in Seattle. "What do the notebooks say?" asked this thinner, less trustworthy Mr. Schaub, reaching out to pat her gloved hand.

Dulcy shook her head. "Nothing that makes sense." She kept her eyes on the hunting-scene wallpaper, the gray marble floor, the tall buildings across Second Avenue (no one else falling, currently—how often did someone jump?), and only gradually became aware of the man's confusion.

"I don't, though, understand. I'm not sure what Mr. Remfrey had in mind here, asking you to protect these accounts. Mr. Maslingen doesn't have any access to these funds."

She had not mentioned Victor. "I don't know that my father really had Mr. Maslingen in mind," said Dulcy. "I'm only doing as he asked."

"Well, there are four separate joint accounts in each of his children's names." He pushed a sheet of paper toward her. Not more than five thousand in each, and all of it deposited around 1900; this wasn't what they all had been looking for. Dulcy gave him New York addresses for Carrie and Winston and Walter, but she asked for hers in cash. While Mr. Schaub shuffled papers, she stared down at the little bit of blood visible on her wrist, above the glove, and she thought about the other banks in other cities. *He may take revenge*—she wondered if Victor was anything but a victim, but she veered away from doubt. She wanted to believe Walton on this particular day.

She took the trolley to the next bank, the Metropolitan on Seneca ($2,100 per child), walked on to Washington Trust on Pine ($845) and First Columbia on James ($1,319). At each, she had her brothers' and sister's money mailed, and she took her own in cash. Rain began, a sprinkle and then a deluge, soaking through her coat and overwhelming her boots. She tried not to focus on faces, because all the people around her looked stretched and strange, but she started to melt on Western Avenue, and she ducked into an alley near a hop basement. Twenty feet away some drunks watched her from under an awning. She pushed Walton's notebook against her face to block their view and wondered belatedly if the ink had transferred, if it looked like calligraphy on her cheek and lips.

She was still two blocks from the Butler when Henning ran toward her and circled, a large, frantic herding dog. He'd lost every shred of his Viking aplomb. "Why are you out here?" he said. "Why would you be walking around this city at such a time? We thought you'd thrown yourself in the ocean."

The notebook was tucked inside her coat; the new money was in her bag. Henning wrapped an arm around her. She burst into tears and truly couldn't stop.

• • •

Grief: it was really just a swim in and out of love. That night, Dulcy heard someone on the sidewalk singing a song Martha had loved:

What do I love? I love you.
Why do we love? I don't know, but we do.
Tell me true, love you blue, tell me why we do these things we do.

When Dulcy's mother died, Martha put the big, bent farmhouse through a ritual cleansing. She stripped the windows, sold the bed, painted the walls robin's-egg blue, and installed an art desk, a piano, and a set of the Britannica ninth edition in what had been Philomela's bedroom. And when her husband, Elam, died—still fond of Walton, still not understanding his daughter's illness— Martha's reaction was similarly abrupt: she leased the pastures and sold the prize hogs and cattle. She dyed her hair back to black, then to a hennaed black like nothing in nature, and wore it down. She looked like a native witch woman, which fascinated some of the children of Westfield, and terrified others. Older women usually took on a watered-down look, but Martha's expression was still terribly sharp. She stopped doing anything she didn't enjoy: no more church, or excessive cleaning, or visits to neighbors she disliked. She turned more fruit into wine and brandy and cider than jam, and she started to drink the results.

It drove Dulcy's nervy aunts, Grace and Alice, to fits. They'd spent their lives teaching at Miss Porter's and had moved back to Westfield to help care for their addled father; they hoped to relax after the trauma of his raving deathbed. Martha, the reliable presence in life, was supposed to comfort. "What's *wrong* with you?" asked Grace.

"Nothing at all," said Martha. It was years before she tipped face-forward into her peonies. She wasn't a faddish woman, but peonies and clematis were her weak spots, and she never asked her farmhands for help with "frippery gardening." She'd gone out to deadhead the spent blooms, and had been about to say something about Carrie's beaux, or the cooking stains on Dulcy's skirt, before she turned toward an excitement in a flock of cranes and dropped. She made a small recovery, but her heart faded, and her lungs weakened, and with the next attack, she sank like a fish with a broken tail, silently and quickly.

• • •

The next morning, Dulcy was sure that Walton's note was another delusion, and as he was being prettied up for his box, she showed Victor the Seattle accounts and the scrawl she'd taken to Schaub.

"Schaub may take revenge?" asked Victor. "Little Schaub in the Gold Building?" The brown journal was open on his desk; she'd once again removed the Butte and Denver pages. His nice green eyes were red and bruised-looking, and his hands vibrated while he turned the pages one more time.

"No," said Dulcy. "You."

He looked down at his hands; she did, too, and felt sick. He pushed the notebook back toward her. "None of it was mine, Dulcy. Put it away for a trip." He tapped the desk an inch from her fingers. "I'm ready to try a ship again, myself."

On the other hand, he seemed to think a magic box would open up now that Walton was dead. He asked the coroner if Walton might have swallowed a tube with paperwork. He had every book in the library shaken. He ordered Henning's youngest, blondest brother to search the bedrooms, rip up the carpets, crawl the floor for loose boards. Everything Dulcy and Carrie owned was spread across the music room floor while they watched another Falk cut open the trunk linings. Victor fidgeted.

"Please don't be offended."

Dulcy thought Carrie might spit at his feet. "How would we manage that?"

"I'm not suggesting you've hidden anything. I'm hoping that he did."

Victor insisted on a wake and had Walton's coffin placed in the parlor. The January windows were open, and there was little need for ice around the casket. There was really no need for a viewing, either, since though Walton had always been good company at a dinner party, he'd known few people in Seattle. This wake was being held to prove to investors that the cause of death was a rumor, despite an item in the paper about an unnamed man leaping from an Elliott Bay window. The unnaming was all Victor's doing; he was still a part owner of the *Intelligencer*, and he'd insisted on an open coffin for the same reason—how could a man fall so far and look so untouched? The mortician had been paid one hundred dollars to make a flat man look round and full and youthful. Nevertheless, Walton was bleached to the color of the inside of an oyster shell, no layer of fat to turn him candle-colored like Martha.

People Dulcy had never met circled the coffin. Victor, who disliked talking to people at the best of times, had given up whiskey for port, but he was drinking quite a bit of it. The women circled him, too, but he stood near Dulcy and only paid attention to what the men suspected. He'd designed the black-rimmed memorial card—a globe in one corner and a pickaxe in the other, nothing about the ultimate earthbound man taking to flight—and he'd written the *Intelligencer* obituary:

WALTON JOSEPH REMFREY,
ENGINEER AND INVENTOR, DIES SUDDENLY

Walton Joseph Nectan Remfrey, a regular visitor to our city, died yesterday at the Butler Hotel apartment of his partner, Victor Maslingen. He had been ill for several years.

That much, at least, was true.

Mr. Remfrey, well known in the scientific community for his forthright views and honest practices, was born sixty-three years ago in Perranuthnoe, Cornwall, and quickly orphaned. He came to San Francisco in 1868, later making his way from the silver mines of California and Nevada to the copper mines of Montana and Michigan. Mr. Remfrey was an inventor of many devices and a part owner, with Mr. Maslingen, of several mines in the Transvaal. At the time of his death, his properties included investments in Chile and Mexico. He is survived by a brother, Christopher John Remfrey of Pachuca, Mexico; two sons, Winston Austel and Walter Selevan Remfrey, both of New York City; and two daughters, the misses Clarissa Mabena Galatea and Leda Cordelia Dulcinea, who attended him in Seattle at the time of his death. They will accompany his body back to Westfield, New York, for burial at the Old Saint James Cemetery.

Walton, who didn't believe in God, had been fond of Cornish saints' names, Shakespearean names, pompous names. His own hated namesake had been Nectan, a Cornish saint beheaded by pig thieves. Dulcy's older brothers Winston and Walter (sons, after all, of a woman named Jane) had gotten off lightly in the naming wars, but when Jane had died giving birth to a third son, Walton, unfettered, named the blue baby Gabriel Maximus. After he married a woman named Philomela—nightingale!—he completely lost his mind. Galatea! Dulcinea! His last children, Philomela's kitten-sized twins, needed an outsized headstone to hold their names: Perdita Dido Isolt Victoria and Edmund Orlando Pelleas Albert.

Dead Jane was not on Walton's conscience. She'd wanted more babies, and things went wrong all the time, the child a little turned, the leg a little in the wrong position. A little this, a little that; so much of the world ended or began that way. Philomela was another matter. She'd been short like Dulcy, willowy and silky and blond like Carrie, and she really did have a beautiful voice, even if she'd been named for an uncle named Philo instead of Ovid's nightingale. She died a few years after the twins, ruined by and ruining Walton. But everyone had been ruined by something; that was the great lesson of following Walton to destroyed cities.

Now Dulcy sat in a parlor with his body, thinking of a different sort of end, listening to sanctimonies. They might as well have been in John Wesley's pit in Redruth. *Home to his dear sweet Lord. Such a wanderer. Such a thinker. A genius, a saint in his way.* Even Victor looked queasy. Walton would have said *avoid these pretentious fucks* (a phrase that brought back the lost accent: *praytaintseeous fooooks*);

they *brim with fecal matter.* Most of them knew she had once been engaged to Victor; what did they think when they heard him refer to *his fiancée* and gesture in her direction?

What she thought: fear and alarm, like the flash across Henning's face. But she decided this was just another panicked way to save face, and so she sipped tea, nodded endlessly, tried to ignore the cloud of bad toilet water and tuberose, the scent of Walton's body (not rot, but a breaking-open), the smell of the city's coal fires and horseshit that swirled through the open window. She took her meals alone in her room, which had once been the custom when a dead man lay in a house; no one used to eat near a body. Carrie claimed to not eat at all, but at night, Dulcy heard Emil pad down the hall, bearing something that smelled like melted cheese. And later, other footsteps in the hall, but now he just stood in front of the new lock on the hall door. It was over, she thought; there was no point to him trying anymore, because he'd only ever wanted the money.

At night, to keep from listening for footsteps, she made herself hear Walton sing through the bedroom wall, and in the dark she felt like she saw him clearly for the first time in years. From a distance, he'd seemed pale, tall, and fragile: a gentleman. He'd loved clothes and dressed well, with a fondness for soft gray wools and silks that didn't abrade the imagined sores on his back or legs. But closer up, the face had seen sun, whiskey, death, and long dark hours, God knew what female parts; the hands, however beautifully manicured, were miner's hands, down to the flattened left little finger. How did you get that? asked the girls when they were little, on a trip to Michigan. It takes talent, said Walton. It takes an affinity with a fulcrum.

He'd never once been in a fight, and he'd seen no need to manufacture violence. No broken bones beyond the tip of that finger, no whorehouse brawls, no other injury to the body beyond syphilis until he hit the sidewalk on Second Avenue at a hundred miles an hour.

• • •

A religious sect had heard that a man had *defenestrated* from the Butler. They believed that flight was a route to rebirth, and the placards the members carried as they marched on the sidewalk below the hotel read *Float High in His Heavenly Kingdom* and *We Are His Birds.*

Dulcy and Henning followed the show from above while they smoked on the parlor balcony a few feet from the casket. The men wore brocaded shirts, the women smock dresses, and the placards were peacock blue. "What religion do you follow?" asked Henning.

"Nothing."

"What was he?"

He cocked his head toward the open window behind them, and the casket. "Methodist, geologist," said Dulcy, trying to drag out her cigarette. "Catastrophist. Please let me take him home."

Henning flicked two pennies from the balustrade without any reaction from the marchers below. "You don't want to kill anyone, do you?" asked Dulcy.

He'd reached into his pocket for more coins, but now he looked at her: not a warm look, but she hadn't spoken with innocence. "What cow shit did your father tell you?"

Henning still got phrases wrong. "That you killed your brother-in-law."

"Oh." He flicked another penny.

• • •

She packed Walton's trunk. The velvet lining had been restitched badly. Soft suits, shaving kit, five pairs of glasses, the lumps of copper and gold and silver, all the journals, even the green one, her book. She closed the lid as Victor watched, and she changed the label from *Wm. Jos. Remfrey, The Butler, Seattle* to *Remfrey, 109 East 19th St., Manhattan.* She used this address on her own trunk, too, though a welter of messages had landed from her brothers, grief giving way to rage and recrimination, avoidable telegrams to the telephone. They would meet their sisters in St. Paul and travel with them up to Westfield for the funeral. Dulcy said that Carrie had to go to the city first (Carrie, who had already locked herself in her room for the night, who had such belated remorse about her father that she said almost nothing to anyone), to see Alfred as soon as possible. "Nonsense," said Winston. "She's in mourning. They can talk later. You must both keep your heads down."

The Boys had been joyful and loud until they'd finished college and shrunk into life as it should be led, away from their father the libertine. Their wives were sweet but stupid, their politics basted with religion and money—they tended to conflate the two. They said Dulcy had made it possible for Walton to continue on his ludicrous path to ruin, allowed him to spray money every which way, allowed him to die. The money could have gone to charity or power, instead of whores, quack doctors, and first-class cabins. They didn't give a shit for the great wide world Dulcy and Walton had waded across, and the hint—she'd only hinted—that Walton had lost any mining proceeds added to their rage. She should have followed him to Africa, once Martha was gone, "instead of flirting in Manhattan," said Winston. "Just as you're flirting now, in Seattle."

Dulcy tried to imagine the dialogue once they knew the truth. Victor's financial loss was huge, but the Remfreys had stood to clear more than one hundred thousand dollars. During this last telephone call, an experience like dragging her face over gravel, Victor paced in the library, ostensibly because he fretted about the connection, possibly because he worried that Dulcy would open her own window. Henning came in and out; Dulcy tracked them both while she listened to the rage on the other end of the line. "These accounts— did he have the numbers wrong?" asked Winston.

"Not according to small Schaub."

"And this 'do as the journals say'—we have to read all ten thousand pages?"

"No," said Dulcy. "I have. I assume he meant the words he added at the end."

Boil me, burn me. The last page in every journal, written within minutes of the window, funeral wishes Walton might have borrowed from his fables. Dulcy thought of an officer they'd met on a long-ago visit to Yellowstone Park, who'd described what it had been like when a soldier had fallen into a boiling spring and had not been found for four hours. "Boiled shin," said the officer. "And the meat smelled as if someone had dressed it with mustard and vinegar."

Maybe they were meant to drop Walton in a caldera, so that he could erupt anew like a steaming, randy phoenix. Dulcy tried the word *cremation*.

"That's nonsense," said Winston. "Had he become some sort of addled Buddhist? We'll bury him like a good Christian, just as soon as we can get his spotty body in the ground. 'Boil me'? How far gone was the old idiot, anyway? Jesus suffering Christ."

Far gone enough to jump out a window, thought Dulcy. She let the tinny shrieks echo, but Winston wasn't in the mood for reflecting on his own cruelty. "You gave him too much morphine. You wanted to keep him there," he said.

"If he'd had too much, he'd never have reached the window. And I'm not sure he cared to go anywhere, ever again. What was home, anyway?"

"He had *my* home whenever he wanted it," Winston snapped. "And real doctors. Why aren't you on a train yet?"

"We're finishing up. Dad left things a mess. We'll make the noon train tomorrow."

Victor, who'd had a bottle of wine at his very healthy dinner, had been quiet on the couch, but he now twitched out of a daydream. He disliked her brothers, and Dulcy found this no longer offended her. Henning was reading a telegram in the doorway, shushing a maid.

"Bring the contracts," Winston barked.

"We're sorting them out."

"'We,'" snapped Winston. "That's how it is again?"

She shut her eyes, but when she opened them, Victor was still staring at the ceiling. "Go to hell," said Dulcy calmly. "You believe in it, after all. Don't meet us in St. Paul. I don't want to have to talk to you."

"We don't care what you want," said Winston. "What you want has been entirely unsuccessful for the last ten years, and you allowed Da to run himself into his seedy little grave. We'll meet you Monday morning and ride back with you. Then we'll set up an income with what little's left, and you can do what you like."

She put the phone down and thought: I can't bear this. She couldn't stand her own skin, all the things the Boys could and would say to Victor, the future that kept bobbing into sight. Her sense of dread was elephantine. She didn't want to be herself anymore.

Henning, in the hallway, met her eyes and pointed in the direction of the elevator: some problem. Stay, she thought.

"Don't leave Seattle," said Victor. "Don't leave me."

"I have to get Carrie home." And Walton, she thought.

"Marry me." He touched the cloth of her skirt.

She snapped it away. She could hear Henning's voice fading in the hallway as he talked to the maid; she could hear the elevator climbing toward their floor. "You're asking again because you think I have the money."

"No," said Victor. "I'm asking again because I love you."

His head was thrown back on the divan. In the past, when he'd say something like that, and look right at her, just an inch away, she'd want to change it all. She'd want him to feel some extreme, she'd want to seduce; she'd want, as Walton would have said, to light a fire under his fucking ass. But now her skin crawled, and she felt clammy, and she could hear the elevator retreat. Henning and the maid were gone. "No," said Dulcy.

"With you, now, I don't need to explain. Can you imagine what a relief that is? I hadn't seen it that way, when I knew we had to bring you out here—so much anger, you can't imagine—but now it is so lovely to simply be, and it makes me understand how close I could be, with a little effort, with someone who did understand."

She watched his fingers edge closer; she had to pass him to reach the door. "You know it's not right," she said. "You know we wouldn't be happy. You can't seem to be happy, not that way, and I want a little joy, Victor. Think about it. We like each other. We don't want to make each other miserable."

"We don't just *like* each other. It's not as if I don't have emotions, Dulcy."

"I know." She could have ended it, but she said, "It's not just that. But no."

He had an odd look on his face: excited, smug. "You could do as you like."

"You deserve better."

"No," said Victor. "I don't. I deserve you."

His hand closed on her skirt and pulled. She jerked back, and he knocked her down on the couch, a sweep of the tweed arm, no skin involved, and pinned her with the same arm while he worked on their clothes, a pillow over her mouth. He clubbed her on the side of the head when she kicked him; in the end, she turned so she could breathe while he slammed into her, and his breath streaming over her skin was the hardest thing to bear.

Afterward, to prove the point, he pushed her down the hall to her bedroom and lay down next to her, "as lovers should." He pretended to sleep while she sucked the blood off her teeth and felt her body ache. He kept his shoulder against hers, and she could feel a shiver whenever he moved, but when she heard Henning return and jerked upright, he pushed her down and kept his hand in place, right on the skin of her chest, while he talked and talked: he would follow her to New York, they would marry without waiting for the end of mourning, this roughness was only an anomaly, because she should have understood, she'd forgotten how hard things were for him; if she screamed, if she lied, he'd throw her out the window and tell her family she was a whore. She should think of how fine it would be, how easy always ever onward. She should understand he'd do this to her until she loved him again.

She lay back in the dark and let him talk, and talk, more hot breath poisoning her skin. What he said had nothing to do with her, because she would leave the next day, and he would never see her again.

MY IMPORTANT TRAVELS

1862: Falmouth to Allihies (one visit home, 1864).

1867–1868: Falmouth to Bluefields, Chagres, Valparaiso and Cerro Blanco, Panama City to San Francisco.

1869–1872: California, Nevada, Arizona.

1872–1877: Between Michigan and New York, ad infinitum; to Redruth with Jane, and back.

1878–1879: Colorado, Montana, New Mexico, Arizona, California, Chile.

1880–1882: To Plymouth, retrieving the Boys; Keweenaw and Butte and Colorado.

1883: To Cerro Blanco and Pachuca and Paris.

1884–1890: Keweenaw and Butte; Arizona, Idaho, Pachuca, Cerro Blanco; the Transvaal (several trips to each).

1891: To the Transvaal and New Zealand and Australia.

1892, March: To Keweenaw and Montreal; August: To Persia and Syria and Hungary.

1893: To Paris and Berlin and Vienna.

1894: Pachuca, Chile, Hawaii.

1895: Madrid, Seville, Lesbos and Smyrna, Constantinople, Trieste.

1896, February: The Transvaal; June: California and Montana and Minnesota.

1897, January: Pachuca; April: Barcelona, Florence; August: Japan, the Transvaal, Assam.

1898, January: Butte; March: Iceland, Amsterdam, Berlin.

1899, January: Crete, Damascus, et cetera, Vienna and Copenhagen; October: Johannesburg, et cetera.

1900, January: London, Paris; June: Butte and Seattle; October: Cape Town, et cetera.

1901, January: Cuba, Pachuca, California; India, Cape Town, et cetera.

1902, January: England, Lisbon, Cape Town, et cetera, Sicily, Salonica, Naples, Pachuca.

1903, January: Cairo, Alexandria, Turkey, Munich, Bucharest; August: Cape Town, Santa Barbara.

1904, February: To Nice, Athens, Paris; July: Cape Town, et cetera.

—from Walton Remfrey's gray notebook

CHAPTER 5

THE SEA-GRAY BOOK OF TRAVEL

•

When Dulcy was fifteen, Walton decided she should come along on his trips. He needed an aide for his work and his health, and he argued that while she had finished all the schooling Westfield offered, she was too young for university. He had to argue, because Martha was in charge.

Dulcy wanted to go, despite misgivings about a life of uninterrupted Walton. Her aunts thought this was an awful idea: if Dulcy was too young for Vassar, she was too young for Walton's life. Martha had mixed feelings; she was worn out by Elam's illness and worried about a neighbor's bored sons: one had impregnated a doctor's daughter; the other had bombed a Civil War memorial in the town square. Dulcy was the closest game in sight. So she gave her blessing, with the understanding that Dulcy would begin college the following year.

On that first trip, Walton assessed ancient, derelict tin mines in Spain before they sailed east toward a Turkish earthquake. Dulcy began her collection of cracks-in-the-ground snapshots and averted her mind from the almost visible stink coming from under a collapsed rug factory. Walton sometimes claimed parity of carnage, but that was an illusion: palaces stayed upright; huts collapsed. When cholera broke out they retreated to Constantinople, where Walton disappeared for three days, then made their way to Trieste for a hastily arranged clinic.

Walton, who aimed for places in the habit of collapsing, almost always ended a trip with his own collapse. He thought he saw a sore begin in Trieste, and nearly killed himself with mercury; after they came back to Westfield to recover, he traveled to Africa and ruined himself all over again. The next summer, after wandering around the West, he stalled at a clinic in Minnesota until Dulcy missed the beginning of another college year.

Dulcy the traveler: she had spent more than a year of her life on a boat, and easily another year on trains or other wheeled conveyances. Though most subsequent summers were spent with Martha in Westfield while Walton traveled to southern Africa or South America on mining business, every fall they'd set out together for destinations selected more for disaster than commerce. They'd each board with a steamer trunk, a valise (novels for Dulcy, his own prose for Walton), and a grip for her toiletries and one for Walton's potions. If Walton planned to test new equipment, or hoped to bring back specimens, he brought an extra trunk. The family apartment on 19th Street bowed under the weight of samples.

Dulcy usually stopped being sick after a first day's diet of crackers and coffee beans. Walton, despite testing lemons, chloroform, creosote, and weevily biscuits, always persevered, eating breakfast and blustering up to the deck as if there were no issue, then rushing to the side. His stomach always settled at cocktail time. "Why don't you just drink all day?" she asked once.

"Stopping is difficult when you reach dry land," said Walton.

She had her days to herself, and would take to the deck with a book, holding it up to her face and wearing her blue glasses for extra opacity. The chaises lounges were usually bolted down, but the fastenings were almost always loose; she read to a sway-lurch rhythm. Sometimes, to escape the wind or her fellow man—ships' doctors were often handsome, but there was always some good reason, gradually revealed, that they were marooned on a boat—she read in the nooks behind lifeboats. After the first few days she'd talk to people, and play: cards on still days, chess or dice or shovelboard when it was windy. Ringtoss was more exciting in high seas, after dinner and wine; after dinner and wine, she'd become a social butterfly. In the morning, the fact that she always found this transformation surprising depressed her.

On land, outside of cities, the reality of travel was difficult. Walton packed an India rubber bath, which liked to collapse suddenly, and his medicines often shattered, the fumes poisoning fellow travelers. Travel meant being wet and cold or dry and hot; it meant hours in enclosed spaces with people who stank of urine and bad meat and heartbreak. Pushy, mustachioed men in uniform, demanding imaginary paperwork at sudden borders; dusty telegraph offices and banks with wayward hours and false coinage; mysterious meat, leathery fruit. It meant *chalets de nécessité* that either disappeared or overflowed, insects skittering over mattresses or rappelling down at high speed from dark ceilings, the flutter of bats and whisper of mice. Even the best hotels had paper-thin walls, so that she could hear Walton snore or hum badly or—most nights—treat her to the suctioning sound of bodies on bad mattresses. He'd opened the wide world for her but sluiced away her joy.

Dulcy was good at washing out clothes, pinning her hair and hat for the wind, daydreaming miles into submission. She was hopeless at speaking anything beyond bits of French, but she could read several languages and was evocative with hand gestures. She knew all about train and ship menus and was particularly well versed in post-disaster hotel menus, tentative stabs at normalcy. After an earthquake, the bread always tasted of plaster dust, and scraps of meat were always high. She'd developed a fondness for lentils and garbanzo beans after nights spent huddled near open stinking pots. She trusted very old cheeses.

• • •

On her last morning in Seattle, Victor crept away from her room before the apartment began to wake, before the world had any color, a gray shape in gray light. He'd been staring at her for an hour, believing that she was asleep; he would believe anything, sometimes.

She scrubbed herself at the sink and slipped away, too. She'd had plenty of time to think, but only a few hours before the train left for errands that were now necessary. When she came back, Henning's head jerked around for a long look, but she shut her door in his face. They had all misjudged.

When she opened the door again that afternoon, he was waiting with a bellboy, and they made a last trip to the Seattle station. Victor hadn't emerged to say good-bye, but he'd given Henning a note to pass on, and Henning didn't look at her directly when he put it in her hand as he helped the sisters onto the eastbound Empire Builder. They stood in the train passageway and listened to Carrie retch in the cabin toilet. She'd already been sick on her mourning dress.

"What will you do?" Henning asked. He was braiding the silk strings on an extra luggage tag.

"I wish I were dead," she said.

"No, you don't," he said, turning to leave. "You wish you were dead to some people."

She didn't watch him go—he'd failed her. She left Carrie to her misery and walked down to the lounge as the train began to roll. No one paid attention; her damage was under her hair, under her clothes, though her lips were swollen and beginning to darken. Her muscles ached, her vulva ached, and she felt almost as nauseated as her sister, but the train would soon reach the east side of Lake Washington, and leave Victor in the fog. She found a seat, and then she made herself think.

And by the time Carrie had joined her, Dulcy saw no reason to accept life as she knew it. She'd worked herself into a new daydream, a new past, a bit of salvation: she'd had a husband, and he'd been:

a. Handsome, intelligent, and sane. Yet somehow (of necessity) tragic.
b. A wastrel, with a divisive, disowning family.
c. Someone in between, someone she hadn't imagined yet.

Her eyes passed over a quartet of women playing whist and landed on a pale man who'd entered the car and paused, taking his time before choosing a seat. He didn't bother looking at the sisters Remfrey, but that didn't mean he hadn't sized them up from the beginning. Dulcy liked the way he looked, and his expression: both bemused and indifferent. She decided that her husband had been pale and tall and dark-haired, romantically gaunt, nothing like Victor.

The train climbed out of coastal rain and into snow, leaving gulls for crows and ravens. Dulcy faced east with the movement, and the large flakes whipped out of tall dark conifers, aiming at her eyes. Carrie dozed with a magazine on her lap, plump lips open, making small horking noises. Dulcy leaned the side of her head against the window, trying for a position that didn't hurt, but her skull was bruised, and the glass glowed with cold, and her pride couldn't quite bear it—one sister snoring, one pasted to a window like a halfwit.

She kicked Carrie's ankle, and the *Harper's* slid from her lap to the floor, but she didn't wake. Dulcy scooped it up and found bilge:

Ah, that foolish dream of mine had proven true: I knew her, I knew her, unmistaking, without doubt or hesitancy—and in the dark! How should I know at the mere sound of her voice? I think I knew before she spoke!

Carrie had changed dresses, but she was still aromatic and stained, her pale blond hair flat on her head. She looked like a pretty strand of kelp with a doll's porcelain face. Their better clothes were buried in the luggage car with Walton's coffin.

It didn't do, thinking of the lost world, and so Dulcy left it again. The pale young man, who had chosen a seat across from a stocky man who talked loudly about the insurance business, was big-boned, with a good wool coat, an expensive hat he now placed on the seat next to him, and thick, well-cut hair. He didn't seem quivery, or agitated, or prone to exclamation points, but he was thin, with a kind of diminished look that might have come from illness, or alcohol, or shot nerves. Dulcy couldn't tell if he was twenty-five or thirty-five, but she liked his face, and she could tell he deeply regretted his choice of seatmate: the insurance man hadn't stopped talking.

Run now, or regret, she thought. But the young man raised a finger for the porter, and his pragmatism pulled her back to the newly imagined husband, her necessary creation. Dented, she thought, but not weak. Sick was not weak, until the heartbreaking end of things; she'd be good at these details. This husband had died young, not more than thirty. Perhaps a tropical illness—not a sexual one—with consumption as a nail in the coffin. They had traveled widely, spending their time alone together in anonymous places, and he'd left behind little sign of his existence.

The cardplayers were insulting each other, dropping cards in mock disgust and giggling, wheezy and raucous. They were wearing black, too: the world was made of mourning women. Someone was always dying, and someone was always dusting off black silk. The thick insurance man must have liked this notion: "They might not all be dark complexioned, but they think that way. Warm climates, you know. I'm of the hope that the Irish will simply kill them off."

The younger man tapped the pages of his open book—shield of the traveler—and beamed up at the very, very dark porter, who'd arrived to save the day. When he left, his companion started in again, but in a strained whisper; here was a man who didn't want the staff to add anything extra to a meal. "They're trying to join all the orders."

"Dark people?" asked the young man.

"Slavs, Italians, Spaniards. Not to mention the truly dark ones."

"And who are your people?" asked the young man. The question sounded polite; it might not have been. His eyes drooped, and he curled his lip well; in that sense he might have fit into Carrie's short story. He could be a Pinkerton; Victor couldn't resort to Henning's brothers again, but he might have hired a detective—would a

Pinkerton have a sense of humor? And what did it matter, anyway, if someone was following them?

Dulcy moved in her seat, and felt her damage, and wondered why her brain felt so strange and shuttered and peaceful. The window gave her a thousand more spruce trees, a million more snowflakes: she felt like she was watching her mind dissolve. Someone had opened a pane, and flakes touched her face and pushed the stink of cigars to the back of the car.

"Scotch and German," said the insurance man, oblivious.

Her sharper Remfrey brain, the one she would never shed, thought *xenophobic prick*, and she floated away again to her promising, very dead husband. Tubercular or feverish, possibly wounded: an American back from the Philippines, an Englishman who'd served in Africa? She wouldn't know enough to be believable; Walton had been a flawed parent but adept at steering his daughters away from soldiers. She circled the idea of a mountaineer, but she'd seen so many crushed and splintered animals and vegetables and minerals that self-inflicted injuries—injuries of amusement—lacked nobility. Though how was climbing any riskier than sleeping with everyone who volunteered?

The porter reappeared with large brown drinks, and the young man put his book down and used the same hand to take tip money from his pocket. The big talker seized an opening. "In any event, we're flooded with thieves. All of them highly sexed."

"Oh God," said Carrie, eyes still shut. "Get me some water. Who is the person who drones?"

"You'll see him soon enough," said Dulcy. She was fascinated by the young man's expression as the insurance man blathered on, a look that was both tight and wild-eyed. He was cornered, and he looked it. Maybe he'd drink too much. Maybe he'd scream, or have a fit.

"Of course, real tradesmen are another question," said the big man. "These people are good with stone. A man of ability will always be recommended and make his way, don't you think?"

"No," said the young man, though he smiled enthusiastically and reached for the glass, again using his right arm. Dulcy was sure now that something was wrong with the left. "I don't think that, at all. I think for some reason you would rather have bad work from a Scottish mason than brilliant stuff from a Sicilian or Romanian."

A normal flush started on the neck; the insurance man's nose turned the color of a raspberry. He looked around for an escape, but there were no empty seats. "It's only a guess," said the young man. "I'm happy to admit I'm often wrong. Stay and argue with me."

Dulcy smiled as she turned to the window, temporarily in love with the world again.

• • •

In the dining car, Dulcy gave Carrie one of Walton's pink stomach pills. They watched passengers and made guesses out of boredom, mostly unkind: the bearded men in the back sat too close to each other; a little man who stared at the ceiling like it was God must be a dipso. Carrie thought the blowhard college boys in one corner were charming—fictional heroes should be morose, but real men had to be sunny. Alfred honked like a goose—a wealthy, intelligent goose—and had a scrubbed, optimistic face.

Dulcy guessed the college boys were spoiled weasels, but at least they didn't look like they were related to Henning. A handsome blond man was unreadable: he had classic features, but the set of his face never really changed, which could be indicative of deep thought or none at all. A woman with gray hair and a gray blouse—she looked as if she were in the process of becoming a ghost—cut up meat for an ancient man whose bright eyes scanned the people on the train. Dulcy didn't think he could talk, but he'd studied the menu the way she did: earnestly. "Are they married?" she asked Carrie.

"Of course not, nor biblical. Impossible. She's his nurse, or his niece or daughter. She avoids even thinking of birds and bees."

Unlike those well-raised Remfrey girls. Dulcy ordered oysters, a salad of beets and apples, salmon with Chablis sauce. Carrie had vol-au-vent à la Toulouse and saddle of lamb, with asparagus and hollandaise on the side. Dulcy hoped the pill kept working, so that neither of them had to see any of these dishes twice. They had glasses of Heidsieck and slices of citron cake with boozy berries and thick cream. The mood improved. Dulcy shut out the things that had ended, the things she couldn't change and that Carrie didn't understand. Neither of them brought up Walton in the luggage car, and neither felt self-conscious about this. Dulcy emptied Carrie's champagne flute; Carrie finished the cake crumbs on Dulcy's plate and nattered about finding a wedding gown with a forgiving waist.

"After I find a forgiving funeral dress," she added. "Do you supposed Victor will actually get on a train?"

Dulcy watched one of the college men snap the other with a Princeton scarf, a Victor flag.

"I imagine he'll become calmer once he makes the money back," said Carrie. "What did his letter say? That he loves you again?"

"It doesn't matter," said Dulcy.

"Of course it does," said Carrie, but now she was watching the attentive ginger-bearded men incline toward each other, ever so slightly. "And how odd are they?" she asked.

"As odd as they'd like to be," said Dulcy.

"What do they do, when they're alone with each other?"

"You'd like me to guess about this out loud?"

"I would," said Carrie, leaning forward. Her cheeks were pink again, and her wide blue eyes wanted fun, or a fight. But Dulcy was watching the porter hand a fresh whiskey to the thin man, who surrendered his book to take it. All was revealed: the third and fourth fingers of his left hand were missing, and the back of the hand was scarred.

"Do you think it was an explosion?" asked Carrie, miner's daughter. "A captain? He's awfully well-dressed, but he's young enough to have gone to one of the technical colleges."

The train lurched, and the insurance man turned to reassure the unworried cardplayers. The young man downed half his drink and reclaimed his book: *Nostromo*. He looked hunted, as well he should. "No," Dulcy said. "He's a veteran." She slid back into her story: my husband was a soldier. She'd have to read up. You needed a man to really disappear.

• • •

Sometimes, while they traveled, Walton had talked about the West as a dreamscape, a place like the steppes or the outback, and he would describe how sun-blasted and moon-blasted and immense it had seemed at first. The landscape made him think of Spain, and it made him feel a little like Don Quixote. And so Dulcinea: this was meant to be her landscape.

She thought about this when she woke up to a jolt of worry about whether the door was locked, confusion at the way her neck and ribs hurt, before she understood the train sounds and heard Carrie's breathing in the lower bunk. They were passing through another bleak town, wood buildings so fresh people could probably watch them warp, on their way up to a plateau with long slow humps of winter wheat. The snow was a goose-down blanket over an infinity, a death march, of dirty gold grass.

Dulcy's new landscape: not New York, not Seattle, no place Victor knew or could possibly understand. She lurched into her clothes and made her way back to the dining car. Onward Christian soldiers: the breakfast menu didn't offer much of a virtuous middle ground between health and excess. She considered oatmeal and fresh fruit before asking for coffee with cream, sausages with fried apples, hashed potatoes, a poached egg. She watched the rest of the diners, but in this harsh light, a day later, no one seemed Victor-sent. The beards were too interested in each other, the talky insurance agent was far too self-involved, and the man with the wounded hand so lacked interest in anyone that he hadn't come to breakfast. The volume in the car went up as the card-playing ladies in black entered, laughing again. Mourning—who was to judge? Maybe there'd been no love at all, only duty. They drank cider with their hash and rolled their eyes at the landscape. The handsome blond ate a whole egg with each bite, and while his elegant jaw moved like a stamping press, it occurred to her that he hadn't read a word since he'd boarded. She thought of the way that Victor ate—his eggs would have been hard-cooked, sliced into a half-dozen bites—and suddenly wanted to be sick, wanted to be off the train, wanted to be hidden and still and anonymous, vanished, a blank. She lost all doubt.

She was seated near the galley, where the black porter was talking about what he planned to do on his break in Spokane—see his mother, drink whiskey, watch a play. Dulcy pulled paper and a pen from her bag and finally replied to Victor's letter. She waved to the porter and gave him twenty dollars for a few favors: he would mail Victor's letter, redirect Walton's trunk, and forget he'd done either of these things.

• • •

In the cabin, Carrie was still folded like a handkerchief in the bottom bunk. The train was ripping around curves like a bobsled, catching up with itself, as Dulcy climbed into the upper bunk, smoothed her map, and confirmed that due to the snow they'd be at least twelve hours late on the seventeen-hundred-mile trip to St. Paul. The Boys would cool their heels at a good hotel, relieved to have the reunion postponed. Spokane had become a daytime stop, and the mountain towns of northern Montana had no outlet beyond this east–west route. Too early, too late. If she had anything in mind, anything at all, it wasn't a mountain pass or a prairie.

The train inched into another narrow-canyoned lumber town, and passengers picked their way across frozen mud toward ugly taverns. It was the kind of place a low winter sun never reached. In a few days, Victor would pass this with his eyes squinched, not understanding the size of the landscape, the way anyone could disappear. Still, people got off at all these stops, mostly from the tourist cars. Which was a bit of a joke—surely she was the tourist, and these battered people were on their way to another war.

"What hole are we in now?" asked Carrie. "And would you stop rattling that paper? What are you looking at?"

"Nothing worth talking about," said Dulcy. She climbed down. They watched a young woman slide on the boards along the track, nearly dropping a baby and a corduroy valise.

Carrie looked away. "You'd tell Martha. I would very much like to talk to her now," she said. "I miss her so much, and I feel worse for not missing Dad a bit."

Dulcy curled around her, and for a while they were quiet. Dulcy reached for the novel Carrie had been reading, wedged between the train wall and the bunk. She flipped pages: portents, seductions, revelations. It was about a Boston girl who boarded a ship for France after being seduced, *ravished*. Her rapist had a dream of guilt and pursued, but learned on the docks of Marseille that she'd jumped overboard; he vowed to be a better man.

Ravished. Did ravishers exist, in a pleasant way? Dulcy didn't think so; she made herself remember what it had felt like, Victor holding her down, ripping at her, and any last bit of blur disappeared. "Do you think you'll ever get your mind back?" she asked, climbing off the bunk.

"I don't understand anything you say," said Carrie from under the blankets. Even her voice sounded green.

Dulcy tugged at the window and hurled the book against a wall of pines. It started a small landslide of scree. "I might have read that one," said Carrie, one eye open. "What happened to your lip?"

The evidence of Victor's very deep, truly profound emotions had ripened overnight, so that Dulcy's lip no longer looked pleasantly bee-stung. Her mind was doing the same thing, losing its facade, letting its bruising up to the surface. "I dropped my book while I was reading."

"There's my point," said Carrie. She smiled. "We should both read lighter books for a bit."

• • •

That afternoon, the young man with the missing fingers, having hidden successfully all morning, was pinned down again as the insurance man launched into the Russian-Japanese conflict, the unrest in Moscow, and the wayward nature of automobiles, a boon to his business. For once he was timely: as the train slowed at the outskirts of Missoula, they passed a crushed green Rambler, and the conductor explained that a driver had misunderstood a train the week before. This same train.

Misunderstood. They mulled it over while they waited for a freight to go by. The bright green curl of metal looked like a giant had stomped on it, then gnawed it in half; it couldn't have looked worse after an earthquake. "Is he dead?" asked one of the card-playing ladies. She had loose pale eyes and a thin red mouth, but she wasn't as grim as her features, and she smiled often.

"Oh, they all are," said the conductor. "Before the snow, you could still see blood."

Heads swiveled. Dulcy knew the passengers wanted to rush to that side, and she wondered if trains could tip over, like ferries. They might have tried it, but the conductor interrupted the moment and announced a reroute through Butte, rather than Helena, because of more snow slides.

Dulcy stood as the train slowed—she had to get out, at least walk on the platform, but the old man and his gray companion blocked the aisle, and she waited just behind the young man with the missing fingers while the couple wrestled with a dropped cane. He was studying the crooked wall of a firetrap theater, where a recruiting poster for the war in the Philippines was half covered by the generous shape of the actress Anna Held, a cloud of a woman who did whatever she wanted to do when she wasn't attached to a building. He held a notebook instead of a novel, and his script was tight and even. She read a line marooned in the center of the page, above and below dense paragraphs:

I'd do better with someone else's plot.

She studied the clockwise whorl in his chocolaty hair. He smelled nice, at least for someone who'd spent two days on a train. She wondered what he really thought, and if she'd like it, before the old man moved and she hurried down the aisle.

Dulcy wandered down the platform, thinking past the reroute and one more ruined plan. She sucked in new air, the smell of dirt and different trees. It was almost fifty degrees; she heard a splashing sound by the baggage cars, ice beginning to melt under Minnesota-bound shellfish. Walton would be warming up, too.

Back inside, the passengers dozed. Carrie had been stung enough by Dulcy's criticism to plow through *The Soft Side*, and Dulcy returned to her quest for a husband with a military history in Victor's last issue of the *Atlantic*. William James against the Rough Riders' world:

> The plain truth is that people want war. They want it anyhow; for itself; and apart from each and every possible consequence. It is the final bouquet of life's fireworks. The born soldiers want it hot and actual. The non-combatants want it in the background, and always as an open possibility . . . What moves them is not the blessings it has won for us, but a vague religious exaltation. War, they feel, is human nature at its uttermost. We are here to do our uttermost. It is a sacrament. Society would rot, they think, without the mystical blood-payment.

It would have been convenient if Victor, instead of boring the world to death talking about the war in Cuba and the Philippines, had enlisted, been shot, and never met her, and this got to the point: she wasn't sure she could imagine being married to someone who would have volunteered. She hadn't been part of the fever, and now even newspapers were tired of it, which couldn't compete with the way the men stuck in the Philippines felt about the mess.

She dozed, and looked up to locate a hissing sound, a flurry of motion: the insurance man was waving a newspaper at the young man with the missing fingers, whose eyes were closed. Dulcy thought he was pretending until she took in the half-open mouth, the long, outstretched leg in the aisle, and an equally unfettered pyramid at his crotch. The insurance man threw his newspaper on the younger man's lap, and his eyes flickered open as the paper slipped off. The older man stared pointedly, and the younger man looked down. He reached for his derby and dropped it on his lap, without apparent embarrassment.

The insurance man, as ever, relied on conversation. "What do you write about, then?" he asked.

"Unions and immigrants and politics," said the young man. "Brown people and the Irish and lynchings, and nasty, selfish Anglo-Saxons such as ourselves. Plenty of things to say."

The insurance man finally changed his seat.

• • •

Dusk, Butte: half of the passengers climbed off and headed for streetcars. These were the paler immigrants, the city people, not the red-faced farmers who'd disappeared into the frozen grass of eastern Washington. Dulcy studied a dozen skinny clouds rising from the city on the hill. They looked like volcano plumes, dragon exhalations, and it took her a moment to realize she was seeing steam from the mines. When she'd come through here at sixteen, Walton had explained, ad nauseam, the strangeness of a city built on an anthill, tunnels that stretched a mile down, engines rumbling below department stores and fancy hotels. Dulcy had thought it might all cave in, but he'd said that Butte was no different, really, than Paris or Rome, any city built over old mausoleums and sewers. The rock and ore underneath wouldn't dissolve like the salt mines in Normandy or Austria.

Though these tunnels were much, much deeper. She wondered if the city was somehow steam-heated, and if the steam smelled like metal, and if the metal smelled like blood from all the men who'd died and never been brought back. There were no trees, and there was barely any grass. This was the place that had made most of Walton's fortune, where his two real patents for hoist parts had panned out (as it were), but most of his time here had been spent fine-tuning his magnometer, an invention to warn the world of earthquakes. Butte was only a hundred miles from Yellowstone Park, where the earth shuddered every day, but the magnometer had failed. It hadn't been able to foresee any of the Yellowstone vibrations, or even distinguish them from dynamite blasts in the mines.

The dining car was mostly empty; next to her, Carrie was halfway through another letter to Alfred. The cardplayers and the red beards had left in Anaconda, and no new passengers wandered on: however grim Butte looked, no one seemed to want to leave it. The man with the missing fingers was out on the platform, trick bowler firmly on his head, taking in the raggedy view of the hill. He paced with more energy than he'd shown on the train; she watched his breath turn white and followed his view and realized that one of the dozen plumes rising from the hillside was black, not white, smoke rather than steam. A boy carrying a hot box sold him a meat pie. When he bit in, there was another explosion of steam, a miniature replica of the background fumaroles.

"Might be a terrible thing," said the disaster-loving conductor, looking at the plume. "Of course, you don't need a fire to kill people down there. Those hoists go down, rocks go down. And gas. You know, they look alive when they pull them out after that kind of accident. Pink-skinned."

Carrie looked up, annoyed by the piping, asinine voice. Both the sisters Remfrey, one-time daughters of a one-time mining engineer, pursed their pretty lips at the idiot civilian.

• • •

Gas victims didn't stay pink for long. The first time that Dulcy and Carrie had been on a real trip with their father, in 1892, they'd visited the copper mines of Keweenaw Peninsula of Michigan, where many of Walton's new hoist mechanisms had also been installed, and where he was testing another warning device, a machine for the detection of dangerous gasses. They took trains and ferries west from the huge depot at Buffalo. The trip had been wildly exciting, and Walton had been patient and wonderful. Philomela had been dead for two months, and he let his daughters wear her flamboyant, too-large hats.

But after a week of Calumet and Hecla dinners, ice skating, and drilling contests—wiry violent men with picks, sparks flying—an explosion occurred without Walton's warning device chiming, crippling one of Walton's unstoppable hoists. An hour later three crimson-skinned blond men lay in the snow, looking like photo negatives. Carrie and Dulcy darted around, trying to escape weeping housewives, while Walton bellowed at the engine crew. Any ground that wasn't covered by snow glittered with shards of quartz and feldspar, and Dulcy worried that the dead men would be cut open unless someone put a blanket underneath them.

On the way back to Westfield, Walton had been in a suspended state, rage as a kind of jelly holding his mind in one piece. This time they rode the northern route and took a suite in the St. James Hotel in Montreal. Walton bought them books and games, and told them to order anything they wanted from the kitchen, and to go anywhere they wanted within the walls of the hotel. He disappeared for the next five days, then bundled them home without explanation. For a long time Dulcy assumed that this was when he'd made himself sick, but she later understood that Walton had earned his syphilis in Paris just after Carrie was born. He'd given the disease to Philomela, and to the twins, and it had killed them all.

• • •

East of Butte, another rockslide, another "short delay." Dulcy tried to enjoy the battened-down chaos as the galley staff served courses at an angle. From the uphill side of the table, she watched the liquor in the last of the Seattle oysters dribble toward Carrie, a wine sauce oozing away from a partridge in viscous waves. Carrie kept down a cheese soufflé and veal. Dulcy didn't joke about this new fondness for chewing up baby animals. In the far corner, the handsome, blank-faced blond man still stared into space.

"Does Alfred read?" she asked Carrie.

"Of course he reads," said Carrie. "I can't claim it's any good—it's all adventure stuff—but I believe he's still recovering from college."

Dulcy, who hadn't gotten to go, disliked Alfred for complaining. Sadness percolated into pettiness, on its way to a truly evil mood: there were so many ways to make Carrie not miss her. She signaled the porter. "You're a lush," said Carrie.

"You're a brat," said Dulcy. "Let's not be hard on each other."

They simmered, they were sorry, they loved each other. Their lives had been filled with passing tiffs, and this too would pass if it were given time. An hour later, after the train finally began to creep uphill again, she told Carrie she felt ill. "If you think you'll give me something, warn me now," said Carrie. "This is the first day I haven't been sick in weeks."

"So many people left the train," said Dulcy. "I should see if another cabin is available. We need to think of your health now."

There were four open cabins, and only one party boarding before morning. Carrie blew a kiss good night and floated off to her private kingdom just as the train began to roll again. No backward glance, no instinct for the moment. It should have been a relief, but Dulcy had trouble grinding her way through a conversation with the porter: she requested a bottle of mineral water and some shortbread, declined turn-down service or tea. She didn't want to be bothered at all, even for breakfast. The porter, worried that she'd mess up her cabin in some horrific fashion, returned with towels and a bowl and a little sign for the door: *Quiet is Appreciated.*

When Dulcy was finally alone, she locked the door and curled on the lower bunk and wept: shuddering, galvanic sobs. She felt like her brain was being exposed to the air; she wondered if the pillow would still be wet when they looked for her in the morning.

But she was running out of time, and when she finally rose, she stripped off her clothes quickly, ripped lace from the sleeve of her black dress and tore more strands from her thin shawl, then wound the dress and shawl around the brick blanket warmer she'd hidden the night before and tied the bundle tight with her stockings. She'd hidden a canvas bag within her other luggage, and she changed into the warm navy stockings and sturdier boots, the dress and wool coat she'd bought on the last Seattle morning while Victor hid in his room, things Carrie had never seen. She waited at the window, swaying as the train caught up with the map. When it curled and lowered its head somewhere after Whitehall, she tugged the pane down, and when the sound echoed and she could almost smell the cold water below, she guessed at a trestle and threw the bundle—the things Leda Cordelia Dulcinea Remfrey would have been wearing when she killed herself—into the dark. She stuffed the scrap bits of lace and wool in the corner of the window and pulled it up an inch to trap them. Then she waited again, holding on to the frame—open just wide enough for a woman's body—until her fingers froze.

The brightly lit Bozeman platform came as a shock: it was filled with men and women in ball gowns and furs, half of them carrying champagne bottles. It took a moment to recover, and Dulcy was about to leave the window for the corridor when the crowd parted for the two-fingered man, her own very tired veteran, who vaulted down from the still-moving train with such youth and grace that he was almost unrecognizable. As people pushed past, he reached down to change his grip on his bag and looked back up at the train, straight at the stunned woman in the window, who wore a red hat after days in mourning black. He smiled, the kind of glowing, frank smile he would never have given if he thought he'd see her again, and then he walked away.

Dulcy stepped back into the shadows of the cabin and listened to the fancy-dress drunks invade the corridor—*Kiss me*, howled a man—as the train creaked away from the station. She dug out the guide. These idiots were getting off in Livingston or Big Timber, but it was a long, long ride after that, a bleak world of small towns where people—people who weren't drunk—would notice anyone new. She thought of the emptiness she'd seen to the east on the earlier trip with Walton, and she began to panic. As the train rose and fell over another pass, she tilted the guide toward the moonlight, and when it slowed again, she pushed into the corridor, leaving the *quiet* sign on the door behind her. She launched herself down the metal steps to the cold half-lit bricks of a platform and paused, shocked by the size of the grand brick depot, before blending into the opera crowd as it invaded the building, looking for warmth until their rides arrived. A woman in a feather boa ran by singing a solo from *Aida*, and a man scrambling after her fell on the wet marble. The eastbound train began to roll again, and through the depot's tall windows, Dulcy watched Carrie and Walton disappear.

She was second in the ticket line, behind a confused old man who spoke only Norwegian, and she booked a ticket for a cabin on the next westbound train, due through at ten. She walked toward a wooden bench to wait, a little surprised by the sound of her steps in the emptying depot, by the first subtle sounds after days of listening to an engine, a track, movement.

Dulce:

Know that I do blame myself, that I can only assume my very poor example has somehow infected your mind. But for the same reason, I am aware that you know better, and I hope you will understand you cannot treat people of fine intention like shit on your pretty shoes. If, as you state, you do not even love the poor fellow, I must assume you did this thing out of sheer perversity, perverse curiosity. Was it meant as some sort of test? You have harmed your body, you have harmed his heart, and I can only imagine what I will need to do to redeem the business relationship. You must learn not to drag people back and forth on a chain, the direction according to mood and no rational notion whatsoever.

If you will not reconsider, you and I will leave tomorrow, to do what we can to repair the problem. I suggest you send a letter of apology to Mr. Maslingen before we sail.

—Your loving father, WR

CHAPTER 6

MISS REMFREY IS LOST

•

A woman gets off one train and onto another, and no one human sees both moments. Of the people who notice her at all, the men remember thick dark hair (worn up: a married woman), her shape and nervousness, and the women see the red hat, the hint of the blue dress. She was pale, not so pretty as to be worth long study, and her good taste might have been accidental. They remember that she did not wear mourning, and that she was alone, and self-possessed. They assume she was well traveled, and married, and not a crazy girl who'd fling her body out of a train window.

• • •

Walton liked to introduce Dulcy as "a child of my dotage," which was annoying, given that the dotage was of his own making. Every trip began with a virtuous air—a promising mine to be checked, a surprising earthquake to be researched—and then the relief of having done his duty would light Walton like a firework, and he would slide off to fuck himself to death. He never, truly, saw it coming. While different hues of doctors treated him with mostly identical means—mercury and iodine enemas, purple potions and electric therapy—Dulcy learned to be anonymous. By the time she disappeared, she knew how to move, and how to be alone.

The only true anomaly was the trip to London in early 1902 after the engagement. This time, she was the patient: the best clinic in the world, but things went badly, and painfully; the pregnancy had been tubal, in the wrong place all along, and would have killed her in a month or two. The doctors sewed her up and told her she would now never bear a child.

She wondered sometimes if her aversion hadn't just been to Victor, but to fate. She liked children; she liked being alive. Despite any number of horror stories, she'd assumed these two things would go together.

After she seemed to recover, Walton took her to Cornwall. In Redruth, she met her great-uncle Edmund, who was elongated and dark like Walton, religious like Walton's brother, Christopher, bitter like neither of them. She saw her grandparents' graves in the pretty seaside town of Perranuthnoe. Away from the coast, Cornwall was a raw, sad place, boarded-up adits and slag piles, but when she pointed this out, Walton forgot his own disdain for his birthplace. Weeks of anger at having to deal with someone else's drama burbled out: Dulcy knew nothing about grubbing underground from infancy on to an early death, about her relative good fortune. He'd shown her tragic childhoods, everywhere they'd gone.

In early March, they sailed on to Lisbon and saw the damage still evident from the earthquake of 1755: fifty thousand dead, many in churches that collapsed during the All Saints' service, most in the tidal surge, some in the final fire. Walton said one hundred thousand, and that the same wave drowned the Azores and cracked the Galway city wall. Edmund, the sour uncle, had been told as a child that a wave had hit Penzance after this event. Walton claimed to be dubious, but she knew he was thrilled. He loved the notion of waves.

Dulcy looked down on the city from her hotel and wondered at how arbitrary Lisbon's hell had been—death by water while the city burned above, burning alive while water was visible. The blue-black harbor was still and deep and inviting, and the urge to drop into the sea stayed with her to Cape Town. She was seasick for the first time in years, and as she dangled over the edge she tried to come up with an equation to balance the cold and violence of the drop with the nausea and hopelessness of the deck. She worried about what she'd see before she died, as she sank. She didn't want to panic; she didn't want to see a beast rise up to meet her.

The plan in 1902 had been for Dulcy to stay with Walton all the way to the Transvaal, but by the time they landed in Cape Town she was ill, not seasick. Africa was a long hallucination. She'd read an account of the Siege of Mafeking (a dizzy blend of bicycle races and decapitations), and she was braced for starving blacks and Boer children in camps, but her fever kept her in a coastal villa so Cornish that it might have been in St. Ives, if it weren't for the plants and the bird calls, the servants with gold-ringed toes. She sat on a veranda above the ocean, imagining shark fins cutting through the surf while dozens of Cornish engineers trouped in and out, talking diamonds and gold, copper and silver. Smoke and voices spooled through the shutters of Walton's office, every man and thing smelling of tobacco and saddle soap and curry, scents that clashed with the heat and the cloying flowers from the garden. These men looked and sounded the same in Chile, Keweenaw, Butte, as they had in Cornwall; they all tended to look like Walton, Celtic instead of Anglo-Saxon, lean and dark instead of rosy and blond. They looked like the Irish, though you couldn't say that to either group. Only Robert Woolcock was distinctive: he had a great knob of a nose and tiny happy blue eyes; he used a deep bass voice on a huge repertoire of dirty song lyrics, all set to church melodies, and his was the only voice Dulcy enjoyed as her fever worsened. Walton said they drank more because she was in the next room and sick, but she could mark the moment each night when they forgot she was there, a half-dozen men cackling and crooning and passing a decanter. Not a bottle—that would have been Irish.

Then she worsened, Victor's child killing her again. Walton found a turbaned doctor who sliced her open for a second time and fed her iridescent medicines with an ivory spoon, while Walton lurked around the room. The doctor thought Walton was beside himself with worry, and he probably was, but Dulcy knew he was circling the doctor's medicines, looking for the exotic, for a cure, for orange pearls of tropical wisdom, liquid green marvel.

Walton and Woolcock disappeared for the mines to the north and left her in a world of ceiling fans and tropical flowers, days spent with little memory of anything between vanilla ices served by dark servants. She remembered watching the ice melt. Where had they found it? She couldn't imagine. Great ships waiting in the harbor, blocks sunk in sawdust in the hull—still, nothing could have lasted so long in that heat. But she really did remember ice, and seeds from a vanilla pod, and Indian mangos that were as sweet as Martha's peaches.

Toward the end of the trip to Africa, she'd listened to the men blather deep into a night, more talk of gold and copper and cunny, claustrophobic glory dreams echoing down the hall to her hot room. Walton laughed about an adept English colonel's wife, and Dulcy, trapped with these voices and the probable fate of the woman, left her bed for his room, where she drank most of his last half bottle of Armagnac and broke his seven thermometers one by one, pouring their contents out in a shimmery puddle on the top of his nicest shirt. He could take his mercury pure; he had to stop spreading the doom. She arranged the broken glass on the shirt, too, and walked across the compound to the nurse's quiet, airy cottage, where she was given another vanilla ice (never as cold or delicious as the first) and put into a cot.

Walton was attentive for the next two days, but by the time they left, he was back on himself, fretting about a relapse and muttering as the ship pulled away from the dunes about the copper he'd helped wrench out of the place, the diamonds and gold he was sure were under the sand of Namaqualand. This was his story, and he could only comprehend someone else's life for an hour or two at a time. His mood sweetened when they landed in Sicily. He sent off a salvo of triumphant telegrams to Victor and trolled for beauty through the narrow alleys of Palermo, while Dulcy sketched Etna and ate through the menu of the Hotel du France.

In June, in Salonica, they were greeted by Mehmet Akif, a banker Walton had met at a spa in Austria (Mr. Akif had suffered from a far more innocent disease) and done business with in Africa. Salonica was a perfect destination: earthquakes, ancient mines, and equally ancient medicinal springs. Mr. Akif's family—Dönmeh with the huge brown eyes of Coptic mummy paintings—served cherry juice and sweet wine, lamb and octopus and olives. Dulcy tried to learn the Greek alphabet and swam badly—despite growing up a mile from the lake, no one had ever really taught her—while wearing a balloon-like muslin shift. She visited an open-air cinema with Akif's daughters and avoided his sons' stares during table tennis and billiards.

The clinic was in the foothills. They shared a balcony, and when Walton wasn't being dosed or plumbed, she usually found him forgetting the book in his hand, watching one of the maids cross the tile below. "What are you doing?" she asked one evening.

"Well, Dulce, she's quite lovely."

The maid had long cherry-colored hair and a tiny waist. "And all of sixteen."

"Twenty, and widowed." The girl disappeared into a doorway. Walton waited for her to reemerge, a dog on point. It took years off his face.

"You must be fair to others. You mustn't ruin their lives."

"It's important not to be judgmental, Dulcy." His expression dared her to say more; she didn't usually bother, since she'd given up her high moral stance. "I have my ways."

Walton's ways—some of the time—were expensive sheaths; he liked to pretend she didn't know about them, despite the fact that he'd instructed doctors to speak to her directly, despite the fact that she handled his affairs and paid all his accounts. He went inside to dress for the evening. Two joined dogs lay in the courtyard under an apricot tree. She watched them pant and avoid each other's eyes, and her mood grew bleaker. Maybe she would run away.

On the evening of July 1, they joined the Akif family in the shaded courtyard of the white-walled Hotel Leonidou near Apostolon Square. They ate cheese and eggplant, game and fish and fruit, paper-layered cakes of honey and nuts, while doves rustled in almond trees, people laughing in air that felt silky on the skin. Walton was in the midst of an elegant toast when Dulcy realized that her straw-colored glass of wine was sliding away from her. Walton paused. There was a sense that the air in the town was sucking inside itself, that the trees were shrinking and the tiles of the courtyard swelling. Then everything broke apart and shattered, and the family and their guests threw themselves under the long oak table while windows and plaster descended from the hotel above.

The smell of dust, the beginning of smoke. The members of the dinner party stayed entwined under the table, all of them spackled with shattered glass and sticky wine. Dulcy's ears made a grinding noise, like a boat sliding on a gravel bank, in the very momentary silence before someone began to scream. Marble dust settled onto her arm, and she watched the shadows of birds veering about in the last of the sun. A donkey brayed, and she thought of how they'd once come upon a half-dozen starving goats in Turkey, marooned from their flock by a quake slide. No one ever talked about the animals in newspaper accounts, but in fallen towns, she'd seen people weep while they listened for the sounds of trapped cats and dogs.

The Hotel Leonidou had shifted two feet, but the pillars stood. A few blocks away, a pension had collapsed and caught fire, trapping and killing a group of Danish tourists.

"We are very fortunate," said Walton, later. This careful near-piety may have come out of the shock of seeing Mr. Akif drop to his knees and pray to the invisible new moon. When they returned to the clinic, they found the springs had cracked open, and the water had disappeared. Walton vanished, too, off with the caramel-haired girl, and when he was located, Dulcy herded him onto a ship bound for a fever clinic Mr. Akif had suggested, north of Naples.

• • •

On January 17, 1905, while her old life rolled on toward St. Paul, Walton's runaway daughter took the line west as far as Spokane, then changed to a Utah train at dawn. She wore her hair up to show diamond earrings above the red collar and blue dress, a blaze of color in a bleary morning. She sat with a nice woman named Lahey from Chicago and introduced herself as Anna Mendelson. She talked about visiting an aunt in Houston, about music (no, not those Mendelssohns, sadly), about the weather.

Mrs. Lahey would remember "Anna," who had brown eyes, dark brown hair, and a face and nose that had previously been described as long and English, as *that nice Jewish girl heading home to California*. Dulcy took a train to Pocatello, instead, then Omaha, where she spent a day writing and destroying apologies to Carrie. In the morning, she boarded a Topeka train, wearing a new wine-red dress.

She left a ribbon of fibs across the West for eight more days. In scrubby towns, the hotels all seemed to have the same carpet, the same lurching Otis elevators and anxious guests. Dulcy lay on identical beds, watching cooks drag garbage down alleys, pale men leave Chinese basements or tiny apartments with polka-dotted curtains. Stray dogs, dirty snow, women walking alone, wearing black; every city was populated by an identical army of men in black bowlers and black suits. She began to have an eye for the strange as it blurred by: there would be one bright dress besides her own in every crowd, one misshapen face or body; the odd cow in every herd—a monolithic black Angus changing out a herd of scrubby longhorns, a Holstein or Jersey Sabine in a gang of orange Herefords—would be the only one that bothered to lift its head to watch the train pass. In Colorado, she saw a bear sit back on its haunches, taking a pause in a menu of train-splattered carrion. She saw many small children, alone. She saw no one she recognized, anywhere, but every other day, she glimpsed Walton from behind.

She headed west to Denver and checked into the Brown Palace. She bought a plain gold ring, a shearling coat, a pretty blue tapestry purse, and black and mauve dresses to be tailored quickly, and she scanned newspapers while the order was tallied: two earthquakes on January 18, in the Caucasus and Veracruz. Walton would have maintained that the same great sucking gob of magma had caused both events.

• • •

The shock of the first account of the missing Leda Remfrey, found in the late edition of the Omaha *World Herald*:

> The sisters Remfrey were accompanying the body from Seattle to New York. It is believed that the missing girl departed the train between Miles City and Dickinson, though no witnesses admit to seeing her after Butte, when she stated she felt unwell. It is hoped that she became confused, and will be found in one of the towns along the Northern Pacific route, but though Miss Clarissa Remfrey denies that her sister was distraught following the death of their father, an official allows that evidence found in Miss Remfrey's cabin—a lowered window, fabric caught in one corner—suggests that the poor girl flung herself from the train, to her certain death, her body lost to wolves on the prairie.

This satisfied Dulcy, though she wished she could save Carrie and her aunts from the image. "Lost" was fairly gentle; soon vultures would pluck her eyes out, which was better than Victor finding her and doing the same thing. She ordered a tray, put a *quiet* sign on her door, drank most of a bottle of Corton-Charlemagne, and lay in the bathtub, adjusting the temperature with her toes. She dripped water across the room and stood naked at the window, at least for a moment. She danced, she lounged on the chaise and the bed, she played with herself, she felt some self-disgust but finished the wine.

She flipped through the newspapers and scribbled down ideas on the hotel notepad. She didn't want a tinny name.

• • •

The snow began in earnest, weighing down the hotel awnings. It fell too quickly to be colored black by coal and wood smoke, but at night all the frozen dust combined with streetlights to turn the city a glowing rotten lilac. The staff muttered about train delays, guests who were unable to leave, guests who failed to arrive. The bar and restaurant downstairs grew louder, and the room-service menu slid inexorably from shellfish and salads toward beef and potatoes.

On the third day, when the trains stopped entirely, the doormen looked at her in disbelief as she headed out: to a bookstore, to keep from losing her mind; to a stationer to have calling cards and notepaper and luggage tags printed. At the last moment she had the initial *D* inserted, then tried to beat down her panic as she floundered on to a picture show. *Cleopatra*, staged with midget pyramids and a bantam Marc Antony, palm fronds everywhere—she sat there, befuddled in a miasma of clove cigarettes, and wondered at people who seemed to believe a chubby woman in a horsehair wig had something to do with Egypt. Henning would never have inflicted such crap upon the world.

The suicidal Leda Cordelia Dulcinea Remfrey continued to appear in the newspapers, but her middle names were rarely mentioned. In a week-old New York *Tribune*, Dulcy found the photograph she'd dreaded on an inside illustrated page. Her hair was flossy and long, body skinny inside a jumper. She had not yet grown into her nose. The Remfreys had gathered, even the Boys—tall and fake-grim like Walton—because Dulcy and Walton had been about to leave for Mexico, to see his brother, Christopher, in Pachuca, a city that managed to combine agave and copper and white Cornish houses. It had been her first true trip.

There are two dueling theories. The first, whispered by friends of Mr. Maslingen's parents in New York, is that Miss Remfrey had always been unstable and eccentric, a tendency that strengthened during her strange, unchaperoned jaunts with her father. How else to explain the way she broke things off with Mr. Maslingen years ago? These people suggest that she is somewhere in the West, having now utterly lost her already eccentric mind; they also deny that Mr. Maslingen had again proposed.

The second theory is that she quite deliberately committed suicide, in despair, despite her renewed engagement with Mr. Maslingen. This rumor comes from Seattle, from people who have recently seen the man himself: he is unstrung with love and claims that only death would keep them apart. He vows to search until he finds her body; he has hired teams of detectives to scour the country.

Why would she think she could hide? He would kill her if she didn't kill herself: why wait, in dread? Some things were not survivable. All the adrenaline—whatever fear and love that had gotten her through Seattle, Walton falling, Victor, and her own flight—evaporated.

That evening, after more spendthrift wine, Dulcy dressed carefully and walked into the hotel's balconied hall, open to the lobby seven stories below. The irony of the floor had not passed her by, and the stained-glass roof was almost close enough to touch. She leaned out over the balcony, and her breasts started to slide out of her dress at the same time as a child ran across the floor far below, and a table of men happened to look up.

Poor people. No one but her had seen Walton hit, and the people who craned in afterward deserved the image that lodged in their brains, a man whose body looked like a badly judged pressing, a flower too thick-petaled and moist to be preserved. She pulled back, woozy and abashed. If she could have walked off a train during a warm storm and been incinerated by lightning, she might have managed it, but there was no way around leaving a mess.

And in the morning, despite a hangover, Dulcy found she didn't want to die. She emptied one of Walton's two Denver bank boxes— two keys, two imagined names in two different handwriting styles— stuffed her old clothes into a church charity bin, and headed north to Billings, an arbitrary choice, under one final, sentimental name: Martha Wooster. She'd steamed her face, scrubbed her mouth, taken some Walton pills, but her eyes still felt like they'd lost their curve, and her balance was off, and the people on this last train seemed to speak a foreign dialect.

That afternoon, when the porters offered drinks, she was the only woman to accept. She told herself she didn't care; she told herself that the young man sitting kitty-corner was worse off: he reached to his whiskey with a shaking hand but never quite brought it to his mouth. He had huge brown teary eyes, and between attempts at the drink, he used a Parker filigree pen—Walton would have killed for this pen—to fill pages with dense, crooked writing.

At the ten-minute warning for Billings, she watched as he put the pen and paper down, belatedly drained his glass, and left the lounge car. A moment later, the train braked, and a woman began to scream, and Dulcy, blind to her book, understood. The people around her milled to the window and said *well of course* and *anyone could see he was a drinker* and *bits of him everywhere—he dropped straight down. They're still looking for pieces of that girl on the prairie.* And: *one wonders how many delays are due to people who do this to themselves? You can't stop for every lunatic, but any lunatic can stop commerce.*

Suicides were inefficient; suicide was selfish: they'll be sorry when I'm gone, rather than they'll be better off without me. She roused herself and picked up the man's papers and warm pen and sat in his warm seat while she waited for some sort of authority to fetch them. She hated these people: who were they to judge the difficulty of a leap, any leap, how hard it had been to stand between cars in the cold and noise, willing the end. When the conductor came through, looking for the man's belongings, she held the papers away from her fellow passengers; it was none of their business.

"Well, aren't you a special lady," said a woman in purple velvet.

Aren't I, thought Dulcy, who hadn't handed over the pen; Walton wasn't the only one with a fondness for strange talismans. When the train finally rolled again, and the fatuous turds around her stopped talking long enough to detrain in Billings, she decided she wouldn't stay in this place. On the next westbound train, she kept her valise with her. The express followed the Yellowstone River upstream, barreling through a half-dozen scrawny towns. It slowed for Livingston in the failing light, and when she saw the railroad's massive brick machine shops, she realized that this was the town with the champagne crowd and the boastful depot, the place she'd once stayed with Walton, the place where she'd stopped being herself. The buildings looked raw and wet in the just-lit streetlamps, and a group of children skittled down an alley. Perhaps five hundred houses, none very large: it surely wasn't big enough, but she stood anyway, and walked off.

Get your facts, first, and then you can distort them as much as you please.

—Mark Twain

CHAPTER 7

ANOTHER COUNTRY

•

Walton, who managed to believe devoutly in the end of time without lending it a shred of religious significance, had come by his own revelations, and ultimately to the American West, in a salvo that began after he sailed out of Falmouth Harbor with Christopher in 1867. Walton was four months free of a six-year apprenticeship at the copper mines in Allihies, Ireland, and two months free of an engagement to a girl named Ellen, whom he hadn't seen for three years. He'd returned to Cornwall from Ireland to find that she was dying of tuberculosis. She let him go gracefully, having greater concerns.

The winter voyage to Veracruz took almost a month at the worst possible time of year, and when they reached the port, after they made their way between rows of Maximilian's French soldiers, they were stunned by color and heat and smell; dizzy with rum and thick coffee, the strangeness of citrus and snapper and tamales and avocados. Walton could not adjust to the idea that the air could be wet and hot at the same time, outside of a mine. He drank too much and found the women's houses near the harbor, while Christopher, during calm evenings in the arched courtyards and gardens near churches, talked to priests and gardeners, and worked on his Spanish. He began to enjoy chilies.

They traveled south to Chagres and walked across the Isthmus. Bugs and greenery fascinated Christopher—he would happily have stayed in Veracruz for the rest of his life, muttering about the female shapes of orchids—and terrified Walton, who preferred his claustrophobic environments rocky and sterile. At the Pacific coast, they continued south to Chile to visit their friend Woolcock at the Cerro Blanco mines, landing at Valparaiso and moving back up the coast before crossing the Atacama. They passed evidence of ruined towns and of the tsunami that had hit far south thirty-three years earlier, after the earthquake Charles Darwin observed on February 20, 1835:

> The motion made me almost giddy: it was something like the movement of a vessel in a little cross-ripple, or still more like that felt by a person skating over thin ice, which bends under the weight of his body. A bad earthquake at once destroys our oldest associations: the earth, the very emblem of solidity, has moved beneath our feet like a thin crust over a fluid.

One wave-drowned village was still marked by the stubble of its cathedral and the shell of a boat deposited far inland, and as they walked through the ruins toward a northbound coach on February 21, 1868, the brothers felt the sharp tremor of a new event. The driver screamed and the horses bolted. The Remfrey brothers waited some hours, in the company of untroubled locals, before a fresh driver came by.

The quake made an impression on Walton: the ruins glowed in the light of a moon he remembered as full, and this was the beginning of his obsession with a seasonal, tidal theory: he believed the moon exerted pressure on the bumpy skin of earth, pulling it like taffy. Christopher suggested coincidence, or God, and Walton called God lily-fucking-livered, and the brothers had an argument so profane and violent that the offended driver ordered them out of the coach, marooning them for a day with a flask of water and some corn flatbread.

After a third coach found them, and they continued across the plain of the Atacama, they observed dried wrapped bodies, exhumed by the wind. Walton had a fever, and he assumed this was a vision (he assumed as well that he had consumption—he'd managed to talk Ellen into a show of affection before he left, arguing that she was leaving soon, anyway, in a more complete sense, and didn't she owe herself all possible experience?), but the driver said these mummies did exist, and were in fact ancient. Though Christopher was a rational Methodist, he also had a fever, and the barren air beat at his reason. He fell to remembering horrible stories he'd been told in the Redruth workhouse: the *bucca* trying to mate you or kill you deep in the mine, *Blunderbore* eating you on the path out, *piskies* fucking with you everywhere. Christopher did a passable job of delivering these stories in Spanish, and they were once again put aside to await another coach.

Sometimes Dulcy thought of checking the date of that earthquake, the phase of its moon, the notion that Chile had drowned cities or mummies or any of it. But if she looked into it, she might hate Walton more than a quarter of the time, and abandon him, and be left with herself.

Walton and his brother spent the summer—the winter—at Cerro Blanco, helping Woolcock install hoists and man engines, playing cards, two of them whoring. When the Remfreys sailed north again in July, Christopher told Walton he'd decided to join up with a group of Cornish engineers in Mexico, and Walton said good-bye to his brother in Panama City. He boarded a Pacific Mail steamer named the *Golden City* and arrived in San Francisco on the evening of October 20 with 305 other passengers, 152 sacks of mail, and some 8,000 packets of fabric, food, and hardware.

Walton found a rooming house and headed out for oysters and fried salmon, apples and whiskey and women. He was up at eight the next morning, having coffee and side pork and biscuits with a lucky double-yolked egg while he considered the street scene on Sansome and his plans. Should he make his way to Nevada, where he had a captain's job with a silver-mining crew, or should he risk a delay for another happy night of love?

Then every pigeon in the city flushed straight up, the air buzzed, and the shaking began. The street split, and the glass window by his table shuddered and dropped, and the frame grocery across the street folded like a piece of stiff fabric. People in the harbor swarmed uphill, screaming; people on the hill ran down. Walton stepped through the now-open window of the restaurant, walked up to the moving crevice in the street, and stared down at breathing rock. Until that moment he'd thought that his hangover had taken hold, or that he suffered from *mal d'embarcation* instead of *mal de mer*. He thought at first he would be sick—this all happened in forty-five seconds—but then he felt as wonderful as he had for a few glancing moments the night before, in the grip of a big blond woman. And he could talk about this experience, which he did on a daily basis for the next three and a half years.

In early 1872, Walton left a captain's job at the Mary Harrison mine in Mariposa County, California, and headed east with a group of friends to Inyo and a new silver claim. Two months later, on the night of March 26, they were well underground, but Walton was off shift, playing poker on a warm spring night, under a waxing moon. Their valley had begun blooming: redbud and poppies, wallflowers and shooting stars; they played on the porch of one of a half-dozen wood and adobe shacks in a wide clearing, surrounded by overhanging cliffs, and Walton was losing, having not yet gotten a feel for the game. He never would get a feel for the game, but on this occasion he was suddenly unable to feel the floor of the porch: he and the other men were spilled onto the dirt in front of it, and they watched as the surrounding frame houses hopped "like frogs"—though unlike frogs they shattered on landing—and their adobe neighbors crumbled, and boulders sent down from cliffs grumbled by in a sudden game of giant's marbles. Everything that hadn't shattered or rolled had moved some dozen feet, including the town's four trees, and Walton gained a tighter grip on his own version of God.

Years later, in a spa library, Dulcy read John Muir's account of the same night in the *Atlantic*:

> The Eagle Rock, a short distance up the valley, had given way, and I saw it falling in thousands of the great boulders I had been studying so long, pouring to the valley floor in a free curve luminous from friction, making a terribly sublime and beautiful spectacle—an arc of fire fifteen hundred feet span, as true in form and as steady as a rainbow, in the midst of the stupendous roaring rock-storm. The sound was inconceivably deep and broad and earnest, as if the whole earth, like a living creature, had at last found a voice and were calling to her sister planets.

Walton had brought Dulcy west when she was only sixteen. He had failed to regulate his medication during a trip the previous winter, and he'd been so ill that Martha had refused to let Dulcy go overseas with him again. It was a bluff, but Walton backed down, and wandered through California that spring like a bored dog, while Dulcy kept a loose, rattled hand on a leash. In July he abruptly decided that his real affliction was a brain tumor, and he made plans to visit a sanatorium north of Yellowstone Park. Dulcy didn't ask how this diagnosis explained the wonderful things that were happening to the rest of his body; she assumed that he wanted to spend time staring into geysers or revisiting the idea of the failed magnometer.

In practice, the trip to Yellowstone meant standing on very fragile-seeming rock near very hot water, waiting to feel an earthquake. Dulcy saw her first elk and moose, geysers and hot pots. They visited Moran's deep canyon and the waterfalls, and their guide gave her berries, and the venison was delicious at the lodge. An army officer told stories over dinner about earlier visitors who'd fallen into hot pots, eaten the wrong root, arm-wrestled bears. The park offered all sorts of novel deaths, and the officer's wife looked worried.

The next morning they headed north for the clinic, which was tucked into the mountains near the site of a played-out gold settlement. Beyond the pleasures of a hot plunge, Eve's Spring specialized in brain surgery. Walton normally preferred the sort of places with hot compresses and special menus, and when he took in the cadaverous doctor, the shiny steel equipment, the dozen men with bandaged heads sunning foggily by the steaming blue-tiled pool (rather than splashing happily inside it), he panicked. He'd been relying on coca and morphine, and it had been weeks since he'd made sense. Now he announced that there'd been a mistake: his poor daughter, who suffered from neurasthenia, was the patient. He was worried she might harm herself.

"But who would have recommended us to you?" asked a nurse, while the doctor walked away, the greatest insult he could possibly offer to Walton. "We don't handle rest cures."

"She also has seizures," said Walton. "Fits and fevers."

The nurse eyed Dulcy's cheeks and correctly diagnosed her flush as humiliation. The next morning, after Walton had agreed to be examined and was once again marooned with his hopeless, shameful diagnosis, they hired a coach back to town rather than waiting for the train. The day was warm, the air shimmery with grasshoppers. Dulcy distracted herself with the dark blue river and yellow rocks, the smell of pine and grass; she counted cows and sheep, and came up with a tie. As they approached a large farmhouse, a vision: a hundred men on bicycles—black men on bicycles, in uniform—pouring out of an encampment onto the narrow dirt road, white bedrolls on their handlebars.

"The Twenty-fifth Infantry Bicycle Corps," said the polite professor who shared the carriage. He was leaving for his home in Minnesota; his tumor was incurable. One eye was bandaged to hide the fact that it was bulging out of his skull, and the clinic had refused to try a trepanation. "Under General Miles. They're testing this method for the army. I gather they're bicycling to the Park."

Dulcy looked at the faces of the passing men, their eyes veering away from her own. They were so close she could see strips of that morning's lather on their necks, red dust from the road settling on their freshly shaven faces. They were pared down, grave, and beautiful. "It's a mirage," said Walton, his eyes yellow with jaundice; mercury had damaged his liver. "My God, if only there were roads in Africa."

She was mortified: her fair-minded father had disintegrated. She wanted to beat him over the head, but she kept her voice quiet. "There are roads in Africa, Dad. You've seen them."

"Bicycles," whispered Walton.

• • •

Nine years later, there didn't seem to be many people of color in this town, even natives, though the weather might be to blame for the lack of bicycles. Dulcy had never felt such wind. Before she'd even crossed the street in Livingston on January 28, her hair unraveled and one of her scarves swirled into the frozen dark. In 1896, when she'd come through this town with Walton, the depot had been tall and narrow; now it was massive, with a slate roof and wind-funneling colonnades. Maybe the old depot had burned like everything in the West—the buildings across the street were new, too, and she headed for one of them, a brick hotel named the Elite.

She wanted privacy, and she wanted her own bath; the Elite provided these things. The large, pink proprietress, Mrs. Knox, talked in puffs while they trundled to the third floor—the hotel had a new elevator, but there were issues with its motor. The tiny porter was only twenty or so, but he also wheezed audibly, coughing discreetly whenever he was out of sight around a bend on the stairs. "At this end of the hall, the train will be less likely to wake you," said Mrs. Knox.

Dulcy had an image of a stalking train, a Cyclops headlight shining into a hotel window, looking for her. She aimed her eyes at the pattern in the carpet, fat ruby-colored roses. "And the newspaper's on that side, too, though we ask that they not run their presses during the night," said Mrs. Knox. "I'm very sorry for your bereavement. Your husband?"

"Yes," said Dulcy. "Thank you. And I am here for precisely that reason, to rest."

"Well, then," said Mrs. Knox. "We'll not bother you. You have family here?"

"No, we passed through here once, and talked of returning. And so, somehow, I thought . . ." She petered out, but she was tired. The explanation was both evocative and convincing, and she had successfully avoided dates or origins. Mrs. Knox twirled a finger, and the elfin porter deposited the suitcase on a marble-topped dresser. The marble was nice, but the dresser itself looked as if it had been made to fit, with a hacksaw.

"I'll wire to have my other things delivered," said Dulcy, and then she regretted saying it. She needed to avoid adding details. After they left, she lifted the window for a moment. She smelled Chinese food, and heard a piano, not a dance hall tune but poorly played Bach.

Never before in the history of the world has there been such a remarkable series of terrestrial disturbances as those which have followed each other day by day over the past three months over an area covering practically the entire surface of the globe. . . . From the original eruption of Mount Pelée to the present time there has hardly been a day when the record has not shown earthquake, tidal wave, or volcanic disturbance. . . . Thousands upon thousands of persons have lost their lives, other thousands have been maimed, towns and cities have been wiped out. . . .

—From "Three Months of Earthquakes and Eruptions,"
The New York Times, August 17, 1902

CHAPTER 8

THE GARNET BOOK OF THEORY

•

A follow-up article on September 28—after eruptions in Japan, Italy, Greece, and Mexico—ended with the phrase "what the immediate future has in store no one in authority pretends to say precisely," but this wasn't quite true. Walton, one of the authorities consulted, had been happy to say what he thought was going to happen next: more of the same. The world's center was ripening and expanding, writhing in discomfort. The end was nigh, and they were all going to die. There was nothing Biblical about this: the earth was godless, unsympathetic, and a grand killer. She didn't give a damn for her inhabitants' physical suffering and puny offerings. Instead of blaming God for the earth's sins, Walton blamed the earth for religion: natural disasters weighed on fragile minds, and fragile minds shattered and subscribed to the notion of an angry god. If people weren't terrified, why, he asked Dulcy, would they be such idiots, over and over again? In Seattle, toward the end, another singsong: *dynamism, dynamite, dice, die, diet, deity.*

But after the earthquake in Salonica in 1902, something seemed to slip in Walton's brain, and he lost his ability to silence himself when a listener's eyes glazed over. He'd always been a marginal man of science, strange but influential and somehow more authentic to reporters than those men who never left the university. He was one of the few authorities (and he loved the word *authority*) with true experience with the world below the earth's surface. Now, though he maintained a competent business front on Victor's behalf, he lost the line between theory and fantasy on his favorite topic, what he liked to call the "dynamic earth."

"A volcano is a pustule!" he howled into the Westfield telephone, home for a week and ten minutes into his last talk with a *Times* reporter. "It enlarges, and ruptures through thinning skin, and the infection spreads!" He now believed that some combination of the moon and the fermenting iron and uranium core of the world caused quakes and volcanoes just as they caused tides; the tides themselves caused imbalances that disturbed the thin parts of the earth, and storms—false tides—were also capable of waking fragile parts of the earth's skin, areas that were already under pressure. But this liquid notion of quakes had been long discounted, and Walton's attempt to ball up neptunism or plutonism with the new theory of radioactivity didn't go over well. He had only a faint, selective grasp of the idea of radiation, and he couldn't prove anything with his calendar, but he would not believe in a random universe. Why would Mississippi suffer a significant earthquake and not Switzerland? Why was Scandinavia so stable, and Alaska in constant movement? Given his knowledge of quartz and copper and schist, these questions were torments. He had a tightly folded map of the world, and he sometimes tacked it to cork, pressed in pins, and strung the pins together with different colors, seeking a pattern. Dulcy had seen a Micronesian island map that looked a little like this: a confused guitar, a drunken cat's cradle. Sometimes he'd paste on colored dots for the samples he'd retrieved; sometimes he added little flags and squinted, deliberately blurring the picture to find a pattern. There were, in his mind, no true anomalies, just bad data.

That fall, Walton returned to Westfield in the midst of a fever. Mr. Akif's Italian clinic had failed to cure his syphilis, and on the boat home he'd taken massive doses of quinine for his newest, deliberately contracted illness, malaria. When they reached Manhattan, he gathered up news accounts of the eruption in Martinique, the greatest volcano of his lifetime, and on the ride north to Westfield he raved on about how thousands of fer-de-lance—vipers—driven out of the mountain forests when their dens turned into ovens, had swarmed the streets of Saint-Pierre. He told Dulcy about how people had dropped, paralyzed, where they'd been bitten; how they had lain in the bubbling mud, snakes sliding over bodies; how this poisoned hypersensitivity might have allowed the dying to feel the presentiment of disaster, the quivering lava several strata below.

Dulcy never saw this piece of reporting in the piles of paper around the farmhouse, and she was dubious. Walton knew she didn't like snakes. She'd been tentative on their one trip to Egypt and later barely left a hotel in Ceylon, despite an intense curiosity about the food. She disliked snakes so deeply that she'd read quite a bit about snakebites, and she'd never heard of a snake outside of Australia capable of dropping a man in his tracks, but she let Walton unwind. "Where did the snakes go, when they were done?"

"Soldiers shot some. The rest slid into the ocean."

Or died with the rest of Saint-Pierre a few days later. Had the seawater boiled when Mount Pelée finally exploded? This thought came out of her mouth as she held a steaming washcloth against the side of his face—gumma fear, again, but she thought he simply had a toothache. "Of course it boiled," he snapped. "Boiled and evaporated. I imagine deposits of salt left behind, dusted with cinders."

While he slept—it was a humid eighty-degree Indian summer day in Westfield, and Walton lay on the porch daybed—she read about other things that happened in Martinique: boiling mud, overflowing rivers and a fog of ash, swarms of ants and foot-long centipedes. On May 5, a tidal wave. On May 7, La Soufrière on the island of St. Vincent erupted, killing off the last of the Carib natives, and neighboring Martinique spent a last night reassured that the internal energies of the Caribbean had turned on others. But the next morning, Saint-Pierre's population burned to death almost instantly in a cloud of "pure temperature."

Dulcy imagined this as steam from a kettle, the blinding puff of an opened oven. She had just opened an oven for a chicken pie, flavored with some of the items she'd smuggled home from Italy. None of the articles Dulcy ever found mentioned the fer-de-lance invasion, possibly because the larger details—three humans alive, thirty thousand dead—took precedence, and possibly because Walton made things up.

• • •

Dulcy burrowed into her lair at the Elite, drowned herself under Mrs. Knox's soft corduroy quilt. She admired the clear yet soothing quality of light, rather than getting back on the Great Northern to New York and a ship. Rather than many things. She beat back a childish urge to bolt for Christopher in Mexico, mostly by considering a life of church and bitter letters from the Boys and Carrie, Grace and Alice. Not to mention Victor. Not to even think of Victor.

She'd worked through a stack of books she'd bought in Denver, and the last in the pile was a roman à clef about the Spanish War by a man named Maximillian Cope. *A History of a Small War* was funny, and rude, and full of convenient detail. The narrator enlisted to escape an engagement, and was put to use as a sharpshooter; he discovered he reacted badly to killing people (he drank, he found women) and managed to escape that, too: he spent most of Cuba in a hospital with malaria, and most of the Philippines in a hospital because of a misfired shell. When he returned to New York he found his fiancée had jilted him, and so he got on a westbound train and seduced a married woman before he reached Chicago. The end offered a refreshing lack of redemption or punishment.

Dulcy, who wasn't in a judgmental mood, finished the book that afternoon and daydreamed her way through it for another hour, reworking her own story.

She had dinner, a gristly pork pie, brought to her room. She'd sent the tiny bellboy out for a newspaper, and he found a *Times*, where she read of a massive blizzard in New York, snow three feet deep on

Fifth Avenue, while she drank a bottle of Cahors and took a long bath. She saw a notice for the speedy Hamburg-American ship *Deutschland*, ninety dollars and up for first class, sailing from New York on February 7 for Genoa. Dulcy thought about the meals and the wind on the deck and the rocking, luxurious berth. She could have one if she got back onto a train immediately. Victor didn't do well in boats, but he also didn't do well in small towns with middling hotels. He'd hate the wind; it would muss his hair, and everything would be out of his control.

When she couldn't sleep, she thought about the letter she'd sent to him.

By now you know I'm willing to die to be free of you, just as my father was. Perhaps you can find some way to be happy in your very unhappy body and soul, but I think no one can help you, no one will love you, and nothing will change you. You cause pain; you are unredeemable.

She hoped the words had ground down on his soul. It would have been so much simpler if he'd been the one to go, instead of her. She daydreamed about his end; it was like counting sheep. Sometimes she imagined the smug look on his face just before he was hit by a train, by lava, by falling rocks (it was important, in this vaporous revenge, for Victor to have moments of understanding that some pieces of the world moved without his approval; hideous pain and public shaming were included, revelations of his cruelty, his physical failures, the deaths that didn't trouble him). In a favorite scenario, Victor was in the gym at the Butler, weeping over her supposed death, when the ground began to shake, and the building crumbled over him, and for weeks the investors who'd taken his money and kissed his ass (somehow in a way other than the way she and Walton and Henning, who always survived these daydreams, had kissed his ass), would have to smell his stinking, unlovely corpse under the rubble.

Victor crumbled, he burned. But that night, in the warmth of the Elite, she imagined him freezing to death in an alley, magpies prying out jewel-sized bites of green eye, and she slept well.

• • •

The next morning, she heard cows lumber through town and the occasional engine on the frozen street. The small porter, whose name was Irving, brought coffee and announced that the temperature was ten below zero. "Don't go out," he said.

"How cold might it get?" she asked.

"Thirty under tonight. Forty." His eyes were uneven, and after he heard a question, there was always a lull, as if he were waiting for an invisible translator to make sense of the line. He wheezed and spat and was not long for this world; Dulcy tipped him well.

She draped herself in black and took the long hall to the stairs and the main lobby of the Elite, which looked like a different country in the daylight, after sleep: airy and high-windowed, but weighed down by trophies of moose and buffalo and Amazonian fish, all with glass eyes that followed her progress like bad actors, like the dozen guests who studied her with unapologetic curiosity and the tall, dark desk girl, who wore a filigree sign on her breast: *Irina*. Dulcy decided that this was not the time to place a telephone call. She walked through the doors as if she knew where she was going.

The illusion of golden warmth shriveled in the wind, and within two blocks she returned to fantasies of Italy. She opted for the first bank she came to, made her deposit with a shiny-faced banker, and took a medium-sized safety deposit box.

"Thank you, Mrs. Nash," said the banker.

Mrs. Nash had a short name and a flowing signature. She tucked the account card and key into her blue bag, and she walked away, mind blinking.

The library was just a block away, so new that only the periodical room was in use, and a banner advertised a grand opening that spring. A long table of women looked up from pots of glue and virgin circulation cards while she selected a stack of novels, and continued to watch while she pulled on eyeglasses and searched the eastern papers.

She didn't find a notice for Walton, but she did for Carrie.

Miss Clarissa Mabena Galatea Remfrey became the bride of
Dr. Alfred Lorrimer, a cardiologist, on Wednesday afternoon, the 25th of January, at the Manhattan home of her
brother, Walter Remfrey. All concerned are greatly relieved
that a ray of happiness will shine upon the bride during
her double bereavement; this happiness was her father's
dying wish.

Small miracles. Dulcy fished around for sadness, but though the idea
of never seeing Carrie again always smacked her in the throat, the
idea of missing the wedding only brought relief.

She scanned the local papers. In neighboring Big Timber, a
smallpox patient had escaped the pesthouse in his nightshirt, danced
down a sidewalk, and run into a busy saloon. In Livingston, Winslow
Mercantile had both fresh oysters and nice oranges, and the town
was going through a winter rash of divorces, dead children, and
poisoned cats: this newspaper, lacking meaningful news, listed every
drama. In the Billings *Gazette* she found an item about the search for
Leda Remfrey, now firmly centered in Miles City, where a girl of her
description had been seen singing dementedly by the river. Dulcy
felt something close to happiness—a little smugness—but on the
editorial page, someone with the byline *S. Peake* brought her out of
a placid mood:

- Why come this far on a train, to die under a train? The
  following souls have recently ended their lives in this way
  on Western lines, and it behooves thinking people to ask if
  the sheer emptiness of the region calls out to the suicide.

- A drunk in Missoula accelerated a green Rambler toward
  the tracks in an automobile on January 8. We do not know
  his last words, either, though the three people with him
  presumably heard them.

- A bereaved girl threw herself from the window of the
  Empire Builder on January 16 or 17, and chose the least

comforting landscape possible in which to die: namely the area between Butte and the Dakota line.

- Young Alexander Tuck, heir to a ranching fortune, dropped between the cars just outside of Billings on January 27. He had been wronged financially by his partner and could not face his family.

- The mangled body of another girl was found near the tracks east of Livingston only yesterday. We have no idea when she took her last ride.

All of these people acted on what could only be profound despair. Our long winter exacts a toll.

These were the people she'd decided not to be. Dulcy thought of Alexander Tuck's beautiful eyes, the way he'd dropped his pen and the pages of explanation. She wondered again if Walton had fallen with his eyes open, and if he'd focused on the sky, or screwed them shut to everything but memory and wind.

She heard a muffled crash and craned her neck to see out of the library window. A cart had blown over on the street, and men ran to help free the horse from its harness, hopping over unfurling rolls of canvas. The tail of the struggling horse whipped the men trying to cut the traces, and their coats pillowed out in the wind.

She flipped back to the front page. The unidentified girl found the day before was described as likely one of the town's "unfortunates," a euphemism that made her brain ache. The cold weather made it hard to be specific about the time of death—she may have lain in the snow for weeks—but the *unfortunate* had been in her mid-twenties with an average build and dark hair, and an undated chit from a Spokane restaurant in her coat. Dulcy wondered if they'd been on the same train on the same night, two suicides waiting for the right moment.

Darling—I should have been patient, but you always wanted me to be capable of impulse, and strong feeling, out of my head and free with delight. I can only do better, and you surely know I've never loved anyone as I love you, and I will continue to try. Your touch and your voice are what I long for; I have proved that now, haven't I? A safe journey, and I will join you at the funeral.

—*Your beloved V, 14 January*

CHAPTER 9

THE JADE BOOK
OF ELITE OBSERVATIONS

•

In her first week at the Elite, Dulcy spoke to no one but hotel staff, the librarian, and store clerks. She had most meals sent up and spent her time reading in the sun of her south window. She read books that annoyed her, about people who (not being real) could die with meaning, and she moved to the east window whenever a train arrived, to gauge its passengers for Victor's spies. When the lobby seemed quiet, she'd slip outside and slide on frozen clay streets, mummy-wrapped in woolen scarves as she zigzagged toward the river—snapping ice and steam and eagles—wishing she'd never left the Elite, wishing she'd never left anything. She would begin to bawl (silently, but this was no polite ooze from a pretty corner of the eye), keeping her eyes down on the black ribbons on her skirt, the warped, icy sidewalk boards.

When these spasms passed—Carrie was better off without her, Walton was better off out of pain, and Victor would ideally spin on a pike and die alone—she would feel like she was holding her breath. She wanted to burst into movement like a child, like a horse losing its head and bolting. No one can make me do anything, thought Dulcy. Running away was childish, but was it cowardly to run into a new world alone? It made her feel tired, and it made her feel lonely in a new, hard way. Aloneness had always been finite: Walton would be discharged from a clinic or die, and she would go home to both Martha and a future. She hadn't considered the oddity of not even being able to write a letter to another being, or the implication: she no longer existed.

This thought took her to Vogt Liquors, and then to bed. After two sodden days, she cleaned herself up, smuggled the empty bottles out to an alley bin, and took to the lobby, an invisible widow who kept her face plain and pointed in books. Mrs. Knox's desk girl, Irina Dis, spilled tea onto Dulcy's plate without apology, letting her know she knew Mrs. Nash was a dipsomaniac.

The chair Dulcy liked best was near a frayed Boston fern, and the people who moved through the room gradually assumed she was one, and went back to their own dramas. Watching and listening chipped away at the problem of having no actual life, and little idea of how to begin one. The fern chair gave her a view of the teatime crowd, and the beginning of the cocktail hour; a corner table in the dining room, perched near the kitchen door, gave her breakfast, lunch, and dinner. One of the newspaper's doors opened into the lobby, which in turn opened onto both a dining room and a saloon, and she watched the paper's staff ply sources. The editor, Samuel Peake, was a slight man with dark hair, a sad voice, a long nose, and putty skin. He'd been the one to write about bodies dotting the plains, but he always looked amused as he and his assistant, a slender young man named Rex Woolley, wined and dined everyone: beer and sausage for police and railroad contacts, whiskey and cheese toasts for businessmen and doctors, claret and oysters for the bankers and lawyers. When the newspapermen were in the restaurant, words like *divorce* and *insane* and *blackmail* and *fiend* left a kind of vibration in the air.

It was stunning what a person could hear in such a hubbub. Dulcy listened hard; so did Irina and the head maid, Rusalka Havic. They were from Trieste and Bucharest, either end of Eastern Europe, and were forced to speak English with each other. Irina was tall and malicious and meant her comments, and Rusalka, a redhead who looked like a curvy peppermint stick, parroted everything she heard. Beyond their contrasting appearances—sulky and dark, bright and sunny—they were alike in being resolutely shallow, with no thought beyond a new man in the lobby, dress, the police chief's bad marriage. They talked about the guests, though Dulcy was never fernlike enough to catch them talking about her. The accountant in Room 204 might be an axe murderer (Irina, disputed by Rusalka); one man long absent from Room 423 (Dulcy, below him in 323, paid attention to this) might have managed to kill himself in Butte or Helena or even further afar; the colorless Leonora Randall in 326, another lobby stalwart, received monthly wired payments from New York and was either in the process of being jilted or fleeing a violent suitor. Miss Randall's lips were thin and chapped, her eyes flat, and her papery sobs itched their way through Dulcy's west wall. They had tea together one day, but Miss Randall didn't volunteer tragedy; she talked quite a bit about nothing: dresses, stationery, and Very Nice People in town.

Dulcy was interested in ruin and duplicity, and she sorted people in her own way: the dishonest (Irina, for example, and the unfaithful police chief Gerry Fenoways, a bullheaded drunk who always seemed to be whispering in the ear of Eugenia Knox, who was his aunt), the mental wrecks (Leonora Randall, young Rex Woolley on a bad day, a man wearing armor who'd stood in the street and screamed about God until Gerry Fenoways bundled him off), and refugees like Samuel Peake and the German photographer, Siegfried Durr.

Dulcy understood that she currently fit in all three of these categories, but she aimed for the last group; they seemed to keep secrets well. No one knew what to whisper about Durr, a Berliner with stiff dark hair and wild blue eyes, a bad limp, and an elegant ebony-and-silver cane. He kept a military bearing, and Dulcy watched Gerry Fenoways size him up and stay away. Dulcy did the same with Fenoways, who was theoretically handsome, meeting his eyes over a newspaper: they dismissed each other. He strutted on thick, too-short legs and brayed, and might as well have been another species.

According to Eugenia Knox, who had purchased the hotel two years earlier, Samuel Peake had come to Montana for his health, like half the town: sufferers of asthma, or tuberculosis, or the pressures of city living. One day he sat next to Dulcy in the lobby, and after a diffident conversation about her past and her reading, he asked: "My condolences, but do you need to be in absolute mourning, if no one here knew your husband? Are you still in the mood to mourn, or has grief begun to come and go?"

It took her a moment: "Some days are difficult."

"Well, hide on those and go out on others. Life is short."

This wasn't the tenor she was looking for: she needed a buffer of tragedy, time to get her past in place. But she couldn't manage outrage, and she was bored, and they started having lunch together. Samuel Peake explained the town in a roundabout way, confirming most of the impressions she'd made and dissolving mysteries about men who might have been interesting: this one beat his wife, another owed more than he owned, a third was dull beyond all imagining. Gerry Fenoways and his brother preyed on female inmates, Peake's assistant Rex Woolley needed to escape his mother, Siegfried Durr was talented but drank more than most, in a town that drank more than most. It was good Dulcy felt widowy, said Samuel Peake, because her options were limited.

He was funny, and sweet, and he did not pry or suggest he was an option. When they talked, when they looked at people together, she began to feel giddy again: the world was rich, and interesting, and survivable. Eugenia Knox tried harder for information, foisting tea and cakes on the widow, sliding a chair close. She seemed to be built out of joined pillows like a Rubens rag doll, not obese but nowhere bony, with a general look of placid exhaustion. She moved ceaselessly but sedately around her empire, scooping surfaces clean as if her languorous arms were magic wands. Her questions seemed equally idle, and as she answered as vaguely as possible, Dulcy fell into Mrs. Nash, and ironed out the story she worked to believe: her husband,

Edgar, had been tragic and flawed and lovely, though she left a sense of a dark side. He had volunteered in New York at the beginning of the war but had quickly fallen sick and seen little action, and had never fully recovered. Dulcy implied that his relatives were wealthy and distant.

You'd have to be an ass to insist on details, and Mrs. Knox would float off toward another dusty surface or difficult guest. But a few days later she invited Dulcy to her apartment for tea, and she surprised her with other guests: a widow named Margaret Mallow; the watery Leonora Randall, who kept the rooms across the hall from Dulcy; and Vinca Macalester, the doctor's wife. Eugenia Knox's quarters were as padded as their owner: festoons of velvet flanked doorways and windows, and the floors were so laden with carpets that walking through the parlor felt like crossing a sandy beach. Dulcy arrived on a bright, snow-blasted afternoon and felt like she'd opened the door to a séance. She made for the crack of light near a window, next to Margaret Mallow, who gave her a reassuring, sidelong look. Vinca Macalester nattered away, and Leonora Randall agreed with everything anyone said. They talked about the weather, about Mrs. Knox's prospective new chef, about Rex Woolley's business prospects, and about Crime (some murmurs from Mrs. Macalester, whose husband had just mended a man who'd been shot at a "seamstress's" house on B Street).

A pause—they didn't know Dulcy well enough to do more than dabble in the risqué, and perhaps it was shallow to discuss misbehavior rather than death. Eugenia Knox struck out for a fresh topic—where had Dulcy taken her husband while trying to cure his illness?

Margaret Mallow squirmed in the only gap of light. "Our last stop was in Santa Barbara," said Dulcy. "An excellent place, but visited far too late. Forgive me, Eugenia, but I don't know—are you a widow, too?"

"Oh no!" said Eugenia. "Drop the thought! Errol travels the West. We have too many investments, and very little time together." She gestured toward a shelf with two photos of a slight, balding man.

"Perhaps you would allow us to see a photograph of your late husband."

"I've put them away," said Dulcy. "They hurt me, and I keep Edgar in my mind's eye."

Their faces pinched in sympathy. Dulcy felt she said too little, too much. She didn't want to be sucked into this world, but she knew that loneliness was liquid, and she was drowning. Sometimes she had the sense that she was tipping off the earth, that she could feel it spin. Her moments of elation, her sense that she could escape alive, would falter.

And so during the day, she kept walking, despite the fact that sniveling out-of-doors left a frozen shellac on her face. At night, her ghosts marched in, but with Walton, she never had the classic sense of shock each morning, the cloudy "Is he really dead?" feeling she'd had after her mother or Martha. She didn't half forget, or expect him to walk through a room, or think she should send a letter, or wonder what he'd like for his birthday. Watching someone hit the ground at high speed erased the typical confusion. Walton was extremely dead.

Her windows faced south and east and took in the strip of shops on Second down to Lewis Street, the corner of Callender and Second, where businessmen met to gossip, and the alley behind the Masonic Temple and the theater, packed with tavern backdoors and three Chinese storefronts: a noodle shop, an apothecary, and a laundry. Only two of the Chinese men in town had wives, according to Eugenia Knox, but the resulting six children ricocheted around the alley, little golems in quilted winter clothing, delivering drugs, food, and laundry, chasing each other around carts and napping drunks, sliding on frozen puddles. Samuel Peake, who looked forlorn when he was alone, used the alley to cut between the *Enterprise* and the courthouse. Irving, who had clearly been dropped on his head as a child, smoked there on every break, hopping up and down in his own cloud of warm, tubercular smoke.

At night, everything took a shift to the strange. Dulcy saw it all through the net of electric lines and telegraph lines, cables plugged into every downtown building. Once she saw a wagon roll past with two caged men in back, fingers curled around the bars like zoo animals while a policeman on horseback poked at them with a stick. Irving explained that the cage was the open-air jail for a town to the north; often the police found it easier to bring the whole problem to the county seat.

No one seemed to pay attention to the cage. But the following week, when there was a fire half a block down the street, flames shooting up several stories in the windless cold, the sidewalks filled. Irving told her it was a cigar factory, and though she thought he had to be insane, this far away from Cuba, when she opened her window—for just a moment, in the bitter cold—her room filled with the rich brown of tobacco. She could see firemen trying to knock ice out of their hoses and hear the crowd *ooh* and *aah*. She wondered if the fire might spread and if she should be worried. When the water-wagon horses started to snort below her window, she thought sparks had traveled, then saw that what had upset them was a new wagon pulling up, wolf and coyote pelts topped with two dead mountain lions. They looked alive in the firelight, and the trapper in the wagon drank from a bottle while he watched the tobacco burn.

She began to recognize the same handful of women at a tavern back door, and one night a chubby girl was folded facedown in the gap by a coal bin, her skirts hiked, one man holding her down while another pummeled her from behind. Dulcy had pulled on her robe, wondering what sort of reception she'd get from Irina if she said someone needed to be saved, then saw a policeman approach. But they all talked: the first man finished, and the officer opened his pants and started in, and when he threw his head back, she recognized Gerald Fenoways' little brother, Hubert.

The Fenoways: the brothers were everywhere. Dulcy heard their mother was dying, and she saw the woman once, eating at the Elite with her sons. Her skull pushed at her skin, and her eyes were pools of pain, huge black pupils on a yellow background. She looked like a piece of muslin, but her face and voice cracked with rage between raspy gulps of air; she glared at her sons with inky, red-rimmed eyes, and they drank and wept. *Marriage*, she hissed; Dulcy wasn't sure if

Gerry was supposed to repair his, or if Hubie Fenoways was supposed to find a bride. That night she heard Gerry in the hallway, drunk, pounding on doors and screaming for his aunt Eugenia to let him in to her apartment.

Siegfried Durr's newly built studio was kitty-corner to her room, with a glass roof that was still shiny and clear on the north side of its second floor, and Dulcy watched him fumble with his lock each morning and evening. Carefully dressed people filed in and out all day long, and sometimes she'd see the explosion of a bulb through the glass roof when he worked into the night. Once she saw a couple carrying a baby's coffin inside. A flash of light, and they left again with their box.

When I say I was committed to pleasure, I do not mean "pleasure" as an abstract notion. I hoped to be loved as often and as well as possible, but entirely on my own terms, and only when the mood struck. I was no different than most bachelors (or married men) in that respect. I wanted amusement, and after I'd been amused, I wanted my own company. If any one tells you otherwise, they likely lie. On waking most mornings, I knew I deserved condemnation; around midnight, I couldn't be bothered.

Miss Dalgliesh told me it should be otherwise, and made her case convincingly, and we were engaged. Within an hour, as the wine faded, I felt a new cold liquid in my veins, like mercury: panic.

I left for Cuba a week later.

—Maximillian Cope, *A History of a Small War*

CHAPTER 10

EVERY WIDOW IS A LOVE STORY

•

The story of the newly arrived Widow Nash, as discussed in her absence by the members of the Sacajawea Club during a meeting at the new Carnegie Library, in Livingston, on February 15, 1905:

The husband's Christian name had been Edgar. He'd been born in London to an English father and an American mother, orphaned in India and schooled in England. Mrs. Knox was quite sure his middle name had been Walter. He had been tall and blond and Anglican, had come to New York as a young man, and had volunteered for the Cuban war immediately. Abigail Tate imagined he'd served in Astor's contingent.

"If he was English, why our war, and not Africa?" asked Mrs. Mallow, whose husband had enlisted in 1898, though he hadn't gone overseas. "And if he was wealthy, why fight at all?"

Eugenia Knox shrugged—she'd told them all she knew. Edgar W. and Penelope Maria Dulcinea Nash, née King, had met in New York, but married in London, and lived there for most of their marriage. (The whole notion of *living in London* was transcendently interesting during a Montana winter.) Maria Nash had little of her own live family, had never been close to her husband's, and was comfortable with solitude. She'd come to town virtually empty-handed, despite her good clothing and untroubled allowance. She said she did not want reminders of her past, and of course most of her good dresses would have to wait until after a period of mourning, but the Sacajaweas agreed it still made no sense.

Mr. Nash had fallen sick soon after he arrived in Cuba—yellow fever? malaria?—and spent much of his subsequent time at sanatoriums. "Did they marry before he was sick, or later?" asked Mrs. Macalester, the club's president. She was married to the youngest doctor in town; she had a certain bloom. "And why no children?"

No one knew. However the war had dented Edgar Nash, the mortal issue didn't seem to have been a wound, or fever, or any tropical ailment. The consensus was tuberculosis. The ladies had been given the impression of a long dwindling, though a minority clung to the gorier diagnosis of cancer. Mrs. Nash had mentioned visiting a clinic in the area; the ladies reasoned the clinic at Eve's Spring, but that led them back to a brain tumor.

Whether Edgar Nash had dwindled or gone out screaming, he'd been quite young—thirty, thirty-two—and any fool could imagine just how awful it had been before his body had been put on a boat to London. Most agreed Maria Nash was in a state of shock, so bereft, so literally at a loss, that she could only drift in her own thoughts and take long, silent walks. Abigail Tate, a widow herself (her husband, a deputy, had been shot by a drunken miner), said she recognized the foggy look of utter grief. Vinca Macalester said Mrs. Nash's reticence was perfectly normal, and that she should be given time to find her way to a more social existence.

"Is she reticent, or cold?" asked Mrs. Whittlesby.

"She's comfortable with keeping her grief in her own head," said Margaret Mallow, not looking up from labeling circulation cards. "She has quite a sense of humor. And she reads."

"I'd like to know why she came here to begin with," said Mrs. Whittlesby, who didn't read. "If she does not want to be thought a snob, she should consider a greater degree of honesty." Mrs. Whittlesby had this opinion of everyone who didn't kiss up. Mrs.

Nash's refusal to confide, to provide tears or a verbal wallow, drove Mrs. Whittlesby into small fits of hysteria. She had been born talking, and silence terrified her.

• • •

Dulcy had seen the real Edgar Nash in August of 1902, at the fever clinic near Terracina, on the coast between Rome and Naples. Fever clinics were a novel cure based on the observation that several men who had suffered from syphilis in the tropics, in India and the Congo and Manila, had managed a miraculous recovery after a bout of high malarial fever. This clinic was one of only three, and it sat on the edge of the infamous Pontine Marshes: men with tertiary syphilis were offered up to clouds of infected mosquitoes.

Walton's symptoms—hysteria, a rash on one arm, an open sore on his leg, an aching spine, an aching liver, a fading in one eye—made malaria seem like the better disease. He joked about mixing some gin with his quinine and looked forward to life again. He loved lava-filled Campania and Lazio: earthquakes, volcanoes, refined physicians, ancient history, good food—all the area lacked was a profitable mine. He and Dulcy toured Pompeii and Herculaneum, the gassy moonscape of Campi Flegrei, where the fumaroles reminded Walton of Yellowstone. They walked through the tunnel between Cumae and Sibyl's grotto near Averno, and picked fruit from a fig tree that grew upside down from the rock at the entrance. The Romans had claimed the lake was the entrance to Hades— Aeneas had descended into the underworld here—and believed that the fumes rising from the volcanic lake killed birds. Dulcy couldn't recall seeing a bird anywhere in Italy, and had heard that they'd all been eaten.

After a week of tourism, they headed north. The driver swathed everyone in netting a mile before they reached the clinic, a pretty yellow villa with high windows and curvy nurses; Walton almost capered, but his enthusiasm withered within hours. He'd wondered over the genius strangeness of the fever concept and the fact that he would be allowed to wander outside like a normal human, but the true nature of the cure—the downside of being encouraged to drink, and eat, and take walks in the open air—involved being offered up to a marsh of buzzing, biting mosquitoes. Walton howled like a child, and the clinic doctor, saying this was a common reaction as patients became accustomed to insect bites, gave him sticky fortified wine, to sweeten his blood even more.

Visitors had to be swathed in netting, and because so much time was spent on intimate digestive complications, the patients' families were encouraged to spend the curative period at other hotels. When Dulcy announced her departure, Walton wept and raged and tore at his sores. She relented and was given a screened room with a view of an unpleasant green pond. She brought a stack of books to Walton's room and read them aloud stoically, cocooned in netting, while he tossed around his still-drab notebooks. She would be there, but she would not listen; he said she did him no good, but he wouldn't let her leave.

On the third evening, Walton went missing from the ward and was caught hours later in the guest wing, rutting wildly with a fresh length of sheep gut dangling from what he sometimes called his instrument of doom. The woman was the elderly wife of another patient; Dulcy, listening to Walton whine in tune with insects, decided she might leave for the coast after all, if they could manage to bolt her father to his bed so that he didn't kill someone besides himself. Walton was entirely out of her control, agreed the doctor, and he congratulated her on her pragmatism.

Bully for me, she thought. She traveled to Gaeta with two women, Enid Poliwood, the young wife of a very advanced patient, and Amelie Nadsonova, a forty-year-old Russian who'd brought her mother, an ancient ballerina who had finally lost her balance to brain rot. Miss Nadsonova laughed about her mother's sexual misdeeds and gave Dulcy and Enid French translations of Turgenev and Chekhov and Tolstoy. She smoked and had beautiful Parisian clothes; she talked about politics and novels, and she laughed about her lovers (real lovers) over wine and grappa.

And so while Walton was being sucked dry at the jungle clinic, the three women took overnight trips to the mountain abbeys, to tombs and catacombs, to beautiful cave-lined beaches. They snickered at obscene frescoes and flipped starfish with bare toes, and in one marsh town they wandered around a drowned, ancient villa, where they'd been told they'd see the world's loveliest clematis, a white *montana*, and some grapes planted in Nero's time. Dulcy had never been to a more beautiful place; she would never see anything that could equal it. They passed the clematis without noticing it and ended up sitting on the massive stone heads of animals (a rhino, an elephant, a horse, an ox) at a fountain in the warm sun, while lizards scuttled around them and Miss Nadsonova talked about ways of avoiding babies. It was a moot point for Dulcy after London, but she enjoyed the knowledge, anyway.

At the catacombs of Rome, she counted shinbones in one room, lace-dressed infant mummies in another cavern. It was horrible but soothing, this ancient and overwhelming death. Everybody died: in the presence of thousands of bones, any idiot had to acknowledge defeat. Dead Etruscans (nameless), dead Romans (Scipio and Agrippina), dead Christians (beyond number), and at the English cemetery, dead Anglo-Saxons (Keats and Shelley and Constance Fenimore).

Enid Poliwood, who'd studied literature at university, began to weep. She was very tall, with a harsh laugh and a great mind, and spent much of the trip trying to talk Dulcy into rebellion. Dulcy would love college, even at this late date; she would get so much more from her future travels, and do so much better than the usual student in class because of the experiences she'd already enjoyed. Her self-reliance might even force Walton to be more competent. But Enid described herself as absolutely lost: not only married to a mess, but also possibly infected. Life was not as either woman had pictured it: Dulcy circled the topic of her misadventure, and Enid hinted that she'd had her own similar trial. One of the points of higher education was to meet people like oneself, to realize that these things happened all the time.

• • •

On the day Dulcy saw Edgar Nash, she and Enid had gone to view gardens near Frascati, where cold and hot springs were routed through the orchards according to the season and the needs of the fruit. Palm trees and bougainvillea on one wall, white grapes on another, growing near espaliered lady apples. In the terraced garden area, an old woman peeled invisible scale insects off the citrus trees with a long ivory needle, following these individual murders with a perfume sprayer of alcohol spirits and water. They ate sardines and a chickpea cake and figs and drank sharp white wine, then made their woozy way back to Gaeta.

A nurse was waiting: Walton needed to see her; he'd had a *difficult* day. Dulcy wanted a bed, but she climbed into a carriage, put on her jungle gear, and plunged into the swarm. Walton was in the midst of being plumbed. She dropped her bag onto a bench and lingered in the hall, fixed on the notion of an empty room with an open bed. A breeze swirled down the long hall, thirty yards of marble and open windows. The air that day smelled of fruit and seawater and was nothing like a *miasma*, let alone *mal aria*, and she peered inside each doorway. If she made out a figure, she let her vision blur.

None of the rooms proved to have an empty bed, but at the last one she stopped anyway. This room had a balcony framed with a jasmine vine and a laden plum tree. The fruit was dusky dark purple and looked as if it would taste better than anything she'd ever put in her mouth; she took a step closer and gave the still, sleeping figure in the bed a sidelong look. His head was tilted away, but otherwise he could have been a tomb effigy: a high forehead, folded hands, long legs straight under a thin sheet. The whole effect—the high ceiling, the flowers and heavy overripe fruit, the man on the bed in filtered light—reminded her of a painting or maybe, more ominously, of a fable. She took another step before she paused, thinking of how these fables usually ended, and turned to look again at the man on the bed. He was young, with curly blond hair, a long straight nose, full lips, dark eyebrows and lashes. Or singular: half of his face was perfect, a Botticelli, but the far side was gone, a pit loosely covered by a black bandage. A harlequin, with a slipped face: she could see the edge of what was hidden underneath, a pitted eye, a rim of dying skin.

She edged on toward the plums, gathering her skirt a little to make a pouch. She could eat, she was alive, she was everything this man would never be or touch again. She reached out to the tree and dropped a dozen plums into her skirt, then retreated. She'd made her way halfway back across the room when a peacock in the garden screamed. The man's untouched eye flapped open, light blue and blind, then closed slowly. He hummed, a hurdy-gurdy sound.

She reached the hall bench, dropping the plums into her bag just as a nurse came out of a room. Dulcy asked, in bad Italian, about the patients who never left their rooms: the man at the end of the hall, for instance. The nurse said that it was all terribly sad: Mr. Nash had been infected very young, and had drunk heavily instead of mounting an assault upon his disease; he had also been fond of hashish. He was a wealthy orphan, an unmarried only child whose account was administered by a London bank and whose relatives seemed untroubled by his accelerated demise and their eventual inheritance. He would not be mourned, and even when he'd been able to talk, in the first week after his arrival, he'd only instructed the staff to dose him for pain. If the mosquitoes worked, so be it.

It was horrible, said the nurse, to have no family to sit with you, and to not mind the lack.

• • •

When Walton did contract malaria, he suffered the consequent high fever, cramps, and pains; he poached and writhed and moaned, but his syphilis plodded on. When the cure's failure was apparent, the staff used quinine to bring the malarial infection to heel, and it left Walton even more addled and temporarily deaf. He threatened to throw himself off the balcony one steamy night, and Dulcy pointed out that his room was only on the second floor, and above a little lily pond; he said he'd drown himself, then, and she explained that the water was only three feet deep. She told him he was the only one of five patients who'd checked in during July who was still alive. He stared at her for a moment and found his inner Protestant, his silent, suffering childhood self, and she reloaded the medicine chest for two diseases and a hundred symptoms.

Enid Poliwood's husband died at the clinic a week after Walton and Dulcy sailed away. A few months later Enid met a magazine publisher and remarried. She was very happy, and Dulcy had seen her twice more, the last time in Chicago, to congratulate her on her new husband, and her pregnancy, and her clear, almost unnerving happiness. Two months later, the pregnancy killed her, but Enid's husband wrote to say that the stroke had happened before labor, before worry: She had walked into her kitchen and dropped, gone. No pain, no warning—a rock had fallen, the earth had opened up, and everything had stopped.

Dishes Dulcy has learned to cook, listed on the occasion of her fifteenth birthday:

Sauces: béarnaise and hollandaise, espagnole, velouté, tomato and cream reductions. Potpies and en croutes. All meats, all game in most forms (stews, sautés, and roasts, fresh and cured). Dumplings, noodles, puréed and rustic soups, eggs, breads, gratins, timbales. Fish whole and filleted, frogs' legs fried or sauced. Potatoes, all forms. Vegetables, boiled or creamed or Italian style, fresh or pickled. Tomatoes, salads and slaws. Puddings, cookies, cakes, fools, pies, crumbles, soufflés.

Dishes to refine:

Shellfish bisques; pâtés and Wellingtons; dacquoises and other meringue-based desserts.

Dishes that she feels aren't worth the effort, or dishes that have failed, woefully:

Layer cakes, candies, aspics, and ice cream desserts: baba au rhum, feuilletés, galantines.

Dishes she would very much like to try, if she ever travels widely:

Fresh scallops and snails, real curry, Italian dumplings, all manner of cheeses, mangos, Chinese things.

Signed by Leda Cordelia Dulcinea Remfrey
and Martha Maria Wooster Bliss,
May 26, 1895

Menu

Caviar frais d'Astrakan
Real Turtle
Saumon du Rhin, Sce ml

Caviar frais d'Astrakan
Real Turtle
Saumon du Rhin, Sce mousseline
Selle d'agneau Parisienne
Noisettes de chevreuil Cumberland
Mousse de foie gras en Belle Vue
Chapon du Mans rôti à la broche
Salade Dose
Fonds d'artichauts Bordelaise
Omelette Norvégienne
Gâteau Génois
Dariolee au parmesan
Dessert

Savoy Hotel, London, 21 Févr. 1900.

CHAPTER 11

THE GREEN BOOK'S GUIDE TO LIFE

•

D ulcy hadn't forgotten to eat since she was ten, the age when she'd begun trying to replicate the dishes she tasted during visits to New York. As her loopy childish penmanship gradually became tight and cryptic, she filled Walton's discarded green notebook with recipes, mangled terms for French techniques, and souvenir menus. She didn't weigh more than one hundred pounds until she was fourteen, but by then she'd worked through most of Miss Corson's *Practical American Cookery* and Maria Parloa, and Martha helped her struggle through the *cromesquis*, cannelons, *bressoles*, and *brissotins* in Ranhoffer. On her sixteenth birthday, when she received *The Boston Cooking-School Cook Book*, she copied down a quote from Ruskin:

What does cookery mean? It means the knowledge of Medea, and of Circe, and of Calypso, and of Helen, and of Rebekah, and of the Queen of Sheba. It means the knowledge of all fruits, and herbs, and balms, and spices—and of all that is healing, and sweet in fields, and groves, and savory in meats—it means carefulness, and inventiveness, and watchfulness, and willingness, and readiness of appliance. It means the economy of your great-grandmothers, and the science of modern chemists—it means much tasting, and no wasting—it means English thoroughness, and French art, and Arabian hospitality.

She had been very serious: she had been sure her life would include a huge garden and house, a half-dozen children, a trip to Europe every spring. Before that time, she would travel, and go to Vassar or Barnard, and have lovers and adventures. She'd have them after, too.

> Victor Maslingen, having sustained heavy losses in the African minerals market (he would be the only person to have lost money in that country, in the boom year since the end of the war) has returned from a brief funeral-going vacation in the Empire State, and now talks of selling the Butler Hotel instead of the Intelligencer. Our misfortune, and yours.
>
> —*The Seattle General,* February 11, 1905

Dulcy stopped holding her breath whenever a train came through town, and she took the local to Bozeman on February 14, where she sent a telegram to Spokane. She made the trip again two days later and claimed Walton's pine trunk, which had been held in Spokane under the name of Amelie Poliwood; the Spokane porter had done his job. Now she had the trunk carted to a side room in the freezing Bozeman freight depot, and she transferred Walton's medicine box and the journals and the clothes she'd used to cushion them into a new valise, including two thin cotton dresses she'd inherited from Martha's trousseau that she'd packed in case she ended up taking Walton to a California or Arizona clinic. She left his clothes and coats and boots and mining talismans, his folder of published articles and reading glasses and shaving set, and tried to pack them as she had in Seattle, while Victor watched. The journals were a risk, but the Boys would probably assume they'd been left in Seattle; the Boys might never look inside. The trunk smelled of Walton in a good way, but he was miles away, years away, down to sounds and fragments. In the middle of the night he was a long novel, but in the light of the here and now he'd lost his edge, done the thing the dead do and begun to fade from feeling to thought. All the brutal, shitty, gravelly reality smoothed and silky, like the new notebook fabrics.

She ripped off the forwarding name so that the original label was visible—*Remfrey, 109 East 19th St., Manhattan*—and when the porter reappeared, she tapped the address and tipped him a dollar. She checked the valise into a locker at the station and waited at the library until after the shift change, when she reclaimed the valise and rode back to Livingston. When she climbed off she thought of how pretty the town was when the light was clear, of how she wanted to stay and not board another train for a long time.

At the Elite (which he called the *Eee-light*), Irving lugged the valise up the stairs, while Dulcy dodged looks from Eugenia and Irina. Alone in her room, she lifted out the medicine box and removed the dozen journals, one by one. Garnet theories, egg yolk cures, red carnage, rose pink love. She opened the peach *My Family and Life* for the photographs: a formal portrait of young Walton with Woolcock and Christopher in Chile; Walton's dead first wife, Jane, deeply religious but with a sensual, Spanish face; Philomela, primped and young and too ethereal for anyone's good. Walton had saved snapshots of his children by the 19th Street stoop; Martha in the kitchen with Dulcy on a stool, stirring a pot (apple butter, Dulcy thought); the girls and a spaniel named Harry wading in Lake Erie. The travel photos were a mix of shattered masonry, pretty nurses, and Dulcy posing before a variety of backdrops: on-deck lifeboats, a tumbled pyramid, a seawall, a coolie, mountains, the sea, a trained bear, trains. She did not always look clean or well fed, but she had been happy.

In the green book, Walton, who'd written *Walton Joseph Remfrey, Transvaal* on every other new flyleaf, had done her the gift of entering just *Dulcy's Book* here—no date, no family name or location. It began with the pages Walton had filled before Dulcy had taken it over: a skirmish with horticulture when he'd first visited Westfield, notes on the possibility of growing coffee or tea in northern Oregon or opium poppies in Montana, where the climate was similar to Afghanistan.

Dulcy's era began with recipes—everything from session pie to chop suey (she'd crossed it out after it proved to taste nothing like Chinatown)—and a first menu from Sherry's on her birthday in 1894 (*huitres et caviar Russe, selle d'agneau de lait avec sauce Colbert, glaces des fantaisies*). The next menu came from the ship home from India, a simple English typescript with innocuous descriptions like *poached chicken* and *green beans in cream* that had meant dishes howling with small vicious green chilies, thick coconut milk, mysterious salted fishes, toasted yellow pastes and nuts and a soapy, strange parsley. A third menu was from the Savoy during an early, happier stay in London. The meal had been caviar-laden but very simple, perfectly balanced, and Dulcy drove Martha batty trying to re-create the *salade Duse* when she returned. She began to eye the leghorn chicks, weighing the advantages of caponhood against the disadvantage of not knowing how to get the job done.

She'd never written down thoughts or a record of her day; she didn't see the point, especially now, since she tended to change her mind, and the world changed around her, and who was she writing it for, anyway, since she was dead? But she was possibly disingenuous, or simply disorganized. She'd pasted down letters, corsages and theater tickets, bits of ribbon and Brownie snapshots, lists—Italian verbs, rose varieties, addresses—in lieu of memories. She still had Victor's calling card from the morning after they met in 1900. Before, destroying it would have meant everything had been a loss, no matter how pompous the card looked, no matter how vicious the memories:

VICTOR BOUWER MASLINGEN
The Braeburn, New York, Ph. Br 129

Now she ripped it into tiny spiteful pieces, turned to the new end sheet in the front of the green book, and added *Penelope Maria Dulcinea Nash* to Walton's inscription. The married name, without the mourning, using the pen that had belonged to the suicide from the train. It felt right; she was a pragmatic widow.

She pulled the medicine box from the valise, fifteen pounds of glass and wood and poison. She took out a dozen vials and dumped the most toxic and least useful in a small wastebasket. Pink pills, mustard-colored pills, horse-choking lumps that looked like they'd been made from ashes and hay—she scraped Walton's name from the labels. She lined up the liquids she wanted to throw down the sink, then had a vision of killing all the fish in the river, of poisoning the livery horses pastured just downstream from the town's new sewer. She put the liquids back, even the arsenic, but the bottle of ipecac wouldn't fit flat, and she reached gingerly into the narrow slot to see what was in the way. She felt a pebble, too small to be another Goa stone, too heavy to be a magic lump of ambergris. She stretched her finger and tried to drag it up the velvet-lined slot, and on the third attempt she retrieved a lumpy marble-sized rock, rough and opaque on one side, icy gray on the other. She carried it to the sink and made a tentative scratch on the enamel; she took off her mother's diamond ring—now her wedding ring from Edgar Nash—and tried it against the pea's translucent side.

Walton the packrat, bringing an uncut diamond home, an expensive token of the last trip to Africa. He'd probably looked for it in Seattle, not caught the rattle in the clatter of his glass vials, or maybe he'd forgotten it, along with everything else, by that time. She held the diamond up, but she was no judge, and she tucked it into the brocade bag with the bank keys, kept next to the Seattle money she hadn't deposited. She rearranged the notebooks according to color— yellow to red; red to pink to blues and black—but she was sizing them as well. They were too bulky for a normal bank box, and she didn't want to stand out by asking for an extra-large anything. She might not need to hide her own book, labeled with a nickname no one would know, but the others, signed *Remfrey* and damning, posed a problem, and she squeezed them into the new valise with the medicine box, tucked the valise inside the larger bag from Denver, and slid the lot to the end of her bed. She threw a traveling rug on top, then one of Mrs. Knox's comforters, then a stack of library books, sliding them into a pattern she'd remember. Irina was a nosy girl.

At dinner, Dulcy looked over the Elite's menu—bad pork and fried potatoes or fishy gray cream sauces over suspicious chicken, all served with variations on tinned peas or corn—and gave up the delusion that she could live in a hotel. This was Livingston's nicest restaurant, and no one cared that the food tasted like sawdust and pickles and rancid fat. She pushed a horseshoe of gray gristle—perhaps a literal horseshoe—around the plate, watching the sauce ridge and fail to relax again in a natural fashion. She was starving to death, melting away, beginning to look like a consumptive or a real widow. She needed a kitchen.

• • •

And so Dulcy looked around with a clearer mind, trying to decide what, given the wind, made this place worth keeping. The brick downtown was flamboyant, the houses on the west and north side were sober and Protestant, the painted bungalows on the southeast smaller and Catholic and immigrant. The grocers were either Italian or Czech, and the bar owners were German or Irish, but no one but the French owner of the burned cigar factory seemed to be truly rich. There were far more taverns in town than churches. The owner of the best wine and tobacco store was Jewish, and there was a kosher butcher on Lewis Street, though no temple. A dozen Chinese, a single Persian couple, a handful of real gypsies, a dozen blacks who'd mostly moved up from Texas with the big ranchers. Members of the local tribe, the Crow, were largely invisible. Most of the clear-cut prostitutes lived on B Street, but a large middle ground of compliant maids and sales girls lived in the rooming houses on Clark and Lewis. Rusalka lived there, above a storefront advertising a fortune-teller who charged astronomical prices, and Dulcy wondered if people were willing to pay so much because of the sudden-death way men made a living out here, mining and dodging trains and trees and errant cattle. Walton, Man of Science, had loved having his palm read, but Dulcy had always assumed there was more to the arrangement than palms.

The point of the game was to pick the most livable house on every block (not unlike a menu, the best blouse on a catalogue page, the most interesting man on a train). The old farmhouses on the east side were too close to the prostitutes' cribs on B Street, a stone place with pretty windows on Yellowstone was too public, a stucco on Third was downwind from a laundry. On South Eighth Street she studied a yellow two-story frame house that sat on the high point of a long clearing—a garden-sized clearing—that faced south to the mountains and river. There was a cart in the yard, and an open door; someone was probably unpacking, and her life felt mistimed.

But she persisted. The temperature rose to a heady forty degrees, and the slush that had seemed to melt away proved to be held in suspension by the clay of the streets, which took on the look of bad pâté, pink slime whipped together with cow and horse shit. During a sleet storm, an algae-green lather formed. Half the sidewalks were still only warped boards, now glazed with slick clay, and little old ladies slid backward regularly into the street mud, umbrellas upright. Some joker made a small fortune using a sleigh to take travelers from the depot to the hotels. When Dulcy stepped off the warped boards of the sidewalk on the fourth day of thaw, one leg simply disappeared into the muck; the photographer Siegfried Durr helped pry her out, an intimate act that was apparently customary in the town.

Durr walked her to Thompsons to buy new boots. He was handsome, but his eyes were a little too open. "When will the mud dry?" she asked.

"When the temperature hits ninety. Then it turns to rock," said Durr, watching Thompson lace her up. "Other than that, I highly recommend the town."

Dulcy made her way back to the house on Eighth Street and found the cart in the yard had been replaced with a sale sign. She stood tiptoe near the wraparound porch, but she was too short to see anything beyond a dangling electric light. The foundation seemed sturdy, and an old poplar at the gate barricaded it from the only other house on the block, where a man had begun to yell—*useless dirty woman eggs with feathers lick them off. God dear God how could you have created her.*

She scurried around to the far side and sat on the steps next to a withered grapevine while the roar next door continued. A handful of scraggly gooseberry bushes ran along a low wall that marked the drop-off to the river bottom, next to a ruined shed. She walked down and scuffed the soil, the same pale clay that had sucked her boots off downtown. She looked up at an osprey nest in a bottomland cottonwood, down at willow and dogwood and paths snaking through the Fleshman Creek marshes and ruined beaver dams to the river.

She wanted it all, despite the neighbor. When she walked into the Elite lobby, Samuel Peake was waiting for Irina to finish with a guest. "You look happy," he said.

"What do you mean?" asked Dulcy.

"Just that. No need to be alarmed." He handed a note to Irina. "Don't read that," he said. "It's for Lewis. Rise above your nature, just this once."

• • •

Samuel talked her into joining him again at dinner with Margaret Mallow and Rex Woolley, and they all drank too much. Rex talked about investment ideas—dams, resorts—and Samuel worked to keep bringing him back to newspapers. Gerry Fenoways, the police chief, was in the far corner with his wife, who looked like a nominally healthier version of his mother. They didn't seem to be talking: Gerry's face was red, and his wife's was rigid. Eugenia swept into the room, ushering in a group of fur-coated travelers, and Samuel crooked his finger. "Eugenia," he whispered, "perhaps you could go over and reassure Mrs. Fenoways that Gerry loves her, and loves her alone."

Eugenia turned a roasted pink, but instead of fleeing she began going from table to table, filling glasses herself, floating around the periphery of the room like a swollen butterfly.

That night, Dulcy woke to the sound of a man howling in the halls and a woman shushing him, and she felt the hotel shudder. A rumble, a shift: Dulcy listened for a train, but there wasn't one; she watched the ceiling, but it didn't fall on her face. Here she was in a brick hotel during an earthquake again—why did this always happen? It happened because she only slept in hotels.

In the morning when she left her room, Irving and Rusalka said they hadn't felt a thing, but Dulcy guessed that everything felt like a passing train to them, now. They were scrubbing the hallway near Eugenia's private apartment; Chief Fenoways had urinated up and down its length. "Until she let him in," whispered Irving.

Dulcy slid her way to the office of the property agent whose name had been posted on the fence of the house on Eighth Street, a man named Nesser. She'd seen him eating in the Elite dining room. His face was bland, but she'd been impressed by the wine on his table, and now she also approved of the way he didn't stare at her mud-splattered coat or her windblown hair, or question her taste in houses. But when Dulcy said she didn't need to see the inside before putting in an offer, he pulled on his hat and coat and signaled his assistant to bring a car, one of the only ones she'd seen in town. "I won't take advantage of a widow," he said.

The widow cringed as a crowd gathered to watch the assistant tinker with the Reo engine, but they spun through the mud, and she found the house was solid, built in 1885 and plumbed and electrified later by a junior banker with a finicky wife. It had fir trim and floors, tall windows and a bathroom with a tub and water closet and sink. The kitchen had a tin counter, a hole in the floor for draining an icebox into the cellar, and a stove space under a large vent, which warbled, in the wind. The two bedrooms upstairs were wallpapered in a pattern of lumpen indigo grapes. The banker's wife hadn't liked light anymore than she'd liked snow, and the couple had lacked children, and so the sunniest room had been used for storage, while the owners had used the dark room that faced north, and the neighbor currently stared at Dulcy and the realtor from his front porch. When the realtor waved, the man walked into his house and slammed the door. "I don't mind not being social," she said.

"He's a minister," said the realtor. "He can't be that bad."

A realtor had to be an optimist. Dulcy thought the neighbor could be that bad, but she still made an offer. They discussed bank transfers, workmen, and weather while she worried about money and whether she'd lost her hold on her circumstances.

• • •

The Widow Nash perked up and continued her social hatch: Margaret talked her into a meeting of the Sacajawea Club at the Albemarle Hotel, where Frances Woolley, Rex's mother, was hosting a meal. Mrs. Woolley usually waited to come north from Pasadena until spring, but here she was, eager to slum with the hoi polloi. Who were naturally happy to slum with her, even Eugenia, who was miffed by the choice of the Albemarle instead of the Elite.

Frances Woolley, mother of Rex and aunt and benefactor to Samuel Peake, was tall, with a long neck and a cloud of what Eugenia Knox called "auburn" hair (Dulcy noted that the same color was described as red on a maid like Rusalka). She was still handsome, with an eye-popping figure, and Margaret said that she was fond of her chauffeur, and that a contingent of men would follow her through the summer season. Frances made Dulcy think of a bored carnivore in a zoo, but she talked intelligently about books, and she'd drummed good wine out of the Albemarle basement, and she worried about Rex quite openly.

The problem with Rex: every idea had to be his, and new. Established good ideas—say, the newspaper business with his cousin (poor Samuel was so patient), or real estate in boomtowns like Los Angeles—didn't hold his attention. He schemed about water and dams, highways and hospitals; he wanted to run the world without knowing how it worked, and his mother had sent him to spend time with Samuel in Montana because Rex had bought some land in the Sierras—water, again—and his partners were being sued.

"Boys will be silly," said smug Mrs. Whittlesby.

"Boys will be stupid," said Eugenia Knox.

It was one thing for Mrs. Woolley to complain, and another for anyone to agree. Dulcy didn't think Rex was stupid, but this was a difficult compliment to bestow. The topic turned to the doom of both Mrs. Fenoways, the elder with a tumor breaking through the skin of her breast, the younger running from her marriage. Gerry's wife had decided to visit family back East: the police chief was on a tear, a jag, a roll, a sodden Sherman's march through town in premature reaction to his mother's impending death or his imploding marriage. He'd broken a man's leg the night before; he especially disliked wife-beaters, and one of the older women whispered that the Fenoways brothers had locked the door as teenagers and allowed their own abusive father to freeze to death.

"Gerald is a fine man and a loving son," said Eugenia Knox. Her face was stiff, and she'd lost her soft pink look. "His brother is another matter. When Errol was ill, who came down to help us? Gerald, of course, the best nephew a man could have. He helped us in our time of need, and now, when he will be so alone, I will help him."

It was a wide world in terms of nephews, thought Dulcy during the ensuing silence. "Well, of course you will," said Mrs. Ganter. "And how is Mr. Knox?"

On the far side of Eugenia, Margaret was grinning. She didn't mince around half-understood undercurrents with Dulcy; she'd told her that Livingston was crammed with ancient vicious southerners trying for their own kingdoms—Baptists and know-nothings, bigots and thieves—but many of the women had a lively, silly eye. They argued about novels, and ethnicities, and dogs: Vinca Macalester liked her dogs symmetrical; Abigail Tate liked random spots. Mrs. Ganter drove the polite women wild by mentioning Mr. Thompson's long legs and Mr. Nesser's large hands.

Maria Nash tried to pry out other people's stories, but everyone always wanted to know about her dead man, and Dulcy had already ruined him: Edgar Nash had come into increasingly bland definition as an amalgamation (an amalgam? Dulcy had a bad habit of thinking in mining terms) of Walton and Victor's least memorable traits, which meant he was mostly Victor. She hadn't caught the tangent until the damage was done: Edgar had been well traveled but finicky, with difficult, wealthy parents. The shift from the dashing wounded man she'd imagined on the train was upsetting. She wished she'd stuck closer to Maximillian Cope's novel and made him a drunken adventurer, a talented wastrel, but when the concerned women of Livingston faced her, refreshments tilting as they concentrated on her words, she'd only managed to solidify the bore: Edgar had been an opera buff and talented businessman, a fair shot and a good though reluctant soldier.

Dulcy had to survive these women; she had to make them believe her. Tonight, after too much wine, new details of the sad story of Edgar dripped out: he'd had malaria in Cuba, but he'd made an ill-considered return to service in the Philippines, where he'd had a close call with guerillas. On a visit to family in Cornwall, he'd fallen ill with pneumonia. He never fully recovered, and he'd ultimately died in California, of meningitis.

"Such awful luck!" said Margaret. "Nothing interesting ever happened to Frank."

"Edgar had a rough time," said Dulcy. "He was very brave, but one thing led to another."

"His war experience sounds close to Mr. Braudel's," said Vinca. "Our first library speaker."

Over dessert, with more sherry, Dulcy's mind slid away from Vinca's ominous comment. The crumb of the cake oozed butter, and the sugar icing smelled sharply of bourbon; Dulcy and Margaret planned a shopping trip to Butte. By the time the meeting broke up—with nothing substantive discussed beyond Easter baskets for the Poor Farm and whether bridge whist was worth learning—it was ten o'clock, and as Dulcy sank into the mud on her way back to the Elite, she thought the clay might give her a better chance to stay upright. Fat

flakes of snow spun around her head. There were still Masons and
Elks and Woodsmen of the World about—on Thursday nights, every
fraternal club seemed to have a meeting—most of them heckling a
drunk who sang in a piercing, marginal tenor:

> *The wind it did blow high and it did blow low*
> *and it waved their petticoats to and fro . . .*

The song was a Walton favorite. She smiled before she remembered
she was wearing black.

> *He tapped at the bush and the bird it did fly in*
> *just a little above her lily-white knee . . .*

She was crossing the street when the drunk changed his tone: "Here
now, what the fuck do the two of you have in mind? Stop that shit!"
A screaming bald man had rounded the corner of Second and Park
at an awkward run, and another middle-aged man was chasing him,
both of them sliding in the mud in a circle around the drunken
singer. The second man had a long knife.

"You're a fucking savage," screamed the singer.

"I'll gut you both!" No one in the crowd stepped forward. The
bald man ran in circles in the mud, sliding and backtracking; the
man with the knife lunged and then lunged again.

They're not serious, she thought, scurrying for the hotel. Things
like this probably happened all the time here—police pissing in
halls, men in cages in the streets. She was tugging the door shut
behind her when the bald man lunged through. Irving ran forward
to slam it closed on the face of the man with the knife.

The glass door shattered; the pursuer recoiled, as did Irving in the
opposite direction. Dulcy was intent on the stairs, but the bald man
tottered toward her. She was about to say *now you're safe*—though
the man with the knife was already trying to rise—when she saw
blood spilling out from under the bald man's vest, splattering his fine

shoes. He slowly lifted his shirt, and they both looked at the puncture in his stomach. It sucked and flowed with his breathing.

"Lie down," said Dulcy, and the man did, dropping to his knees and then onto his back in his own puddle. She crouched down and tried to straighten out his legs. His hands fluttered, and he fixed his eyes on the far wall. The man with the knife struggled to his feet, some of the hotel's glass door in his forehead, but the drunk who'd been singing "The Bird in the Bush" reappeared and clubbed him with the hotel's iron doorstop, and the crowd roared. Still on the floor, Dulcy looked back down at the man who'd been knifed, whose bleeding and breathing had stopped along with the piano music in the tavern.

The lobby blurred with faces. She wiped her bloody hands on his waistcoat and let herself be pushed out of the way. At the stairs she heard a bellow, and she turned to the arrival of Gerry Fenoways of the perpetually dying mother, now complaining that he was being taken from her bedside. He had an actorly habit of turning his entire body toward each person he addressed, and now he was calling for *witnesses, witnesses,* tilting from side to side like a weighted balloon while his young deputy, a pale boy named Bixby, cringed in embarrassment.

Dulcy met Irving's eyes, shook her head, and ran upstairs.

• • •

The bald man was dead, and her hands weren't shaking, but Martha still would have called her *juddery*; she would have told Dulcy to *get a grip, find her brain.*

Martha had never had to see someone stabbed to death. Dulcy didn't know if she'd have dreams, but now she thought again about what Walton might have seen falling, Pip and God's loom, faces and beds looking out at him as he passed the Butler windows, the sound and touch of the sea air fanning his nightshirt and poor sore body before he hit.

She yanked her mind free: there would be a trial, and she would have to testify, and someone would take her photograph, and Henning would see her face as he scanned the national papers, selecting Victor's reading for the day. She rinsed the snaky splatters of blood off her hands, then her coat, before she gave up, tossed everything on the floor, stripped naked and scrubbed herself, found a nightgown and ran to the window.

The police cart had arrived, lanterns swinging, beautiful blurs of light. "Dead as a fucking doornail!" bellowed Fenoways. "Bixby, where's my brother? Find Hubie, and a stretcher, and tell Eugenia to donate a blanket for a fucking cause." A lull, and then she watched Bixby and Hubie move the drained body, lumpy but insubstantial under a tablecloth, through the fat drops of snow. She heard hammering and guessed Irving was covering the shattered door with wood. The snow began to fall even harder, wet and large, and a new train was so muffled by the down in the air that she couldn't tell if it approached from the west or the east. She curled up on the bed as the sound of brakes drowned out the Fenoways brothers' bellows, and she tried to put her mind somewhere else: wading in Chautauqua Creek, the way the courtyard rippled in Salonica, the spice bazaars in Damascus or Palermo or anything that smelled different than Walton or the stabbed man when they reached the ground.

The sounds of voices, bystanders or new guests from this last train, died down. She would read and fall asleep with her light on like an idiot. And now that she wanted her glasses, she finally realized that she didn't have her bag, that it hadn't made it up the stairs. She'd dropped it on the floor when she'd knelt with the man.

She looked for her slippers and gave up, cinched her robe, and padded to the stairwell. Behind her, Miss Randall purred and mumbled, oblivious to death and chaos; below, Irving was talking fast and hacking his little heart out. She tried to wait him out, but her feet were freezing, and now Irving was laughing, probably because he'd just seen someone die, and people had bought him drinks when he had no head for liquor. The stairwell lights were dimmed, which meant he thought his guests were in for the night. She started down, but paused when she heard steps on the marble.

"Night then, Irv," said a man. "I hope tomorrow is quieter. Did Samuel see the show?"

"He's off to Helena," said Irving. "Missed it. Did I give you the mail?"

"You did."

Dulcy decided that she would soon freeze to death, and that anyone on a first-name basis with Irving wouldn't care about Mrs. Nash. She edged to the side when she rounded the landing to make way for the man climbing toward her. His head was down and he was still wearing a hat; he didn't notice her until they were a few steps apart. He lifted his head, and she focused on his pale, surprised face for a second before she took in the hand with the missing fingers on the banister. They stared at each other before the man from the train moved to one side and she edged past.

"Excuse me," he said. "Miss . . . ? Excuse me, but I've forgotten your name."

It was so hard to speak. "Mrs. Nash," she said. "I'm sure we've met, but I can't recall yours, either."

"Lewis Braudel," he said. "Irving just told me the story of your dramatic evening."

"Horrible," said Dulcy.

Lewis Braudel looked down and away from her bare feet. "Good night," he said.

"Good night," said Dulcy, despite the fact that it hadn't been, and her heart was blowing up. She tottered past him, and felt him pause on the next landing to look back.

Irving was humming as he mopped blood from the lobby floor. He nodded toward her blue bag on top of the glass case at the base of the stairs, the one that held little tourist trinkets, statuettes of geysers and bears and Indian chiefs. "I just saw it," he said. "About to bring it up, but I worried I'd wake you."

"I couldn't sleep," said Dulcy. "That poor man. Do you know his name?"

"Well, of course," said Irving cheerfully. "The lawyer Peck, and Mr. Inkster, who owns the stables. But we can't have blood on the marble, even if we liked the person it came from. I'm a happy man that Mrs. K slept through the thing."

Dulcy doubted Mrs. Knox's slumber was natural, but she envied her. She'd be taking the next train, rather than sleeping at all. The reality of the man on the stairs was sinking in: she could hear his voice on the Empire Builder, see the hat on his lap, the smile from the platform in Bozeman. He had been Victor's man after all—she'd been found, and she must run. East, west; how much time did she have, and how to ask Irving when either train came through? "I'd rather no one know I saw it happen," she said. "I'd rather not have my name in the paper."

"Course not."

Her whole body was shuddering. "But the new guest knew. I was so startled to see him on the stairs."

Irving looked dubious. "Well, you're a mess tonight, Mrs. Nash. There's nothing to worry about. That's just Mr. Braudel finally back, the guest I've been worried about. I only told him you helped."

"Oh," said Dulcy. "I don't think so. I'm thinking of a man with missing fingers."

"Well, yes, but it wasn't that he lost them playing with a knife. He's Mr. Peake's old school friend, the one who's kept 423 this last year," said Irving, looking her over. "You have blood on your chin, you know. Can I bring you up something to calm you down?"

"No, thank you," she said. "I'll be fine."

He started to hack again as she retreated, wondering why she hadn't said yes. She wiped off the smear on her jaw and lay on the bed and stared at the ceiling. She could hear someone walking in the room directly above for the first time. *Old school friend*: even her gothic mind couldn't believe someone would have shadowed her on the train from Seattle, only to have her choose a town where he'd lived for months. She hadn't known where she would get off the train, or whether she'd have the courage to leave at all. The leaving was one of the things that still stunned her every night.

Irina's strong, fast steps rumbled up the stairs, then passed to the hall above Dulcy's patch of ceiling. The man moved to his door and spoke, and the notes of Irina's voice rose. The door slammed, and Dulcy heard Irina's quick retreat. Lewis Braudel's window scraped open, and a moment later cigarette smoke winnowed through Dulcy's own window, still ajar.

Mr. Maslingen, barricaded in his Butler castle, is rumored to have received a suicide note from Miss Remfrey, posted in Spokane. The Remfreys, wishing to end this sad chapter, have expressed frustration at not being allowed to read their sister's last words.

—The Seattle General, March 1, 1905

CHAPTER 12

WOMEN OF THE WORLD

•

Dulcy spent most of the morning after the stabbing flat on her back in bed, listening to her ceiling. Twice she left the bed to watch Lewis Braudel cross the street and disappear east, a third time in the company of a laughing Samuel Peake. Between these sightings, she never saw Braudel return to the hotel, and his pacing always caught her by surprise. He liked a counterclockwise pattern.

She didn't know whether to stay or run.

Irving brought her coffee, but his jabber cleared nothing up. Between crime communiqués—the dead man had a pretty wife, and the killer had loved the pretty wife—Dulcy learned that the man from the train was from New York—a state Irving had left as a toddler, whose population and variety he could not parse—and that people paid him to write. Mr. Braudel liked women, but he was fairly discreet; he liked to drink but not to wretched excess. He had been in and out of the hotel for the last two years, since Samuel had moved to town, and he had otherwise traveled, and was often ill. Irving enjoyed Braudel tremendously and had been worried by the length of his last absence. As he said, over and over, without helpful details, when he delivered the day's gore-laden newspaper.

"He travels for business? What sort of business? To Seattle, or San Francisco?"

"He travels for the sake of writing about things."

"What *kind* of writing?"

Irving, who could not read well, looked annoyed. "Newspapers for sure, but a book, too."

Dulcy was supposed to meet Margaret, but she sent word that she was ill. When Margaret came by, openly admitting curiosity about the knifing rather than concern about Dulcy's health, Dulcy took a roundabout approach: why was Irving so worried about a Mr. Braudel?

Margaret was friendly with Samuel Peake, and she knew quite a bit about Lewis Braudel. Samuel and Braudel had gone to Columbia together, and Samuel said Braudel had caught malaria during the Spanish War; this explained much of Irving's worry. There was a rumor—a flutter among the local women—that he'd been with the Astor Battery, the Ivy League crew of young heirs who'd volunteered to fight in Cuba, but Samuel had laughed at the gossips, and said that Braudel wasn't quite an heir, and that after he'd fallen sick he'd simply stayed on in the Philippines as a reporter.

"Ah," said Dulcy. "But why be here?"

Margaret stood at the window, watching the flash through the studio roof as Siegfried Durr worked. "Well, why not, Maria? He's visited Samuel often, and he's written quite a bit about Butte, Clark and all, and I've heard he's having an affair with a woman in Bozeman. It doesn't matter where he is between assignments, and now he writes his own books. He fashions himself lazy, but he's been too many places for that to be true. He wrote his novel under a pseudonym, which just makes it all fun instead of tragedy. It's very, *very* racy, and so he only wants me to tell the ladies about the journalism when he speaks to the club. But it certainly makes him more interesting, and you're a woman of the world—you'll love it, if you aren't offended."

Some sarcasm: Margaret had begun to sense that Dulcy's sensibilities weren't fragile. It was only now that Dulcy realized that

Braudel had written the book she'd read in Denver, the false memoir by one Maximillian Cope, that she'd used for so much of the late, great Edgar's experience. She finally looked convincingly ill.

Margaret left for crackers and bicarbonate, and Dulcy went back to her study of the ceiling and Lewis Braudel's footsteps. She could stay or she could flee for a new place—the Midwest, the South, California, Europe. Some days she felt as if she knew no one on earth, and on others she counted all the people she might see on a new sidewalk, who might remember her from a dinner in Manhattan, a Buffalo wedding, a clinic in Minneapolis, a bank; all the people she'd forgotten to Walton, Victor, a glass of wine, time. If she couldn't remember their faces, how could they remember hers? How could this matter?

But this missed the point. He *had* remembered, at least something. He didn't need to have followed her to recognize her, depending on what he remembered from the train, depending on whether he'd read the news about Leda Remfrey and put the two women together. In the middle of the night, he'd roll over, and open his eyes, and understand.

Perhaps she could pay him off. Perhaps she'd leave and come back after he'd died of malaria or worked his way through the women in town.

She stayed inside for the rest of the day, ordering her meals up. Samuel visited, having heard she was ill. He brought his favorite brand of stomach pills ("Take two or three. Did you eat something blue?") and a deluge of useless information: Lawrence Peck and Albert Inkster had both loved Mrs. Peck, who has not been seen since the day of the attack, and had probably bolted for family in San Francisco. Samuel was hysterical with disappointment: finally a violent sex scandal but the guilty man was obvious. There'd be no prolonged trial, no secrets, no news. It was a tremendous waste of murder.

When he bounced out her door, she listened to him climb the stairs to Braudel's room, and then she listened to them laugh for much of the next hour. It enraged her. Nothing in her life was funny at all.

The next morning, after she heard Braudel head down the stairs and watched from the window as he crossed the street—moving quickly, like a well man—she emerged, and none of the lobby regulars stared at her as if she were a rediscovered confidence woman. A train was pulling in, and she hurried down the block, through the soapy steam from Joe Wong's laundry, worried by whatever ghosts might disembark.

It was March 2, the day before Inauguration Day, and parties would begin early, even in Livingston. The Boys were political animals, and Dulcy imagined them in Washington, rebuilding the family reputation at the balls, publically applauding Roosevelt, whispering to fellow bankers. They were not progressive men, and they never told acquaintances that their father had been a miner.

At the library, she found Lewis Braudel all over the place: *Harper's* and the *Century*, *McClure's* and *Collier's*. Politics; some cruel profiles; talk of the West as a colony, no better or worse than Algeria, India, or King Leopold's Congo; an amusing piece contrasting insanity diagnoses in a rich Scottish immigrant and a poor Irish one; some non-patronizing humor in a profile of female explorers; an essay on Italian restaurants that made her like him too much. She'd read some of these articles without recognizing his name, especially a humor piece called "The Grand Tour of Health," which might have been a profile of Walton. She tried to settle on an opinion, beyond the notion that he wrote well but used too many adverbs. He was a bit of a socialist, though one who seemed fond of certain luxuries. He was not bland.

In the *Enterprise*, to the right of ENORMOUS LOSSES AROUND MUKDEN, she skimmed the news of the stabbing, then landed on a second article:

IDENTITY OF GIRL STILL UNKNOWN

The body of a girl discovered along the train tracks west of our city remains unclaimed. The corpse had been sent north to Great Falls, to be viewed by a family seeking a missing daughter, but these hopes were dashed last week. Her presence has now been requested in Billings; we wonder how much longer she can tour. She is described as being between the ages of twenty and thirty, of medium height and weight, with dark brown hair. Mr. Siegfried Durr, at 117 North Main, has photographs available for viewing, if any citizen feels they might recognize the girl. The pictures have been artfully framed to spare the viewer's sensibilities.

If the girl is not identified, the body will proceed to the Poor Farm cemetery.

Buck up, thought Dulcy. You're not dead. And she realized, finally, that she was no longer willing to be dead to disappear, even in the middle of the night, even if Victor was close to knowing where she hid.

Back at the hotel, Irina waved a note: Mrs. Nash's house offer had been accepted.

• • •

Margaret and Dulcy left for Butte the next morning. Margaret thought it would be the best place to go to find things for the house, and Dulcy, intent on avoidance, said that sooner would be better. Margaret's own house was a tiny brick kitty-corner to the library, with not enough yard—her husband had not cared for the outdoors. The idea that Margaret might want another husband was not a given: according to the Sacajaweas, Mr. Mallow had been a sandy-haired seller of encyclopedias who had lacked curiosity about the text of the books he sold. Dulcy hadn't sensed heartbreak. Margaret said she was waiting out a year of mourning before regaining a teaching job that fall. She was snub-nosed and long-waisted, but she had beautiful dark hair and eyes, and she was so good-humored, so intelligent and empathetic, that Dulcy watched men watch her with openhearted admiration. Margaret was a *good woman*; Margaret was a *funny smart sweetheart.*

Butte was a short jog rather than a full retreat, just enough to make the situation bearable. Margaret and Dulcy dropped their bags at the Thornton and shopped for linens and cookware at Hennessey's, a store whose name Livingston people whispered with the sort of reverence Dulcy had heard used for Liberty's or Altman's. They found rugs from a dealer who looked like he'd been born in Persia, and ordered teak blinds. Mrs. Knox had supplied the name of a furniture dealer who stocked the better leavings of people who'd sold quickly—half of Montana, at one point or another—and they found a secretaire with actual secret drawers, two nice sets of pawned silver, and some pretty Brussels lace draperies. They bought clothes, not all widowy: nightgowns, dresses in blue and mauve, summer skirts, white hats, canvas aprons for cleaning and gardening. Margaret never asked why Dulcy hadn't sent for the belongings she'd presumably accumulated during her marriage.

Margaret went back to the Thornton to rest before dinner, and Dulcy set off on her main errand. No one else had the key to this bank box, but she worried that Henning might somehow know about the account, that he'd pulled the brown book from under Walton's pillow, too. Coming here for a pittance might reveal her existence, but she had to try: she had enough money to stay in Montana, not enough if she ever had to flee again. At the bank the manager was faultlessly polite, and politely disinterested, as he had her sign the log that showed no visits since 1900, before the African mines. She wrote *Miranda Falk*—if Henning followed her, and paid the manager to show him the log, at least she could leave a clue that she'd expected him—and waited for the manager to leave her alone with the box.

She kept him waiting for a full ten minutes while comprehending the forty-three thousand dollars in English and American notes, with some Austrian gold for good measure. Walton had loved hiding things, and now he'd allowed her to hide. She'd hoped for a quarter of this, and outside on the street with a full satchel, she walked slowly, mind veering around theories of how Walton might have collected so much. This wasn't a revenge on Victor; the dates were wrong. Had he cheated other clients, or spent less than she'd ever imagined on women? She tried looking at a stand of narcissus, a candy store, a window full of fabric, but she shriveled a little as she passed the Sons of St. George Hall on North Main and listened for Cornish ghosts, mining voices. She took the side entrance to the Thornton.

"Was your business all right, Maria?" asked Margaret, looking up from her book.

"It was all right," said Dulcy.

"You're sad," said Margaret.

They had shellfish and caviar, wine and brandy, and Dulcy's worry eroded again. Afterward, they smoked cigarettes and drank champagne above the people strolling down East Broadway: bankers and prostitutes, blacks and Chinese. All of them were well-dressed city people, not a cowboy in sight.

"Maybe the men are more interesting here," said Margaret.

Dulcy scanned the sidewalk, and didn't think so, and didn't think Margaret meant it, either.

When they arrived at the station the next morning, Margaret felt woozy and retreated to the bathroom. Dulcy bought a pasty on the platform and ate it hot there and then before she climbed into the first-class cabin and pretended to be a proper lady, lacking appetite.

• • •

She paid for the house with a portion of the cash and deposited the rest, rattling on to the man at the bank about the need to keep an extra thousand for furnishings and repairs. She wasn't sure if he hated or envied her or both, but she had her first sense, watching the black-suited men eye her in the bank lobby, of what it meant to be a young widow. She tucked some cash into the satchel in her room, but she rethought hiding places—Irina searched well and constantly. Fluttery bits of paper Dulcy had left in the closet door and the bureau drawers were dislodged when she checked, and though she was sure the barricaded pile with the journals hadn't been touched, she added another layer, with a note midway:

If you read this, Irina, then I know you're in my things. I am private, and I am not worth your time.

The moth wing on the green journal at the top of the pile stayed in place, but she moved the cash and diamond to the hem of the gray shearling coat, and tied intricate knots with silk ribbons around the satchel and each of the notebooks inside.

She was back at the window, back to watching Lewis Braudel come and go. She didn't know what to do, what to worry about, how to react to his presence or his apparent disinterest. She fretted about the talk he was scheduled to give the club, but tried to believe in the idea that everything in life really was coincidence: she wasn't living in Walton's world, anymore.

Dulcy resorted again to a corner of the library, Braudel having destroyed the refuge of the Elite lobby. She read every magazine, and tracked the misfortunes of the world and the statewide travels of her doppelganger body, who was due to visit Livingston in the next few days. She'd gradually worked through most of the titles on its half-dozen shiny shelves, and today she ended up with a fat volume on Chinese customs. She hoped to find an answer to how long the town's Chinese restaurant would be shuttered. There was a sign on the door of Ah Loy—*closed for a funeral*—and Eugenia, enemy of all good food, had claimed that the owners of the restaurant had gone all the way back to China with their body. Margaret said nonsense— families immigrated with a little bit of soil, and would tuck it in the cemetery up Fleshman Creek.

A shadow fell across the page. "Was your husband Chinese?" asked Samuel.

She laughed and blushed, and when she saw Braudel standing next to Samuel, she faded to a mottled white. But she managed, "How are you?"

"I'm well, thank you," Samuel said. "My friend is at loose ends, and needed something to write about, and I suggested he had his choice of horrible things from the last few months' papers. A perfect sport for March. Have you met Lewis Braudel? Lewis, this is the shy Mrs. Nash."

"We have," said Braudel, tipping his head. "The night of the stabbing. And before, I think, but I may be wrong. Were we on train, when we met?"

"I can't remember," said Dulcy. "I've certainly taken enough of them in the last few months."

"You had a sister."

"A friend, helping after my husband died."

"Ah." He looked confused.

"Maybe it would be easier to look at it from the other point of view," said Dulcy. "I went from Seattle to Chicago with my friend in January. What were you writing about then?"

She was proud of herself: she'd lied with near panache, though her hands shook, and she felt wet under her arms, and anyone who knew her would have heard the squeak in her voice. But no one knew her.

"You may have remembered my hand," said Braudel. "I would have remembered your face."

"He's like that," said Samuel. "A flirt. So what shall we look for? Suicidal businessmen, girls who jump out of train windows, girls who lie on the tracks?"

"I don't want to write about dead people," said Lewis Braudel. "You're in the mood—you write about them." He met Dulcy's eyes. "What should I write about?"

"Live people," she said. Her voice creaked.

"You'll be at the talk tonight?"

Dulcy had intended to plead illness or sadness or some other dread *ness* to avoid this Sacajawea Club event. She wasn't proficient with excuses; Walton had been such a good one for a decade. "I'm not sure," she said.

"You should come," said Lewis. "You can be my heckler, so that we have no deadly silences."

• • •

Frances Woolley had made money on California land, and she had the largest house in town, an ugly paste-colored pile of bricks at the corner of Yellowstone and Clark. Her parties were filled with cosmopolitan flourishes: Japanese lanterns and cocktails, the novelty of a long-playing phonograph, a lack of ruffly elements in architecture or clothing or behavior. Mrs. Woolley traveled with three servants: an English housekeeper, a French lady's maid, and a gaunt man named Simms who handled Mrs. Woolley's accounts and drove her automobile, this year a cream Hammer Tonneau with red seats which would remain in the carriage house until the snow stayed away. Dulcy had spent a portion of her life in houses where a housemaid could spend an hour a day dusting aspidistras, and after listening to Samuel, she could guess at Mrs. Woolley's relatives—a distant cousin who had gone to university with Victor, an aunt who had a middling house on Union Square. Dulcy knew that Mrs. Woolley was a medium-sized fish enjoying a small pond.

Still, she made the pond comfortable. Rex Woolley offered drinks with gin and currant syrup, whiskey and rhubarb syrup, rum and lemonade—the Woolley pantry was a sticky place. Dulcy asked for a rye old-fashioned and tried not to guzzle. Mrs. Woolley claimed she hadn't seen Lewis for ten years, since he and Samuel were at Columbia and Rex was still in shorts. She petted his arm. "I was here most of last year," Lewis said mildly. "Just away in the summer."

"And it was the only season I felt brave enough to try. But this year I was much bolder."

She looked like she'd suck him off the top of a drink, like the fizz on her good champagne. Her cloud of hair tilted toward him. She asked Durr to take their photograph.

"Mother collects trophies," said Rex. He was not quite as bland and fretful as he seemed; maybe it was a family trait, because Samuel also changed to suit an audience: with the town's pillars, he was flat, earnest, admiring; with women, he teased. But now she understood why Samuel called Rex the Kinglet: as he mixed drinks, she heard

him telling the people at that end of the room that his family tree
traced back to William the Conqueror.

"Rex's having a mood," Samuel told Lewis. "He negotiated to buy
a touring company in Yellowstone Park without telling us. Carriages
and tents and guides. He's arranged for Grover Dewberry to visit and
film a trip down. He wants to rent a train car and take the town."

"That's an idiotic idea," said Lewis Braudel. "He'll have competitors who know what they're doing. Why doesn't he just write for
your paper? Why don't you give him a little air?"

They argued about Samuel's selfishness, and the man named
Dewberry who would visit soon, the things Lewis might read in a
few minutes, more things Samuel thought he should write about. It
was the first time Dulcy had been able to study Lewis Braudel since
the train, and she glanced and looked away, glanced and looked
away, until she worried people might think she had a tic. He looked
healthier now than he had back in January. She noticed that he had
a pattern of tiny blue metallic specks on his left cheekbone.

He turned and caught her. "I did not stab myself repeatedly with
a pencil."

Samuel kept on: "Why not write about Siegfried?"

"Because he's my friend. Because I don't want to shit on my own
sidewalk. Because everyone should be able start over ten times."

"Why would you write about Mr. Durr?" asked Margaret.

Durr was readying his camera on the far side of the room, using
his cane to position a banker who struggled to hold both a cocktail
and Mrs. Woolley. "There you go," said Lewis. "My point exactly.
What do you see? An alcoholic Prussian, right?"

Possibly, thought Dulcy, but Margaret looked like she would
knife him.

"And I see someone who's survived more than any of us could
imagine," said Lewis. "Did you know he was in China?"

"Of course I didn't know that." Dulcy was beginning to be
annoyed.

"Because you haven't stuck it out in a tavern with him. You haven't
put your life on the line for friendship." Lewis smiled and looked

away. She wondered what he thought about her and Margaret, or about Mrs. Woolley's crowd. Disdain, affection, curiosity—his eyes floated away, but she couldn't pin it entirely on boredom or alcohol or sadness.

But Margaret was waiting, and losing all humor, and Samuel realized it. "He was with the German contingent in Peking, in 1900. He was with that idiot who killed the Boxer boy, and opened the whole mess up. He and Joe Wong barely survived."

"Siegfried Durr brought Joe Wong here?"

Lewis cut back in. "Siegfried brought him to Berlin, and Joe Wong brought Siegfried here. Not what you'd expect, is it? So no, Samuel, I don't want to write about him, or about your friend who jumped off the ship, or your other people who jumped off mountains or trains."

"Think of pretty Louisa Peck—you've met her."

"I did, and she was beautiful, but dumb as a box of rocks."

Walton would have loved that phrase. "Is," said Samuel. "Please, have respect."

"Dead," said Lewis.

"The Remfrey girl, then," said Samuel. "You said you heard a rumor about Victor Maslingen not believing it was true."

"Dead and mangled. I did hear, but consider the source," said Lewis. "And by the way, I believe he's engaged again, and selling the paper. You should point Rex in the direction of Seattle."

Dulcy's skin crept with the strangeness of it all. Her life, not her life; how rotten was her body on that prairie? How many days had it been? When Samuel lit a cigarette, she wanted to rip it out of his hands. "You need a soulful topic," he said.

"I may need it, but I don't want it," said Lewis. "I'm planning a piece on what Pinkertons actually do to earn money—mostly a matter of following women who'd rather not be followed—and another long series on bullshit medicine. Write your own soul."

At the front of the room, Mrs. Woolley waved a smooth arm, and Lewis took the lectern. He began with an essay about why he hadn't intended to enlist in the Spanish War—he felt America's involvement was bullying, manipulative, and crassly financial—but he'd fallen prey to pride and curiosity.

Things had devolved on arrival. A questionable mission, poor planning, boys dropping like insects because of insects. Dulcy could feel unease in the room. "Wasn't *Edgar* in that division?" whispered Mrs. Whittlesby, craning her chubby neck.

"I don't believe they were acquainted," she whispered back.

"It's a mistake to bring up bravery when you bring up this war," Lewis Braudel continued. "The bravest thing many soldiers did was to sleep in a camp that would likely kill them. You can't underestimate the damage done by disease, by the climate—"

Mrs. Whittlesby waved her arm and broke in. "You have so much in common with Mrs. Nash, both of you out of New York, after all. Perhaps you knew her husband, Edgar."

Everyone stared, and Dulcy felt her chest thud. "I regret that I did not," said Lewis politely, "but the point is really that I don't recall much of Cuba at all, because I was sick as a dog two months after arriving. I tried to warn Mrs. Mallow that this is not an heroic story."

"And the rumored novel—"

"No," said Lewis firmly, pulling out a sheaf of pages. "You wouldn't enjoy it, and the polite bits are scarce. I'll read another piece from the new collection."

Dulcy drained her glass and held it to a burning cheek, and while Lewis read about rich men given to bad deeds and young men given to stupidity, she tried to pluck her mind from the novel's autobiographical exploits, the evidence that he was good or at least practiced at many things. Walton had liked to say that well-behaved men tended to be boring, and even though the line was self-serving, and even though Dulcy wanted to disagree (hence: Victor), she had to admit that Lewis was not boring at all, even during the long, inane wrap-up. *Do you travel? Have you met Thomas Edison Teddy Roosevelt Jack London Nellie Bly William Jennings Bryan?*

Rex kept his arm up stubbornly throughout, and Dulcy wondered how he'd add to the inanity. "How was your hand damaged, Mr. Braudel?"

"Fireworks. Like any ill-behaved child."

"And how and why did you decide to become an expert writer?"

"I doubt there are expert writers," said Lewis. "There are only people who try it, and keep at it." Rex waited, a stoic, and Dulcy watched Lewis's amusement fade and his face go flat. "I needed to make a living, and I liked to write, and when I fell sick, I tried it again for the sake of a living."

Mrs. Whittlesby, whose questions had finished pickling, took over. "But surely you had no financial restraints. Your mother is a Weyden, I believe. I am confused by your name."

Mrs. Woolley moved toward the front of the room with the look of a woman in search of a weapon. Lewis folded his papers. "My father was Mr. Blake, and he was married to Mrs. Blake, née Weyden, and the Weydens do in fact all have a great talent for money, and have been invaluable to my father's career. But my mother was a Frenchwoman who died when I was quite young, and the Blakes took me in, and while I can't say it was the world's most affectionate situation, it was bearable. I went to good schools, and I have several half-siblings I enjoy, and I doubt I'd have found my calling if I'd come from a more typical background."

Well. Dulcy could feel the surrounding minds zigzag. Braudel meant nothing to her, Blake and Weyden quite a bit. She knew this story, even without the novel: French whore and sad marriage; smart, bitter, wastrel son; a bad engagement involving a banker's daughter. She very much wished she could talk to Carrie about this.

Mrs. Woolley had paused a moment in disbelief, but now picked up speed toward the lectern. Mrs. Whittlesby blurted on regardless, as if Lewis somehow had his own story wrong: "But I thought you were Mrs. Blake's nephew."

"No," said Lewis. "As I explained, I'm her husband's bastard son. He met my mother on a business trip to Paris, and I eventuated. Braudel was my mother's family name."

No one moved a finger, though every eye in the room pivoted to the floor or ceiling.

"Should I leave?" asked Lewis.

Dulcy made a sound, then went mute in a great wave of blush. "Has anyone heard the Widow Nash laugh before?" asked Lewis. "Maybe I have done something with my life, after all."

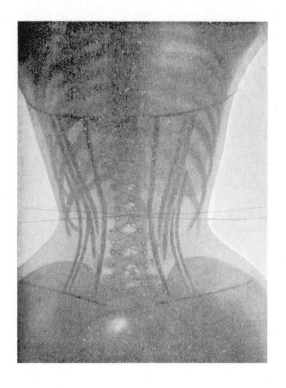

The world is filled with bad luck, surrounded by bad dreams, but if you see a woman three times, in three very different places, you have to be curious.

—Lewis Braudel's notes

CHAPTER 13

THE BROWN BOOK OF INVISIBILITY

•

Something had slipped away: she stopped waking in dread. She bought a six-burner stove and an icebox and a long table with cherry legs and a tin top, some tidy painted chairs and an armchair to tuck next to the west-facing window in the corner of the kitchen. Irina, who hadn't feigned grief over Dulcy's pending departure from the hotel, suggested relatives for plastering and woodwork, fences and roofs, and by the end of the day three had been hired. Now they swarmed through the house, shifting boards and buckets like loud, wiry ants. A cousin named Davor repaired the plaster walls, chipped by the banker's ancestral portraits; an uncle named Sabon would sand and varnish the floors; and another cousin was in line for garden work.

She took the rough diamond from Walton's medicine box to Mr. Hall, on Lewis Street. He was aquiline and bony in a way that made her think—pleasantly—of Walton, and he picked up the pebble, looked at it, looked at her, put it down. "I don't understand," he said.

"I don't, either," she said. "A business partner owed my husband money, and gave him one of these. They bought a horse together, a race horse, with another stone."

"What breed?" Hall's blue eyes were almost aqua. He didn't believe a word.

"A Thoroughbred," she said. "Though perhaps with some Barb. The man was an Englishman who'd spent time in Morocco, but I don't know where he came by the diamonds."

He put the gem down and spun it with a fingernail. "You couldn't know for certain until you cut it, and that would not be here, but it's very fine. A thousand, even if flawed. If you have more like this, go to New York or Amsterdam."

"But if my husband's other investments disappoint, I might have some relief?"

"You would."

"Well, that's lovely," said Dulcy.

"And a real pleasure to see," said Hall. "Let me look it over again."

It gave her a little more bone for her back, even given the money from Butte: perhaps she'd keep finding these tokens from Walton until she was rich enough to buy a house in Italy, too. She telephoned the Persian in Butte and asked him to deliver the carpet she'd liked best, rather than second best, and she decided to replace all the windows in the house. When she asked around about who was best for this job, people told her to use Durr, who'd glassed his own studio. Margaret was especially enthusiastic.

· · ·

Dulcy loved lists, to an unhealthy degree, and every night during her last days at the Elite she made a new one: the names of housepainters, books Margaret or Vinca suggested, a story she might try to write, paint colors. Sometimes she included tasks she'd already finished, for the sake of a horizontal slash. A few nights after Lewis Braudel's reading, she settled into a chair by the east window and arranged her writing board, her pen and ink and green notebook, a glass of wine, and one of Walton's hundred half-used pieces of blotting paper. Tonight's list would be the useful sort, the How to Get Walton Into a Clinic sort, with a new twist. She should be leery about this urge to codify things, but she needed to be organized, now that she was dead, and had a life.

Nursery in town? Rootstock via Salt Lake?
Soil & manure
Cedar boxes? Or dig down? Terrace hill?
Rock walls? Espalier?

She added *seed catalogues* before she moved on to more practical topics:

Mattress
Bedding and linens
Fry pans, Dutch oven, sauté, sauce

This wasn't very organized. She started to write *second sofa*, then felt silly and profligate, crossed it out with too much of a blob, and reached for the blotting paper. She spun it slowly while she listened to the racket in the lobby from a fresh load of train passengers, trying to decipher Walton's mirror writing, all the lost shadows of his live mind. She could make out *accounts* and *temperature*, *clinic* and *ship*, *medicine* and *meter* and *mine*, *all* and *my* and *love* and *rock*, *jews* or *jewels*. Walton had no issue whatsoever with the one, a great love for the other. She squinted and guessed jewels, the repetitive topic in the rosy book of poetry.

She eyed her half-empty wine glass, then wrote:

Everything.

Miss Randall was weeping again, and the sound ground against Dulcy's fragile new love of life. The weeping wasn't a new problem, and when Dulcy had tried knocking on the door of 324 at other times, everything had gone quiet. Still, tonight's noise was a wail, and now she glared in Leonora's general direction, put everything aside, and opened the door to the hall cautiously, leery of Lewis suddenly appearing on the stairs. This didn't, of course, happen, but the sounds deepened to the kind of keen she'd wanted to make when Martha had finally stopped breathing.

Dulcy tapped on the facing door and called out, "Miss Randall," and a tentative, "Leonora?"

Miss Randall stopped; the door stayed shut. Dulcy knocked again.

"I'm fine," said Miss Randall. "Thank you, Maria, but please go away. Please don't bother me."

Bother. All right, thought Dulcy. Simmer in your own snot, you cow. A second later she heard Martha's lecture—life wasn't a series of rewards, godly or otherwise—and had a dizzy memory of standing above the lobby of the Brown Palace, balancing a drop.

Still, having offered, she was offended to be rejected, and she closed her door with emphasis. She thought of the wine bottle but managed some strength of character and filled her empty glass with water. She resumed the chair, the notebook, the window, and saw that the theater cast had emerged, still half-costumed, smoking after the second performance. They had a bottle of champagne, and a board of what looked like cheese and bread rested on the ledge by the cellar stairs. Dulcy was hungry again; maybe she'd have Irving bring up a tray like that, just cheddar and bread. She flipped to a fresh page.

To do (cont'd):
Check electrical, gas, water. Coal dealer?
More shelves? Books!

A man passed through the alley, and Dulcy thought of Henning: it was something about the way he walked, a kind of strut she'd once enjoyed. Another man approached the alley crowd from the west. He took off his hat for a half-bow, and an actress danced over and kissed him on the cheek. She was the pretty lead from the play—Margaret had pointed her out—wrapped in a shawl but still in hoops for the *Pimpernel* dress, and she tucked herself into the crook of his arm.

Lewis Braudel let her, and brushed a soft, fat snowflake from her powdered forehead.

Dulcy looked down at her notebook and tossed it onto the floor. It landed open, and she stared down at Walton's shaky hand:

Boil me. Burn me.
All my love.

Only the green journal had these last three words, added on Walton's last morning. Dulcy, who had let her brothers bury him, instead, felt her good mood once again trickle away. She climbed into bed and pulled the covers over her head; she thought of the Westfield cemetery, Walton and Philomela, Martha and Elam stuck together eternally, dotting a hillside facing Lake Erie. It was probably still snowing there, too.

She turned out the light and tried to fit her mind into a different world. But on still nights, in sudden absences of wind, she could hear everything. That weekend the Elite was hosting a stockman's convention, and the ranchers' bellows mixed with an argument down the alley, geese flying overhead, dogs yipping, a late train. Across the hall, Miss Randall still emitted pigeony coos, and now the same drunk who'd sung about birds and bushes during the stabbing began his nightly warble.

I long for her peaches, I yearn for your apples, but Bella's plums bake up best . . .

Dulcy walked to the bathroom and stopped at the window on her way back. Lewis and his actress were gone, but everything else had an echo: snow would begin to fall, someone new would run down the street with a knife. Durr was working, his glowing glass roof blotting out the stars. A figure approached from the alley, and she thought of Henning again, and wondered if this was a headache coming on, if she'd soon smell dead mice or spices or metal. Maybe she'd only be trapped in sound: a stockman in the lobby howled about *fucking Holsteins* and *that cow*, and a zither-like instrument wailed and blended with the drumbeat sound of a guest dragging a suitcase down the hall.

The radiator hissed, and she stripped off the top blanket before she climbed back in. Miss Randall fussed if the climate was less than tropical, and Eugenia was the sort of proprietress who listened to the loudest complaint. The heat didn't seem to make Miss Randall any happier: her moans had once again evolved into yips, and Dulcy's always tentative love of humanity eroded. She was prone to what Walton called *shit-fits* of rage, and when the drunk began singing about cherry pie, Dulcy lunged out of bed and hiked the window, hissing like a goose.

The singer was directly below, momentarily silent as another man lit his cigar. They both looked up at the sound of the window, and the man with the match met her eyes and turned back to the drunk.

"Quiet, you," he said.

It couldn't be Henning, but it was so much like him that the *no* came too late to save her from the shock, electric fear. Dulcy stepped back without closing the window, then dropped to her knees on the floor, out of sight but with her forehead pressed to the frame. She kept her eyes shut for a few seconds, then looked again, but only made out the top of the man's hat, a dismissive gesture of his hand, and a movement to the right, at the alley: Lewis Braudel rounding the corner, alert but unsteady, Samuel trailing behind. They nodded to the Henning man as if they'd met before—familiar, but without warmth—then disappeared into the lobby, and the man finally turned his face toward the streetlight again.

Not Henning Falk, but she was sure one of his brothers had arrived from Seattle.

She wouldn't have slept that night anyway, but Gerry Fenoways began roaring in the hallways an hour later, pounding on Eugenia's door, pounding on every door. *My mother is dead you fucking cunts get up and mourn her or I'll burn you up.* Dulcy didn't have to go out to the hall to follow the police chief's progress—he stripped his clothes off and flung himself about while Eugenia implored him (*Calm yourself, ducky*) in a keening voice. The Henning doppelganger had been given the room next to hers, and she heard him complain when Deputy Bixby arrived with Dr. Macalester. *How could this be a policeman?*

It's hard to be sane when you're alone; it's harder to be sane when you're alone and drinking and have good reason to worry. After stabbings and fingerless men, a Falk brother was too much to fathom. Part of her brain—her pit brain, Walton had called it—screamed *they're all in league*; while her rational brain had been so frittered by every coincidence since the dawn of time (thanks to Walton, again) that some fragment simply refused this new ludicrous assault. She floated between what she thought she'd seen and what was vaguely reasonable, but there was no one to tell her how she'd drifted. A brave woman, a person who could think clearly about odds and the future, might take a train to Seattle and find the right quiet time to kill her enemy, and for a half hour she calmed herself with scenarios, thoughts of knives and poison and sharp rocks. Imagining it was easy, almost soothing, until she thought of Henning.

• • •

In the morning, Irving knocked, bearing her morning roll and coffee and newspaper. He eyed the bureau that had blocked his entry. "Did Chief Fenoways bother you?"

"I think Gerry has other doors to knock on," said Dulcy, who'd woken up crosswise on the bed.

"We don't all wet the hallways when our mothers die, do we?"

"No," she said, watching his black eyebrows wiggle, wondering about Irving's mother. "Did other guests complain?"

"Of course," he said. "But they could see he was batty, and it wasn't our fault."

"Where did he end up?"

They were alone in the room, but Irving leaned forward to whisper. "Mrs. K's bed."

Irving gave her pragmatism, and with coffee she found equilibrium: she'd been drinking. She wasn't worth finding, and the state teemed with six-foot Scandinavians. The house was worth the risk—there'd been no recognition in the man's eyes last night, and even if this really was one of Henning's brothers, there were a hundred reasons for him to be traveling through town. She was a paranoid mess. She needed to leave this hotel, but not this town.

She was forever padding down these stairs to ask misleading questions, and she paused on the mezzanine to study the battlefield. In the cold, hard morning light of the lobby—every fray showing on the upholstery, Eugenia's cheeks looking like crepe paper balloons—this man seemed less like Henning. He wasn't either of the brothers she'd seen close up, the brothers who had followed her in Seattle, Martin and Ansel. Still, seeing this man again gave her spine a jolt, and she was flushed as she took the fern chair. He kept his blank blue eyes (light blue, not dark and grayish like Henning's) trained on the sidewalk outside the plate glass, and barely noticed the way Irina gave extra twirls as she poured coffee. Surely an attention to females was a family trait, along with a tendency to carefully observe, but this man had no regard for drab women or the men at neighboring tables, who simmered in curiosity at the natty gray wool suit, the fine shoes.

On the other hand, this not-Henning ate a vast, Henning-style plate of food, half a chicken with spinach and fried potatoes. He dropped money on the table and walked past Dulcy to peer through the lobby windows of the newspaper, then paced while she pretended to read. When she looked back up he was staring directly at her but didn't flinch away, and she realized he was actually looking past her at Miss Randall, intent upon her customary dessert of tapioca pudding.

Dulcy looked down at her newspaper, the crisp letters telling her about mendacity and murder and the promise of another snowstorm, and felt a gust: Samuel and Rex and Lewis had surged into the lobby. They greeted the mystery man as Eugenia swooped down on them.

"You'll be trying the new chef tonight," she said to Samuel.

"I will not," he said. "I have too much to worry about."

"What would that be?"

"Dead girls on ice blocks, while Lewis asks horrible questions," said Samuel, moving around her for the door. "My poor mess of a cousin and his rotten investments."

Rex blushed. "Such a nice boy, when his mind is quiet," said Eugenia.

Dulcy guessed she didn't mean Lewis, who'd belatedly noticed her, and tapped his hat with his bad hand. Eugenia was given a mock bow. "Your guests look tired, Mrs. Knox. What was that noise about last night?"

"I didn't realize you spent time in your room, Mr. Braudel."

He grinned, and they were gone, crossing the street to a waiting Durr, and the group started south down Second Street, arguing. Rex kept a sidelong eye on the others, trying to fall into a step that had no collective rhythm whatsoever—these men were all in their own world, like competitors in an odd race, contestants in a strange beauty contest. Rex was so pretty, and so frayed, with loops of artful hair; Samuel had a nice profile, but his skin was gray, and his parts didn't quite fit. Durr limped with fine posture and looked annoyed with all of them. The new man, out in the light, looked harsh-featured and brutally pale, with none of Henning's weird angelic glide. He looked like he wanted to be sick to his stomach; he looked miserable and afraid.

Dulcy's eyes skittered over Lewis, who flexed his maimed hand while he listened to something Durr said, something private while Samuel gestured at Rex and the new man.

They are in league, thought Dulcy, dizzy from mapping out eye directions. She made for the *Enterprise* door. The secretary looked down and up again in surprise, because Dulcy had been distracted enough that morning to come down in her eyeglasses, but she claimed she had no idea where the men had gone. Dulcy sensed a territorial interest, and back in the lobby she tacked toward the front desk, where Irina fiddled with a new compact of rouge, flipped through a catalogue of bows and combs and barrettes. She had to know.

"I don't know if there's room for improvement in your appearance," said Dulcy.

"Hah," said Irina. But she smiled.

"I have a question," said Dulcy. "Who is that new guest?"

"Mr. Braudel?" Irina rolled her eyes. "He is not new. He is simply strange."

"No, the other. Tall, reddish hair. Is he a cattleman?"

The girl snorted. "No, a businessman. He is not one of those cowboys, or trading Jews, or sheepherding Catholic faggots."

When Irina kept her mouth shut, she managed to look grave and thoughtful and lovely. Speech ruined the effect. "Ah," said Dulcy. "He does have pretty blue eyes."

Irina turned another page in her catalogue, but she smiled again. Dulcy's view of the hotel log was blocked by Sears's shirtwaists, and she drummed her fingers, one eye on the other door. "Are you waiting for the wind to stop, for your usual walk?"

"Silly, aren't I?" said Dulcy. She made out an *F* in the signature in the register.

Irina leaned closer, her voice dropping. "But listen, I have a question. Do you know something much about Miss Randall?"

Leonora Randall was still in the dimmest corner of the lobby, finished with tapioca and back to her scrapbook. Dulcy avoided thinking of her own lists. "Beyond the fact that she likes the boiler on high?" asked Dulcy. "Not a thing. Has she been asking about arrivals, too? I've always gotten the sense she's waiting for someone." Eternally.

"No. She's even quieter than you are." Irina's forehead wrinkled, as if she belatedly wondered if this last comment was true. "Do you really think she's from Ohio? Someone asked if she might have a New York sort of voice. A city-like voice. And my ear is not so good, and I thought you'd know, because Mrs. Knox said you've been there."

Dulcy tried to think; she bought time. "I'd have to hear her again. She always sounds so heartbroken, it's hard to recall an accent."

Irina leaned forward. "A guest thought she might have a different name. The man you just asked about, from Seattle. Mr. Falk, Lennart Falk. He is here to see the body of the suicided girl they keep bringing back and forth. That is why he is out with Mr. Peake and

Mr. Braudel, waiting for the body to come. I think he must be not family, but some sort of detective."

"But who is he looking for?" managed Dulcy. "Did he give you a name?"

"Ramsay, I think. So much like Randall." Irina leaned forward again. Her blouse was low, and Dulcy, blood slowly returning to her brain, wondered if Irina would tilt like this for the man from Seattle. If he was like Henning after all, it should do wonders for his attention. "'Do we have a Miss Ramsay,' he asks, 'name of Lena?' 'No,' I say. 'Do we have a brunette girl,' he asks, 'who is new to the town and all strange and lonely?' 'Well, only Miss Randall, of course,' I say. 'And me,' I joke."

Irina's English was inexact, but evocative. Bereaved Maria Nash, who'd hinted at a long marriage, was not a girl. Miss Randall was taller, and ungainly—Samuel Peake said she looked like a flute with mildewed pads—but still nominally a medium-sized brunette maiden. "Lena Ramsay?"

"Something like that," said Irina. "I did not want to ask him to repeat. He does not have a sense of humor, or so much more English than myself. He has said he goes from town to town looking for this girl, and perhaps he is tired."

"Perhaps," said Dulcy. "Does he mean to stay long?"

"No, but look at me, look at you. It happens," said Irina.

"Look at Miss Randall," said Dulcy. It was a foul thing to do, but she was desperate.

"Of course, maybe he will see the body and be satisfied." Irina leaned closer. "But I think he thinks not. I think he thinks Miss Randall is his runaway. Why else follow a girl so plain?"

Irina's stunning vanity often rendered her stunningly stupid, but it sometimes lent clarity. Part of Dulcy wanted to smack her, and a small fragment wanted to protect Leonora Randall, but the largest piece of her heart was ready to run again. She'd thought that she was good at it. "Can't he just view Mr. Durr's photographs of the body?"

"I don't know," said Irina. "Perhaps he has been told to look for something to do with this dead girl's teeth. Perhaps he's been told to look for a mole or a broken bone. Last night before Chief Fenoways drank so much he told me"—Irina leaned forward again, looked sideways, whispered—"told me, just me, that they will look at this dead girl for such things, and bring down one of Dr. Macalester's machines."

This dead girl: Dulcy imagined herself on a metal table, the leg she'd broken when she was little now rotten and stretched out into the green maw of an X-ray. She'd fallen climbing for the first peach after years of bad weather, weather Walton, naturally, blamed on a volcano. The Boys had been there, and they'd known how bad the break had been—the bone had come right through her skin; they could have told Victor about this one identifying mark. But if Lennart Falk was studying a woman like Miss Randall, it meant Victor thought she really might be alive.

Before Walton had jumped out a window, Dulcy had the capacity to think through each act and reaction. She hadn't been a great chess player, but she could at least see three or four moves in the future, even if she couldn't manage her own temper. Now she'd been waylaid by her own poorly thought-out novella, built on panic and wishful thinking, and she made for her room, rabbit to the bolt-hole. Having the trunk sent had been a mistake, going to Butte had been a mistake, not killing herself had been a mistake. She wept—she didn't want to leave this place. She opened drawers and squinted at underwear, forgetting the eyeglasses on the collapsing bun on her head. When she bent for a slip, they fell, and one lens popped out.

It slowed her down. She found the chair by the window, fixed the lens, brushed out her hair, and attempted thought. This man had never seen her in the flesh; this man had looked right through her, which meant that she didn't quite match whatever he'd been told to find: a dark-haired nervous case, young and wandering. If he had a photograph, it might only be the old one from the paper, hair down, no rounding to her body. He was looking for an idea, not a face, and something put her out of contention—the believable tale of widowhood, the expensive black mourning dress with the high neck, the flat, practical boots she wore for walks. Her hair was up, and she'd lost weight, and it must all have conspired to make her invisible.

She shouldn't run or hide, she did not want to be mysterious in her absence, but she needed to do something about the notebooks, the one piece of irrefutable evidence that could reveal her identity. She studied the space behind the radiator, the ledges above windows, the plumbing alcove behind the water closet. She considered the mattress, and she thought of taping a notebook to the back of each awkward botanical print on the walls. She finally settled on the shearling coat, hanging in the closet, already protecting her cash and the diamond. She made a larger rip in the lining and lowered the notebooks in, maneuvering them around the hem until the coat regained some balance but still felt soft at the waist, where someone might put their hand if they pawed through the closet. The pink book was the last to go in, and she flipped it open to an early page, wondering if she should just burn the thing:

> *The earthquake came, and rocked the quivering wall,*
> *And men and nature reeled as with wine.*
> *Whom did I seek around the tottering hall? For thee.*
> *Whose safety first provide for? Thine.*

Walton's first instinct had never been to save anyone, even himself. She smiled down at the flourish after *thine* and touched the corner of her glasses to feel that the right lens was secure. She finally understood: she'd always been too vain in front of Victor and Henning to wear her glasses, even playing tennis, even at the theater.

• • •

She dressed for shopping and sailed back down to the lobby, manic and free of fear. Miss Randall was still placidly concentrating on her big loopy handwriting, and Lennart Falk was back in place, looking strained and pale. He had a copy of Butte's *Tidende og Skandinav* on his lap and didn't give a glance as she passed through the lobby. He had eyes only for the wallflower, despite the fact that Irina swayed like a debutante as she delivered tea. By now he seemed like a poor shade of Henning, and he certainly didn't have his brother's subtlety: he marched between the newspaper and the wire office and the train station on the far side of Park Street, smoking and staring blatantly at Miss Randall through the window. She didn't notice his existence.

Irina, suddenly her friend, waved her over. "They sent the wrong person from Billings," she said. "The wrong iced coffin. It was a fat man, not this girl. Now they wait again."

Dulcy headed out for Margaret's house, where she was the second Sacajawea on the gossip circuit: Vinca Macalester had talked about a body arriving, and a mix-up, and mentioned X-rays with her husband's new machine. She'd also passed on the news that Mrs. Fenoways had died the night before in horrible suffering, riddled and wracked by cancer while Gerry and Hubie howled at her bedside. The sons had been drinking since the morning; now they were waiting for the girl's body at Hruza's Cold Storage.

Dulcy said she had errands in that direction; would Margaret go with her? Margaret would not; Margaret had an aversion to the Fenoways brothers.

Which was only sane, but Dulcy had a compulsion to know the worst. She felt like her own body was arriving on the train. She bought two blouses at Thompson's, a pair of spring shoes at A. W. Miles, a magazine at Sax and McCue's, where a five-year-old boy flirted with her; every little thing helped. She stopped at Wong's for the laundry she knew wasn't ready yet, and she played tiddledywinks with another small boy propped on the counter between bales of linen while Joe Wong's wife counted items. Through the laundry's window she watched Durr and Falk march back and forth between the hotel and the studio two more times while Lewis sat on a bench in front of the studio, just one door down from the laundry, and read a magazine. When Samuel emerged from the newspaper office and waved to him, she followed.

The Fenoways brothers were holding court at Hruza's Cold Storage, moving in and out of the tavern next door while a boy ran back and forth between the telegraph office and this temporary police station to check on the status of the girl's body. Dulcy, pretending to admire dresses through the window two doors down, smelled cold and woodchips from the open door. The crowd of men in Hruza's anteroom stood in a fog of tobacco smoke, talking loudly about dead mothers. When she saw Durr come around the corner, Dulcy hurried into Winslow's Grocery across the street, and Gerry Fenoways' voice followed her like a wall. *My mother's fucking dead, and it's Saturday; let's get this thing into the beyond, send this little lassie back to her own home hell. You know this isn't some effing maiden we're discussing here—so young, but the bits seem quite used. And meanwhile none of you cunts give a shit about my poor bleeding mom.*

In Winslow's, a nervous clerk followed her while Gerry howled on: at Durr to take his portrait and hurry the train, at Bixby to find *that Swedish fuck.* Dulcy fluttered in a circle, then said she needed to pick out things for her house, to be delivered later. Ten pounds of flour, ten pounds of sugar, coffee that had flavor . . . she nattered away while a boy took dictation and politely ignored repetitions.

I could run faster than this fucking train. This girl fucked faster than this fucking train. Go ask again. "Doesn't he know how to use the station telephone?" said Winslow, a twitchy man growing twitchier. He had a gray mustache that seemed wider than his bony face. Dulcy, ordering food she wouldn't be able to taste for weeks, was beginning to be hungry, and she eyed casks of smoked and salted fish, Karkalay and Norway bloaters, Holland and kippered herring, anchovies and mackerel. She bought some smoked eel and was at the cash register when a new sound echoed across the street, someone singing. Everyone in the store walked to the front to see whatever this new noise meant.

> *Che gelida manina,*
> *se la lasci riscaldar.*
> *Cercar che giova?*
> *Al buio non si trova.*

What a frozen little hand. Let me warm it for you. Such sensitivity: Hubie Fenoways, wiry and agitated, was bellowing out *La bohème* as he paced in the street. She'd heard that he styled himself an opera singer, and he really wasn't that bad. Someone jeered, and called him a bagpipe, but he finished, and bowed, then rolled up his sleeves and started for the man. Bixby, who needed to find a saner line of work, held him back, but the mood changed: a delivery wagon with the coffin appeared, escorted by Lennart Falk. Hubie walked up to Falk and poked him—hard—in the chest. A voice whispered in her ear, Lewis: "Avoid those men, at all cost."

Samuel was next to him, gleeful. "The Fenoways are quite something, aren't they?" he said. "They are their own opera."

Lewis took a second look at Dulcy. "Did this just happen?" he asked, pointing to her glasses. "Are you blind?"

"I often use glasses," she said. "And I've had headaches."

"You're vain," said Lewis. It made him happy, and she guessed they'd been drinking. "They make you seem very severe," he said.

"I am severe," said Dulcy, who'd put effort into looking more like a widow that day.

"You are lovely," said Lewis. He nodded toward her purchase; the clerk was just tying the string. "With strange tastes. Eel, Mrs. Nash?"

"Are you watching?" asked Samuel. "Mr. Falk would like to hit the younger Fenoways. He's already had a hard day. He wasn't looking forward to the girl, and the brothers Fenoways were making the most of the moment—"

"Nasty little shits," said Lewis. "Their mother should be relieved to be free."

Dulcy blinked, but Samuel rolled on: the body had been due to arrive from Billings early that morning, but the Billings morgue had loaded the wrong coffin. When they'd accompanied Lennart Falk to the back of the store at ten, they'd peered down at the body of a middle-aged suicide, an accountant who'd swallowed cyanide.

"Worse than a hanging," said Samuel, rubbing his eyes. "Worse than the girl when we saw her in Missoula a month ago, and I vomited on Lewis's boots."

The Fenoways disappeared inside Hruza's, and Lewis headed out. "Here we go again," said Samuel.

Dulcy fled.

• • •

At six o'clock, when Lennart Falk's Elite door slammed, Dulcy listened to him talk to a presumably empty room. This was yet another thing that was her fault: if only he'd think it was the end of the story. But that poor dead girl without the right broken bone would still be dead, and Lennart Falk would begin looking for another brunette. Dulcy had almost managed to feel sympathy for everyone but herself when she heard a soft firm step in the hall. She braced herself for Irina's questions, but the girl knocked softly on the door to the north. Dulcy vaulted off her bed to put an ear to the wall. She heard the click of Falk's door, soft conversation, a salvo of giggles and soothing sounds, and within another sixty seconds the unmistakable wail and thump of a bed subjected to a full-blown rut.

In novels, the heroine has never truly done anything wrong; in novels, heroines languish in their chamber indefinitely, sipping spring water. By eight, as Lennart Falk began to thump into Irina again, Dulcy had found and eaten all five crackers she'd stowed in her bag, as well as some pistachios left from the Butte trip. She cracked the door and smelled roast beef and sugar and shrill perfume, not the best mix.

She shut the hall door quietly. Someone outside was making crooning noises, calling out, but the wind warbled the sound. The heat was pounding out, Eugenia catering to the nitwit again, and when she heard the crooning again, something very close to *Maria*, Dulcy lifted the window. A group looked back up at her, and Margaret gave an embarrassed wave.

"Rapunzel," said Lewis. "Take the stairs."

• • •

She should not have done it—this behavior was not bereaved—but the whole town seemed to be out, and no one would notice her. Within an hour, after whiskey cocktails at the Albemarle, she was tipsy enough to drop fully into the role of a worldly widow and admit what she'd heard in the hotel. Samuel covered his face, but one eye drooped. Margaret blushed, but Lewis only shrugged. "I imagine he needed to wind down," he said, and explained that the photo Lennart Falk carried looked nothing like the bloated face of this dark-haired woman—a different nose, different cheekbones, different neck—

"Hard to tell about the eyes," said Samuel.

"Stop it," said Rex. He dropped his head.

—and Falk had been sick, though there was already vomit in the Hruza's bucket. There was no matching the photo, but the girl Falk sought had broken a leg as a child, and Gerry sent a summons to James Macalester, and the doctor sent a summons back: his machine was not portable, whereas this body had been in constant motion for weeks. Gerry decreed that they could dispense with the coffin or the hearse, and he had his men use a delivery cart for the three-block trip from Hruza's to the hospital, and so the town was treated to billowing sheets (the wind, again) and dead blue feet.

The hospital was a Victorian labyrinth. Macalester kept specimens of amputations, growths, and fetuses, and Falk was sick to his stomach again. In the lull before the beginning of the long green crackle of the machine, while Macalester tinkered with the equipment, Gerry and his men made more bad jokes. The body was rolled into position (or part of the body: the woman had been sliced in half), and Hubie Fenoways did something and said something that made Falk retch one more time and swing at him.

It took an hour for the image to resolve. Hubie left, and Samuel and Lewis took Falk and Rex out for another drink. This body's legs had never been broken. Macalester had heard what Hubie had done, and Hubie would be fired, dead mother or no. Gerry couldn't prevent it.

"But what do you mean?" asked Margaret. "What did Hubert Fenoways do?"

The men looked away, and Dulcy started to go hot at the hairline. Rex, who had been sick, too, buried his face in his hands, so that only his floppy forelock stuck out. Lewis finished his glass of water and pulled a notebook and a pen out of his pocket. He drew the outline of a woman, and then he drew slashes across the body.

"This was how the body was cut up by the train or by a man," said Lewis. "This is where Mr. Falk had been told to check for a broken leg. And this is where Hubie put his fingers."

Dulcy scraped a speechless Margaret off the bench and pushed her toward the door. "Who did he think she was?"

"Wait for us, Maria," said Lewis, pulling out his wallet. "Don't do a runner."

"Leda Remfrey," said Samuel. "You might have read about her back in January."

"No," said Dulcy. "I probably wasn't here yet, and I wasn't thinking clearly."

"Sorry," said Samuel. "Of course. The father had been a suicide, and the daughter might have run, might have jumped—"

"Jumped," said Lewis, dropping coins on the table. "Her fiancé was a renowned prick, the kind of man any sensible woman would escape."

No one had apparently ever said *prick* in front of Margaret, who buckled again. "I've been told she poisoned her father and stole one hundred thousand dollars," said Rex.

This came out in an elided blur. Rex tilted, and his pomaded head left an oil stain on the wallpaper. "Jumped," said Lewis again. "The father was an eccentric in business with the fiancé, a newspaper man named Maslingen; the father came out of a window at the Butler in Seattle. He'd lost some money, but he didn't bother sticking around to spend it, so perhaps it really was lost. There's no evidence the daughter knew, either. Jumped."

"What about the poison rumor?"

"I heard she saw him fall," said Samuel. "So it does seem redundant. And I heard it was more money, but who knows? Everyone lies."

"I'm completely fuddled," said Lewis. "I need to sleep."

At the Elite, Margaret curled up in a lobby chair, and Samuel promised to walk her home. They'd dragged Rex this far, and Samuel argued with Lewis: they couldn't physically get him home, but they couldn't in good conscience expose him to his mother's wrath. As they started in on Irving—couldn't he tuck Rex into a staff bunk?— Dulcy made for the stairs. She was dizzy, but some sense of self-preservation was intact, and she turned on the landing to see that Lewis was right behind her.

"Do I make you nervous?"

She grinned. "You know, you do."

Samuel was calling for him. "I'll give you a head start," said Lewis.

Dulcy laughed and ran up, then slowed. The curtains at the end of the hall billowed away from Leonora Randall's open door—Miss Randall, who loved her privacy and her heat. Dulcy walked slowly down and found that the curtains gusted inside the room, too, every window open over a mess. Leonora had three trunks—she'd traveled heavy, in the parlance of Irving—and the staff had muttered when she'd refused to have her things put away or the trunks removed, which made her rooms cluttered and hard to clean. Now someone had opened all three, and every drawer, shredded the upholstery, tossed all of it into a mound in the center of the room with the torn pages of the violet-laden scrapbook.

Dulcy took a step over silverware and just missed a china shepherdess's painted head, then slid on a pearl, one from a long, broken string. The bedroom floor, partly visible through a doorway, was dusted with feathers, as if someone had taken a knife to the pillows. This was rage, not a robbery. She paused before she managed to walk to the open window near the gutted sofa. The pavement had no body.

Dulcy ran to the stair railing. Lewis looked up from helping Samuel and Irving with a jellied Rex. He smiled—she was calling his name from the mezzanine, after all—but his mouth drooped as he took in her expression. The tavern roared, sound working like bellows on the glass doors at either end of the lobby, and as Lewis dropped Rex with a bad bounce, the door at the end of the lobby blew open. Hubie Fenoways, no longer singing, crawled into the room with Lennart Falk behind, lashing him with Durr's ebony-and-silver cane. It looped so quickly through the air Dulcy could hear it whistle over the crowd and Hubie's screamed imprecations—*duck-dicked motherfucker sardine bait buggering*— and Lennart Falk switched to stabbing at him with the cane, spearing him until the shaft broke and stuck in the man's jaw. Hubert crawled on, smashing into a glass case of tourist souvenirs, screaming *fucker fucker fucker* and choking on blood while the broken end of the cane wiggled in the air like a conductor's baton.

Lennart Falk lifted what was left of the cane, and Dulcy saw Lewis run toward him, swinging the elevator attendant's stool. He brought it down in a slashing motion and knocked Falk to the floor. When Hubie turned to snarl, Lewis kicked him flat.

• • •

Lennart Falk freely admitted to destroying Miss Randall's room. "I am looking for a beautiful woman," he said. "If she is not dead, she has stolen from my employer."

Beautiful—a small stab of pleasure, mixed with a recoil. Lennart had come to believe Miss Randall, *though plain and skinny now*, might be the confident woman he sought. His client was clear about the need to reclaim property.

What property? He couldn't say, or explain why his client might think Leda Remfrey was still alive. Samuel, who witnessed the interview, quoted other phrases like *hunnerts of towwsants* and *ruint in love*. Lennart had searched in Salt Lake and Denver and Omaha, then backtracked and moved along the northern line, asking questions in rooming houses and hotels from Spokane to Duluth. He had brothers who had the same task in New York, Chicago, San Francisco.

He agreed that Miss Randall did not seem to be the thief he sought. He admitted to Bixby—Gerry Fenoways was dead drunk—that he had lost his mind after the stress of seeing the dead girl.

"The scum police officer stuck his finger into her," said Falk. "I protested, and he lied about what he'd done. But I walked away, I tried to be calm."

After the viewing and before the caning, Falk had telephoned Seattle, drunk a half bottle of whiskey on an empty stomach, and decided that his prey was indeed Miss Randall. He entered her room and lost any remaining control during his search.

Then he made his way to the saloon, where Hubie was waking his dead mother or his dead job. Macalester had already marched to city hall to demand his firing, and Gerry had been so drunk, and so upset about their mother, that he waved a hand and let it happen. A rational man would have found a different bar, but Lennart wanted a drink, and while he watched the bartender open a bottle of gin, Hubie let everyone know that Falk's reaction to the body had been to throw up. Siegfried Durr told him to shut up, and most of the men in the tavern said anyone would have done the same, but Hubie kept cracking jokes, and Lennart Falk had three shots of gin—*boom, boom, boom*—while he listened to the merriment.

"After Hubie has a few, he swells into a giant," said Samuel. "Bloodlust sets in. His mind flames, his mouth opens. Mellifluous filth emerges."

Some of the filth: Hubie called Falk a cod-fucker and a fiord-paddler, and added lines about reindeer and Lapp women. Durr tried again to silence Fenoways, but it was too late: Falk drained a last gin, picked up Durr's cane, and speared Hubie in one thigh— "gaffed him like a fish"—then wiped the tip clean with the barman's cloth. Hubie fled toward the door but managed a last insult: he said, in so many words, that the girl's body had aroused the Swede. Falk surged toward him, stabbing at Hubie's back, his legs, his retreating ass; as they broke into the lobby, he flicked off Durr as if he were a bug and sank the cane deep into Hubie's jaw. The silver tip was still where a tooth used to be.

Falk said he regretted having tossed around a nice young woman's unmentionables. He did not regret what he'd done to Hubie Fenoways, but his employer would be happy to make reparations to everyone involved, despite his near financial ruin. Gerry finally left the Mint Saloon to arrest him, and the rumor was that he beat Falk for the next several hours until Bixby managed to lock the Swede in a cell and temporarily hide the key.

• • •

"I don't *have* anything to steal," sobbed Miss Randall, when she and Eugenia returned from the theater at midnight. "Beyond my aunt's necklace and earrings. And I did offer to give those back."

This was interesting. Dulcy, drunk and daubing at the girl's tears, thought that maybe everyone had a dirty little secret; maybe Dulcy wasn't alone in this world. She began to warm to poor, kleptomaniacal Miss Randall, until the girl added: "They don't understand how cruel they were, how much I deserved some sort of present. Why would they send me away?"

Dulcy, who had stumbled into crime, loathed her for her incompetence and greed and self-pity. Her dislike only deepened when she sobered up: the next day, she hated everything, right through coffee and lunch. Her head buzzed and her stomach dipped, and her suffering only ebbed with a larger terror, when Irving told her that Gerry Fenoways, who wanted revenge for his brother's ouster and beating, had insisted that someone travel from Seattle bearing bail money, to personally escort Falk home.

Dulcy made a show of using the telephone and took the train to Denver, telling Eugenia that she needed to meet her sister-in-law, who was en route from New York to Los Angeles. After a few days at the Melton—she didn't dare return to the Brown Palace—Dulcy called Margaret, who was very proud of her recent purchase of a telephone, and said that *an amazing man, so interesting, so strange looking* had come to retrieve his brother Lennart. When Henning Falk had arrived late, he'd found the jail locked tight, no one on duty, and he'd eaten a late dinner with Samuel and Lewis. In the morning he met with Gerry Fenoways, handed over a bag of gold, then bundled his brother onto the next train, after visiting the body of the girl and giving Leonora Randall an up-and-down that had sent her weeping to her room.

Dulcy came home. The next morning, a little man from Utah was ushered into Hruza's and recognized his wife from a pattern of moles on the breasts.

Fruit

I have two apple orchards, one consisting of 150, the other 120 trees, principally grafted fruit: Roxbury Russet, R.I. Greening, Esopus Spitzenburg, Pearmain, Newtown Pippin, Baldwin, Black Gillyflower, Jonathan, Fall Pippin, Honey Heart, Swaar, Harvest, Priestly, &c.

Peach trees, 52: Alberge Yellow, Morris White, Early Ann, Royal George, Early York, Early Crawford, Lemon Cling, &c. Pear trees, 39, including Belle, Barlett, Virgalieu, Swan's Orange, Woodruff, Harvest, &c. Plum trees, 29, including Damson, Greengage, Yellow Egg, Mediterranean, Large Purple &c. Also 33 cherry trees: Tartarian, English, Florence, American Amber, Morelio, &c. 12 large Orange Quince bushes; Apricots, Isabella grapes, &c.

The curculio has troubled my plums some seasons. The pear trees are affected by blight, which I fear will prove destructive; I know of no effectual preventive.

From Transactions of the New York State Agricultural Society for the Year 1848, *Elam Bliss's response to the questionnaire about his farm in Westfield, Chautauqua County*

CHAPTER 14

A GLASS HOUSE

•

This Elam Bliss had been Dulcy's great-grandfather, and all of the trees except the blighted pears, immediately replaced, were still bearing fruit when she was a child in the house of his elderly son, another barrel-chested botanic obsessive. Dulcy had a list of everything that she and Martha had picked in the Westfield gardens tucked in the green book, and she looked at it now with a new eye. Pearmain and Baldwin, both cider apples, ripened too late for Montana. So did Spitzenberg and Black Gilliflower, a smoky, ribbed apple that had been one of Dulcy's favorites, along with Swaar, rich and spicy and mottled green, the ugliest fruit in the orchard. Swan's Orange had been Walton's favorite pear, on his summer visits, but the Virgalieu pear, known these days as White Doyenne, had been far better.

Martha, Elam's daughter-in-law, had taught Dulcy to make a checkered tart with the damson and greengage plums, to make apple butter and chutney, and cider and brandies out of everything. Dulcy spent late summers with a face smeared by syrup from Moorpark apricots and mirabelles and mulberries, newer cherries like Black Republican and Bing, blackberries and raspberries and gooseberries the size of quail eggs from bushes with thorns like medieval spikes.

Martha grew dessert and wine grapes, but Concord vines increasingly circled Westfield, as the Welch family bought up land for juice and Seder wine. Martha blamed the Welches for an onslaught of plant ailments, but the greatest enemy remained the curculio, a weevil. She'd send Dulcy and a spritzer of poison up into the trees in June, then back up in September with a hooked basket for the survivors. When she was especially annoyed with someone, usually Walton, she'd call him *the weevil.*

• • •

Dulcy saw nothing like Elam's orchards in Montana, but that didn't mean they couldn't be attempted, on a smaller scale, in her own backyard. A week after Henning Falk retrieved his brother and disappeared again, she purchased a ruler, draughtsman's paper, and good pencils at Sax & McCue, and spent an evening reading new gardening magazines and sketching.

To order & start inside: tomatoes, peppers, aubergine, melons, artichokes

To plant outside, April: lettuces, parsley, beets, carrots, turnips, celery, cabbage, Brussels sprouts, peas, onions, radishes, potatoes

To plant when warm (last frost when?): beans, squash, cucumber, corn, cosmos, nasturtiums

To order: fruit trees & berries

The next morning she walked to the new house in another snowstorm, nothing soft and ethereal but a fat fog laced with crystals that stuck to her face and melted down her neck. She'd wanted to plan out terraced beds, but she couldn't see more than ten feet, nor could she study the shade patterns or determine if any corner of the yard had soil that was any better than the center, where the wind had scoured enough snow away to show dead gray clay.

Inside, progress: Dulcy had hired one non-Slovak, a painter and paper-hanger named Gustaf Goulliand recommended by the Sacajaweas, and chosen a buttery off-white except for the largest bedroom, for which she picked a sort of apricot, and the small library room, which became sea blue-gray-green, almost the same color as Walton's travel notebook.

Margaret described the former owner's wife as likeable but odd. She'd hated the local climate—she'd emerged rarely, usually wearing a fur coat—and the white tiles were the result of her obsession with cleanliness. Margaret surmised that this fixation on soap and disease had led to the woman's committal to a sanitarium in her home state. Dulcy knew the kind of institution, deceptively homey in its public rooms—lots of light and potted plants—but more like a hospital proper in the treatment areas, with gray marble walls and floors and nurses in love with their own starched uniforms, advertising quantities of grain and oxygen, baths, electricity, and Swedish movements. Walton would love the experience for a week, and then flee for dirt.

"The view of the river depressed her," said Margaret. They were on the porch a few days later, talking about what cane furniture to purchase, and Siegfried Durr was tromping on the ceiling above their heads, measuring for new upstairs windows.

"But it's beautiful," said Dulcy, flummoxed. You could see rivers and mountains, sky, and none of the town. It stunned her: she'd bought the place without ever looking up and out.

"She found it bleak; she was quite morbid. She said it was the same thing, every day."

"I can see feeling that way about the wallpaper," said Dulcy. "But everything here is moving. The river, the wind and clouds and trees."

"I think she had the sense that the water was constantly disappearing," said Margaret.

As opposed to the goddamn wallpaper. Dulcy had her own bleak thoughts, watching Goulliand struggle with a steamer and a scraper, the shadow of purple roses holding on like a rotten body. "Should we give up on the idea of paint?"

"No," he said. He tended to grit his teeth. The hair and beard she'd initially assumed were gray were speckled with whitewash, and his nails were permanently copper green.

"Can I do anything to make your life easier?"

"You could leave the room, Mrs. Nash. I would suffer more comfortably if alone."

Margaret fled. Dulcy walked into her kitchen and slammed empty drawers on her way out to the side porch and her bag and downtown, where she could throw some money at the empty-drawer problem. She found Durr on a ladder and Margaret underneath, holding a putty pot. Three panes had been cracked when a plasterer swung wide with a board.

"You're a man of many talents," said Dulcy.

"I am a man of two or three," he said. He'd started a black beard, and he had a new cane tilted against the bench by her boots, silver clad with a blue glass ball at the end.

He had all his weight on his left leg and was dangling his right on the ladder. "Did you hurt your leg falling from a window?"

"From a horse, in the army. I crushed it, and that was the end of that."

"The army?"

"The army," said Durr.

Margaret gave her a look; Dulcy had confessed to doubting Lewis's story. The move from officer to glazier still didn't make sense, but Dulcy had no right to inquire about anyone's alternate history. She tried to look interested in flaking caulk on the other windows, until Durr felt the pressure to offer more information. "I learned glass from my father-in-law," he said. "In Berlin. Ateliers, palm houses, solariums in clinics."

"Oh!" said Dulcy. "A wife!"

"Dead, then," said Durr. "And so I emigrated." He started to climb down, but Margaret handed him another pane and gave him an expectant eye—please don't stop. Durr elaborated: he'd been depressed, and he'd had a tendency to fight. He made his way from New York to Milwaukee and found a job repairing a studio for an old photographer from Hamburg, who'd known his wife's family, and showed him how to use a camera. And then another fight, and a friend had come to retrieve him, and brought him here.

"Since then I wanted to begin seeing it all fresh," said Durr. He had a floaty way of looking at a person, half there and half anywhere else. Perhaps the other half always had to be sure nothing stray was headed for a pane of glass. During the story, he bent down to show them the dent on the crown of his head where a man had hit him with a metal bar ("a Silesian").

"Fresh? Because of your grief?" He drew a perfect bead of caulk.

"No, no. I used to be violent, very angry. Then it went badly, and when I woke I was different, and everything looked different, and all I wanted was to look very hard at things."

The idea of Durr angry made her uneasy, but that in turn made her feel guilty. He had only been honest, and he didn't wrangle like Irina's men. Rusalka was there helping after the plasterers were done, and Goulliand finished his martyrdom of walls, and Dulcy noticed that Durr studied Rusalka with pale moon eyes while they wiped the place down, hung the curtains, and had the furniture and coal delivered. He watched Margaret the same way.

• • •

Dulcy had told Eugenia she'd need her room until April 1, but she'd had Irving gradually move her things from the hotel. The gray shearling and the blue valise were stowed in the smaller upstairs bedroom, and she kept the door locked. It was her Bluebeard room.

A few days before the official end of winter, she walked back with a small satchel and some groceries and let herself in. She lit the furnace and loaded wood into the stove and left her groceries in a bin on the cold front porch. She made tea and began the christening task of painting her pantry a bright Swedish blue with a pot of paint she'd smuggled in that afternoon. Martha's shelves had been a deep ironic grape color; Goulliand would have been horrified, but

Goulliand was finished and paid, off drinking away the job. Dulcy planned to layer her paint like shellac so that it could be scrubbed without chipping for years, so she wouldn't have to line things with tatty muslin.

When the first layer was down, she opened the pantry window and shut the door, poured herself some wine and twirled around the house, unpacking silverware and linens, moving the bedstead around the south-facing room for the right feel from the windows, walking barefoot to not gouge the freshly varnished floors while she put her very few belongings on her very many shelves, running back and forth. She was giddy; it made her think of running a doll through a dollhouse when she was a child, all errands and no duty, all officious joy, and it reminded her of how Martha had changed everything in her house when her husband and daughter had died, how even in the middle of that hell she'd been silly with movement.

Dulcy's new bedroom still had no curtains, and she watched the snow fall after she turned down the lamp. When she woke up, the coal fire had died out, and the house was cold but muffled by new snow. She found another quilt, and climbed back under. She could sleep as long as she wanted to sleep.

• • •

"It snows in the middle of summer, sometimes," said Samuel, shaking slush from his hat. "I gather people go ahead and plant, and then just cover the little things."

"Cover with what?"

"A sheet, I think. Canvas?"

He had no idea; he couldn't have told the difference between a radish and a beet if they bit his gums. "You'll be flooded, anyway," he said. "The mosquitoes will kill you. You'll have malaria by May."

"No, she won't," said Lewis. "The creek has a good drop. She's ten feet over the flood level."

They'd toured the place before lunch. "I suppose you're the voice of authority," said Samuel.

"I'll do," said Lewis. It was a Saturday, and they were eating at Ah Loy on Main, open again after its mysterious funeral. The place was filled with ranching families in town for supplies, but Samuel, who was wearing a new checked suit and cultivating a spotty moustache, was by far the nattiest dresser.

"I like you better clean-shaven," said Dulcy.

"I'd like to look older," Samuel had answered. "Sterner."

He wasn't a fop; she wasn't sure what he was. Lewis filled their beer glasses while Rex, who dressed in silk and wool like a banker from 1850, spoke nervously about a variation on his newest business plan—he'd had a promising note from a family friend in the Interior Department about a possible concession permit for an area of the Gardner River just inside Yellowstone Park, and he intended to construct a hot springs resort.

"What a lovely idea," said Margaret. "You'll bring tour people to your own hotel."

"The Boiling River?" snapped Samuel. "Who on earth wants to boil? You'll have to rename the spot, or people will think 'boils,' instead of luxury."

"I will," said Rex, flushed. "It makes as much sense as betting on thin paper and bad writing."

Everyone studied the menu. The waiter came, and Dulcy pointed to a dish at a nearby table: it had real dried peppers, and what looked like spinach and fish. Margaret had a noodle dish, Samuel soup, Rex fried rice, and Lewis asked for duck. While Samuel argued with Rex—all of Rex's idealistic business ventures removed money from the newspaper—Lewis studied the sleet outside and the trio of tough young Chinese at the table by the door. He tapped a chopstick against his water glass in an annoying fashion; he looked thinner than he had a week earlier, and Samuel had muttered about *a wave of attacks*. Dulcy didn't remember what they'd told her in Walton's Italian clinic, about how and why malaria came and went. She hadn't heard him walk in circles on her ceiling during the last few days at the hotel, but she thought that the Sacajaweas who whispered that Irina still "ministered" to him were wrong. Not so sure that she hadn't asked Rusalka, in the most roundabout way possible while they were unrolling carpets.

"No," said Rusalka. "She used to, when he very first arrived, but they are no longer fond of each other. I think Rina only thought he *might be*. He had a greater liking for a married lady or widow in Bozeman, but that is maybe over."

"How do you know?" asked Dulcy, thinking of Lewis jumping onto the train platform back in January, buoyant and aimed for pleasure.

"That it's done? Letters," said Rusalka. "The lady writes very dramatic, according to Rina. But you can't tell if that's so true, because Rina is not a reader."

Now Dulcy watched Lewis flip through a newspaper. "How are you?" she asked.

"I've been away," he said, which wasn't the same thing as answering. He looked a little green-skinned, though perhaps the ink of the paper in front of him, the St. Patrick's issue of the Butte *Independent*, reflected on his face. The taverns in Livingston had served green beer the night before, and on their way to the restaurant, the gutters were still chartreuse.

While they talked the cooks dropped piles of noodles—roar, crackle, hiss—into the huge woks behind Lewis, the three-foot metal pans fitting into the round openings of the wood-fired stove, the wall behind so cured with fat it was almost metallic. A little boy threw a log in the side hatch every other minute, and the men at the stove, all of them with the polished skin of the perpetually roasted, dashed sauces in from the old whiskey bottles that lined the stove next to heaps of mustard and cabbage, onion and peppers, and smeared glass jugs of soy. The steam made an unlikely halo behind Lewis's head. He had a nice, austere, saintly profile, but his mouth was a little too wide for the role.

The food arrived, and Margaret picked at her noodles with a worried forehead. Rex was angry and stabbed his rice, and Samuel scanned the Butte paper and made jokes about Irishmen. Dulcy tried not to eat too quickly, and she fanned her face. Lewis reached out and clicked chopsticks with her, as if toasting. "You're good with those. I imagine you've had better Chinese than this in Seattle."

"I have," she said, before her words echoed.

But the others didn't seem to notice. "Or New York, certainly. Or even Butte," Lewis said a moment later. No hint of a smile, no sense that he was playing a game. "Try some duck."

He reached out and she opened her mouth. She gave him a bite of the mystery fish and noticed that her hand was shaking. "What will you plant, Mrs. Nash? Flowers, vegetables, an orchard? You have a large yard to fill."

"All of it," said Dulcy, watching him stab another bit of fish off her plate.

"We'll help," said Lewis. "I know how to shovel."

"You stun me," said Samuel.

"Bodies," said Lewis. "Yellow fever."

"May I ask what happened to your hand?" asked Margaret. "Samuel says it wasn't really a fireworks accident."

Samuel signaled for another pitcher of beer. "You should ask what happened to my head instead," said Lewis.

"Your head or your mind?" asked Dulcy.

"My head," he said, tapping one of the metallic freckles on his cheekbone. "Unless you have some fresh insight."

"No, I don't," she said. "But what happened?"

"A man blew himself up a few feet away from me in Manila. I was on the other side of a pillar, reaching for a drink. Nothing heroic. My dinner companion was not so fortunate."

"Poor man," she said.

"Woman," said Lewis. "A recent acquaintance, but she seemed quite nice. She was tasting some wine."

"Why do you tell people it was fireworks?" asked Margaret, after a moment.

"If I'm trying to find out something, it's easier if some people think I'm a fool. I'll usually never see them again." He smiled and pushed a plate of sweet wafers in her direction. "That was in another country, and besides, the wench is dead."

"I don't enjoy you as much when you're arrogant," said Dulcy.

"All right," said Lewis. "I'll keep that in mind."

• • •

Livingston's trees were either new and spindly or crippled and writhing in the wind, as tortured as the trees of what Walton refused to call the Holy Land. The dead gardens she passed on her walks were simpler, messier versions of Martha's: wide rows, mounds for squash and corn, branch supports for cucumbers and tomatoes. The only thing that distinguished Livingston's efforts was endless howling wind and the use of pretty red dogwood twigs for these supports.

Nothing could look bleaker in March. Mrs. Whittlesby, the most aggressive gardener of the library women, liked a fancier, faux European variation, patterns of zinnias or petunias interspersed with ugly pergolas and statuary; she didn't mention that this collection, and her garden soil, came from the monument business owned by her husband and the Protestant cemetery managed by her brother: the angel a couple couldn't quite afford for a baby's grave, the dirt overflow from an especially bulky casket.

Dulcy's garden would be different. After weeks of listening to the operatic wind spin around the Elite, she'd thought on new terms, anyway. The old cottonwood next door swiveled, and her neighbor, the minister Brach, swiveled too, lurking just beyond the fence when she was outside, plinking away at his piano until he heard her door. The Sacajawea ladies said Brach had a history of alienating his parishioners by sermonizing about a fast-approaching apocalypse with no mention of salvation opportunities or, say, Easter. Mrs. Brach, who would once have been a pretty blonde, seemed to exemplify the notion of I *myself am hell* without drama or arrogance. She didn't speak, even utter a simple hello; she simply stared, a shriveled ghost. Her husband was openly malign: he dumped his stove ashes in her yard and talked loudly to himself about Rusalka being a prostitute. He kicked his dog, and probably did worse to his wife. Dulcy had taken to locking up, and she tested the lock by sliding a piece of paper at the top of the jamb, just as she had with Irina. It was there when she returned, but she didn't feel like a fool for having done it, even though she imagined Henning would notice it from across a room.

She did not think of this possibility often, but it never left her.

From the north upstairs window, the Bluebeard room, Dulcy saw the minister pace his perimeter, and she thought: brick or stone. Another Irina relative, a spidery great-uncle named Abram, had been a mason in Trieste and had no problem with the idea of a six-foot garden wall, or any quibbles while Dulcy toured the corners of the brickyard for a shade she liked. "Like a blushing peach," he said.

"Exactly," said Dulcy.

"A dozen cartloads, but cheap, all in all, for the privacy."

She loved watching the wall snake up from the old foundation at the bottom of the yard. When Abram finished a rough frame, she hopped up and down in her dirty garden skirt to see if she could see out. She couldn't, but she had him add another foot. The garden beds were staggered down the slope, with a double line of stakes spaced for fruit trees along the east edge of the property, and the day they were filled, snow fell again.

She walked around town the rest of that day, the last official day of winter, wide-brimmed hat collecting snow, and though it melted and ran down her back in gouts every five minutes, she did in fact see coverings in yards over patches that seemed planted, quilts and burlap and sail cloth pinned down with stones. Some people knew how to grow things here, but she hadn't found a way to phrase her questions, and she didn't knock on their doors.

At the nursery on Clark Street, she hit another hiccup: the owner refused to order peach trees for her. "I am not a fool," he said. "How could you think such a tree would be suitable? I would no sooner give you a gun if I thought you were going to use it against me."

She couldn't speak for a moment, but he didn't look up from a receipt for the indoor things she'd already selected: two nice figs, a lemon, a holly fern, a big jasmine and a melon abutilon. "The blossoms come out during a warm patch and then freeze," he said. "Of all silly notions."

He was a Scot named Buchanan, not obviously dramatic. If he'd explained his reasoning with humor, rather than with condescension, she might have stayed sane; now she'd grind his bones to make her bread. "I see," said Dulcy.

"It goes warm, it goes cold, cherries and peaches and apricots explode, split right to the ground. You'd best give up on fruit. Raspberries, maybe. Strawberries."

Now he'd offered some information—she didn't like the sound of this tree-splitting issue—but still in the wrong tone. "Strawberries," hissed Dulcy. A small voice in the back of her head reminded her of Samuel's jokes about people leaving after every winter, driven away by cold and wind. Some inner rationality whispered that this nursery was the only source in town: catalogues were good, but seeing was believing. Beyond the peaches, she'd intended to order apple, plum, pear, and apricot trees, she'd chosen four types of grape vines, she'd hoped to purchase gooseberries and currants, not to mention roses and clematis, peonies and iris. She needed this little gnome.

It was hard, though, to see this nursery in April—empty benches, a small hut for bare-root storage, dirty panes on the small greenhouse—and feel a relationship was essential. Buchanan's thin mouth twisted: he liked to win an argument. So did she. "I'm building a conservatory," said Dulcy. "It should be tall enough for espaliered peaches, but perhaps I'd be better off with figs and quince, and I understand now that you'd rather I find another source, even for my plums and pears and apples."

"Well, now, apples. Apples I can get you through Krohne, out on the island—"

"Perhaps I'll ask my friends in England for cuttings. Are you using Spy for rootstock?"

"I'll ask," said Buchanan, who'd lost his glow.

"Any chance you'll have any Adams, or Grimes?"

"I can see if they're available. He may have Wealthy, and Wolf River—"

"Have a lovely year," said Dulcy. "I'm off to order my grape trellis. *Trellises.*"

She let the door slam, hoping that she'd hear a tinkle of glass. She'd given up on the wide-brimmed hat, and she pulled a wool knit cap down hard on her head. The sun was out, but the gusts were icy, and the street was covered with shattered branches from last night's wind. She slid on a stick, and her rage deepened. She found Siegfried Durr at his studio, and he promised to build her a glass house.

SPRING (AS DEFINED FROM EQUINOX TO SOLSTICE, MARCH 21 TO JUNE 20)

March 23, 893, Ardabil, Iran, 150,000 dead.

March 26, 1872, Lone Pine, 30.

April 3, 1868, Hawaii, 77.

April 3, 1881, Chios, 7,866.

April 6, 1667, Dubrovnik, 3,000.

April 18, 1902, Quetzaltenango, Guatemala, 2,000.

April 28 & 29, 1903, Malazgirt, Turkey, 3,500.

May 3, 1481, Rhodes, 30,000.

May 8, 1847, Nagano, Japan, 9,000. A fire.

May 19, 526, Antioch, 250,000.

May 21, 1382, Canterbury, (the Synod earthquake).

May 26, 1293, Kamakura, Japan, 23,000.

May 28, 1903, Göle, Turkey, 1,000.

June 3, 1770, Port-au-Prince, 300.

June 7, 1692, Port Royal, Jamaica, more than 2,000. A wave.

June 12, 1897, Assam, 1,500.

June 15, 1896, Tohoku, Japan, 22,000. (The greatest waves observed after such an event, 125 feet.)

—from Walton Remfrey's red notebook

Easter Greetings

CHAPTER 15

EASTER

•

On March 26, 1905, the thirty-third anniversary of the Lone Pine earthquake John Muir and Walton had shared, Abram framed in new walls on the old shed foundation, and Durr began the greenhouse. Dulcy sketched out what she wanted—glass on one end of the old shed and frame on the other, bowed metal ribs to give height and width (the peach trees, again)—but Durr brought up constraints of finance and timing, repair and venting. Above all, he brought up the question of wind, and in the end they compromised on a plain lean-to design against Abram's building, tall enough for two dwarf trees to be espaliered against the back wall and two smaller plants like figs trained up string ladders at either corner of the front walls. Dulcy would buy some cane furniture, and she would go there to read books and daydream and nap; maybe she'd try to paint for the first time since she was nineteen. She knew she'd be better off getting a teaching degree, or applying as a secretary at the newspaper. Samuel thought she should apply at the courthouse, but only because he wanted a spy.

Durr did not have much business now, anyway. Spring was the wet season—snow in the mountains, rain in town. During the slow, steady splatter, he photographed a few fraternal gatherings and school groups, but the tourists had not arrived yet, and poor people were always poorest at the end of winter. He talked while he measured for the metal frame and she worked on the new garden beds, Margaret giving prompts: about how much portraits differed in bad weather and good weather, about how when the wind wailed Durr's subjects had a pinched look, as if they worried the glass of his studio would shatter onto their heads, about how little time it took to tell if a couple loved or loathed each other. If his subjects were farmers, they were preoccupied by temperature and rainfall, and if they were businessmen, they worried the summer wouldn't save them. The children in class pictures were out of their minds with boredom, and old people were as fidgety as toddlers.

"When are people at their best, then?" asked Dulcy.

"Early summer," said Durr. "Or almost anyone at their own wedding. You would think an infant, but with a child they're too worried that a photograph will be all they have left."

Durr always brought the conversation back around to death. It was a character flaw, though his approach to the topic was never predictable: he could go from freezing to plague in a minute, then an hour later wonder aloud if different races of men rotted in different fashions. Margaret somehow felt comfortable enough to tell him everything of her husband's every last moments, every fluid and sound that emerged. Durr confessed he sometimes fantasized, when walking through a city, that all the dead were walking with the living, which had been part of the reason he'd wanted to learn to capture faces. He thought, especially after his time in the army, that people should consider the alternative when they whined in the midst of their limited time on earth. Walton would have enjoyed him, especially given that all the macabre talk fizzled at the sight of food or alcohol or anything lovely—a painting, a piece of pottery, a girl.

On the day she visited the studio to see glass and frame samples, Dulcy came in just behind a nervous couple, the woman a wash of violet water, the man stiff in a dusty suit. They weren't dewy—the man was bald, and the woman windburned—but they seemed happy enough. Durr called them up, and Dulcy wandered around looking at the portraits on the wall. She recognized teachers, bankers, waiters from the Elite. The Fenoways brothers were posed with their mother, who had the stretched look of someone being eaten from the inside out.

Upstairs, the couple laughed nervously, and Durr asked them to hold still. Dulcy saw the greenhouse catalogues on Durr's desk in the corner, but she lifted two albums first. The first had a county stamp, and after the first page—a glazed-eyed wraith with the notation *lost three children Feb 99, found wandering*—she realized she'd stumbled on the album of the Poor Farm in town and closed it hastily. The second album held police booking photos: the inside docket sported *Ger. Fenoways C of P* in an inch-high flourish. She flipped through with a jumpy combination of aversion and fascination, like a baby watching a fire or a sheltered girl facing her first fig-leaf-free David. But on the last page she stopped breathing.

"You cannot say what you've seen, you know," said Durr, who'd come behind her. "You'll remember this one. The man who stabbed Hubie Fenoways with my cane."

"But when did this happen?" Lennart Falk had been beaten— saying *to a pulp* didn't do it justice. An eye was closed, a cheek split open. The aquiline nose was a bumpy squash, lower lip a pillow.

"When he was in jail," said Durr. "It happens to all of them, but usually they have me take the photograph before, or wait. This man needed to be released to his brother."

"And this is how he looked when the brother came to fetch him?"

Durr looked at her; he understood. "You know the brother?"

"I know of him," said Dulcy. "I know the situation."

"I was there," said Durr. "Mr. Fenoways should worry about that one. The one who came, he wanted to get his little brother well away, but he'll not forget."

• • •

On April 7, she read that an eighty-four-year-old man from Denver named George Wilder, who'd never left home before, never seen tropical waters, mangroves, or hammerheads, had nevertheless traveled to Galveston, boarded a ship for Key West, and jumped overboard in the middle of the Gulf. He'd left a note: *I am worn and tired out and I thought I would put this old frame where there would be no inquest save the sharks.*

This item was well inside the newspaper, because a huge earthquake had shaken the Kangra Valley in northern India, killing tens of thousands, even some of the English elite, destroying temples and bridges and livestock. Walton might have found the will to avoid the window if he'd known what he would miss. *The mountains heaved and swayed for a full minute, and then three severe shocks, each lasting a few seconds, were felt in quick succession. Orthodox Hindus declare that the heinous sins of her children make Mother Earth tremble.*

Dulcy knew she'd have bad dreams about pinioned babies and the smell that floated out from under crumbled buildings. Maybe these dreams would displace the vision of old George Wilder dropping into the warm blue dark.

• • •

The weather turned dry and warm. Her cabbages had come out fast, carrots and onions with hairlike slowness. She'd ordered from True Blue Seeds and L.L. May and started tomatoes inside—Magnus, Grandus, Stone, Aristocrat, Large Rose Peach—along with seeds she'd brought back from trips (a pink aubergine, artichokes, astrantia and eryngium, optimistic melons). The ones that germinated were a little triumph, a tendril of the strange past growing secretly in her very proper present.

Dulcy's trees arrived a few days after Irina's crew left to plant hops in Washington State. Durr was in Butte, buying a new camera, and anyway had a crippled leg. Abram had pleurisy, and Irving, who weighed less than Dulcy did, staggered when he coughed. Dulcy dropped a note at the newspaper, and Irving arrived wheezing with a response from Samuel an hour later. She studied him, and worried, and then forgot her concerns when she read: *You've mistaken me for someone who knows what he's doing.* Dulcy wetted down the burlap around the roots and dragged the trees to the shady side of the house, then wandered around, poking stakes into the ground to mark planting sites.

Late the next afternoon, Durr was balanced on the greenhouse frame while Dulcy repotted tomato seedlings on the back porch. Her apron was covered with soil, and the cuffs of her blouse were filthy. When a figure came around the side of the porch, she gave a little shriek but did not drop her Peach Blow Sutton seedling.

"We had a parade," said Lewis. "Or a clown show." He wore stained canvas pants, and Samuel was next to him, wearing stiff new dungarees, staring morosely at the river and the greenhouse and Durr suspended against the blue sky. He was holding his own shovel, and Irving appeared behind them with a wheelbarrow, still in half his bellhop uniform.

She showed them the six marker stakes and the burlap-wrapped bare-root trees. Lewis scuffed the ground with his boot and sent Irving out for a pickaxe. He talked her into moving the two plums, which was a sign of how he'd rattled her, and she was very happy. She put a chicken in the oven, and sent Irving back out for some bread and beer and lemons, a bottle of whiskey, potatoes, and Margaret Mallow.

The trees took nearly an hour, and though Lewis kept swinging the pickaxe, his sunniness cracked. Dulcy started some cheese biscuits and filled a wheelbarrow with manure. For an exercise devotee, Samuel was not very helpful, nor did he notice Lewis's growing resentment. When they began to argue about a large rock, she asked Margaret to finish the biscuits and mix spiked lemonade and used the pick herself, working around the edge of the hole to loosen the soil. She should have shown them how at the outset.

"You've done this before," said Lewis, sitting on the freed rock.

"I have." She handed it back.

"In the secret time before your life of married luxury?" he asked. "Did you ever play games?"

"I did." She sipped the whiskeyed lemonade and thought of kites and tag, tennis and running like a boy at dusk. She hadn't had enough of it, and she missed her brothers, at least as they'd once been. If she'd said that Edgar had died earlier, she could be silly now, done with mourning, done with constraints.

"And how long ago did your husband die? How long do you have to wait to play again?"

Was she so transparent? "That's very insensitive of you, Lewis," said Samuel, who had asked the same question earlier.

"Even if it was less than a year, you saw it coming for so long," said Margaret. "And Frank made sure I remembered he was dying every day."

For a moment, there was only the sound of the pick. "Well, don't extend the martyrdom," said Lewis. "Don't hide your light—what's the phrase?"

"Under a rock," said Samuel.

Lewis handed him the pick. Margaret, who still hadn't developed a head for alcohol, bubbled in: "My husband died on May 30. I win the race."

"What killed them?" asked Samuel, watching Durr maneuver glass. "Gardening?"

"Frank had a bad heart," said Margaret, with a sliver of irony. "And Mr. Nash had several issues."

"A variety of things, in the end," said Dulcy. "Meningitis. Pneumonia."

"And your father, the doctor, couldn't help?" asked Lewis.

"He was ill himself, and a specialist, anyway." She finished the glass, thinking of the mental flaw that had led her to tell Samuel or Margaret that her father had been a doctor.

"What sort? Heart? Liver? Brain?"

This had to stop, and a dose of truth would be key. "The male sexual organs," she said. "With a stress on how they interact with the nervous system. He specialized in wealthy syphilitics."

Samuel's face turned a hot red, and Margaret's eyes glazed over. Lewis, on the other hand, crowed: pure glee. "This is fascinating," he said. "A cock doctor."

They ate on the porch steps; Dulcy bullied Durr down from the greenhouse roof. At dusk, it was still sixty degrees, and for the first time in weeks there was no wind. The chicken had been roasted with most of her new tarragon plant, and she'd picked most of her first lettuces. She loved the way Lewis ate: a little wild-eyed and abstracted, thinking about what he put in his mouth for one intense second before he swallowed and asked another question. Had she read any Russian writers, and had she ever been to the southern latitudes? Did she like horses, or did they make her sneeze? Or both? Did she follow a religion, and had she ever slummed to Coney Island?

Sometimes Dulcy lied pragmatically and with ease, and sometimes she loathed herself an hour later, but she was enjoying this dance. He clearly knew that some of what she said wasn't true at all, but he let her say it. She wondered what he'd done, and who he'd done it with; she wondered how different the women seemed to him when he was touching them, or if it was all the same, at least in hindsight. She wondered if he'd slept with the woman in the story before he'd seen her blow up, and if she was now part of his body, ink for the tattoo on his cheekbone.

Mostly, she wondered how to become someone who did things, rather than trying to imagine them. How did it all start? Not sitting at the house in Westfield, never again with Victor, and if she hadn't managed much of her own drama while traveling with Walton, maybe she was hopeless, and she'd sink into this town like she'd sunk into the mud that spring. She'd be left to only care about bad novels and food and the people she'd never see again.

• • •

On April 23, Easter Sunday, Mrs. Woolley gave another party, ostensibly for the benefit of Grover O. Dewberry, moving-pictures cameraman. For the occasion, Dulcy shifted from black and gray to the nicest of the marginal widow's weeds she had purchased in Butte: a lilac hat with smoky feathers, a matching dress that at least showed her collarbone. There'd been another soft snow, and the early-budding trees in town were draped. They passed children carrying bright Easter eggs, others hurling egg-shaped snowballs. In the untrampled snow of Mrs. Woolley's yard, protected from such children by a forbidding iron fence, Dulcy made out bursts of narcissus glowing under the ice.

The man of the hour had worked since the war making actuality films, and now he wanted to form his own company. Mrs. Woolley and Samuel wanted to invest, though Dulcy guessed it might simply be a way to redirect Rex, who was still intent on his spa project. Dewberry was handsome like a Gibson boy: his thick hair had a soft curl, his jaw jutted, his lashes were long, and he said things that were witty. He'd taken Miss Randall's apartment in the Elite, Miss Randall having taken Dulcy's, and Irina was probably peeling herself off his door nightly. He was shiny and fervent and everything he said was meant to be amusing—he didn't stop, or allow for a pause, or realize that the relentless nature of his personality was not entirely to his advantage, at least not in Dulcy's eyes. She realized her dislike was largely competitive: people swarmed the cameraman rather than talking to Margaret, or watching the poor freezing children outside, looking for eggs in snow banks, and Mrs. Woolley's impressive buffet cooled while her staff grew irked. Within an hour, the guests all seemed to call him *Grow-vy*. Even Margaret turned a dusty pink in his presence despite Grovy's constant references to his beautiful, beautiful, quite absent wife.

They ate, which was at least part of what Easter was supposed to be about, and the snob in Dulcy had to admit it was all wonderful—silky *dauphinois*, salmon *en croute* with a capered sauce, a lemon soufflé. Mrs. Woolley had real wine, and even the cigars smelled delicious. Dewberry talked on and on about what he intended to film as he established a new company: the growing cities of the West, the wonders of the national parks (particularly the wonder of Rex's new empire in Yellowstone). The point, said Grover, was that there was no war on: "And it's very hard to catch an earthquake or a hurricane in the act. I am moving on to narrative. I must do whatever's necessary."

"Grover believes in drama," said Lewis, who had arrived late. "If warfare fails, he'll provide. His friends worried about how he'll cope with peacetime, but he's managed to be creative."

"Travel," said Grover.

"There's the other stuff," said Lewis. "Will you show snippets of *Mary, Queen of Skirts?*"

"Be my friend, Lewis," said Grover, gesturing to Durr to help him set up the projector.

Dulcy ebbed to the back of the claustrophobic living room, thinking about her wet, cold feet. Samuel and Durr were wound up in the mechanics of Dewberry's presentation—the white screening curtain kept wrinkling—and Rex honked on nervously about the weather, and what it might do to the trip he'd planned for the following week to Yellowstone Park, the one Grover intended to film. Everyone planned to go, if the weather improved. Dulcy heard her name, Margaret promising that they'd both pack furs and boots and treats for the train. She didn't protest; she would back out later.

The snow outside made it difficult to darken the room, even with drapes as heavy as Mrs. Woolley's, and Grover fretted about invasive beams. Dulcy stayed on a windowsill in the far corner. It was hard to see over the sea of plumed Easter hats, colors only slightly muted by the effort to darken the room, but the director gave a helpful narration: snippets from Cuba; British troops marching along an African river, chased by dust; zoo footage of elephants and giraffes; an automobile screaming past a crowd; a cannon firing. A volcano (Grover said it was Etna; Dulcy, knowing it was Vesuvius, and that he must have bought someone else's footage, could say nothing), pyramids near Memphis, the Fuller Building going up (Dulcy squinted, trying to find a Remfrey in the crowd), bathers in the Fort Myers surf. The World's Fair, the ocean, an acrobat, Constantinople.

Damascus, she thought, recognizing buildings. She wasn't sure if she was seeing her own past, or Walton's, or Maria Nash's, but it wasn't Grover's. The projector crackled. Florence appeared, then Paris, but the gardens were Cluny, not the Tuileries, people promenading for a full, boring minute, long enough for Dulcy to think of how it had really looked and smelled, and how much better Henning might have done with the same film if the money hadn't disappeared.

Lastly, Grover showed footage of the Galveston disaster, children climbing on ruins, bodies floating on the Gulf, bodies being piled in carts. Dulcy had seen photographs, but movement changed everything, and even in these scratchy images the stiff flop of ballooned bodies allowed you to smell the rot, the salt, the heat. Drowned Galveston would be all fresh wood and brick now, and the bodies from the 1900 storm had become shrimp shells and marsh grass. They were picnicking by Lake Erie the day the headlines reached them in September, and Walton worked even this tragedy into his private world. He'd stared at the waves and only heard the suck of the global undertow. Everything happened in concert. It was no coincidence that the Gulf was shaped like a volcanic crater. Dulcy wouldn't have been surprised if Walton had tried to link August's grasshopper infestation in Kalamazoo to tidal weight, or the radioactive core of the earth, or whatever variation currently monopolized his mind. Something bad was always happening on the planet.

Ah, but it's a wonderful land, [Yellowstone is,] with its snow peaks, its canyon, colored like the sunset; its burning geysers, its seething ponds, its mud volcanoes, its blow holes for steam that smells so like Long Island City . . . When you hear the crust crack and feel your heels suddenly growing hot and the panting and groaning of hell sound louder below and around, you almost instinctively go somewhere else—some quieter, cooler, dryer place, where you can think of a different set of thoughts. You never know where you're going to be steamed.

—C. M. Skinner,
*Yellowstone Park: A Land of Enchantment That
Even Caucasian Savages Cannot Spoil*

CHAPTER 16

THE ROSE-PINK BOOK OF VERSE

•

April of 1905 had been so warm that Dulcy's neighbor, the minister Brach, had announced that End Times had arrived—sin had tilted the earth on her axis (Brach said "his")—and that he would be holding a sort of exorcism behind his church, a tottery log cabin by the river. Samuel and the congregation showed up to find that Brach had quietly accumulated every image of a naked woman he could find in town—an old ferryman's prized figurehead, a dress model, bits of a second-story frieze from a building on Main Street, pried off the night before, a treasured French oil robbed from the Bucket of Blood saloon—and now hammered them to bits and set them on ceremonial fire while the crowd watched.

Gerry was drinking, and couldn't be bothered. The injured parties said they'd file suit against him, too.

Dulcy turned the page on Samuel's story to see the italicized high and low temperature records on the second page of the *Enterprise*, and noted they went back only twenty years. At ten a.m. on April 29 it was already seventy degrees Fahrenheit, and she unpacked her shearling coat and found some linen for the Yellowstone trip. She was going because Margaret had begged her, and Samuel had begged her, and because she was lonely. Rex was desperate and needed to prove himself with this business venture. They must support him.

She'd spent the early morning making pasties. She began efficiently but quickly frayed, mismanaging her stove and overheating the kitchen. She opened the windows, which meant she had to keep paper over the meat to ward off an unseasonable hatch of insects; she put rocks on the paper to keep it from flying off when she propped the door open, too. The lard softened so rapidly that she had to keep the dough in the icebox until the last minute, and she threw so much of the disappointing chuck to Brach's ratty terrier that she heard it retch into the shrubbery. The potatoes were hollow-hearted, half the onions had turned to slime, and she used all her new parsley. An hour before Samuel had said he'd swing by, she was red-faced, spackled with fat, dredged in flour, and filled with rage at the whole notion that she'd thought this was a good idea. Three of the pies broke on the sheet, and she finished shattering them when she crammed them into the overworked icebox, the ice block down to a four-inch square, the drip of melt as annoying as the flies ricocheting around the house.

She ran a cool tub and jumped in, rethought the extreme in a matter of seconds, and got out to heat some water, then looked at the clock and gave up. She cinched a thin white blouse over a charcoal lawn skirt. She piled up her hair and stabbed her scalp while trying to secure a new hat, simple bleached straw with a pretty mossy-colored ribbon. She lined the hamper with newspaper, pulled the last of the pasties out of the oven, and lugged everything to the gate.

Samuel looked breezy and cool and annoyed her all over again. Seersucker, a new hat—he'd picked one of her little apricot pansies and stuffed it in his buttonhole, and she didn't bother telling him he'd chosen the wiltiest flower in the yard. He did not comment on the redolence of the pasties, and he was not apologetic when he said that she was his first stop. He did not pull up the buggy top for shade when he strolled into the Elite to roust Lewis from his den and Eugenia from her carpet-walled kingdom. Eugenia, who'd feigned enthusiasm, would inevitably not come, but she'd want Samuel to put up a struggle. Dulcy seethed in the buggy for ten minutes, then walked to Vanzant's for a soda.

They gave her a vanilla ice, very different than the one she'd had in Africa. This one had egg and cream and no spice, but it cheered her up. She flirted with the soda jerk, and he put her in a better mood, too, as did the fact that Samuel was annoyed when she walked out to find him circling the block for a third time.

Lewis was in the back, pale and thin-faced. He asked for a taste of the ice, then reached out and wiped a smudge of cream from her lip.

"I gather you were out last night," said Samuel.

"No. I had the fever again," said Lewis.

"Truly?"

"Truly," said Lewis. He didn't smile. When the whites of his eyes were tinged with yellow, his irises looked hazel instead of gray.

"Does he smell of whiskey, Maria?"

She was tired, and she imagined burying her face against Lewis's neck. She began to understand that he might disappear for good. "No, Samuel, let it go. Where's Eugenia?"

"Not coming. I wasn't in the mood to beg. She says her husband is planning to visit."

"Do you believe it?" asked Lewis.

"No." They passed two men putting up posters, jingoing up the town for the centenary of the Lewis and Clark, the rodeo and parade, the county fair, circus, traveling Shakespearean troupe. The city fathers were ready for the summer tourist trade. When Samuel pulled up at Margaret's house, Dulcy and Lewis sat in silence. A gust sandblasted them—a hot, alien sirocco, nothing springlike—and she clutched her head.

"How many pins does it take to anchor that thing?" asked Lewis.

"I don't want to remember," said Dulcy.

"It mostly disguises the flour in your hair."

She felt for remnants of dough. Margaret started out her door, then turned around for some forgotten object. Dulcy had never seen her make a clean break of it.

"And on your neck, too," Lewis said, wiping gently at her nape. This was the second time he'd touched her that morning, but she let it happen. She twisted to reach into the hamper for a piece of one of the already-broken pasties. "Christ," said Lewis. "That's a dream."

She gave him another sip of the ice.

* * *

There were twenty in Rex's group, and he ran around the depot with red panic dots on his downy cheeks. He'd reserved a full car, and seated proper citizens toward the front, riffraff in the back. Dulcy, Margaret, Lewis, and Samuel were sorted into seats two-thirds of the way down the car, behind the Macalesters and an architect named Denison. Mrs. Woolley was a distant egret-feathered hat up front in a clutch of bankers and East Coast ranchers, while Durr, who had been hired to help Grover film the wonders of the park and the birth of Rex's new business, had been wedged into the last seat. People muttered about the lack of a guide. The former scout who'd worked for W. A. Chadfield Touring, the company Rex had purchased in Gardiner, had just died of peritonitis, and now they all listened to Dr. Macalester describe the mistakes the doctor might have made: operating, not operating, not washing his hands, missing rot, nicking a blood vessel. "Another guide is waiting for us," said Rex stiffly. "Please don't fret."

Macalester tilted his head back and shut his eyes. He was a transplanted New Yorker, a fly fisherman; the hatch was on, and he'd wanted to be on the Clark Fork this weekend, but Vinca wanted to see people.

They rolled into the widening valley, the river low despite the heat, mountains still white-topped with a stubble of hacked trees on the slopes. They'd been logged since Dulcy had been here in 1896, and she could have claimed a memory with Edgar Nash, but she was tired of volunteering lies, increasingly bent on keeping her problematic mouth shut. Rex was asking for business name ideas, both for the tour company and the resort he intended to build on the

Boiling River: Wonderland Rides? Wonderland Nights? Soothing Springs?

"I hate to repeat my suggestion," said Samuel, "but 'Boil Away Boils' seems admirably direct."

"The waters are truly curative," snapped Rex. "They have nothing to do with hemorrhoids."

"Do you know that for a fact?" said Macalester, whose idea of a vacation included sleep, and whose eyes were pink with exhaustion and resentment. "The problem is terrifically common."

"Please don't ridicule me," said Rex, passing around soda and beer, trying to find his mood. "Think of a mountain fastness, a Swiss sort of spa."

"Fastnesses are what you want in a siege," said Lewis. "Not in an initial sales situation."

"Humans are fond of warm water," said Rex. "Tell me if you disagree."

Dulcy wondered if a subtler intelligence might hide beneath the dewy locks, the checked tie, the relentlessly self-absorbed wall of slang. She pulled out a novel but took in a fragment of the spiel: instead of staying at the hotel in Mammoth, they would camp in the luxurious tents Rex had purchased from the W. A. Chadfield: platform floors with Turkish carpets and soft cots and quilts, fine comestibles and a talented cook. They would pass the spa site tonight, picnic there tomorrow, then dine and swim at Eve's Spring, an older resort that was another investment possibility, on the way back.

Dulcy wondered if the staff at Eve's Spring had changed. Not that she was memorable.

Frances Woolley's plumed hat turned slowly in her son's direction, and Dulcy thought of the kind of bad cathedral tours she'd taken in Europe while Walton was in a clinic. Grover and Rex talked too much; everyone talked too much. Samuel began to lecture Lewis about the shoddy wisdom of visiting his family when he was so ill. Lewis planned to leave the following week, and what was the point in wearing himself down for people who didn't care?

"They care," said Lewis. "In their way."

The pasties were gone within fifteen minutes. Mrs. Woolley's cook had made lobster sandwiches for the swells up front and the people who ricocheted between worlds like Grover, who had a blob of mayonnaise on his resolute chin. He grabbed at Samuel's slice of pasty, trying to have it both ways while he told them he intended to film everything that moved in the park—wildlife, water features, soldiers, all of them frolicking in Rex's new fine springs. Two pretty spinster teachers named Audrey and Beryl bounced from seat to seat; Grover threatened to film them, too. "You won't film me," said Margaret.

Grover gave her a half smile, as if to say: I hadn't planned to bother.

Down the valley, ranches and the first mining towns; people talked about whether the mines were played out, the likelihood of dredging bringing in any meaningful profit. Near the front of the car, Rex said a new medium in town was popular with many miners' families, who begged for séances: one could imagine the miners' ghosts *tap-tapping*, looking for a way out.

Dulcy thought of the sound of real hammers, the weird roar of a mine, the idea of dying in the dark. Beryl and Audrey started telling knock-knock jokes. After Emigrant, they passed a quarry and a sawmill. The valley tapered into another canyon, then a steaming hillside with an ungainly lodge that was Rex's third-best option as a spa investment. This landscape had ridges of red rocks instead of yellow, pure desert: Dulcy looked down on tiny cactus when they slowed for Electric, then lifted her eyes to see a dozen miners waiting for the northbound train with a coffin. They were wide-cheekboned men with thick hair—half of Rusalka's relatives mined coal down here—all permanently grubby, permanently heartbroken. The coffin was expensive, black and brass.

"There's your *tap-tap*," said Lewis.

• • •

In Gardiner, they met their guide: Hubert Fenoways waited on the siding. He held a hand out to Rex, who took it sheepishly, and shook it weakly. "I don't understand," said Margaret.

"He had no choice," said Samuel. "I can't explain beyond that."

Dulcy watched Lewis and Durr wake up to the situation. Hubie's right jaw, pierced by Durr's cane, was still bandaged, and he didn't meet many eyes, but he looked sober. He explained the current problem: he'd arrived to learn that Chadfield, their original guide, had left town an hour after Rex had wired money. The horses and harness had been sold, and the only wagons left were broken. The tents remained, but none of the other mechanics of adventure: no cots or lamps, stoves or chamber pots or hatchets. They'd all been sold to Wylie, the main competitor, whose massive storehouse dominated what passed for a skyline in Gardiner.

Rex stood blinking on the siding, and the women broke for the toilet in the log depot. "We'll go back," said Samuel. "It's been a pretty ride down, a lovely day trip."

"No," said Rex. "We'll carry on. I cannot bear the failure."

"Well," said Samuel. He was angry with Rex, but didn't want to see him humiliated. "We need a big Portland coach and a hotel, then. I'll wire ahead. Mammoth? Canyon?"

"Canyon," said Rex, trying to recover.

Hubie Fenoways headed off and returned with two smaller coaches and ragtag drivers. They seemed amused: where on earth did Rex think they could go, so early in the year? Canyon wasn't open yet. The *road* wasn't even open yet, and the staff wouldn't show up for another fortnight. How could Rex have been so misinformed? Had he just moved to their fair state?

W. A. Chadfield had claimed that the roads were in fine shape, said Rex. "Well, he lied," said one of the drivers. "Though they might be, under all the snow."

"I'll hunt him down," said Hubie.

Maybe he'd be the right employee, after all. They climbed in for the ride to Mammoth, where some rooms were kept open to serve the army base and explorer types. The road climbed steadily, and Dulcy, who helped Durr balance his camera and had a rear view, imagined the runty horses sliding and allowing the overloaded coaches to roll backward over the edge.

When the driver stopped with a bellow—*"Boiling River!"*—it took a moment to take in the moonscape, the funnels of hot wind, the dun-colored rock. To the west, a long gravel-covered rise; to the east, a gray ridge and the river. No trees, no grass, no graceful building site: a tiny thread of steaming water emptied into what looked like a mud puddle in the Gardner River proper. A bighorn sheep watched from the ridge, and a buzzard loomed above the facing cliff.

They climbed out. "Darling, what did Cousin Percy tell you about this place?" asked Rex's mother.

"A golden opportunity. He would talk to people." Rex burst into tears.

"Should we just go back to town?" asked Samuel.

"No!" Rex yelled.

People retreated to the coaches. Dulcy stayed on her feet, less out of compassion than misogyny. "Well, then, would you like to explore now, or come back tomorrow?" Samuel's voice was gentle. Rex's whole face quivered, and she heard his mother, Frances, weeping in the coach.

Grover put on blue-lensed eyeglasses, oblivious. "I'd *love* to find something to film in Mammoth before the light dies. Something a little more dramatic."

"All right," said Rex. He rubbed his eyes. "We'll wait until tomorrow to study this situation."

"I'm sure you could perch some sort of log structure down there," said Grover. "Run a pipe. Perhaps a small, round pool . . ."

"No!" Rex hissed. "No logs, nothing small. I don't want to be small."

At Mammoth, they looked at the pin-neat army buildings with longing. The hotel manager, amused, said he had a few other ignorant, optimistic tourists on his hands, and he'd open up a few rooms and *scrounge together* some food. The Dewberrys walked away, presumably to suss out just what Cousin Percy had in mind with the spa location beyond a better share of family funds. The rest of them wandered around the steaming terraces in small groups. The hissing sulfur made the air seem even hotter, and Dulcy and Margaret scrabbled down a still-icy path to the river, where they splashed their necks and wrists and flinched at every cracking branch. The pine smelled sweet, and the whole world seemed to buzz. When Margaret left to find out when their rooms would be ready, Dulcy found a covered gazebo near one of the showier terraces. Fumaroles: it looked like Italy, without the ruins and good food. It was mesmerizing, watching fizzing white froth in the heat, but it was not a varied experience, and she began to doze.

The bench shifted as someone settled next to her. She opened a stony eye and edged away while the leg next to her bobbed. Twenty feet away, three men in tweed suits circled a formation with a measuring tape, a long glass rod, and a sketchbook. One was older and tiny, one was round and middle-aged, and the youngest was slight and pale.

The rude knee on the bench next to her made contact with her own, and she jerked around. "Sanborns," said Lewis. He held a flask. "Insurance men, mapmakers. They'll be working in Livingston this summer."

"And this?" She nodded toward the flask.

"I took it from Hubie," said Lewis. "He promised to stay dry, when Rex allowed himself to be blackmailed."

"Really blackmailed?" The oldest surveyor slid the rod into the formation. "Do you know what they have on him?"

"Yes." Lewis's leg bounced again, and he tapped the flask in time. "There's a photograph involved, but it's not such a horrible thing. Or it wouldn't be to some people."

The men in tweed bent in unison to stare at the tip of the rod. She thought of pinching Lewis to make him tell, as she would have pinched her brothers, but pinching Lewis wouldn't feel brotherly.

"I'll think of a price to put on the information," he said.

"More blackmail."

"Affectionate blackmail."

• • •

The manager found lamps, and they ate on trestle tables in front of the hotel. Rex had pulled out the treats he'd meant for a camping trip—cheese and Utah strawberries and cases of champagne, so explosive after the jouncing trip that Dulcy slid a bowl underneath to catch the overflow of each bottle—but these treats were gone quickly, and they were left using the manager's frozen beer to sluice down a dried gray roast and undercooked half-fried potatoes, slubby with old grease. They ate with a wary English family and the Sanborn engineers, and Samuel and Lewis set up bocce on the lawn in front of the hotel—it was a big game in Livingston, an import from the Italian grocery families—as well as a freeform version of croquet. Rex brought out a Victrola, but only two disks had survived the trip unbroken. This brought on another snit, but Dulcy was relieved to have the session cut short after twirling badly to one song with Samuel: she was no better at dancing than she was at swimming, because Martha hadn't danced well, either, and if Martha didn't know how to do something, Dulcy hadn't learned it. She tried to keep her balance by looking down, watching her shoes move through last year's live things, wild strawberries and remnants of sticky geraniums.

Audrey and Beryl, the young teachers, danced on with the soldiers, but Dulcy retreated to the embankment of widows and wives. When they went inside, some of the men, subtle as a pack of monkeys, scratched the hotel windows and made ghost sounds. It was all silly and happy, even for Mrs. Tate, a genuinely sad widow. Dulcy lay in a corner bunk, giggling woozily with the others while Mrs. Whittlesby, who'd insisted she hadn't had champagne in *years*, snored like a troll.

A whisper through the screen: "Is that the sound of the Widow Nash?"

"No, Lewis," said Dulcy. "It isn't."

"Mind your health," said Margaret.

"Mind your business," whispered Lewis.

• • •

In the morning, as the temperature rocketed from frost to sizzle, the Sanborn surveyors had already returned from an abortive bicycle ride to the Obsidian Cliff by the time Rex's group reached the lobby. Every one of their tires had popped, and the manager told them the wrong gravel had been spread the year before—he brought out obsidian specimens to prove his point, and Stromberg, the oldest of the Sanborns, saw Margaret pick up a piece. "Watch how you squeeze that," he said.

She opened her hand and they saw a trickle of blood, a thin slit in her forefinger.

Rex's river still looked terrible, like a Biblical parable or a sarcastic mirage, but when they finally climbed down the slope they found that the oval puddle was large enough for several people to soak, if not swim. Rex slipped skinny white toes into the water; Grover dipped a hand and said the temperature was perfect, lovely. Mr. Denison, the architect, found a safely distant rock and began to make sketches. They all talked about the way that rocks could be moved and a better pool achieved, travertine patios and fans and propellers. The Sanborns weighed in with information on similar resorts in other cities, and the Englishman on tour with his family, a lung patient on his way to the clinic at Eve's Spring after a winter in Tucson, made the case for having a solarium roof. The park could use one true year-round hotel.

Hubie had brought fishing rods, and unloaded a folding table, the bocce set they couldn't possibly use on this slope, towels for the swimmers. Dulcy saw him swing Rex's remaining case of champagne down onto a rock while Macalester stalked off to fish, and Samuel and Lewis wandered after him, arguing about flies. Dulcy and Mrs. Tate read guides about everything they weren't going to see in

Yellowstone until at least June. Audrey and Beryl fluttered down to the men at the shore. Audrey had her eye on Denison, and Beryl had her eye on Grover, or Rex, or Samuel.

"Good luck with that," muttered Margaret. "Look at them argue," she added, watching Lewis and Samuel. "Is that really how you fish?"

"I don't know," said Dulcy. "Probably not."

Frances Woolley, whose lobster salad and *sablés* were long gone, had elected to ride on directly to the train and Livingston. She'd wired ahead from the hotel and waited apart in the cleanest carriage, parked in the lone smidgen of shade near a tall rock. Mrs. Whittlesby's snores and Rex's miserable judgment had taken a toll. Dulcy was fairly sure the Macalesters would try to bolt with her, and within an hour, when a new carriage arrived, James Macalester put Hubie's rod down quietly and slid inside. Vinca, who had looked forward to leaving her house and her young children, did not protest.

A moment of reckoning had come at the pool, precipitated by the fact that the English family had found a rock to change behind, and waded in like a line of ducks. Grover fiddled with his camera, but Dulcy didn't think he found this subject interesting. Rex had brought down men's suits, and they took turns behind the rock, coming out in black-and-white costumes, all but Hubie looking sheepish. He had the smallest, tightest costume, and the marks from Lennart Falk's attack were bright red on his sturdy white thighs, glowing from a distance. Dulcy could hear Samuel snicker while Hubie proclaimed temperatures, giving updates as the water reached his ankles, shins, knees; a hot pot, a cold plume.

Rex marched in, bubbly again. "Come in!"

"Piss off," said Samuel. He was still laughing, wiping at his eyes. "Where're you going to put the hotel gardens? How will you block the wind?"

"Come on, Samuel. Let's see you wet," said Grover, who'd been filming Hubie getting in and out of the water. "I'll film you jumping."

"Not deep enough."

"Well, the rock isn't high. I want the splash, and you're well built."

Dulcy didn't want to look directly at Samuel, to see his reaction. "Please come in." Rex tried Lewis, now. "I'm so relieved by how wonderful this feels. You can't imagine."

"It's not hot enough to show my lily-white ass," said Lewis. "But I'm happy for you."

Dulcy left to help spread the food out. When she walked back, Grover floated on his back, yelling commands to Durr, who filmed from above. Hubie still checked depth, bellowing estimates at the architect, who didn't seem to be listening. The Sanborns kept their own counsel at the far end, and the English family was drying quietly on a rock. Samuel and Lewis and Rex were waist-deep toward the front of the pool, tossing rocks over the side of the barricade. "You reconsidered," said Dulcy.

"I crumpled under pressure," said Lewis. "Come in."

"I'm dressed," she said. Stupidly.

"Undress, then," said Lewis.

"I'll swim tonight, at Eve's Spring," said Dulcy. "I'm supposed to tell you that it's lunchtime."

"All right. Wait."

She dipped a soggy slipper while he dried off. They scrabbled up the path. "Was it nice?"

"It lacks regulation. Move a toe and you're either freezing or poached." They stepped around the tethered horses, too many of them chewing through too little hay. Two of the English children rocketed by them on the path.

"Are you fast?" asked Lewis. He was walking ahead of her now, with the towel around his shoulders. Little ribbons of water ran down his calves.

"I don't know. I've never raced anyone since school."

"Even your sister?"

"I was always faster than my sister," said Dulcy.

The sister she would never have mentioned, since Mrs. Nash didn't have one. A flush and a surge of anger before her next step landed: he was enjoying this, and she was too easily caught in his game. She tried to focus on the path rather than the way the water ran over his skin. Then it all moved, pebbles bouncing, air buzzing. The world rumbled, gave a small scream—it was nothing like Salonica, but it was truly happening. Dulcy turned to watch the cliffs on the far side of the river. Lewis moved his feet wide apart like a drunk or a sailor, but he kept his back straight, military-style, as did the Sanborns and Durr. The other men thrashed out of the water and crouched with their mouths agape like gargoyles while Audrey and Beryl screamed.

Acts of god, Dulcy thought. A scattering of rocks growled down the face, and the hum faded. The horses had pulled their pegs and ran in loose circles from one end of the flat to the other, heads up and neighing. Dulcy only realized that she was smiling when she met Lewis's eyes. "I gather you've been through one of these before," he said.

"Such a strange feeling." But when they looked at each other it was still about what he'd said before, about the sister.

The champagne bottles spilled onto the dusty gravel. Margaret scrambled around trying to salvage a few cups. Rex and the English children hopped up and down in sheer anxiety, and Grover railed at Durr: one camera had tipped on the rocks. Dulcy enjoyed the fact that Durr ignored the rant for the sake of filming the slowing horses.

While they ate dry bread and moldy cheese, Dulcy felt two more soft long tremors, but no one commented. Durr showed Margaret how to use one of Century cameras, and Dulcy kept her face averted and talked to the Englishwoman, who was packing to leave ("before we all die in *lahhhva*,"). Rex cranked up the Victrola, and Grover herded Hubie down to the water. He wanted at least one more jump recorded, but Samuel and Lewis wouldn't budge, and Durr ignored him, and Rex apparently lacked the desired physique. Grover and Hubie weren't natural companions, but Hubie was at least game, and so, Grover said, he would be the *immortal one*, the man to put droplets in air, into sunlight, on film.

Lewis sat next to her and rubbed his eyes. "When we get to the springs I might hide in my room. Maybe they'll have food there."

"How can Samuel bear listening to Grover?"

Lewis gave her a look—in hindsight, disbelief? Amusement? Out of the corner of her eye Dulcy saw a jump, heard a splash, heard Grover bellow *Great one!* And then screams, a hyena-like sound that popped through the melody of the phonograph, bled into the tinny violin; rending, echoing wails that bounced off both sides of the mile-wide canyon. They were on their feet as Hubie staggered, still screaming, out of the pool toward Grover. His skin was a new shade of pink. He knocked the camera over and fell to his knees. "Look out!" howled Grover. "Whatever is wrong with you?"

"The water was fine," said Rex. "It was fine."

"I'm not fucking fine," roared Hubie.

The men helped him down to the cold part of the river, the fresh melted snow flow, and the screams turned into whimpers when Hubie was submerged. But his legs and torso were a bad orangey pink, and he pawed at his privates but howled at everyone not to touch. "He needs to stay there until you know what to do with him," said Stromberg, the little gray-haired Sanborn. "You keep him here until you have a way of keeping him cool, snow or ice."

Snow was miles away. Rex babbled: during the earthquake, something new must have come up from below. The burns might not really be that bad. Who knew what could happen to the earth's plumbing after such a shake; who could know what might happen next?

"What do you think?" Margaret asked Samuel.

"I think it's bad," he said. The youngest Sanborn man ran down the hill with a thermometer and a jerry-rigged rod, a candle tied to its line. His first cast fell short, and the candle was intact when he reeled in. His second reached Hubie's spot, and after a half minute he raised the tip. The wizened, melted candle slid out of its noose.

The ground murmured, and a sliver of shale moved a few centimeters near Dulcy's dusty slippers. When she looked up they were all watching. "These happen afterward," she said. "For hours. We're outside; we needn't worry."

"We should if the cliff decides to drop on the road," said Lewis.

A decision was made to go to Eve's Spring rather than waiting for the train to town. They soaked cloth scraps in cold water and loaded Hubie, but within minutes the keening began again. Even his face was burned, and they wrapped him like a mummy, with slits so he could breathe and scream. They found ice in Gardiner, and at dusk they reached the resort. Dulcy, pinned in a corner of the last wagon next to Durr and Margaret, saw a scurry of people in white, a stretcher, everyone disappearing into the building beyond the large plunge.

They piled out and wandered past proper guests who were bemused by the frayed look of the new arrivals, a little alarmed, though not alarmed enough, by the noises coming from the man in the stretcher. A gaunt girl at the desk gave them rooms, and they found tables in the dining room and had indifferent food and big whiskey cocktails. Rex jammed biscuits in his mouth and said the doctor didn't know what to think. The people at the next table began to mutter about the noise coming from the back and talked about the news of a quake in Yellowstone, geysers acting strangely. None of them had felt a thing.

"Let's swim," said Lewis. "I'm worried that if I don't try it now, I'll never do it again."

They'd been given the last few rooms at the end of the old wing. A maid brought a selection of swimming costumes—wide, narrow, wool, silk, all bad stripes and polka dots. "I don't want to do this," said Margaret, who kept towels wrapped around any visible patch of flesh.

"I think it's a different sort of night," said Dulcy. "Try not to worry."

When they crossed the lawn to the covered plunge—an ungainly white barn, nothing like the beautiful stone palaces she remembered from Budapest or Prague or Vienna—they could hear Hubie: *Help me help me help me.* And sometimes a higher note: *Jesus.* Dulcy tried to remember the soothing waters at Walton's spas, the wonderful way she'd slept afterward. Maybe swimming would allow her to sleep through Hubie Fenoways' wanting to die. When they entered and hit a wall of moist air and echoing laughter, she nearly turned around and ran, but she could hear the men behind them. It was time to disappear. She looked down at her grubby white feet, let go of the towel, walked to the cracked tile rim, and dropped off the side like an ungainly ladybug.

When she opened her eyes, Lewis was sitting on the edge. "I admit to being surprised."

"I do, too," said Dulcy.

In the beginning, the men put on a show: cannonballs from the deep end, back flops at the middle. A war broke out, then became male-female, ungainly water birds at an elaborate dance, a ritual of splashing approach and pretty retreat, arm-waving and ducking, the woman finally seized and tossed through the air, passed around like a ball or towed along behind like a dingy. Dulcy's brothers had done this with her when she was little, but she hadn't gotten water up her nose since then, or paid attention to her brothers' skin and what was underneath the woolen bathing suits. Now she felt hunted, and she panicked. "Stop!" she yelled.

Lewis did, momentarily abashed by the whole transparent nature of the game. They caught their breath but watched each other. No one was nearby; no one paid attention. The dozen people in the pool had broken into distinct groups: Samuel and Grover had stopped quarreling to race, and Durr explained the sidestroke to Margaret.

"Would you like to get out?"

"No," she snapped, holding the edge.

He went under and headed straight toward her like a seal, twice as fast below the surface as he would have been above. He came up along her body, arms around her legs, and he lifted her. Dulcy started to scissor. "Lie back," he said. "I'll spin you. Just give it a try."

He kept a flat palm under her back, and twirled. She made herself relax and looked up at the rafters, the blurred moon through the dirty glass of the roof.

Someone whooped. Grover and Samuel were swinging from the rope twenty yards away while Audrey and Beryl oohed, and Rex had found his way into the water, though he had his arms on the tile edge and his head down. "I'm afraid he'll drown himself," said Dulcy.

"He won't," said Lewis. "He's too worried. He just wired Gerry."

"I've heard the pain of a burn usually improves after a day," she said.

"Only if it doesn't kill you," he said. "The doctor thinks it's already infected. He's talking about gangrene, but where would you begin to amputate, or stop?" He gave her another swirl. "You don't really know how to swim, do you? Do you want to learn?"

Dulcy smiled. "Maybe later."

"We have time to kill." He towed her a little deeper. "I can pry things out of your head while we're at it. What's your favorite poem? You must like something."

"Of course I *like* something. I like Yeats, these days."

"A love poem," he insisted.

"Why would I have thought of love poems in the last year?"

"Jesus, Maria. I thought you liked to read."

"Jesus, Lewis. I thought you were a gentleman. How about 'true love is mute'?"

He smiled; he liked this turn in the conversation. Audrey and Beryl ran by, and Lewis towed her further away from the edge. "It's your turn," she said.

"Well," said Lewis. "I like Yeats, and I like the loony French, but what's wonderful about Donne is that he goes both ways. He can talk about air and angels, or he can say, 'Enter these armes, for since thou thoughtst it best, not to dreame all my dreame, let's act the rest.'"

Dulcy focused on the back of his neck and thought about the strangeness of holding on to someone else's arm this tightly. "Or," said Lewis, "'Licence my roving hands, and let them go before, behind, between, above, below.'"

"Take me to shore," she said.

"It's not a shore," said Lewis. "It's cement. Are you blushing? The water makes you look blue, and it's hard to tell. Do you think, 'Oh poor Lewis, he's missing some fingers, no wonder he likes a hand poem. He must worry about his abilities as a lover.'"

They were in the far corner, out of the ring of light. "No," she said. "I don't think you're worried at all, and I can't believe you're saying this to me."

"Who else would I want to say it to?" He slid his arm around her waist. "And what else should I want? Not to waste my life? To be happy for a while?"

"That's all?"

"Of course not," said Lewis. "I want to eat you up. If you pull away, you'll drown."

They kissed, then paused and looked at each other. He pushed her up against the edge and they kissed again before the door opened and they were flooded with cold air and the sound of Hubie screaming in earnest. Rex ran by without noticing them.

Everyone left the pool and slipped off across the dark lawn. The towels were too small, and Dulcy was still wet when she ended up in a bunk above Margaret, who would not stop talking about all the bad things she wished she'd never said about Hubie Fenoways.

• • •

In the morning, their carriages were delayed by a flock of sheep, and the train reached Fridley an hour late while Hubie cackled on a stretcher. They saw another casket on the siding, this one simple pine, but the sky was blue and the rocks above the mining town were cinnamon-colored. Dulcy had a corner seat against the window as they moved north, next to Margaret and across from Lewis and Samuel. No one had slept through the screams the night before, and now no one talked, not even Audrey and Beryl.

Dulcy fell asleep and woke with a start at a bend south of town, roasting in the afternoon sun through the train window, sticky and parched, terrified by a dream she'd already forgotten. She could not place herself, and she looked for Carrie before she was back to the burned man and the plunge, the way Lewis watched from the facing seat as if he could track her alarm, as if he remembered everything they'd never talked about.

Lewis handed her a flask. He'd gotten sun on his face. He had to be exhausted, but he looked younger and tighter, healthier, better in all sorts of ways. "Water," he said.

"He's not leading you astray," said Margaret.

She was amused by everything, wrong about everything. Lewis watched Dulcy, and the expression was both sidelong and direct. "You're an optimist, Margaret," Dulcy snapped.

"I am." Margaret was hurt by Dulcy's tone, and it was her turn to stare into space.

They reached Livingston at four in the afternoon, and the thermometer at the station told Dulcy it was still eighty degrees. They'd arrived at the end of the May Day parade, and it looked as if both senses of the holiday had been celebrated: the streets were still full of banners and miners, clerks and laundresses and children wearing flowers, dressed in white.

She faded away with her blue bag while the others sorted out luggage and the wounded man. At home she stripped off every pinching bit of polite lingerie, put on an old dress, and walked down to her garden, willing her mind free from what she'd done and seen in the last two days. She'd put on her muddy moccasins but kicked them free when they kept gathering pebbles. She thinned lettuce and radishes and nibbled on what she pulled; she loosened soil and drew a row for a second planting of peas, emptying the packet into the palm of her left hand, dropping them into the double furrow at two-inch intervals. It was a relief to concentrate, to be away from voices, to be alone.

The wind swirled and caught the seed packet. She turned to reach for it and saw something white on her porch: Lewis, sitting on the steps, watching her. Dulcy scooped soil over the pea seeds, looked around for the moccasins, then gave up and walked toward the house.

"Giving shoes up entirely?"

"A nice idea," she said. He had already been inside to find glasses and wine and a corkscrew, but was not so patronizing that he patted her own steps as an invitation. She dipped her dirty hands in the rainwater pail, sized up her options, and aimed for a spot on the far

side of the bottle, wiping her hands dry on her skirt while he poured
a glass. She kept the part of her mind that might jump into the future
blank, and as a result the here and now was magnified: the birds in
the river bottom, the coin-like fresh poplar leaves across the street,
Lewis's surviving fingers, sunned and practical, working the cork
free from the screw and forcing it back into the bottle.

"What were you doing out there?"

"Peas," said Dulcy, looking at her nails. "Not thinking."

"Because your thoughts are unhappy?"

She took a long sip of wine.

A pause. "Should I apologize?"

"No," said Dulcy.

"Would you like to get married?"

She hadn't expected this. "No. I don't want to be married. Do
you?"

"I didn't think I did," he said. "But in this particular situation, I
felt I should ask. I want to do all sorts of things."

He flicked a piece of grass from her ankle, and she didn't move,
even though she felt as if she were about to blow up. "I like you," he
said. "I like seeing you, I like talking to you, I like touching you, and
you seem to feel the same way. I'd like more of all of it, and usually,
when people want this, they consider marriage."

"But Lewis, you don't love me."

"I don't know you well enough to know."

She wrapped her hands around her knees. He reached out and
touched her arm. "Please look at me. What do you think?"

"I would like to have everything," she said.

She watched him put down his glass of wine. Maybe she'd been
about to say more; maybe she wouldn't have thought of anything to
say even if he'd waited.

• • •

This was what people talked about. This was what the books were
all about; this was why people did irrational things that had no

relation to the violence of Victor. She wasn't as divorced from the physical as many women: she'd walked in strange places, worked outside on hot days, eaten and drunk to excess, nearly died from a pregnancy. She knew intellectually that one kiss was not like another, and lovers had nothing to do with rapists, but this was not so much a novelistic blur but shock and joy and propulsion. This kind of immersion of touch and mood, skin to skin, using a mouth like a third hand—she felt stupid to not have understood. She went from being someone who hadn't been naked in front of another human in twenty years to someone who would lie back on a bed in the daylight.

All of it stunned her, but by midnight, looking for something to eat in the kitchen, she only wore a blanket because she was cold, and she sat on his lap while they ate it because he was naked himself, and cold. She had finally peeled off her old life, lost her ability to fret over secrets before this new one. Cheese, sardines, canned peaches, being carried back upstairs, snickering at the effort. Over and over, she was shocked: they were lovers. She hadn't understood, and now she did; this was what the word meant.

1. ANT-EATER FLY.   2. LARGE APE, OR OURANG OUTANG.   3. PIGMY APE.   4. TUFTED APE.   5. ARCTIC BIRD.

6. ARGENTINE.   7. ARMADILLO.   8. LIZARD AST.   9. TEN RAYED AST.

Widows, like ripe fruit, drop easily from their perch.

—Bruyère

CHAPTER 17

THE DARK BLUE BOOK
OF ANOMALIES

•

Walton hadn't seen fit to send her to university, but he did shove history down her throat. There were no anomalies, he said, lecturing always. *With history, Dulce, you understood that every human, every living thing dies, whether or not it is or has food, whether or not it has a god, whether or not it understands how consistently this happens.* He certainly hadn't carried the no anomalies rule over to his own personality—he was sure that there was no one else like him, and he was probably right—but she hoped he'd found a universal ending comforting as he approached the window.

Nevertheless: if something seemed anomalous, Walton maintained it was simply a matter of missing data, undiscovered or forgotten knowledge. To that end, he kept track of mysteries: at the close of every year after 1872, he picked one oddity that had outlasted others and flouted his theory, and added it to a list on the inside cover of the dark blue book, under the heading of *Things Without Explanation*:

31 Dec 1879: Huachuca silver seam variations.

31 Dec 1883: The disappearance of Krakatoa: the color of the air.

31 Dec 1885: Praseodymium.

27 Dec 1892: I need not wait for the last day of this year to know that my rarity will remain Isobel's unimaginable cunny.

31 Dec 1894: The patient in the next room last April. He had a third nipple and a third bollock and had survived our illness since 1863. Perhaps the manner of acquisition, reportedly a Hawaiian octoroon?

31 Dec 1897: The bubbling springs and stones of Assam.

31 Dec 1902: The eruption of Pelée or my daughter's illness. Is this sort of difficulty really so common?

And the last, two weeks before he died:

31 Dec 1904: The strange gem middleman in Futter's Wheal, or Victor Maslingen, a rich man who dislikes rich things, be they food or fucking or conversation. May he be troubled by his own mysteries.

• • •

Three days after the trip to Yellowstone, as Lewis gathered his things for the train, waves of slush dribbled out of the sky. He would be gone a month, visiting his half-sisters and ill father, on a trip that had been planned for weeks. "Will you be all right?"

"Of course I will," she said. "You're the one with fevers."

"But if you're not all right, you need to get word to me."

He gave her a stepsister's address and took off half of everything for another ten minutes, and when he ran for the train he let the door slam in daylight despite Brach's prying eyes. Dulcy lay on the wrinkled bed in the gray light, endless fat snowflakes twirling slowly past the window, and felt bereft: he would not return. She thought of his skin cooling as he moved toward the station. She thought of how altered she felt, and wondered if she looked as strange.

• • •

By the time Hubert Fenoways died on the night of May 3, he was a pus-filled mess, a stinking pillow of blisters. Macalester had resorted to giving shots of morphine in Hubie's head and neck, and everyone assumed that he'd quadrupled the last few doses.

Dulcy heard this after Margaret rousted her for a meeting of the Sacajawea Club, throwing pebbles at her bedroom window until Dulcy opened the door. The Sanborn Insurance men were in the lobby of the Elite when they arrived for the meeting, surrounded by boxes of equipment as Irina checked them into rooms above the bar. They would begin surveying the town the next day, and though Eugenia tried to look miserable about Hubie's death, she radiated joy. The Sanborns would pay, would eat, and were unmarried: for Eugenia, it all came down to cash and appetites.

After days spent helping Hubie die, Vinca Macalester was cross, and she brought the topic back to the parade. Dulcy, thrumming along in her new private world, supposed such things had to be dealt with in advance, but thought she might be coming to a parting of the ways with the civic-minded ladies. The theme would be the Lewis and Clark centenary, the inescapable duty of any town on the explorers' route: Clark, at least, had camped somewhere below Dulcy's garden, though not until 1806.

"That doesn't mean we can't march as Liberty," said Mrs. Whittlesby. "We can't all wear skin hats and carry paddles." Despite a lack of visible collarbones, she had been fixed on the idea of marching in a toga-style drapery for months.

"I suppose not," said Vinca, too tired to argue. She passed around a list of entrants. Dulcy had never heard of the Improved Order of Red Men or the Knights of the Maccabees, and she hadn't known the cigar-makers had their own union.

"One hundred and twenty entries, not counting our ladies," said Margaret, looking for the bottle of port. "A gross." She was in a fine mood, bearing down on the end of her first year of widowhood without any pretense of grief. She'd planned photography lessons from Durr, and she'd talked Dulcy into the idea of tennis if the rain ever paused. "I will be free of so much," she said. "Black, keeping a straight face, stuff I hated even before Frank died, for God's sake."

Samuel had given Margaret a book called *Widows, Grave and Otherwise*, and she loved to offer up the quote of the day.

May 1: Widowhood is true freedom. (A nugget from Mlle. Desjardins.)

May 2: Easy-crying widows take new husbands soonest; there is nothing like wet weather for transplanting. (Oliver Wendell Holmes)

May 7: Widows are a study you will never be proficient in. (Thomas Fielding)

May 9: Why is a garden's wildered maze / Like a young widow, fresh and fair? / Because it wants some hand to raise / The weeds which have no business there. (Thomas Moore)

The sane part of the Sacajawea Club cackled with glee and had another glass. The other half looked sour, and ate extra cake.

• • •

Immediately after Hubie died, Gerry Fenoways asked around, calmly, about his brother's last days, but he asked for no firsthand accounts, and almost immediately, no matter how truthful the version Rex or Macalester or Samuel had given friends when they reached town, the story mutated according to resentment, amusement, alcohol. Durr (arrogant immigrant) had been supposed to jump in the pool, and somehow sensed the problem, and let Hubie go without warning him; Rex (spoiled brat) had told Hubie he'd be fired if he didn't jump; Samuel (sissy boy) had promised to be Grover's actor at the outset, and had been so unmanned by the earthquake that he walked away from his duty. There was no mention of Hubie blackmailing his way into the job, and Grover's role as conductor of the tragedy was suspiciously absent from all accounts.

Gerry's theories remained unclear, because once he collected accounts, he began to drink so much he couldn't often talk or walk. He made no pretense of living in his empty house, and Irving was constantly dragging him down an Elite hallway.

"I bet he can crawl," said Samuel. "Don't throw your back out, Irving. Try rolling him."

The wake had to be postponed. Hubie waited in an iced box at Hruza's, which was only fitting.

• • •

A few nights into Gerry's binge, Siegfried Durr was woken by Joe Wong's wife, Ruby, and he jumped to his feet gasping in a room of smoke. The fire was out by then—Joe had assumed the smoke came from an iron, and then traced it to the cellar he shared with Durr's studio, where he poured tubs of laundry water on a pile of smoldering rags. Everyone imagined Joe Wong was the target, and his wife told Dulcy she wanted to move to Butte, where they wouldn't feel like darker pebbles on white sand. Durr could move, too—they were good at sticking together, and Butte had almost one hundred thousand people, some large percentage with money and the need of a photograph.

But Durr didn't want to move. He told Samuel that he was fond of a woman in town, and Samuel told Dulcy that Durr and Rusalka had spent one night a week together for at least a year. "I would not call it a romance," he said, and he nodded toward Margaret, who'd just entered the ruined studio with Durr. "And I wouldn't say it's just one woman."

Margaret was oblivious; she studied the stacks of smoked glass and told Durr he was lucky. His paper stock and portraits were ruined, and the cameras needed to be taken apart and cleaned. It was the cusp of his busy season: graduations, weddings, spring dances. Dulcy told him to sleep in the loft of the framed side of the greenhouse, and said he could use it for his business until he made repairs. Her cellar could serve as a darkroom.

She didn't have to bully him. Durr bought an old chalkboard from one of the schools to hang photos, and he put up shelves and drapes. He brought his old carpet, a very nice Persian piece, but it stank of smoke until Rusalka, arguing with him over every detail of the move, blotted the whole thing with waxflower water and worked on the back with vinegar and lemon; Rusalka, who Dulcy now noticed came late and left early on her cleaning chores. Durr put a sign on the street and posted a forwarding note on the old studio, and soon she could see a steady procession of clients from her upstairs window.

"Is this a good idea?" asked Samuel.

"I trust Siegfried," she said.

"It's not Siegfried I worry about," said Samuel. "It's Gerry. Who do you think's trying to burn the town? He can go from dead to walking in an hour or two, and then drop again."

A night later, a four a.m. fire damaged Samuel's rooming house. His ancient landlady nearly died, but he hadn't been home when he heard the fire bells. He took a room at the Elite, on the premise that it would be the last place Gerry tried to burn down, and he told Dulcy he sometimes kicked the police chief when he found him down the hall, sleeping in front of Eugenia's door.

• • •

Despite having lost a small fortune, despite having done nothing to egg his blackmailer on, and despite having been splashed by the water that had boiled the blackmailer, Rex insisted on going to Hubie's much-delayed wake, and he insisted that Samuel go with him. He'd spent time on the piano in the Elite lobby, playing songs like "All Going Out and Nothing Coming In," then passed into a less charming phase filled with wonder at his many misfortunes. Rex didn't drink often, but when he did, he drank badly, and he did so now out of sheer guilt over Hubie's untimely demise. It brought out a kind of defensive pomposity that probably wouldn't mix well with Fenoways-style grief. Samuel said he'd stick close to him. He said that if Gerry was going to do something, he'd find a quieter, darker place, because he was going all the way back to his ancestors on this one—he was angry at Rex for allowing himself to be blackmailed; he was angry at Durr for siding with Falk and Macalester about what Hubie had done to the dead girl. He was angry with his mother for dying, so that both brothers needed to be drunk that day. Samuel said Gerry was angry, period, but nothing would happen in a church with fifty weepy old ladies on hand.

But Hubie Fenoways' funeral was scheduled for May 10 at the Elks Hall. Gerry had argued with the priest at St. Mary's before he argued with the minister of his wife's church, Dulcy's neighbor Brach. Gerry didn't want anyone talking about damnation, or suggesting that Hubie's death had some greater point. He didn't want any goddamn bells. When the men of God resisted these conditions—Dulcy could imagine Brach's response—he said he didn't give a fuck what they wanted, or what God wanted, and Hubie certainly didn't care anymore, either.

Samuel told the story very slowly when Dulcy and Margaret met him the next day in the Albemarle lobby. He said that the few women who toughed out the funeral left before the wake. Samuel and Rex and Grover sat together, and everyone drank. Gerry stood up front for the duration, a master of ceremonies. He forgave those who were responsible for his brother's death, no names specified, but he toasted in the direction of their table: it was over, nothing to be done. More toasts followed, some earnest, most dirty. Gerry sang bad opera in tribute to Hubie's good voice, and three dancers appeared. One was especially stunning, with thick black curls and long kohl-darkened eyes, the rest of her face and stray body parts covered by veils. She could *swivel*, said Samuel, who didn't usually notice. She was *just amazingly mobile*. It made *a person's eyes pop out*. Grovy said he *had to have her on film for his other movies*.

"What other movies?" asked Dulcy.

Samuel waved the question away. The performance was so extreme, especially as the veils dropped away, that he'd forgotten to be vigilant, and only belatedly worried when Gerry gave the girl a five-dollar bill and pointed at Rex.

"What was the girl wearing, by then?" asked Margaret, a little squeak to her voice.

"A kind of loincloth," said Samuel. "Gold and very small, with paste jewels sewn on."

"And above?" asked Dulcy.

"Gold disks on the tips of her lovelies," he said. "Rosettes. She *swayed* over . . ."

He paused, thinking his way through.

"Just say it," said Dulcy.

The girl with black curls swayed over, danced around Samuel and Grover with little caresses, and bent over Rex, rubbing her breasts against his face. Then she knocked him over with one sharp heel, and kicked the chair away as he lay on his back, and jumped in the air and landed right on his face, right with her *fundament* on his face, and bounced.

Dulcy and Margaret waited, their coffee and pastries cooling. "Broke his nose," said Samuel. "Flattened that delicate thing, blood everywhere. You should see him. Not that his mother will let anyone near him for weeks and weeks."

• • •

Dulcy was mostly comfortable with the way memory fell away. But on Walton's birthday, as she passed a mailbox on the corner of Geyser for the hundredth time, she missed Carrie like a body blow and almost wailed out loud.

Some days, the real didn't stay that way; some days, now that she had a house, she talked to herself or to her lost people, floating through time and wandering at midnight. The dead were kept in boxes in her mind, and she tried to open them gently. But that night she dreamed them: she was in a kitchen, putting food on a table for Walton and Carrie and for a naked man. No one seemed to notice he was naked, except for her; they joked, and passed food, though instead of plates some sort of board game covered the table. Green-yellow light, storm lighting: Martha walked in, smelling like lily of the valley, and Dulcy worried she'd notice the man. A moment later she was alone, and she panicked—she hadn't touched Martha when she had a chance, and Martha was dead.

She jolted awake in her new bed, to a burning rubber smell, and after she understood that it was a headache, not Gerry burning down the house, she dragged herself to the bathroom and poured some aspirin powder into a glass.

One of Walton's clinic nurses, a Breton woman, had insisted that all dreams were a mixture of the past and the future, and that one had to decipher which was which. Back in bed, the true memory gave her something to play with, to soothe her twisting head. She tried to remember what food she'd put down for the man—she could not begin to see his face, and now she wasn't sure she'd really seen Martha, either. Instead, her mind landed on a memory of Walton in his underclothes on a leather couch, having his reflexes checked with a little hammer, surrounded by the smell of soap and poison while a doctor bent over him and a nurse stood to one side and hummed Martha's song.

What was a memory, a dream, a headache? She couldn't place the clinic—Walton had dealt with the little hammer in a dozen cities. She curled up and pressed on her temples, outwaiting the pain, and for his birthday, she let Walton come back, all the good parts, everything she missed: the weird sliding smile when he saw a pretty woman, the way his step shimmied walking over ruins, his humor, and the fact that though he had more illusions about science than he did about mankind, he stayed a humanist. "I believe in the individual," he said. "We make our own way, and every man and woman is equal."

He did not whine about his blighted childhood, despite having endured food riots and the Redruth workhouse. He'd had no education past the age of ten, but he'd read every fragment of Shakespeare and Jonson, every tedious essay in every magazine. He could parrot on about Roman emperors until he cleared a room or was stumped by a bigger blowhard, and he'd never given up on finding the struggle between the Aristotelian elements—earth, air, fire, water—in every geological event. He knew his modern physics, mathematics and chemistry. He did not lie about being fluent in other languages. That said, he believed some ludicrous things, like phrenology, and he had a weakness for tarot. He was curious about everything, even if he was incapable of admitting error, and he constantly synthesized: in the months before the last trip to Africa, when a loyal friend at Columbia made a study of famine and allowed Walton to compare notes, Walton came to believe he could prove that every period of starvation could be tied to an eruption, and every eruption to a previous earthquake.

He loved his children and his friends, without expecting them to celebrate every facet of his personality. He knew he was a mess and often managed to be self-deprecating. He had endurance, and a huge tolerance for suffering. He loved women to a fault, or to their death, and he acknowledged that this was his *fatal flaw*. Even his favorite deck of cards, purchased in London, showed naked women playing their own game, the deck broken down to blond diamonds, redheaded hearts, brunette clubs and spades, and each suit represented by a mishmash of rarities—Hawaiian, Sioux, Polynesian, Tuareg, Hottentot, Persian, and so on. The queen of spades was a geisha, the ace of diamonds an Amazon. Henning had tucked the deck into the coffin.

Sometimes, during a fever on a ship, Walton hadn't been able to tell if he was on moving earth or moving water, and in his last week in bed he thought he was on both. She thought of how long that in-between had lasted in Seattle, memories and dreams, his childhood roaring up to greet him, air meeting the ground.

• • •

Every day was cold and wet. The healthiest thing in Dulcy's yard was a rhubarb plant she'd found in a corner behind the mason Abram's leftover bricks. The old grapevine had survived, and miniature clusters snailed out all along the fibery vine, toy bunches for a dollhouse, each grape the size of the dot on a ladybug, each cluster a fingernail. The new trees blossomed, and she watched for bees and dug in wild bursts despite the cold, wet weather, and a fretful Durr, who brought brides and students into the temporary studio. Rusalka had deserted him, and Dulcy watched him clean at night through a growing veil of plants.

As the rain continued, a sense of apocalypse deepened. The river bubbled up in low-lying areas, turning the bottomland below Dulcy's wall into a marsh. An old man drowned on a dissolving riverbank, trying to pull a calf out of the water, and one of the bridges a few miles north of the park collapsed. The Sanborn survey men wore yellow slickers and glowed at a distance, splotches of color glimpsed down alleys.

Things the Sanborns found, while measuring Livingston's hastily built foundations: a split cannon, a forgotten graveyard near the hospital, a petrified tree, and a surveyor's chain that the youngest Sanborn, in a rare fit of enthusiasm, was sure had been dropped by William Clark on his return trek east ninety-nine years earlier. They found a stolen buggy, a lost rooster, a cache of coins buried in a chamber pot, and on May 15, they found the missing Mrs. Peck covered in maggots and straw in an unused stable, beaten and broken, stripped and splayed.

Inkster, the man who'd stabbed her husband, spent his time in either a frenzy or a stupor after being beaten by Gerry ("He's not like a child," said Samuel. "Children care. He just stares at walls and tries to bite"), but he pled guilty in the hearing, and his sentencing was passed despite a diminished mind. His execution was set for May 24. This additional failure to extend or magnify the most sensational crime in years made Samuel miserable, and he was reduced to photographs and maps and hints.

On May 18, as Dulcy headed out of her gate, the postman handed her a letter from M. Cope, East 67th Street, New York, addressed to Mrs. Edgar Nash, 509 South Eighth Street, Livingston. She left her gloves dangling on the fence and went back inside to read.

To quote Herrick, he wrote:

I dream'd this mortal part of mine
Was Metamorphoz'd to a Vine;
Which crawling one and every way
Enthralled my dainty Lucia.
Me thought, her long small legs & thighs
I with my Tendrils did surprize;
Her Belly, Buttocks, and her Waste
By my soft Nerv'lits *were embrac'd*
And found (Ah me!) this flesh of mine
More like a Stock, *than like a* Vine . . .

I hoped you'd enjoy the gardening allusions.

If you prefer food:

I will not be sworn but love may transform me to an oyster

Fondly, M. Cope

She liked his handwriting, and she liked having a secret. She was a little stunned at herself: hadn't she had a secret before? Why would this change so much?

• • •

She neatened the Bluebeard room and installed a desk and chair under the window. She told herself that it wasn't for Lewis, that she might write stories or draw, but she mostly watched birds and the minister's sunken wife: whenever Brach left, his wife would sit on her back steps and stare straight ahead. Dulcy hid the notebooks deeper in the closet, and thought again about throwing out the medicine box.

It rained, another two inches in four days. It would have been nothing in Westfield or Seattle, but in Livingston the streets turned to soup again, and when the rain finally stopped, the world steamed. When Dulcy visited Samuel at the paper, a rancher with a Biblical beard was in to report on the coming catastrophe: trees tilting down the valley creeks, ice dropping in sheets, mud rolling down ravines. All during the next week, as her dresses grew paler and lighter, she watched spring telescope—yards that had just sported crocuses sliding toward tulips and lilacs, while peonies and rosebuds swelled and took on color. What took a month in Westfield began to happen here in days. When she walked near the milky, turgid river, she saw blue and green speckled duck eggs dotted in the brown reeds and wondered if they would hatch before they floated away. Bats darting on high, a whistle she couldn't quite hear. A mosquito landed on her arm; the world was full of reasons to think about Lewis. She flicked it with a forefinger and thought she saw a pink mist, herself in midair.

Dulcy was helping Samuel with editing one or two days a week, working on boring, baroque profiles of local businessmen or the weekly social scroll, and he talked so much that she got very little done. She didn't complain, because some of what he wandered through, what he stored and let dribble out in bits, was key to her existence. Some of this information: Eugenia may have never been married, Irving had survived a Polish pogrom as a child, Durr had killed people in China, Gerry and Hubie had beaten their male inmates but shortened female inmates' sentences in return for sex; their father had beaten their mother, and they had standards. Samuel said that Lewis had nearly died of malaria twice in the last year, and that the reason that Lewis hadn't written a great novel was that he'd fall in love, and fall sick, and by the time he was better he'd realize he was no longer in love with either the woman or the story. He'd lose his inspiration and he'd even lose his anger. No love, no rage— what was the point? Lewis only wanted to write about things that were mysterious, and he simply wrote too slowly.

"And what is he writing about now?" asked Dulcy.

"More about bad medicines, I think," said Samuel, not noticing her relief. "There seems to be an endless supply." He wanted her to go to Inkster's execution, but he only wanted someone to stand next to, while he muttered about mobs. She wouldn't, and he went alone.

The rain began again that evening, and when Samuel showed up on her porch that evening, soaking wet, it only took him an hour to drink everything she had in the house. He said a thousand people had watched; he'd helped Grover with his camera, because Durr had refused to attend. He said he'd witnessed too many executions and preferred to spend the afternoon replacing Margaret's cracked attic windows.

She wondered what Durr had seen—deserter hangings in Germany? Beheadings in China? "Why would Grover want to film it?"

Samuel squirmed. "I did say to him, 'Grove, hasn't it been done? Those Japanese? Topsy?'" Topsy was the name of an elephant Thomas Edison had electrocuted on film. Henning had ranted about it: Edison was the animal. Dulcy watched Samuel smile at his Topsy joke, lose the life-and-death plot of the afternoon, regain it.

The short version: the hangman hadn't arrived from Dillon, but Gerry, sober, announced that there would be no delay. He blamed the condemned man, Inkster, for a third murder, the girl whose body had toured the state, and he said that therefore Inkster had killed his beloved brother Hubert, who had wrongly been accused of desecrating the girl's body, and who had thus taken a job with someone who was "criminally idiotic," and ended up dead himself.

This unified theory of recent disaster left the crowd uneasy, and Gerry hustled Inkster onto the scaffold. He dropped the noose, forgetting the hood—Grover had been very excited (Grover, thought Dulcy, was beyond redemption)—but the crowd had wailed and Bixby had forced Gerry to use the hood. Only a second later, he pulled the lever: no warning, no last words. The trap opened and the body dropped.

And the rope broke. Inkster flopped around on the ground, one leg at an angle, sounds emerging from his crushed throat that made the crowd cover its ears, a *cack cack cack* like a sandhill crane. His leg bone thrust visibly through his pants, and Gerry bellowed for another rope, plunged down and hauled the man back up the scaffold stairs. Deputy Bixby spoke up and Gerry knocked him down and everyone else was paralyzed and Inkster was strung up again, gurgling and hacking in a pile on the trap door. This time the rope didn't break.

"I did wish Lewis was here," said Samuel, "to give me some phrases for this travesty, but he'll be months."

"June," said Dulcy. "I think I remember him saying June."

"That's never how it happens. He likes his family more than he admits, and he'll eat well, and he stays on good terms with all his old mistresses."

Through the open porch door, there was still just enough light to see a new stream running between the garden beds toward the river. "We're all going to drown," said Samuel.

He spent the night wrapped in quilts on her sofa, and when he left at ten, after vomiting coffee and bacon by the gate, Dulcy turned to see Brach gripping the fence, ten feet away.

"Babylon," he said.

"Don't be silly," she said. "He stayed because he was ill. You just saw him be sick."

"Harlot," he said. "Vile crawling sin bag."

She took two fast steps and smacked him hard with the kitchen towel she'd just used to wipe Samuel's face. Which was funny, though the incident left her shaken. She wouldn't be able to fully explain the story to anyone but Lewis.

• • •

On May 26, her birthday morning, she woke up to a room full of beautiful light, poplar leaves shadowed and dancing on the new paint of the empty bedroom walls, the mountains to the south fixed and massive, clouds scudding high above. She was twenty-five.

She pulled herself up and out and bought a rosebush and another grape from the Scotsman on Ninth Street, who gave her a winter-burned clematis "as a peace offering." She almost liked Buchanan now, and bought two roses instead of one. She planted them all along the porch and ended up having dinner at the Elite with Samuel and Margaret and the Macalesters without mentioning the occasion or complaining about the food.

The ground dried, and she finished planting. Her skin sizzled and tightened. They could mummify anything here: Bozeman's town fathers advertised neighboring Gallatin Valley as "Egypt in America," talking up the wheat crop, but they had no idea how unflattering the similarities were. All that water in the river and none whatsoever in the air, no more English-style rain, no Midwestern waves to cool the eye and skin. From Martha's porch, you could see just a sliver of Erie. From Dulcy's porch, she watched the Yellowstone River turn into a lake.

The sun blazed, and she resorted to larger and larger hats in public. In private, she often skipped the hat and wore one of Martha's comfortably indecent day dresses, and she was wearing the one with lilies of the valley on the last Sunday in May when Margaret showed up with Irving and the Elite's buggy. Dulcy had forgotten that it was Decoration Day, and that she'd promised Margaret that she'd go along to the graveyard. Frank Mallow's widow was wearing pink, dropping her *annus luctus* with a vengeance. "We'll be quick," Margaret said.

Dulcy looked down at her brown wrists and fingers: bug bites, scratches. Carrie wouldn't recognize these hands. Maybe Dulcy could hide herself in plain sight by going entirely native, turn into one of the old Italian ladies at the produce store.

"You're fine," said Margaret, brushing pollen off the dress. Dulcy covered up with a black shawl, the wearing of which nearly killed her when they left the buggy's shade. Margaret didn't ask anything inane about graves Dulcy should have been visiting, and Dulcy didn't comment on the brevity of their visit with Mr. Mallow, whose spot had greened over nicely. The cemetery was packed, and when news spread that the river was cresting and that the bridge to McLeod Island was likely to collapse, Irving packed the carriage and took all of them to the rise above Miles Park where a party had formed, flood watching as a sport.

Dulcy spread the shawl on the ground. They were just in time to see the small bridge give way, a faded cracking sound under the ongoing roar, bobbing rails sucked down in liquid that looked like hot chocolate. For once she approved of Grover, who'd propped his camera close to the edge, interested enough not to fret over facing a crowd with his substantial ass.

"Here we are," said Samuel. "Look what I found on the three o'clock train."

She craned around from her spot on the blanket and peered into the sun. "Early, for once," said Samuel. "He must be sick."

"I'm not sick," snapped Lewis, sitting next to her on the grass. "And I said I'd be back."

"Looks wrecked, doesn't he?" said Samuel.

Lewis was a little in front, and Dulcy's view included the side of his face, the tight skin on his right cheekbone, the whorl at the back of his head, the tense neck. She curled her scratched hands under her legs, but Lewis was paying no attention, talking to Margaret while they all watched a fifty-foot length of cottonwood bounce off the far bank and twirl.

"Did you have a good trip, then?" asked Margaret, touching his arm. Margaret could make that kind of easy gesture. "You do look frail, you know."

"It was an easy trip," said Lewis. "And please stop saying that. This is quite a show."

Samuel swatted a mayfly. They watched Bixby charge by in one of the police wagons. James Macalester muttered about automobile accidents, and what a Model A looked like after a driver hit a bull. Dulcy counted the trees that shot by, racing toward the Dakotas, and thought that it was like watching a long earthquake. She stretched her legs, then saw Lewis look down at her ankles. He reached out and brushed an ant off her skirt.

Her blood hummed into her face. She was a horrible actress, but there was nothing she could do. "I have something for you," he said. "A silly thing, a late birthday present."

"When was your birthday?" asked Margaret, surprised.

"A while back," said Dulcy. "A busy day." She couldn't remember telling anyone in this town.

"We're going to a play in Bozeman tonight," said Samuel. "If anyone would like to come along."

Lewis finished a bottle of lemonade. "I won't be climbing back on a train today," he said.

They watched Grover crouched by the bank, muddying his knees, crumpled and intent behind the massive black camera. "I'm sure he'd love to go," said Margaret, climbing to her feet. "*I'd* love to go."

"I need to go home," said Dulcy, standing with her. "I was in the middle of a thousand things."

Lewis pulled himself upright. "I'll walk you. I'm done for the day."

Dulcy started off, but by then the Macalesters had repacked their basket and joined them. James asked about Lewis's trip—pleasant weather in New York, the siblings and father all fine, no compelling scandals or fashions to pass on—and then segued into the Hubie mess, and how Gerry's wife had telegrammed Eugenia that he'd already abandoned the cure, and they would divorce.

James rarely talked this much, but almost nothing that Dulcy would have wanted to say to Lewis could be said, anyway. When the Macalesters remembered where they lived and turned north on Sixth, Dulcy and Lewis walked in silence as a line of carriages passed, with Nesser the realtor in the sole automobile. He turned, and Lewis stared back while Dulcy waved. When they reached Eighth Street, Brach was on his porch. He only nodded in response to Lewis's greeting but watched them openly as they reached Dulcy's gate. Lewis touched his hat. "Have a fine evening, Mrs. Nash. It was good to see you again."

He walked away, not bothering to acknowledge the gnome a second time. Dulcy made her way to her back porch steps, where she waited to cry. It would take a bit: she could feel a wave behind her eyes, but the rest of her body was ringing. She tried to look up at the sky—it was hard to cry while looking straight up—but her eyes still filled. Brach had begun singing, badly, about God, and as she watched his chickens peck by her wall, she decided to kill them. A tortoiseshell cat watched them from the sunny top of the wall, flicking its tail like a metronome.

Dulcy looked down at her hands and tried to remember what she'd been doing when Margaret had pulled her out of the yard. A chickadee landed near her feet, but when she checked for the cat again, it was looking in the same direction as the chickens, all of them watching the alley. She turned to see Lewis drop into the yard from the wall. He landed, and pulled off his jacket, and walked toward her as Brach continued to sing.

• • •

In 1899, Walton had been recovering from a flare in his illness and Copenhagen's version of treatment when he managed this lecture: "The world is all about touch, Dulce. You don't believe it now, or you only think about it in terms of food or plants, which is the only way your poor sour grandmother understands the concept, but you will know what I mean by the end. It's all about touch, even if it's the temperature of water or wind on your skin, and everything will truly change when you understand another human hand or mouth."

At some point that night, Lewis said, "Old Ed Nash wasn't much of a lover, was he?"

"No. He wasn't."

"What did he like to do?"

"Nothing," said Dulcy.

The next afternoon Lewis slipped back to the hotel for clean clothes, and when he reappeared at dusk, he brought two things. Dulcy had not been belabored by gifts from men. Victor had been so consumed by anxiety that an offering became a test, fraught with pitfalls: bright diamond earrings, some careful books, the emerald ring she'd returned. But Lewis's English nursery catalogue was like a fat bouquet in a secret language, like someone knowing you only liked one very particular kind of berry, or opals, or Turkish perfume. The other gift was a soft blue jumper of Afghan wool, and she wore it as a robe in the middle of the night.

(3) When barbiine were cast over waiting hours a bitterness so deep.
Copyright Brown University & Co-citation

Malaria: an Italian colloquial word (from mala, *bad, and* aria, *air) . . .*
A single paroxysm of simple ague may come upon the patient in the
midst of good health or it may be preceded by some malaise. The ague-
fit begins with chills proceeding as if from the lower part of the back,
and gradually extending until the coldness overtakes the whole body.
Tremors of the muscles more or less violent accompany the cold sensa-
tions, beginning with the muscles of the lower jaw (chattering of the
teeth), and extending to the extremities and trunk . . . Sleep may over-
take the patient in the midst of the sweating stage, and he awakes, not
without some feeling of what he has passed through, but on the whole
well . . . The paroxysm is followed by a definite interval in which there
is not only no fever, but even a fair degree of bodily comfort and fit-
ness; this is the intermission of the fever. Another paroxysm begins at
or near the same hour next day (quotidian ague), which results from a
double tertian infection, or the interval may be forty-eight hours (ter-
tian ague), or seventy-two hours (quartan ague) . . .

—*Encyclopedia Britannica,* Eleventh Edition

CHAPTER 18

LEWIS BRAUDEL'S BLACK BOOK

•

Dulcy didn't know whether Lewis's illness was tertian, quotidian, quartan: it sometimes came daily, then not for months. He acted as if malaria were no worse than a cold, but she knew the illness tilted on people despite quinine, and luck ran out. He had two attacks in the first week he was back, but afterward he'd eaten, walked, talked, and he was at her again within hours. Walton would begin to echo in her head, and then Lewis's clarity and youth and vitality would banish these thoughts. And who knew how long any of them had: in the last month, Dulcy's forty-year-old butcher had dropped dead of a stroke, and Margaret's second cousin died a week after her first child was born.

Lewis usually worked during the day at the Elite, but sometimes in the middle of the night he'd leave her bed and she'd find him sitting in the Bluebeard room, scribbling on the graph paper she'd used to draw out her garden. He had meant to continue two long projects from the year before—on immigrants and quack medicines, both topics that could go with him anywhere, but he said he was tired of thinking about illness, and didn't have the mind for anything long. It was tempting to question Gerry about his abandoned cure, but Lewis didn't want to think of alcohol any more than he wanted to think of illness. He'd fiddle with other topics, but he didn't know where they might travel in six months, and he didn't want to limit the future.

His notebooks—stationary pads, not fancy bound things like Walton's—were all piled on the floor of his room at the Elite. Walton's notebooks were buried in the Bluebeard room closet, and the tiny piece of tissue she's used to mark the doorsill remained untouched.

In mid-June, he headed for Salt Lake to write a piece about the aftereffects of the second manifesto against polygamy, or the Mormon missionary program—he thought of calling the article "The Mormon Missionary Position"—and Dulcy slept ten hours the first night he was gone, dead center in her bed. She declined invitations to a seasonal frenzy of parties and felt smug, but after a third night she missed him, and on the fourth she woke at midnight, knowing he was back. It was windy, and she didn't so much hear him as feel the vibration of his steps, catch the sound of the cupboard or icebox, the scrape of a chair in the kitchen. She pulled on her robe and slipped down and he grinned at her, scrounged leftovers and a beer on the table. His shoes were off, his shirt was open, but he looked well. "It's been hot," said Dulcy.

"Not like Salt Lake. I'd douse myself in water, and dry myself, and be wet again by the time I hit the street. It was like being in Atlanta, or Toledo." He handed her the beer, and she sat sideways on his lap while he finished his plate of smoked salmon and bread and beet salad, and then she swiveled around to face him.

This was what it was like, then. But Lewis said, no, this was only what it was like for them, and most people were never this lucky.

• • •

Rex reemerged, face still discolored but in a fine mood, sunny and calm. He'd spent the last weeks in a little rented house on the far side of town, so that his mother's guests wouldn't see what had happened to his nose. The bruising had gone from his eyebrows to his collarbone, and he joked (to Lewis and Samuel) about what had gone through his mind as the girl had headed toward his face: nothing but admiration. He'd been so well cared for during his convalescence, and read so much, that his view of the world was entirely changed. He'd read Greek plays that he'd lied about reading in college, Marcus Aurelius, Casement's report on the Congo. He was renouncing God (in whom he had not, in all honesty, invested much effort) in favor of rationality and humanism. He would dedicate his time and surplus money to good deeds (schools, the poor) and rational plans: he'd scrapped together "the bits of his inheritance" (more bits than most people) and doubled down on California land. He was done with water as sport, and all in on necessity—dams were the new thing, and he'd begun to eye the narrowness of the Yellowstone canyon just upstream of town.

They were all having lunch at Bacchi's. It wasn't very good—Bacchi served rubbery cheese and called raviolis *tamales*—but any attempt had to be rewarded. Samuel put down his fork. "Say all that again. The last two minutes or so."

"I have decided that there is no just God. There is no solution beyond the better angels of our souls." He smiled at Dulcy and Lewis, who sometimes forgot that they sat too close. "I haven't organized my thoughts on charity, yet, though of course there will still be money to help the paper grow, Samuel. Eugenia tells me the Poor Farm is much in need of help." He stabbed a noodle pillow and popped it in his mouth. "God hasn't shown his face there, lately."

"Is all this happening because God showed Her face to you when the girl dropped on it?" asked Lewis.

"Possibly," said Rex, smiling.

Samuel finished a last chewy bite and put his fork down. "You're a fool. Eugenia suggested such things because she and the Fenoways own the Poor Farm. He beats people until they're feeble, and then the county pays him to put them up."

"Well," said Rex. "Something must be done, but in the meantime another charity, then. Would you cheer up if we bought another newspaper? Seattle's for sale—are you ready for a city?"

"I like where I live," snapped Samuel, in a foul mood. He'd planned to golf with Grover, but Grover was at the hotel, "coping" with his newly arrived wife, Clara.

"Did he use that word, *coping*, or is that how you see it?" asked Lewis.

"He used it," said Samuel.

"A little naptime," said Rex, oblivious. He laughed and rubbed his hands together.

After Lewis came over the wall that evening, he explained the story of Rex's recovery: after the incident at Hubie's wake, the veiled dancing girl felt remorse and came to the cottage where Rex was recovering to apologize. She'd apologized so thoroughly that she now spent all of her time there, and when Mrs. Woolley sent spies, they were told she was a housekeeper. As she had been: Rusalka had worn a black wig to the dance.

Dulcy, who assumed no one knew a thing about her past life, couldn't imagine how this could go on without people knowing, without Rex recognizing Rusalka.

"Because there's no moral to the story," said Lewis. "Rex probably wasn't looking at her eyes, but I think he always knew who it was and wasn't in the mood to complain. It was Samuel who didn't have an eye for detail."

"Has he ever been in love?"

"He thinks he has. I'm not sure that he knows, yet."

Once, when he was tipsy, Samuel had told Margaret and Dulcy about a love affair. He'd said that there'd been no question of meeting the parents, and then, "gone."

"She left?" Margaret had asked. "She died?"

Samuel had nodded his head, and a tear trickled into his moustache.

"Died how?" Dulcy asked Lewis now.

"If it's the object of affection I'm thinking of, his appendix burst," he said. "I didn't like him any more than I like Grover. He was hard on Samuel. I've made myself forget the name."

He made fun of her later in bed, making love again, when her shock still hadn't worn off. It was a wide world out there. Surely, given her upbringing, she'd had a little insight?

Dulcy pulled away and watched him in the lamplight; he watched her back. "I was referring to your father's medical expertise," said Lewis.

"Ah," said Dulcy. But she thought about his mention of her birthday, her sister, Seattle, and she climbed out of bed.

"Stop," said Lewis. "I'm sorry. Come lie down again. Don't leave me this way, Dulcy."

The room echoed. He grinned—he pointed skyward, still intent on the moment, and didn't realize what he'd said. She took his bowler hat from the bedpost and lowered it gently on top of him. She wondered if she was about to lose everything.

"What's my name, Lewis?"

He looked down at the hat and up at her face, and his smile flattened. They watched each other.

"You said you loved me, and you wouldn't lie to me."

He took the hat off his lap and sat up. "I love you, and I would never lie to you."

"But you have."

"By using the name you wanted me to use? By loving you even though you were lying to me?" He spun the hat across the room. "Fine. Maria, then."

She was shaking. "Who did you talk to, when you were in New York?"

"I had friends in the city who'd known you. They were talking about your death, and they called you Dulcy, not Leda, and I guess that's how I've thought of you ever since. But I already knew. I remembered you from the train, and when I read the papers, after you disappeared, I could see your face, and it was horrible to think you were dead. So, you know, it was quite nice to see it again at the Elite. And quite interesting." He stood and walked slowly toward her; he kissed her neck and wrapped his arms around her.

"Interesting," she said, into his neck. "Why didn't you tell me?"

"I didn't want you to run away," said Lewis. "I would do anything to keep you with me, and keep your secret, and keep you safe. Don't doubt me. I don't give a fuck what your real name is, and I don't even mind that you've lied to me. This is all about survival."

• • •

Everything was brighter in Livingston, all the time, than other places she'd lived. It was different than the bleached light of the seaside, or a lakeside town like Westfield: desert light, and desert temperatures, but sometimes the wind sounded as if it were coming from an ocean, rather than roaring down an ancient mountain or arriving directly from a thundercloud above. At five in the afternoon it was ninety degrees; at five in the morning, forty. She finally listened to the women who told her to shut the house down in the morning and open up at dusk, and when Lewis managed to retreat to the hotel before light, he left at exactly the point she wanted him for warmth.

But the light: out here, you could see everything headed your way. There was less of a looming sense than she remembered from storms coming over water, but when the scalding light gave way to a wind and black clouds, the fear was just as immediate. She had moved to a place where parasols came to die, were inverted into shuttlecocks and torn from hands, moving like squid. Samuel published a brief account of a rancher's wife who'd invested in an extra-sturdy model and lost an eye to a rib. Livingston was supposedly too mountainous for tornadoes, but the air still turned green, and from her bedroom window they were lucky enough to see the moment when a cottonwood on the river bottom corkscrewed and slammed flat.

A spark started on Macalester's roof, and the doctor's wing and plunge at Eve's Spring burned to the ground. Despite talk of lightning, Samuel made noises about delving into the string of recent fires, or simply hiring a Pinkerton to follow Gerry. They all took a drive to see the charred resort at Eve's Spring, and Dulcy and Margaret wandered around collecting broken bits of azure tile from the cracked pool, hot water steaming up from the fissures.

A few days later, Lewis took the train to Helena with Samuel for a dinner at the Press Club. She didn't expect to see him the next night. When Irving knocked on her door, Dulcy was surprised, but Irving looked astounded to be making this trip at all. He wouldn't meet her eye.

"Mr. Braudel is sick, and he asked me to get you."

"He doesn't want a doctor?"

"He only asked for you to come. I don't think he's so sightly, but he said don't fret."

Irina was arguing over a bill with the Sanborns and did not see Dulcy take the stairs. The door was unlocked, and when she pushed it open to a gust from an open window, she had a flash of Miss Randall's room after Lennart's search, but this was controlled chaos, and the open window was a relief. He'd been sick, and he'd overdosed himself with quinine and rendered himself temporarily deaf, but he bellowed apologies and deranged sallies while she motioned to keep his voice down, so that the people in nearby rooms wouldn't hear lines like *Can't you do that without clothes* or *I am so sorry just put me down you don't need another invalid.*

She didn't; it was true, but Walton's illness had been hopeless and revolting and made her angry. Lewis's made her desperate. By nine he'd stopped shaking, and she hiked the window and waved a book for a fan. He and Samuel had seen a friend, drunk too much, been stupid. "Is this attack any different?" she asked. "Does it ever change, if you drink or you're tired?"

Lewis still couldn't hear, and he wasn't yet a lip reader. "I was sick by the Philippines."

"Too sick to misbehave?"

His eyes were lazy, but he understood. "You've been reading novels. Serves me right."

"What does it really feel like?" she asked. "Do you hallucinate?"

"No," said Lewis. "I just feel so sick I don't mind giving up. I used to look for opium or hashish—why not be in a trance?—but I don't want to leave now."

Dulcy asked Irving to bring some broth and watched it put Lewis to sleep. She sorted through a box of books he'd shipped from New York and decided she wanted to read all of them. She poked through the piles that dotted the room—she could date the trips taken by the top of each mound, a train ticket or a newspaper. One stack of tropical linen, layered with a stack of torrid letters postmarked from Bozeman, seemed oldest. She made herself tuck them back, mostly unread, but skimmed through fond notes from his sisters, asking about his health, talking about plays and scandals, a dead girl they'd all known, a runaway car.

"Dulcy, are you there?"

He thought he was cold even though he was burning up. She undressed and lay down next to him, wet towels in a basket for later. When he was asleep, she reached for a thick notepad near the bed and read through dated pages of fragments, beginning the summer before:

> Fever dream: birds bleeding onto the ground as they flew
> overhead.
> Samuel needs to find a larger town for his appetites.
> Chicago after a pipe, watching a girl's head bob. She seemed to
> be ten feet away, but she was having an effect.

What he thought about: not nice things, but honest, and it was all him, fresh and violent and bored and depressed, ill without being in any way languid, and she buried herself into it enough to not hear the lock. She was half covered, propped up on an elbow, when she looked up at Irina in the doorway, hand to her mouth. "I thought he might need help," Irina squeaked.

"You do this all the time?" asked Dulcy. "Walk into this bedroom?"

Irina shook her head, eyes locked on the scene: a feverish man on a bed with haphazard covers, arm wrapped around the equally naked Mrs. Nash. "I heard Samuel say he was ill."

"Go away," said Dulcy. "We're fine."

Which was true, all in all. She imagined Irina's voice streaming across town and wondered how she'd play the idea that she'd let herself into a man's room, thinking she could help.

Dulcy picked up the notebook again.

Sometimes, another human comes on you like a vision. You feel you already know her, you're familiar with the line of her cheek, or the way she looks away, the way she studies a menu. You don't know her, of course, anymore than you know a Venus in a painting, but because you have that sense you decide you will now, and it will make all the difference in your life. It's the American Way.

Lost and found: the West as a place to disappear or a place to be reborn.

Beginnings disappear here, but endings are dramatic. People come here to remake ruin or to drop into emptiness.

Poor Rex, Poor Samuel. Dulcy is fine, all silk skin and good mind and appetite. The question is not how to be happy but how not to ruin it.

She began to have the sense that he really only cared about staying alive, and enjoying life, rather than being a great writer; this meant that the snippets he put down were easy and loose.

"What did the lovely Irina want?" asked Lewis, as if he'd just heard them speak.

"To inquire after your health."

"I never fucked her." He reached out for a cup of water, and Dulcy watched his whole arm vibrate. He looked at what she was reading, lay back, and shut his eyes. She turned back to his notes, probably from about April—he was guilty of lists, too: *laundry, moderation, talk sense into Samuel, $ and goodbye to P.*

P was possibly Priscilla, the Bozeman mistress. Dulcy decided to face the clippings she'd glimpsed labeled *Leda R.*, glued down near handwritten notes from February:

A girl in the dining car, the blank look of an open future. Pale and dark and tired. She seemed stunned by the landscape, by other travelers who rambled on (the look on her face while she watched the man who brayed at me about politics), by books that bored her. I remember her because she was pretty but odd-faced, and I liked her shape. Sometimes her expression fell away, snapped like an icicle.

No one leaves a train and what he or she loves in life for any one reason. She was distracted, dressed in bereaved black. She was, moreover, dealing with another girl who seemed to be her sibling, and who was evidently difficult, or at least ill and petulant. We did not talk. How did I know about the father's body? The blowhard conductor.

But I recognized her. I knew already: the fallen man on the sidewalk, while people gawked. And so knowing—hindsight is cheap—that this might be the Remfrey girl, I am on the one hand surprised, and on the other not at all. I could not swear to recognize her in a group of similar women, in a different season, in different light and mood; I'm not sure that I didn't want to create a drama around a face. But I remember the face as I last saw it, as I left the train, and it was filled with energy or fear or the excitement that comes from having made a decision.

She flipped to the last entries, started to avert her eyes from scribbled accountancies, then gave up her selective morality. He'd made a good sum on his journalism and the Cope book, and he had some sort of family income. Geometric doodles, a sketch of a crooked house, a naked girl in profile scattered around lines like this:

She can die, or she can die to her old life. The argument after the fact is annoying. She wanted to disappear. Running away from something, running into something. There would have been so many easier places to land.

And:

What was it like to grow up with such a father? No lightweight eccentric.

I told myself I wasn't sure because I wanted her.

I don't want to write this anymore.

She lowered the notebook to the floor and reached for the pile of New York newspapers and clippings, probably untouched since his return at the end of May: business scams, digs at Clark, a car accident that had killed two Columbia graduates, and this small corner item:

FAMILY REQUESTS
THAT GIRL BE DECLARED DEAD

On the occasion of what would have been her twenty-fifth birthday on May 26, the family of Leda Remfrey has requested she be legally declared dead after months of fruitless searching. Miss Remfrey's brothers, Walter and Winston, bankers of the city, maintain that their sister, lost from a Northern Pacific train on January 15 or 16, flung herself to death from a train window somewhere in Montana or North Dakota. A small service will be held next week in the city, the location and time to be announced, and a stone will be placed in the family plot in Westfield, New York. This ends a tragedy that began when Walton Remfrey, Miss Remfrey's father, died in early January.

Lewis rolled around her. "Argue with me," he said. "I've been so fucking bored. I can't find anyone who'll agree with me for the right reasons."

Later, when he was lying in a lukewarm tub, creating his own steam, she asked him questions: Who had really cared for him? (A nanny, his sisters.) What had he liked when he was a boy? (His dogs, drawing maps, women, reading.) He'd been kicked out of Andover for one of those things, finished up at a military academy, done well at Columbia.

Dulcy watched him turn the spigot with his toe. "Why did you come here to begin with?" she asked. "And why did you come back after the first time?"

"I didn't really want to be anywhere," Lewis said. "I stopped to see Samuel on my way to Butte for some interviews, and the room was cheap and so I left bags when I made a run down to Denver for a different story. The town was so strange and pleasant. People are holier than thou everywhere, but this place had a sense of humor."

"You're cherry-picking," she said. "You really swan around, thinking nice things about the citizens?"

"Honest things," said Lewis. "But I understand your sarcasm. Don't you want to lie down again?" he said. "I'm not so hot anymore."

She did, though he was. She hiked the windows, and they climbed back in bed. She didn't think of pitying Lewis since spending nights with him, despite his sweats and his miserable childhood, despite running her fingers over his ribs.

"Why don't we marry?" he asked. "Marry me."

"I like having a secret," she said. "Having a lover, and no one the wiser."

"Lover," he said. "All right." The wind gusted through the open window, blowing his clippings around, but he had an arm clamped around her. "Why Dulcinea? Did your father read *Don Quixote*?"

"Yes," she said.

"It's better than asking why Leda or Cordelia."

"Yes." She turned on her side and watched the tips of his eyelashes, batting off sleep and some greater weariness. He was too thin. She shut her eyes.

"Dulcinea," said Lewis. Another gust and they turned away from the window together, spooning against each other, thinking about wind, windmills.

SUMMER (JUNE 21 TO SEPTEMBER 20)

June 29, 1170, Aleppo and elsewhere, 100,000 dead.
July 8, 1730, Valparaiso, unknown. 300-mile wave.
July 13, 1605, Qiongshan, Hainan, China, 3,000.
July 21, 365, Crete, 20,000. A wave to Alexandria.
August 8, 1303, Crete, 10,000. The same.
August 12, 1042, Palmyra, 50,000.
August 12, 1157, Syria, 20,000, largest in a sequence.
August 13, 1868, Arica, Chile, 25,000. A wave.
August 17, 1668, Anatolia, 8,000.
August 26, 1883, Java, 100,000; eruption of Krakatoa.
August 31, 1886, Charleston, 60.
September 5, 1694, Puglia, 6,000.
September 10, 1509, Constantinople, 10,000.

—from Walton Remfrey's red notebook

CHAPTER 19

THE SKY-BLUE BOOK OF
SUMMER DAYDREAMS

•

Late June was the time of arrivals in Montana, of tourists and ballet troupes and suspect royalty. People who kept grand sporting camps or bred horses, local bigwigs' wives who wintered in the East and deigned to visit only when the average daytime temperature reached sixty, wealthy fishermen from England and Germany, who didn't entirely understand the pattern of thawing and flood, and had to seek out still-clear spring creeks while the café au lait river raged on. European wilderness enthusiasts, oil-well con men, logging crews, union organizers, vast clotty herds of sheep and cattle heading for early market by train before the summer heat could kill the load.

The women of the Sacajawea Club, sultanas of their world, had been galvanized by scandals, stabbings, canings, executions, and a flood. Now the world had gone flat, and the proverbial mud was drying. It was hot, and they arrived at the meeting with great rings under their arms; they forgot the handkerchiefs they'd stuffed up as they drank, and by the end, the inside of their blouses by the wrists were wringed with damp crumpled cloths and melted cornstarch and soda. The arrivals were a relief—mysterious, or reassuringly cyclical, or fizzily open-ended. Local rumors were the same old thing: Eugenia's husband was again expected to visit, Mrs. Woolley had broken it off with her chauffeur, Rex's lawyer had managed to hunt down the man who had sold him nothing in Gardiner, and both Samuel Peake and Lewis Braudel seemed to be spending their nights away from their rooms in the Elite.

"You can't believe that nasty piece of work Irina," said Vinca Macalester. "They probably both turned her down, and she's having her revenge. But I heard a different rumor: Eugenia's husband is dying. A friend who lives in Provo heard something about a heart attack."

"Hard to die if you don't exist," said Margaret. "Do you think they're even still married?"

Dulcy had been thinking the same thing, but Margaret surprised her. Now they fell silent because Eugenia had just entered the dining room: she was showing off her new cook, and her shell-pink silk dress made her seem like the single largest item in a room of beefeaters. After a winter of dormancy, she'd had every inch of the hotel scrubbed and spruced; after months of accepting Gerry's drunken body as drapery in her hallways and apparently in her aunty bed, word was that she'd sent him home to his empty house, and that he'd once again sobered up. "He's dry drunk now, and mean," said Samuel. "This is when the drunks of town should hide."

Dulcy began to understand that Eugenia's pattern of lassitude and furious action was a kind of seesaw: she stayed still as long as she could, then burst into action, then fell quiet again and stored up a fresh batch of worry. Now she was her own volcano, and her flossy hair and pearls billowed as she handed out the new menu. The chef was *from Europe, very exciting*, but Dulcy wondered if *Europe* meant one of Irina's cousins. The waiter used sign language to steer her toward safe appetizers, but he was hint-free about the main course. Now, as he delivered their plates and she peered down at a beige pile, she was sure she'd been right.

Leonora Randall was having pale food, too: scallops in a cream sauce, with mushrooms and baby onions. "Lovely, isn't it?" Eugenia asked, sticking to wine. Margaret, profoundly nice, and lucky in her choice of chicken, said it was all delicious, and Vinca, who was pregnant again, said she didn't have much of an appetite, and Dulcy said the effort was promising.

"You wound me, dear," said Eugenia. "Have you even noticed the new awning?"

Dulcy and the others had mostly noticed that Gerry Fenoways had entered the room, and was walking straight toward Eugenia, who had her back to the door. He looked leaner and years younger. He greeted them all now as if he'd never not been perfect, but what was his alternative? He put a proprietary hand on Eugenia's cushioned shoulder, and she looked up at him as if he were a spider on the ceiling and she was judging the distance for a swat. "My dear," he said, "I need to have a brief word with you."

"Well, Gerald, I'm entertaining. Perhaps in the morning?"

"Perhaps in the lobby, now," said Gerry.

"No," said Eugenia.

Gerry studied her. Margaret began to search through her bag for some unknown item. "Things have been a bit of a blur," he said, "and I haven't handled myself or my business well, but the time has come to have a heart-to-heart with Uncle Errol about our investments."

Eugenia sipped her wine. "You know he's fragile, dear. Didn't he address your questions in his last letter?"

"I can't recall what questions I asked, in all honesty. I intend to visit him. He would be my uncle, my blood. You only married the man!"

He laughed, and though Dulcy did think he made a point, it was a horrible sound. They all watched Eugenia reach for the glass again.

"I can't allow you to exhaust him, Gerald. I'll see him soon, and I can pass on your concerns."

"Maybe we should visit him together, Aunty."

Dulcy had some insight into the look that Eugenia and Gerry exchanged: they wanted each other dead. Vinca rose and said she felt unwell, really had to go. Eugenia and Gerry didn't notice—he reached down for Eugenia's wineglass, twirled it, smelled it, put it down hard enough to splash.

Eugenia pushed away from the table, not a very ladylike gesture. "I will not be humiliated by you in public, and I will not let you bully an unwell man. What would your mother say about you foisting yourself in this way on her little brother? Perhaps you'd like to discuss breaking the partnership. It would be easier to do this before Errol buys the next property. We'd rather have the hotel to ourselves."

"I have no fucking intention of giving you anything you want."

"Gerald, perhaps you should simply drink. Not drinking isn't making you any happier."

"You'd like me to kill myself."

"I'd like you to be at ease. I hope that you can achieve some happy balance."

Gerry stared at her, probably wondering what it all meant. Not good things for him, thought Dulcy, getting to her feet to leave while Margaret did the same. Did Eugenia have his trust, or just his money? Had it been both, and now might it not be either?

• • •

The beginning of summer, over three occasions:

They were all invited to a garden party down in the valley, thrown by a man who Grover hoped would invest in his movies. Grover wanted Lewis to go, because he could "vouch for me professionally," and Lewis wanted to go because he was thinking about writing a piece about the humorous ways wretched excess—serious Eastern money—played out on a frontier landscape. Their host had six thousand acres, a spring creek, a mile of river, and a house that had employed most of the region during construction the year before. The owner, Mr. Bartle, had bought boats for guests, and brought in five hundred pheasants and the newest targets. The river was still muddy, and the pheasants were presumably nesting, but a target-shooting picnic and spring-creek fishing would be a fine time.

Samuel was excited, Rex was excited, Dulcy and Margaret planned to be snobby about the house.

That morning Lewis left early for the hotel, hoping for a telegram about his last article. When she saw him a few hours later, waiting for their buggies outside the Elite, he looked ill and angry.

"What's wrong?"

He looked away. "Nothing. I'll tell you later."

They ended up riding with Grover's wife, Clara. She had chestnut curls and a moppet voice and a fitting nickname: Bubbles. She was *beyond happiness* to be reunited with Grovy. "Love him," she said. "Love him, the silly man. We hug and hug."

Maria Nash had limited experience, but *hug* wasn't the word that came to mind when she thought of lovers' reunions. Nevertheless, she smiled along with all the other women and tried to not dwell on how much Clara Dewberry, amazed and happy at *every little thing*, sounded like a pet monkey. Dulcy made herself deaf, and she looked out at the world through the buggy fringe as if she were looking at a stage, the screen of a moving picture, a window on a changing museum.

The house was new, ungainly and brick, a Victorian pile set ostentatiously on a bleak Mongolian plain instead of the lush river bottom. Their host, Mr. Bartle, was extravagantly friendly, gratingly intelligent; his wife wore a plank of turquoise silk that ended midway down her concave shins, and she staggered on nail-thin heels as she led them down the stone path to the gardens and through the bland, velveted main rooms of the house. Rex ran around calling *drinks, drinks*, just as he had at his mother's house, and the host asked questions: should they test the boats today, or wait? Should they play badminton, or shoot a few birds after all?

Someone sane pointed out the mud in the river, the wind in the air, and the fact that the spring creek had sprung a temporary leak. A second and third round of drinks was served, and they milled, waiting for the lunch bell—"a cowboy bell!" according to their ever-enthused host. Samuel kept moving away from Clara, and Clara kept following him. His aversion was palpable, and she seemed to be attached by a string. Grover ignored both of them. Dulcy watched this from the center of the lawn as she listened to their hostess tell plump Margaret about her new diet—only dairy—while Margaret munched on creamed crab toasts with a half smile. They were on Dulcy's right, and Grover and Lewis were on her left. She heard Lewis say quietly, "Take care of the people who love you, Grover. Don't be a shit."

"I don't give a rat's ass, Lewis. Read your own lecture."

The food was good: crayfish bisque, asparagus, chicken potpie. Dulcy let herself drift in and out of overheard conversations. She watched Lewis—she always loved to watch Lewis, but she tried not to be obvious about it—and wondered about his mood. Grover was wooing his host with information about the film company he thought they should invest in, perhaps take over, at the very least ally with. It was revolutionary, bent on telling full stories, whole plays—

"What kind of stories?" asked Lewis.

"Arthurian legends," said Grover primly. "This company—Globe, isn't that perfect?—had an unrelated loss, and the timing would be ideal for an investment."

Bartle, alerted by the word *loss*, made a grinding, inquiring sound in his throat. "Human vagaries," said Grover. "An insane engineer *lost* the money. I'm not quite straight on this, but Mr. Maslingen made a killing on mines after the Boer problem, and then the profit went missing, and then they had to sell a newspaper—"

Dulcy felt the kind of cold-lipped dizziness that came with a faint or stomach flu. She felt so sick she couldn't find any pleasure in the idea of throwing up on Clara, who was so fascinated by the conversation that her chin was almost hooked on Dulcy's left shoulder. Grover rolled on. "And then the engineer's daughter, a *crazy* girl, jumped out a train window. She put them through *hell*. The man's engaged again now, but still."

Lewis finally met Dulcy's eyes. "She killed herself, and that's the beginning and the end of it," he said. "But it does sound like its own long movie."

They all walked to the range; he passed behind her, touching the small of her back, and said, "Keep your head up."

So she did. The men shot first. Dulcy had used a gun once at a friend's farm near Cold Spring, at a candidacy party. People had loved to have Walton at such events because of the way he worked his accent around the normal nasty American political vocabulary. What he said, if a person truly listened, was not in fact complimentary. Clara launched into a monologue on biting insects. Grover bellowed politics, his voice swelling in the air. Lewis, drunk as a skunk, shot very well—she heard people mutter *Philippines*—and claimed all the shards in his cheek heated up next to the warm barrel, and a Bozeman woman he seemed to know—had she known the last mistress?—touched his cheek to see if he was lying.

The idea of Priscilla the mistress worked its way through drinks and panic. It made Dulcy miserable in a new way, and misery made her surly. When Lewis finally met her eyes now, she looked away. She thought of walking down by the river but guessed she might be shot. Dulcy took a turn with the gun and only ticked one out of six disks that Bartle's boys threw in the air. "Try again," said Rex, beaming with his newly happy eyes over his newly bumpy nose.

"Did you remember your glasses?" called Lewis.

This time she obliterated three of the six.

More drinks; onward to the river, which was still huge and brown and deadly. While the guests politely admired the impressive riverboats, some locals tried to explain to the host that pulling them into the river while it was this high, and they were this drunk, was a bad idea. Dulcy wandered off into the cottonwood bottomland. It was green, high-grassed, orchard as a cathedral. It would be a wonderful place to live, if the river didn't rinse you out every few years.

Birds flushed behind her, and she turned. Lewis was running toward her.

A few minutes later, down in the grass, she said, "You knew and you didn't tell me. You let me feel safe."

"You are safe. I'll keep you safe. What the hell do you think happens in my head, when you look at me like that?" he asked.

"Did you know the woman who petted your face?"

"No."

She could have said, did you know her friend, but she left it alone. "Why were you so sour earlier?"

"My sister telegrammed me. My father died."

He went back out to the crowd first. From the voices she guessed Bartle was persisting in putting people in boats, if only to estimate how many would fit. She walked the other way for a few minutes, plucking at the bark and grass stuck in the pleats of her blouse, wanting to be away from these people. She cut back to the river path for easier walking but heard something and moved behind a tree. Through branches and wild clematis she could see Samuel standing ten yards away. He stared blindly at the river, then tilted his head back and closed his eyes. For a horrible moment she thought, he has a gun, and he's going to kill himself, but then she saw that Grover was kneeling in front, and had Samuel in his mouth.

She slid back into the party. No one had noticed she'd been missing.

• • •

Lewis was not going to the funeral, because his stepmother wouldn't have it. He'd just seen his father, and he'd known it would be soon, and they'd left each other on better terms than usual. Dulcy had to understand how different it had been: her father might have been difficult, but she'd loved him and been loved in return.

He explained this later, in bed. She told him what she'd seen in the woods, that Samuel had to be careful. "Leave it," said Lewis. "Samuel's lonely." This had been going on for years, and it was hard on Samuel, because Grover would sleep with anything, male or female. Lewis said she shouldn't waste her pity on Clara, who was willfully blind to all of it (Dulcy hadn't actually thought of Clara), and Grover's wayward affections were only part of the story: he made gentlemen's movies. One was called *Wild William Tell*, but instead of Tell's son and the apple, Grover filmed girls wearing only hats and cowboy chaps, wiggling body parts at Indian archers, who inevitably had to walk closer to check their aim. Sometimes the cowboys got there first.

She giggled until her face was wet. "He showed that?"

"He did," said Lewis. "During filming the rubber-tipped arrows caused unhappiness, but he made piles of money, especially in England and Germany."

The second film was called *Take a Poke at Polly*, and featured girls on a bingo board, with male winners who stepped forward to claim their prizes. "Maybe Grover will try chess for the up market," said Lewis. "More costumes. Think how much fun he'll have with the bishops."

• • •

A week later, Independence Day: the state might not be twenty yet, but its citizens were serious about patriotism, and because of this boosterism and the town's proximity to Yellowstone Park and the train line, the Livingston parade was the largest in the state. Miles Park was packed with milling bagpipers and Masons, Shriners, and tuba players. A Washington and Jefferson flanked a man in a cannon costume, who looked so much like something else that Vinca laughed hard enough to smear her green face paint. The Hunt Club horses were skittish, as were Mrs. Woolley's pacers and a quartet of dapple-gray Arabians. The bicycle club members rode in circles, the grocers' floats handed out candies and fruits early, and the bottling company doled out waxed paper cones of beer and fizzy drinks.

All of the women were costumed but Dulcy and Abigail Tate, who resorted to widowhood for an excuse, and old Mrs. Ganter, who'd resorted to a heart attack. Two Demeters, grain braided into their hair and belted around their waists (Margaret looked quite nice), two matronly Sacajaweas, and three Valkyries (which made no sense at all). The realtor Nesser's knife-nosed fiancée was a cornucopia: Indian corn for a crown, green tomatoes and currant strands dangling in her deep cleavage. One tiny woman was a firework, but they talked her out of lighting the sparklers threaded between patriotically dyed plumes in her hat. Eugenia Knox was Liberty, held together by pins that threatened to give way, suddenly and painfully. The float was designed to look like a Lewis and Clark–era dugout, but it wasn't as beautiful as Joe Wong's, a ship with dragons and fireworks painted on junk-shaped sails. Mrs. Whittlesby, a rigid Manifest Destiny at the prow, hissed down at the spinning ring of candy-seeking, costumed children as the parade began to move: pirates and Brownies, a dragonfly, princesses and Caesars and one very skinny Joan of Arc with a fringed skirt designed to look like a pyre. They darted around the floats, rolling smoke bombs. The horses were wild-eyed, in a trampling mood, and the wails from phosphorus burns would begin soon.

Dulcy walked up Second Street toward the depot, bunting blurring the town. The world was a swarm: people on the sidewalk, pigeons over the depot arch, insects, the wind that didn't quite dislodge the mosquitoes from her neck but made her hat swivel violently and ripped her hair out at its roots. Lewis appeared in his window at the Elite, and she watched him take in the crowd. He saw her and cocked his head; she shook hers, but she began to warm up to the idea.

The lobby was packed with men having five variations on the same political argument, all of them already spilling beer, and no one noticed her climb the stairs. It was strange having her old view of the street while being had from behind, pressed and panting against the window frame while the parade began to roll below.

"Bagpipes," wheezed Lewis. "How fitting."

She curled up with him for a few minutes, then left him flopped on the bed. She'd planned to watch with Samuel, who'd said he'd find a spot in the shade of Sax and McCue's awning. She crossed Second in a gap between shiny backfiring autos and threaded her way between the people who lined the street, and when she turned to look back, she saw that Lewis had roused himself to the window again, and was watching her, smiling and looking beautiful. The bands clashed, block to block, as she made her way, almost catching up with Durr, who paused off and on for shots. And then Samuel called *Maria* from across the street in a lull between drums, and she turned toward him.

Through a gap in the marchers, Grover Dewberry trained a camera on her. "Smile!" yelled Samuel, thinking it was funny, thinking this moment was light.

Her ears roared. Grover kept the camera focused on her as she crossed toward them. She could imagine her own eyes on film, looking out at Victor. Samuel read her face and seemed to draw back as she approached without moving his feet. "No, please, you must take that out," she said. "Please take me out. Can you do that?"

"Of course I can, but why on earth should I?" Grover asked, moving on to the deafening brass band that was marching by. "Don't you know that you're lovely? Not showy, but handsome. Don't you like the way you look?"

"That's not it," snapped Dulcy. "I'm a widow, Grover."

"Which is why you often wear black."

She wanted to smack Grover's face, but he kept it down, an eye on the lens. Her cheeks burned. "Which is why I'm quite embarrassed to have gone to a parade, all happy and waving, and would prefer my husband's family to not see me doing so."

"Are they modern sorts of people? What are the odds they would see something like a film?"

Horribly likely, she thought. "Of course he'll take it out," said Samuel.

"Of course I will," said Grover, looking peeved. "I imagine you're unrecognizable, but I'll do it. And if you're really so worried about your reputation—"

"Why leave the house?" asked Dulcy.

Samuel roused himself again, eyeing the street. "She asked you politely," he said. "But see who's coming up on you now, Grove."

Grover lifted his head and took in the scene he'd been attempting to fit into focus: the police in blue and black, sweating alongside the paddy wagon and the new black-and-yellow automobile, Gerry skipping around from the far side, six-guns glinting in the sun while he waved his arms. The police were trying a new fashion, smocklike shirts with pointy hats, and they looked like Prussian medical assistants, or butchers, or pregnant bakers.

"Film *me*, Mr. Dewberry! Just don't ask me to jump in a river! I have no family left!"

The crowd laughed, with some nervous high notes.

• • •

During the rodeo that afternoon, with Lewis pushing his knees into her back in the row behind, Dulcy covered her eyes like a child when a bull trampled a downed rider. Everyone wore their best summer hats, but no one had plumes like Clara Dewberry. At dusk, during a baseball game played in high wind between teams from Spokane and Idaho Falls, the Livingston women watched Clara's egret and flamingo plumes swivel like a bug's antennae, and by the time the hat was silhouetted by the fireworks show, the feathers were broken strings and straws. Everyone drank gin and lemonade and beer and ended up sticky and dusty at a dance in the new fair buildings, which did not yet smell of shit like the old barns in Westfield.

At the house later she was woozy in the bathtub while Lewis reassured her: Grover would take her out of his idiot film, he would make sure, she needn't worry ever. He washed her hair, her toes, fitting dirty lyrics to patriotic songs. Hands everywhere.

• • •

The weather stayed hot for a week after the rodeo, and the river level dropped. On July 11, she planted more green beans, and popped a first cherry tomato into her mouth. Lewis left for Portland to do an article on the *Century*, and when he returned on the midnight train she listened while he dropped his things and walked directly to the stairs, his hat whirling against the bedroom wall. To fall asleep in the middle of the night now, Dulcy could shut her eyes and see Lewis sitting in the kitchen, reading in the sunlight with his legs akimbo, his face tired and shirt crumpled.

A few days later, a trunk arrived, made out to Lewis at her address. The delivery boys were oblivious, but the people at the station had to be buzzing. When Lewis arrived that evening—he still took the alley to evade Brach, an easier task now that the grapes had grown wild—he was happy to see it, this final gift from his father. He handed her a letter from one of his sisters and lifted out photographs, books and a black cashmere coat, cufflinks and watches and thick portfolios, a sword, a pistol—he checked to see if it was loaded, and when it was, he muttered—an oil painting of a port town, children's books, journals.

He sat back. "That's it, then. We have money, a gun, and a house in France. Not bad." He put the sketch on the windowsill above the kitchen sink. "We could go this winter."

"All right," said Dulcy. "Just this once, I won't argue."

• • •

The idea of a river flotilla persisted. Bartle had purchased more boats, special safe boats, and they'd take them all the way to town. His men had tested everything, and the ride would be only three hours at most. Lewis wanted to write about the notion of traveling along a river for pure sport, and they climbed out of buggies into a late-season cloud of mosquitoes. Dulcy wrapped her scarf around her face and throat, stuffed her hands in her armpits, and took in the scenery through gauze, thinking of Edgar Nash's last clinic. "Notice they don't bother biting me," said Lewis.

James Macalester had ridden with them, sorting flies and waxed lines, nearly poking out eyes with a cane rod while he talked about having delivered six babies in the last three days—what had happened the previous fall? Vinca talked of picnics, but Macalester wanted to fish, not talk. He was sick of talking, and Vinca's vacation ideas had a way of backfiring. He asked Dulcy if she thought they'd be having another earthquake, or possibly a volcano; strange things happened when they tried to relax together.

She smiled. "I don't want to think about it."

"Did you know that you say that often?" he said. "I think it often, when I'm at work, but you say it: *I don't want to think about it.* I hope saying it works."

The women all wore their oldest shoes, skirts and blouses that were flattering but opaque, their best slips, trying to cover the variables of potential wetness. Lewis had wanted Dulcy to wear one of the Martha dresses. He loved them, especially if she didn't bother with wearing other things underneath. Today she agreed to the dress with a thin sweater, but rebelled with a petticoat and drawers, because the idea of what the river current could do to her skirt temporarily outweighed the idea of what he might do with her skirt.

Bartle was still annoyingly jolly. There were four boats of different shapes and sizes, two barge-like things that could hold eight, two squat little flat-bottomed canoes with square backs meant for only two passengers. The men argued about whether they were Eastern riverboats or Indian boats.

Dulcy was a lake girl, raised to fear waves and undertows. When they pushed off in one of the big barges, she could feel wood twist under her feet, and each jolt on the rocks rattled her, and it took a while to grow used to the groaning planks and trust Bartle's men. When she did, when even Clara quieted down, the world was beautiful, and everything moved with the river: trees and birds in the wind, clouds scudding downstream, racing the boat. She'd brought a green tapestry bag with her green notebook, and now she scribbled down a list of the wildflowers she could see on the hills. Passing under a bridge, swallows peered down out of drippy nests.

They stopped when Bartle decided to explore some caves. Lewis waited until he was halfway up the cliff. "Snakes," he said.

"Pardon?"

"Rattlesnakes, Cornelius. Watch where you put your hands."

They reached a wide, slow stretch. The sun burned, and the wind tugged on Dulcy's flower bower of a hat, her sloppily pinned hair. Taking it off to fan herself meant never anchoring it again; she roasted and weighed options while Clara piped on, now claiming she'd seen a stream run uphill. After Dulcy watched Lewis lower his hat in the water and flop it onto his head a second time, she finally took out the pins one after another, dipped her hat in the water, and only gave it a token shake before she plopped it back on her head. Cold water ran down her back and over her collarbone, between her breasts. "Better?" asked Lewis.

"Yes." But the pleasure had worn off by the time they stopped again. She peeled off her shoes and stockings and stood in the river, letting the water numb her ankles. Lewis walked over and looked down at her blue feet, then back up at her face. She could smile back; she could strip him to nothing without anyone knowing.

They picnicked under cottonwoods, on grass flattened in circles by bedding deer. Rex had brought beer, and Bartle's cook had made dried-out meat pies. Grover never aimed his film camera at Dulcy; he hadn't talked to her or to Lewis at all. After the parade she'd sent a note, and Grover had given Samuel a little melted twisted bit of celluloid. Durr had been coming through the yard when Samuel passed it on, moving his studio back downtown. "Where did Dewberry have it developed?" he asked.

Samuel didn't know; why did it matter? Grover had done as Dulcy asked, and Durr needed to stop thinking the worst of people.

Now Margaret photographed Durr photographing the trees. Rex had brought Rusalka, a quiet debut, and they wandered out of sight around a bend in the river. Dulcy lay back and watched the cottonwood tops move against the sky. The trees made popping noises as they swayed, but Grover was talking again, explaining how he was a *visual man*, as if any of them had thought otherwise, as if any of them cared beyond Clara, who said things like *you are such a poet, darling*.

"I'll quote a poem," said Lewis. "'The thing for me is a drunken sleep on the beach.'"

"You're welcome to it," said Grover.

"You have no idea, Grover. Pipe down. Mrs. Nash, would you accompany me? You're the quietest person on this beach."

She lifted her green bag, with her glasses and the green book, into the little canoe-like boat. She wasn't sure that Lewis knew how to handle it, but she was wild to get away, while Grover announced that he was taking the other small boat with Samuel and Macalester's rod. Would Durr film them trying to fish with it?

"I don't think it would be advisable from that boat," said Macalester, taking the rod away.

"I have my own photographs to take," said Durr, climbing into one of the barges with Margaret.

Dulcy clambered into the little canoe. Its sides felt like paper, and the water looked violent. "Keep your eyes in your head," said Lewis. "We're all right. We'll find a place and swim and take a little nap."

He'd left his hat in the barge. "You're getting a sunburn," she said. "Would you like mine?"

"You'll burn your pretty nose."

"Not in the fifteen minutes it'll take to save yours." She dipped the hat again and lowered it onto his head.

"Jesus," said Lewis.

"He doesn't hear you," said Dulcy. "What are you doing?"

"Slowing the boat down, so everyone goes ahead. Then we'll take that channel."

"Do you think it goes all the way through?"

"I don't know," said Lewis. "We may regret it, but right now I only regret not being wet and not ripping your dress off."

"All right," said Dulcy, watching Samuel and Grover disappear.

They found a pool that was just deep enough, and she spread the blanket behind a downed cottonwood. Bodies had never looked so white; sand everywhere despite the blanket. When their skin dried and tightened they went into the water a second time. "Someone will come looking for us," said Dulcy.

"It doesn't matter," said Lewis. But back in the boat, in the main channel, the pace of the current picked up. Dulcy squinted ahead to an obstacle course of rocks and downed trees.

"This was a horrible idea," muttered Lewis. "I'm going to kill us both."

"Pull out," she said. "We can just leave the boat and walk." They came around the bend and had a glimpse of Grover and Samuel.

They were having the same problems with their boat, and Samuel was yelling.

"Hold on," said Lewis. She saw a tree just under the surface ahead, and he pulled hard to the left. Her bag flew into the water. She saw her green book inside it as if it were one of Walton's crackling X-rays, and lunged for it, and went over into cold and gravel and violence.

Under the cottonwood, she opened her eyes. She was tied to the tree and her hair and arms were being pulled from her body. She tried to push up onto her back, to get her legs up into the current, but the water held her down, and something began to wrench at her waist.

It was Lewis, underneath her and then upstream. Her feet found rocks and she gulped air before he dragged her into a sandy backwater. The bag was gone, along with the boat, their shoes, her glasses, and she wept. Lewis fished her braid out of her ripped dress and weeds out of her braid, lowered her on the warm sand, and lay down next to her, with an arm around her head.

They stayed there for a long time, and when they looked up, a boy was standing next to them. "Hey there," said Lewis. "Do you live near here?"

"I do, sir."

"Do you think someone could give us a ride to town?"

"I do."

"We've lost our things. If you find a bag sometime, a green bag with a green book, can we give you a name, and you'd find us? It's very important to the lady. Will you remember the name Mrs. Nash? You could take it to the Elite. Have you seen the Elite Hotel?"

The boy, a burnt gold version of Irving, said *I have* and *I do* again, and Lewis resorted to repeating himself, then pounded the point in by finding a half-dollar in his wet pocket and handing it over. "So," he said finally, "could we find your father and ask him for a ride?"

"All right."

"Do you understand?"

"I do," said the boy, looking downstream.

"Do you have a problem?" said Lewis. "Can we help you with something?"

"Well, not really," said the boy. "I was to get a hook and a rope and bring it back."

"Back where?"

"Back to the drowned man."

He said *drown-ned*. Lewis ran.

• • •

Grover and Samuel had made it another quarter mile before they hit a rock. The barge with the Macalesters and Rex had tried to save both men but managed neither. Samuel had swum to the bank, and they'd stopped him from going back for Grover. Clara and the people in the other barge would now be almost to Livingston, still in ignorance. Dulcy could hear people talking, asking if Grover could swim, but swimming didn't mean a thing in a world of boulders and branches, pressure and broken bones. Grover had anyway hit his head on a rock when the boat first tipped: everyone on the close barge had seen it, and no one thought he could have survived the blow, even if they'd reached him immediately. "Not a chance," said Macalester, sitting next to Samuel on a rock, both of them soaking wet. Margaret and Vinca wept on the beach, and the others walked up the lane to wait for Gerry and the firemen.

"Do they know where Grover is?" Dulcy asked. "Shouldn't we be walking the shore?"

"He's in that hole," said Macalester, pointing. "In a whirlpool. Every few minutes you'll see his arm rising."

When Gerry Fenoways arrived, he asked—clearly knowing the answer—who had drowned, and then he said that he felt the world was just, and his brother was revenged: he couldn't have made this happen, but he could be happy that it had. He watched from shore while Bixby and two firemen tied themselves off to the engine wagon and waded to the nearest rock, climbed on top, and pushed down into the pool with grappling pikes and a noose.

A single arm rose high like a dancer's, and then the body sank again. The second time they hooked Grover and dropped the noose around one of his arms and his head, and they slapped the horses to pull the body free from the pool. His right temple was dented and bloodless, and his eyes and his mouth were open. Samuel knelt down and tried to close both.

DIES IN JAIL: JOHN KLEINMITTILA
PASSES AWAY AFTER DEBAUCH

. . . But why should Park County's citizens be surprised? Six men and one woman have died or endured brain injury while under Sheriff Fenoways' care. Kleinmittila was a well-known character, often seen at all hours around the German Beer Hall. His death followed seizures on the jail floor over this last weekend, when even the other inmates, of necessity a heartless and dissolute lot, begged Sheriff Fenoways to call for medical assistance.

Other incidents: Albert Inkster, executed last month, was rendered an idiot by alcoholic seizures and rumored beatings following his arrest for the stabbing of Lawrence Peck. Mervin Knaab, a former choir director who had also fallen victim to the demon rum, was imprisoned like Kleinmittila, and had treatment denied like Kleinmittila. He has spent the last six months, vacant and ruined, sitting on the porch of the Poor Farm. He is luckier than Myrtle Duncan, arrested following an illegal operation and held on a bond too high for her family to manage, who died of infection after two days of begging for a doctor. Sheriff Fenoways chooses now to prosecute her abortionist, rather than question if his dereliction hastened her death. Finally, Lennart Falk: we provide his full story, as well as a photograph taken before he visited our city, another taken while under Chief Fenoways' roof, and as he appears now, despite the best medical care possible.

—The Livingston Enterprise, August 1, 1905

CHAPTER 20

THE PEACH BOOK OF LOST THINGS

•

People drowned all the time in Westfield, mostly health-seekers on Chautauqua Lake and people doing stupid things that involved the Lake Erie breakwall. Boys would leap in and be trapped against the rocks, roll like a pebble in a polishing drum until they had no skin. The men who fished out of Barcelona Harbor had been in the habit of dying, too, especially when Martha and Elam had been young, and cargo and passenger ships had still moved between Buffalo, Cleveland, Toledo, and Detroit.

Martha had been full of stories about dead boys before Dulcy's brothers headed off to school. Philomela had been the world's most luxuriant stepmother, but Martha never warmed to them, and they reciprocated. Her tales were elliptical, cagey, manipulative: stories for the boys about Chester *who had jumped from the mast and hit that thing in the water . . .* There was a girl watching on the dock in every story, which made Dulcy wonder what Martha really had seen. The strangest telling had a ghostly vision appear to the Dock Girl as she walked by the harbor alone one night: *Naked, but smooth all over. No parts, nothing left like that, erased with his soul by the rocks.*

That got the Boys, at least until they stopped believing in anything but money.

• • •

Samuel didn't write the article immediately. The night of the drowning he tried to jam a butter knife into his chest, a half-hearted but nonetheless anguished effort, and Lewis and Durr took turns sitting with him. The next day they found that Clara, who had banished the town's women and slammed the hotel room door on Eugenia, had packed through the night to load Grover and their things on an early train. She'd given Irving ten dollars to facilitate this and keep his mouth shut until she left town. She'd headed west, and she talked of Portland.

Dulcy wouldn't mourn Grover: she hadn't liked or trusted him. She had a harder time about the green book. The fat tears rolling down her cheeks that night were for the symbolism of her small idiot loss: did this mean that her old life had disappeared?

"I'm not going to dignify that with a comment," said Lewis. He said it sympathetically, naked in bed, wiping her snotty face, being kind even though he'd had a hard time with Samuel, hiding guns and belts. "We'll buy another book. You can write down everything you remember, and I'll ask questions, and you'll remember more."

"I think I'm better off just living," said Dulcy.

Samuel had been trying to alternate sensationalism with wholesomeness in the *Enterprise* (hopheads flanking baseball photos, accounts of historic murders above profiles of the town's lovely unmarried teachers). He'd packed June with brides and stories of Chinese prostitution in Billings, and July with parties and William Clark's newest sins, but now, in August, he gave up on balance. The world, lately, had been all about sensationalism, anyway. A week after Grover died, he published two stories, one a description of the Poor Farm scam, the other a detailed account of Lennart Falk's saga and beating and failure to recover. Samuel had bribed the jail warden with a printing job and published a list of two dozen beating victims who'd gone on to spend time at the Poor Farm, with accounts of their damage. He described the female inmates who'd been forced to service the Fenoways brothers, though he had to be roundabout with details.

"He writes about how Falk is doing now," Dulcy said. "How would he know?"

"He contacted the man who retrieved Lennart," said Lewis, poker-faced. They were having lunch with Margaret; Dulcy was quite sure Margaret knew they slept together. "Apparently one brother will be coming through soon. Not the one who came before."

She left town for a walk with Margaret and the Macalesters on the day of the visit. They made it most of the way up Livingston Peak, and they only gave up when they nearly became part of a landslide of scree. By the time they got back the story had spread: Lewis and Samuel had met Ansel Falk at the Elite, and walked with him down to the police station, where they found Gerry asleep on the floor behind his desk—he was off the wagon again, still celebrating Grover's death. Bixby was on duty and recoiled, but Ansel Falk greeted him quite pleasantly, thanked him for having tried to defend his brother (Bixby admitted to Samuel that he'd put in only a token protest at the time of Lennart's beating, but Lennart had remembered some moment of kindness), and began to slap Gerry across the face, trying to wake him for a fight.

Gerry, who retched blood between benders now, wouldn't wake. He lay on the floor, mouth open, tilting his head from side to side like a carp looking for life outside the fishbowl. Ansel Falk tried a few more blows, then gave his own head a little c'est la vie shake, opened his trousers, and urinated on Gerry's face, into his open eyes and mouth.

Falk buttoned up while they listened to Gerry choke. "He is bringing it into his lungs," Falk said. "Perhaps he'll die of pneumonia.

Please send us a wire if this is the case, and otherwise let him know that one of us will be back. We're taking our time, not forgetting."

Samuel's life was filled with unprintable tales. Despite his account of Lennart's beating, and the abuse of Gerry's prisoners, the city fathers didn't force the sheriff out of office. He gave up his Poor Farm stake—Eugenia's part of it hadn't been made public in the article, which Dulcy thought was cowardly on Samuel's part—but Gerry still knew more about the mayor and town bankers than these men thought they could endure.

• • •

Lewis bought a typewriter and took over the desk in the spare bedroom. He enjoyed watching Brach in the yard below, trying to understand the man and his constant noise, and while he worked, Dulcy pulled out the surviving notebooks and lay on the room's small bed. She worried that the peach family book might make her resent Walton's failures, and she started with the pink book of verse instead, flipping to the last pages she'd skimmed in Seattle, searching one last time for clues to Victor's lost fortune.

He'd been intent, near the end, on what money did to the soul. Dante, Shakespeare, Ben Jonson, Benjamin Franklin. *Money has never made man happy, nor will it.* In August, as Walton seasicked his way to Africa, he'd shifted to gold—*Love is the only gold; A man who hoards up riches and enjoys them not is like an ass that carries gold and eats thistles*—and then to diamonds: *Nature has made a pebble and female. The lapidary makes the diamond, and the lover makes the woman.*

He'd always loved Hugo. Before the *boil me, burn me* note at the end of every journal, he reverted back to ominous generalities—*Jewels being lost are found againe, this never, / T'is lost but once, and once lost, lost for ever* (Marlowe)—and ended with Aeschylus, and the essence of the problem: *Inscribe it in the remembering tablets of your mind.*

Perhaps he'd intended to move on to opals and emeralds. Dulcy had never known him to take an interest in a rock once it left the ground, and she wondered again if simply he'd gone to a Cape Town slum and given the money all away. He lacked religion, but not guilt.

Brach's refugee cat watched his owner from the half-roof, and Lewis lifted the window to let it in. The cat lay down next to Dulcy and purred, eyes like translucent aquamarines in profile, and she reached for the peach book to kill time and keep the cat close.

She looked at the last real entry, made in Cape Town on September 22, 1904—*The bookbinder's wife, so beautiful in lapis silk, looked only at my right eye. She knows that it will fall out. Perhaps she could cure me*—then toughened up and went to the beginning. She'd expected rants, but it wasn't that way. A front section was given to short entries for people he'd never see again: the way a dead friend had looked after a cage accident in Ireland, his first sight of miners in Africa, the glimpse of a lonely little boy weeping with a nurse in Paris.

People Walton loved earned their own pages, with new leaves pasted in when he ran out of space. He wrote about only remembering his mother's long brown hair. He recorded the Boys' growth and commented on their brilliance. He described Carrie as an infant, swaddled and wrapped and placed in points of honor like *an ornament, a silver dish*. He liked listening to her play piano when he was sick; he anticipated her loveliness and her laziness; he raged at her lack of interest in travel and the *lack of balls* in her beaux.

Of Philomela: *They should have named her Filamenta. There is nothing to her. What am I to do? I tried this joke on her, and she grew angry, then just as suddenly good fun.* And later: *Of course I am guilty. I have killed her, sooner or later. I have some relief in the notion that she has never really lived, anyway.*

Of his father-in-law Elam: *My, how he'll hate me when he knows what I've done to his daughter.*

Of Martha: *Last night, watching her tease the girls on the porch about spiders, it finally occurred to me that we would have done much better together than I ever did with the daughter. Of course she lacks my kind of curiosity, but still, I had a pleasant rest this afternoon imagining an awakening.*

Every time Walton saw Woolcock after an absence, he was sure that Woolcock's nose had grown, and he'd pasted in a profile with penciled measurements: he thought his friend suffered from the same disease as J. P. Morgan. Dulcy's eyes slid over her section, but one entry from the end of 1901 caught her. After the engagement was broken, after she'd hidden in Westfield, she'd returned to the city to sail to Southampton and Africa, as had been planned for months. Walton, still ignorant of the pregnancy, had been enraged—there was no way for him to disentangle his financial ties with Victor, and the situation was wretched and awkward. Walton and Henning met for a drink (and perhaps a ramble, but she'd have to cross-reference with the black book).

I confessed my fears, not that he should feel sympathy; I said I wished to make her change her mind, but Falk said she should not, she was better off even if she's ruined. He maintains that M is an angry man, a violent man who has killed two others in fights, when drunk enough to erupt; after the break with D, he had Falk bring him a girl, and he beat her. He can achieve the mechanics of the act, but he cannot truly enjoy it, and Falk maintains that sooner or later he would lash out at Dulcy in this manner.

At any rate, it's done.

She left the notebooks out for Lewis to read. A few nights later, he said, "You have to get rid of these, Dulcy. You can't have your father's name everywhere in this house. Anyone you hired to clean, anyone with a nose who finds a way in while we're traveling, will see that name."

But she couldn't cope with the idea of destroying them, or even ripping Walton's name out, and so the next morning they carried his notebooks and trunk out into the framed-in side of the greenhouse that Durr had vacated. They piled the trunk with pots and bags of soil and plant potions, the cane furniture that Dulcy planned to lounge on someday, but bits of Lewis's new knowledge leaked out over the next weeks: Would she ever want to go to Constantinople again? Did she want to try making cassis that fall?

They went to the fair and watched the horse races, and Dulcy, scanning the vegetable entries, felt smug. Lewis, in a period of literally rude good health, worked every day and came to the house every evening. She was sure she'd love him even if she didn't get to see him climb a wall nightly for her benefit, but there was something wonderful about the way he crested the thing, dropped, and pulled off his collar while he was still walking toward her. Maybe this was the only point left to him keeping a room in the hotel: silliness, abandon. Let us unfetter each other, he said, moving down the buttons on her blouse.

From the shady bedroom they could see the minister at his kitchen table, staring fixedly at Dulcy's street-side porch, or sometimes watch from the bed while the couple tweezered leaves off their velvet lawn. "What's her given name, anyway?"

Dulcy had no idea. They lay across the bed on their stomachs and watched Brach's cat as it traveled along the rock wall. "He likes me better than that old shit," said Dulcy.

"Of course he does. Did you have one when you were a kid?"

"I did," she said. "A gray longhair named Puck and a black cat named Bucca Dhu," the only animal Walton had ever liked enough to name. "And I had a crow named Pixie and a turtle named Piss-Willie. And spaniels named Pearl and Earl and an Airedale named Maude."

"Jesus," said Lewis. "What's a Bucca Dhu?"

"A storm fairy. Did you have pets?"

"My father had setters. I had good mutts and a cat. My sisters called it Percival."

"What did you call it?"

He grinned. "Dick."

Lewis said he might write about Brach, if only he could bear the idea of inhabiting that brain. He'd thought about writing a series of interconnected short stories, profiles of real people. He showed her a few pages about Durr in Peking, during the Boxer Rebellion, trying to do the right thing, remonstrating fellow soldiers who killed on a whim, loving the food despite the ruin of his intestines. When the German ambassador was assassinated, and the odds of being hacked to bits became overwhelming, he'd stopped caring. Lewis said you could watch Durr's eyes while he talked about it, and wonder what else they'd seen, and let your mind swivel about. A person could be in Africa or Asia as a tourist, and see awful things, and think they knew how bad it can be, but it was different to be there as a soldier, watching a bunkmate kill someone for amusement, or wondering what it would be like to be torn apart.

He wrote a little about his father, trying to imagine how his father could have forgotten his world enough to fall in love with his mother. But the problem was opaque: Lewis barely remembered his mother, and this version of his father was unrecognizable. If he'd been a man who'd invited empathy, ever professed to have an imagination or shown love, something might have been possible. "I don't want to write about an idea," he snapped. "I'd wind up with something completely symbolic and idiotic. And I can't imagine being someone like him."

• • •

On a rainy morning in early September, Eugenia Knox came down to the lobby in black and told Irina that her husband was dying, and that Irina should tell Gerry she'd return as soon as possible. She boarded a train for Utah. The ladies felt a certain relief. "Well, *finally*," said Vinca. "Maybe she'll be fun again when she gets back."

Dulcy, who was in a foul mood with a sore tooth, didn't recall a time when Eugenia was fun. The pain gnawed into her mind, burrowed right through her terror of a dentist, and after she writhed through a second night, Lewis pulled out Walton's medicine box to rub some lumpy cocaine on her gums. At the first vague glimmer of light, the roosters across the street dueled, the town magpies erupted in anger, and Brach began to sing a hymn.

"Say the word and he's dead," murmured Lewis, face in the pillow. "No one will ever know."

She mixed more aspirin and bit down on a wet cloth. "His wife would know."

"His wife would clean up after me."

Dr. Hickman's office was on the corner of Callender and Second; he looked in her mouth and winced, numbed her gums with a stronger paste that made her brain jump, slid in a needle while an assistant told her to shut her eyes. She couldn't manage that, and he resorted to lowering a mask onto her face, which cured the problem of the jumpy brain. In the meantime she'd pressed back so hard that her fingers had turned white, and the leather on the chair arms remained dented after the assistant pried her hands free, after the mask had taken effect.

When she woke with a gap in her mouth, they left her slumped in the chair. She listened to them prep their next victim through the thin wall, a cocky man circling dread. The assistant slid back into the room and murmured that people were often *difficult and confused when they first came around.* Dulcy managed to turn her head and lift her arm; her wristlet told her it was only ten in the morning. Her view took in the roofline across the street, deep blue sky above rich red brick, Joe Wong's children and other workers pinning up laundry to dry on the roof.

A few minutes later she was back on the sidewalk, rocking on her heels and blinking in the light. She resolved to try for the Elite, a block away—she could ask Irina for the key: who would care, anymore? But the Sanborn surveyors, almost at the end of their Sisyphean task, stood in the middle of Second Street, gesturing at Joe Wong, yelling about tunnels. Dulcy thought first of a fire—Durr stood by the laundry and the studio, looking as if he'd inhaled smoke—but even if her face was too numb to smell, her eyes still worked, and no one seemed to be calling an engine, though onlookers gathered. "What is wrong?" she asked Durr.

Her words probably hadn't come out clearly, but he didn't seem to notice. "A dead man," he said. "In the basement. In Joe's storage area."

"Not mine!" yelled Joe. "Under the hotel. The tunnel door all of a sudden open, boxes all over. I have no keys."

"Not his," said a Sanborn. "Just in one of those tunnels under the hotel, but certainly dead."

• • •

Gerry, in a fresh rage over Eugenia's departure, was summoned. He told Sam's competitor, the *Post*, that Livingston had a Ripper. "A Frankenstein. This body has been butchered to a level beyond my long experience. Eviscerated and reattached."

This body was too aromatic for Hruza's Cold Storage, so Deputy Bixby had ice blocks loaded into the shed behind the police station where the disassembled scaffold was stored. Bixby asked Macalester for help, because the county doctor had shingles, and Macalester—retching—took two minutes with the body before he slammed into Gerry's office. "Your murdered man was autopsied and embalmed," he hissed. "Badly, but there it is. I assume the death was natural, because the heart, returned to the chest cavity, was malformed."

"Who?" asked Gerry. "Why?"

"I took the liberty of removing this card from the casket," said Macalester, flicking the piece of stained paper onto the desk. It was the death certificate for Mr. Errol Arthur Knox, dead since September of 1904, survived by Eugenia Knox, disposition pending.

Within hours most of the story was clear: Eugenia had hidden her husband's death—hidden her husband—to avoid foreclosure and to continue receiving Errol's army pension and other payments. There was no money in the Elite accounts, and when Gerry inquired into the real estate the Knoxes had used to secure the loan for the hotel, he found a building with an address fifty feet into the Great Salt Lake.

Gerry owned nothing, and he owed a great deal. He refused to pay for the burial of his uncle, his last relative, and he splintered Eugenia's apartment until the heavy carpets were crunchy and glittering with all of her gaudy cut glass. Then he sobered up, and the town waited. Lewis thought this was interesting—Gerry might possibly be better off without any family at all.

• • •

A few nights later, they woke to a woman's screams from the Braches' house, on and on, interspersed with smashing glass, a huge slamming sound and silence. "He's killing her," said Dulcy.

Lewis was already getting dressed, hopping into the Bluebeard room to see while he struggled with a pant leg. Lights were on up and down the street, and the screams resumed and blended with Brach's bellow. But someone had a telephone, and an automobile whirled around the corner: Gerry driving the new police car, Bixby in the passenger seat. Dulcy and Lewis watched from the window as the men ran into the house and a moment later dragged Brach out onto the sidewalk. Gerry kicked the minister until he was as bloody as his wife, who watched from her lamp-lit doorway. There was no wind; they could hear the neighbors protest, and Bixby attempted *that's enough, sir, surely*, while Gerry raged. "I'm breaking your hands so you can't use them on her again," he howled, winded but still flailing and stomping. "Your feet so you can't kick the lady. I'm tempted to blind you, so you can't lecture from that fucking God book again, but maybe she'll just burn it while you're rotting in my cell."

• • •

On September 10, after reading about an earthquake in Calabria— five hundred dead? five thousand? the pope wept to hear the news— Dulcy was making jam when someone knocked. Her fingertips were a bad blue, dead-man blue, from pulling off grape skins to chop with the sugar, the way Martha had taught her. Dulcy had thought of using a new recipe that dispensed with this skin worship, but she'd chickened out, and now she had a steaming copper pot of purple paste.

When she opened the door, it took a moment to recognize the boy standing there with a burlap bag, and more minutes to go find a coin for his reward. He left the mess in the burlap, and she went ahead and jarred the jam. The metal lids (no wax, a real rebellion against

Martha) were sealing in the background—*pop pop pop*—when she finally reached inside the burlap for the lost green bag, and into the green bag for her mangled eyeglasses and the lost green book.

It was more or less intact, but the spine felt full of gravel, as if the river had forced its way in, though she could find no hole. She didn't know what strange African substance had been used to pad the cover, what kind of horse-hoof glue would coagulate back into something as hard as the source. She pried apart the wet pages, trying not to mind that some ink had been washed clean. The poppy petals from Salonica had dissolved, but left an imprint on the pages, and that was good enough: she felt as if she'd found her childhood. She carried the book up to her bedroom and left it on top of the bookshelf to dry.

Beware the fury of a patient man.

—John Dryden, "Absalom and Achitophel"

CHAPTER 21

THE FALL

•

At the end of September they went to Butte for the reckoning. She'd been tired for weeks, not ill, just sleepy. She'd stop in the middle of a task to curl up in her bed or on the couch or inside the hammock down by the greenhouse. She could be mid-row picking beans or halfway through a recipe. On her usual book-sorting day at the library, she fell asleep at the table, and she missed flagrant errors in Samuel's purple prose.

She explained while Lewis was going up and down a ladder, loading the bookshelves Durr had helped them build in the Bluebeard room. "We saw the best doctors in London," she said. "I had no reason to doubt them." But really, had they been good? They'd saved her but they'd botched the surgery, and nearly killed her again. When she saw their faces, she remembered the general drift, rather than specifics: this thing had happened because she'd been inherently flawed, both physically and mentally. It had been enough to set Walton off on a rant about St. Augustine and original sin.

Now she hated them all over again, even as the whole warm notion they might have been wrong about everything settled in. Maybe she could have a child. Maybe having one wouldn't kill her.

Lewis reached down for another stack of books; he was smiling. "Well?" she said.

"Hand me that last stack and I'll come down and carry you around the house. It's fucking wonderful as long as you're happy."

She thought she was happy. She handed up more books. "Or at least," said Lewis, "this is wonderful news as long as we find a very, very good doctor."

"Not here," she said.

They sat across from each other in the lounge car for the ride to Butte, friends who happened to find themselves on the same train. She'd brought along an issue of *McClure's* and read an Ida Tarbell piece on what the Standard Oil Company had done to Kansas: bad pipelines, price manipulations. What should Kansas do? What *could* Kansas do? She watched Lewis sleep, scribble rants against quacks, stare out a window.

At the Thornton, they had a grand dinner. They had never openly shared a bedroom together, but there were many things they'd never done together. In the morning she made him wait at the hotel so that she could walk to the appointment alone. It was a nice practice, the kind where she was the only person waiting, very briefly, on an overstuffed couch. Once inside, she gave a bowdlerized version of what the doctors in London and Africa had said, of the sheer impossibility of what seemed to have happened. She couldn't tell if the doctor, the young president of the hospital (Lewis had outdone himself) believed her or not, but he was clearly used to unraveling women, and he tried not to patronize: She had two fallopian tubes, and the one on her right was perfectly healthy; no idea why these men she'd seen hadn't thought so. She was perfectly healthy—her ectopic mess had been chance, just chance. If Mrs. Blake feared a second ordeal, he wanted to reassure her. Chance killed people every day, but it wasn't going to kill her this time, because she was—he said again—perfectly healthy. An April baby, he guessed. Perhaps she should take some time to think, but otherwise his congratulations to Mr. Blake, and please, they shouldn't worry, and should continue to do *whatever they wanted. Doing things* kept couples fit—the doctor and his wife had three children, and a happy, perfectly healthy life. After the baby he'd give Dulcy some items to delay a second child.

Lewis was waiting outside; they had some fun calling each other Mr. and Mrs. Blake, which gave Dulcy a little time to let it all sink in. He said there was a fire downtown, and they walked over to gawk with everyone else. Though the city hadn't yet filled with smoke, the color of the sunlight had changed to the yellow magnetic feel of a tornado, the whole nature of the world shifting as they passed through. The air gave everyone high cheekbones and a consumptive dark-eyed look, and Lewis watched the fire like a little boy, beautiful and in awe. Dulcy was sure she felt a vibration under her feet, not an earthquake but the buzz of the engines and pumps that kept people alive in the honeycomb under the sidewalk. The wind grew, the flames shot higher, and then suddenly the clouds opened to a drenching rain, dousing the fire and turning the sooty streets to rivers.

• • •

She didn't argue about his proposal this time. "I'm not going to be the father of a bastard," said Lewis. "It's unkind of you to think I might, given my childhood. It upsets the hell out of me that you have a moment of doubt about this."

"I don't have any doubt about you," said Dulcy. "It's everything else."

He called her "doom girl" for a few days, and then they got back on a train for Fort Benton, which seemed out of the way enough. She wanted to sign her real name for this real marriage, but he talked her out of it; in the end she pruned her lies down to *Maria Dulcinea Braudel*. They had a nice night in a hotel—a second hotel—by the Missouri.

Lewis wanted to leave, despite a lack of news about Victor or Falk brothers, despite the fact that Leda Remfrey had been declared dead. He wanted a city doctor for her, and he wanted anonymity. But Dulcy wanted fall, and even a dwindling garden was better than no garden. No sweet leaves here like Westfield, flat wet fermenting layers; it was a dry, clear place. She wrapped herself in a blanket most afternoons for a nap, but the dreams and half-dreams of Victor dying returned: one night she cooked his arm, and in another she watched him tacking back and forth on a sailboat on the Yellowstone, looking for her. The harder nightmares were peripheral: hearing the scrape of a chair in the kitchen in the middle of the night, and somehow knowing it was Lewis, but the snakelike arm coming up the stairs was Victor's. That night, she screamed and pulled herself out of the dream, and then was bereft when she realized Lewis was still away. Another dream had her waking to a man watching her from the chair by the bed, and she was back in Seattle, in sea air and the smell of Victor's weirdly cloying cologne. This time when she screamed Lewis was home, and he finally talked her into the idea of leaving for California within the next few weeks. Soon.

She thought about the child constantly, moved it though the future—toys, terrifying illnesses to avoid, first books, what apples to make sauce out of this fall for a first meal next summer, what the baby would call them, whether it would still be snowing when it was born, if they didn't leave for San Francisco. She wasn't sick to her stomach like Carrie, and she moved through the house and town believing, most of the time, that the world was normal. But she did abnormal things, like failing to cover her garden during the first frost. She lost most of her flowers, and half of her tomatoes, but she couldn't find the energy to think it mattered.

Brach stayed in Gerry's jail, and his wife never looked in their direction when she sat in her backyard watching birds. Lewis stopped bothering with the pretense of leaving for the hotel. They hadn't told anyone yet, about any of it, but it was a matter of cocooning themselves, and thinking it through, and Lewis traveling. Samuel was all about revenge; Margaret had her own life, and her own secrets. No one said a word to either of them about Lewis's obvious presence, and Dulcy found she didn't care about what people thought—there were ways to pare down a life other than running away. Storekeepers did not seem to regard her as sinful, and when she dozed through the next meeting of the Sacajaweas, no one offered more than an extra slice of cake. Life skidded by.

But in early October, Lewis woke up sick, and kept being sick, and she called Macalester to the house without bothering to explain. The salvo of fevers shook her out of her daze. He was worse than she'd ever seen him, and it made no sense: surely he would have stored up strength over these last few weeks of good health. Macalester said he was worried about Lewis's liver and heart.

Dulcy couldn't imagine his body disappearing. Each time his fever broke she wanted to curl up into a ball next to him. She didn't understand why some people did well with this illness and others didn't; she didn't understand how he could have so much life in other ways and not throw this off. When she woke up with a jolt of worry about Walton instead of Lewis one morning, it threw her into a day of rage and resentment before she settled into all the things that were different: this was Lewis, youthful and her lover. He was a survivor, without self-pity. This was just bad luck.

After a full week of intermittent fever, he sat up one morning, ate most of the food in the kitchen, and wrote ten pages on the piece about bribery in the national parks. He'd have to go to Denver to finish it. She said she wanted him to see a specialist while he was there; he said he'd wait for California, or wherever they ended up. Did she want to go to New York, instead? He'd find a blond wig so that she could take in every restaurant she'd missed.

She'd been cooking obsessively, trying to fatten him up, going on her own tangents: three days of tomato sandwiches; sudden yearnings for shellfish, root beer, plums. But when she thought of New York she didn't think of food. On the day Lewis left, she handed him a package to mail from Denver. He looked down at *Mrs. Alfred Lorrimer* and put the tiny sweater back on the table.

"She'll only be worried. It's selfish, Dulcy. And he'll find out. Save it for our own."

"This can't go on and on like this," said Dulcy. "I can't bear this." But what, as he pointed out, had she thought would happen when she threw her life out the train window?

It snowed the day after Lewis left. People talked about how this would pass, but she pulled out the gray shearling and walked to the library to look up the town in France where Lewis now owned a house. She peered down with her river-bent glasses: it was right on the ocean, only a few miles from the Spanish border. There were vineyards there, and fishing boats, and a market. Lewis said the house had a rock wall around the garden and high ceilings.

The next day a huge warm wind blew over town, and she ripped out frosted plants in the sunlight, wearing herself out in the right way. She went to bed early, and woke a little after midnight, thinking she heard a chair scrape, and that he was back, before she thought of the wind, and all the other reasons for noise. It would be days.

She opened her eyes again to a flare of light, a cigarette and then the lamp, a man in the chair by the bed. Pretty taffy hair, green eyes, a little worn at the mouth compared to her memory.

"Sorry to wake you, Mrs. Nash."

She wanted to roll away from him, curl up and shut her eyes again, but her spine and the back of her head would be vulnerable. When she looked into his face she knew he wanted her brains on the floor.

"Say hello," said Victor.

"Hello, Victor."

"Aren't you dead? So many nights I dreamt I'd killed you, and I went to your funeral. Then I saw you in the film," he said. "Henning said he didn't believe it at first, but you know that I always look too long at everything. I saw you in Yellowstone Park, sitting on a bench, and I saw you crossing a street toward me, angry, so entirely yourself. Henning had to agree that it was you, and that you might likely still be in the town where that sorry little grubworm Grover Dewberry filmed a silly parade. His idiot widow made us take the film. A deal's a deal, said Henning. He's sorry now; he always did try to protect you."

Dulcy watched him, her head still pressed into her pillow. Victor leaned back, and the chair creaked. He was bigger than she remembered, with a sharper nose. "So we came here, with a photograph—a bad print—and showed it to the girl at the hotel Mr. Dewberry used. 'Perhaps Mrs. Nash,' says the girl, 'but I'm not sure her figure is that good.'" Victor seemed to enjoy this. "Isn't envy interesting? At any rate, 'What's she like?' Henning asked. 'Dull,' says the girl. 'Maria likes to garden.'"

Victor laughed, the real laugh. "Dull. Imagine. And a greenhouse, built by a German photographer: there it was with the first interview, no need to ask around, which would anyway be problematic. We checked in, and Henning put in some time with the girl while I sat in the window and watched for you on the very street I'd seen in the film. The girl told him that you had lovers—maybe the German, maybe a man from the newspaper, a little Jew surveyor, a doctor, a police chief. On and on. She is no friend of yours. Have you been having your way with all these men, being a merry widow?"

Dulcy could only assume that Irina hadn't mentioned Lewis because she wanted to protect him. Or maybe she had, and Victor was waiting to get to the point. "I was alone," said Dulcy. "For the first time in my life, I was truly alone."

"I don't believe you," said Victor. "If you lied about being dead, why would you tell the truth about any of it? And there's the matter of this hat, dangling on your bedstead like a flag on an alp." He held one of Lewis's bowlers between two fingers. "A good hat, I must say. Not a drunk cowboy's hat. Maybe the newspaperman, after all, but Henning thinks he's found the right person."

Now he twirled it on one finger. Dulcy watched it spin and shut her eyes.

"Let's leave the scene of your lover's triumph, why don't we, and go downstairs."

She climbed out of bed, tugging at a blanket. She did not show yet, but she was only wearing a shift. Victor's eyes veered away and he jerked open her wardrobe, found a shawl and threw it at her. She wrapped it around her shoulders before she stopped. He wouldn't touch her; he didn't want to touch her. "Why must we go down? What are you going to do?"

"Because we have some things to do, before we get on a train together," said Victor. "I want my pound of flesh. I mourned you, Dulcy. I sniveled like a baby for months. You were going to make everything better again, and instead you made it much, much worse." He noticed the open green notebook, forgotten and finally dry by the window, and picked it up and threw it hard enough for flakes of plaster to pop out of the wall. He threw the book again as she ran for the stairs, so that it tumbled down into the kitchen in front of her, and he roared on: he'd had to get on a train to find her, to go to a new place, naked of protection; she knew he hated new places. She had run away, she had chosen to be away from him but not die, she had lied, she seemed perfectly content.

The wall of rage followed her to the bottom of the stairs. A man who looked like Henning stood by the kitchen door holding a mallet. He handed it over as Victor's hand closed around her wrist, recoiled, took hold again and latched on to her skin in a way he'd never have been able to if the touch were tender. Victor jerked her out the door into the cold dark and dragged her toward the greenhouse, swinging the mallet in his other hand. She looked down at the paint already rubbing off her porch steps, felt the way the ground under the crisping grass was stiff with frost. She was moving too quickly to see anything ahead of them clearly, but as they lurched along she saw flashes of two men watching them approach, only Falks, no Durr, no Samuel, no Lewis.

"Where's your brother?" said Victor.

"Looking for the man," said one of the Falks. He looked young and miserable; Ansel, probably. It was one thing to piss in a man's mouth, another to commit oneself to actual violence.

"There is no man," screamed Dulcy. She thought the mallet would come around but the brothers watched and Victor froze with the thing in midair, looking like a bad actor.

"Hold her," he said, but none of them moved. Victor cackled in rage and dragged her along while he smashed the panes of the greenhouse. He didn't seem to notice that glass was flecking his arms, and her feet were too cold to feel it. When he'd broken every pane he could reach, he hurled the mallet up into the air and splintered the glass in the loft, then let go of her and stood and simply breathed.

It was too windy for anyone to hear up the street, and Brach was in Gerry's jail. If she wasn't deaf from blows, Brach's wife probably thought this was a lover's waltz.

"Did he build this for you? I'll gut him with his own glass while you watch, and then I'll burn him up."

"I built it for myself," said Dulcy.

Victor reached back down, his hand quivering again at the effort to take her arm. Back across the lawn; now she felt the glass in her feet, but she focused on the wrist bearing her along, and as they went through the door, she bit him. He pulled her off by her hair and pushed her—fingertips only—into a chair at the table. He looked in the icebox and the pantry and put a bottle of cider on the table, but he didn't seem to know what to do with it and paced around, opening drawers. "I will have you pack your things. Henning's finding your lover. He'll put him in that greenhouse alive, and we'll burn him to death."

"I don't have a lover," said Dulcy. "I didn't leave to have a lover."

The skin tightened on Victor's face. She ducked just as his arm came at her, so that he only clipped the side of her head. She rocked in the chair but didn't fall. "That was a mistake," he said. "Where's your luggage?"

"No," said Dulcy.

He hurled the remnant of the green book, and she heard the river pebbles finally break out of the spine, ricochet against the tile. Outside, someone called unhappily in Swedish. "This isn't me anymore," said Dulcy. "I'm someone else now. I'd heard you were, too. I'd heard you were getting married."

"I'd rather not. She doesn't understand, Dulcy. She isn't good company, like you were."

She kept her voice even. "I don't have the money, and I don't know what Dad did with it."

"I'd rather think you ran away because you'd stolen the money than found me unbearable, but I'll admit you don't seem to have it. And so I'll forgive you, and we will begin again. I will have found you, and it will be a love story." He pulled out a chair and sat down next to her. "Go upstairs to pack. Henning and Carl will be back with the man, soon, and Ansel and Martin will keep watch."

Henning's army. In the glow from the kitchen light, Dulcy could see Ansel sitting on her porch swing. He looked nervous. She picked up the bottle of cider. "Are you going to kill me?"

"Of course I'm not going to kill you. I'm going to bring you home."

"No."

She swung the bottle of cider against his head and gouged at his face with the jagged stem as he rocked back. Have a scar, she thought. Feel it.

Then she ran in her head; in the real world, she made it two feet closer to the door before he slammed a fist into her skull. She lay on her back in a blurred world and listened to her own breathing and the putt of a car engine on the street. Victor bent over her, dripping blood onto her face. "Pack your things, or go without them."

"No." She slashed at his arm with the bottle's broken neck.

Victor screamed and began to kick at her, howling to the men outside that he was bleeding to death. She curled up and felt cold air flood the kitchen as Henning surged into the room and knocked Victor to his knees, then flat.

"You fucking idiot."

"I'm dying," said Victor. He was glassy-eyed, terrified, staring down at his leaking arm; his blood ran across the floor toward Dulcy.

Henning found a rag on the counter and tied a tourniquet. "We'll find a doctor to stitch you, and get you on the train." He crouched down, peered at her face, waved his hand, seeing if she really saw him, then stood.

"Don't speak to me that way," said Victor.

Henning climbed to his feet, stepping around Victor's blood. "How should I, then? You said you'd only talk. Why do you ruin yourself?"

"Get her packed," said Victor.

"She won't go with you, Victor," said Henning. "And if you've killed her, understand you'll now have to kill half the town, after the girl at the hotel finishes discussing our visit."

"I want him dead."

"He is dead. Go look in the greenhouse. We brought him back in his car. Get to the train with Carl, and Ansel will light the fire. We'll follow in a few days."

Victor crawled toward her; she felt his breath on her cheek. "Go," said Henning.

And they were gone. Dulcy opened her eyes and watched a spider move across her ceiling. But there was Henning again, and for just a moment, before he smiled down at her, she wondered if he was there to kill her. He touched her stomach. "Did he know?"

She shook her head. "Good," he said; he stroked her cheek. "I'll have the little boy from the hotel bring a doctor. He liked you, for sure, not like that bitch of a girl. I want you to know, down there in the greenhouse, it's not him. It's not your person. All right?"

He held up his bloody hands. "All right," said Dulcy, starting to love him again.

"It was my person, for my poor brother. And I want you to know that I knew you were alive, I heard from a banker in Butte but said nothing; I wanted you to have a chance. Even after he saw the stupid film, that waste of money, I didn't think he would do such a thing as this. I will not let him again. What will your friend do?"

"I don't know," said Dulcy.

"You ask this man to let it go, to get well." He bent down and kissed her forehead. "Don't worry about the fire. It won't travel."

And he was gone. She thought about how she would kill Victor when she could move again, just as he'd wanted to kill Walton, just as he would have killed Walton if Walton had only remembered where he'd hidden the money. She'd kill Victor just as soon as her vision cleared and she had her rage back.

She rolled on her side and watched Victor's blood dry on her pretty white tile, all around the bits of the green book, the pages the river had rinsed and the gravel that had lodged in the spine. To live is to suffer, Martha would say. Have a piece of cake. Have that whiskey, just one glass.

The light in the room had gone orange, and for a moment, before she realized the greenhouse was burning, she thought she was dying. Above the wind she heard more glass break and a popping sound, a gun or the metal ribs snapping. She reached out and rolled a pebble from the green book's binding in her fingers, held it up to the glow, reached for another. When Irving and Macalester ran through the door she had a handful, and they thought she'd been trying to clean the blood on the floor; she had to tuck the pebbles under the sink when they weren't looking.

• • •

When Lewis arrived early the next morning, her face was a swollen, stitched mess; Macalester wouldn't let her out of bed for the baby's sake. Lewis moved around the room, putting fresh clothes in his valise. "Stay."

"Of course I'll stay." But he lied. He meant the rest—that he felt this was his fault, that he should have known—but she could see his eyes planning on leaving even when he was an inch away from her, tears running down his face. He had a kind of a blank *I'll do what I fucking want to do* look. The unthinking part of him would fade, she thought, before he had a chance to act.

When he left, Margaret came to stay, with Samuel coming in and out. Dulcy let the official story float up the stairwell, her friends' overheard conversations with the people who stopped by: Gerald Fenoways, Dulcy's deranged admirer, had discovered that she'd married Lewis Braudel, and beaten her, and made a pyre for himself in her greenhouse. Gerry had been dining at the Elite, wooing the hotel's new owners, when he'd received a note and run out to his car. Fenoways' body had only been half-burned, and he was still holding the gun he'd used to shoot himself in the head as the fire took hold.

On the second day, Margaret hid upstairs with her from a visiting Mrs. Whittlesby, and they listened to Samuel elaborate on this story. Beyond people like Mrs. Whittlesby, no one seemed surprised about the Lewis part of the story, though it gave people something happy to natter about. Of course they'd all guessed, and they were a little offended that the couple hadn't simply told their friends, but who would have imagined Gerry was capable of any secrecy whatsoever, and what a horrible thing that he'd even dream she'd reciprocate.

Dulcy wondered about the note Henning had sent into the Elite, what the bait had been, how he'd made sure that Gerry was alone, what he'd said and done to Gerry before he killed him, what damage the fire had hidden. But some of the answer was obvious, the longer she heard Samuel's calm voice rise up the stairwell: *who on earth will mourn that man?*

On the third day, she put on her clothes and walked downstairs. "Please get Lewis to come back."

"He's fine," said Samuel, bland and cheery. "He had to meet a *Century* editor in Denver. He telegrammed to check on you this morning."

Samuel had probably been half in love with Henning, too.

• • •

Lewis returned two days later, on the noon train. It was a pretty Indian summer day, and Mrs. Brach had taken to playing her piano, and Dulcy, who noticed she preferred Mozart to church hymns, was listening on the porch when he appeared. He put down his bag and kissed her. "Are you feeling better? Should you be up?"

"Macalester says I'll be fine." She watched his arm shake as he took a long sip from her water glass. "But should I ask James to come check on you?"

"Let me rest, let me sleep, and then let's get out for a bit. I know we thought of staying here for another month or so, but I'd rather go sooner, tomorrow or even later today. Does that make sense?"

He watched her; she nodded. "I've been dreaming about the hammock for hours. It's such a beautiful day." He reached for the quilt she'd put on the swing and started down to the hammock he'd strung between the new wall and a cottonwood. He ignored the charred pile that had been the greenhouse. "Just an hour or so."

She watched him climb into the hammock, then went into the kitchen and pulled his clothes from the valise, thinking blankly about washing things, getting a girl in to help if they were really going to leave. She started to toss the dirty clothes into the cellar instead of carrying them down—she would never be Martha—but paused at a stain, wondering how much wine a man could possibly spill, before she understood that the stiff dark blotch on his shirtfront was blood. She reached back into the bag and pulled his father's gun from the inside sleeve, turning it over in her hands. She dipped a dishrag in her glass of water and wiped away the red-brown smudge, then dried the gun and tucked it into a kitchen drawer. She climbed down to the cellar to salt and soak the shirt and the silk waistcoat, spackled in more blood.

Back upstairs, she pulled his notebook and a folded Denver *Post* from the valise. He'd saved the Bozeman–Denver ticket, and he'd scribbled notes about a meeting at the Brown Palace with a fellow reporter, an account of the area's swelling wealth. He'd saved a reccipt for his room, too, and she wondered why he'd even bothered with this ruse, and how much time he'd been forced to kill in a lobby easy chair, surrounded by fancier potted plants than the Elite could manage, far below the balcony where she'd stood so many months earlier.

Dulcy was about to close the valise when she noticed a scrap of pale blue paper, crammed in a crack in the leather lining. She pried it out, and held it for a long time:

> *The Film Society of Seattle presents*
> *a lecture by Mr. H. Falk, member of the London Society,*
> *on the Importance of Adapting Shakespeare to the Screen.*
> *Eight o'clock in the evening, October 26, 1905.*

She smoothed out the Denver *Post*. Lewis had left it open to the appropriate article.

THEORIES ON SEATTLE DEATH

Businessman Who Leapt from Hotel Window Described as Depressed; An Echo of His Beloved and Her Father

Despite theories that mining magnate Victor Maslingen owed money to the wrong sort of people, and rumors of newspaper unions or a jealous husband, Seattle authorities now assume that his death yesterday was a suicide.

Due to his financial losses suffered a year ago, Mr. Maslingen had sold his interest in the Seattle *Intelligencer*. He subsequently decided upon selling the Butler Hotel, where he maintained an apartment; he felt little affinity for the city following his partner's and fiancée's deaths. Though a buyer had been quickly located, earthquake damage had been found in the foundation during preparations for its sale, and the price of the property was in question.

Immediately following Mr. Maslingen's leap from his study window on the seventh floor, police located his close associate, Mr. Henning Falk, at the Film Society, where he was in the midst of a lecture. According to Mr. Falk, Mr. Maslingen had increasingly shunned companionship and indulged in black moods and suspicious thoughts; he habitually kept the door to his study locked, and it was so when police arrived. A housekeeper sleeping on the floor above heard no shot, and no visitors were noted in the hotel lobby, or by the elevator operator.

It would appear from the scene, and evidence of bleeding at his desk, that Mr. Maslingen fired a pistol into his abdomen and paused for a time before finishing himself in the window.

Though a pen and paper were ready, he did not write a note; though a shot to the head would have seemed sensible, all attest to Mr. Maslingen's vanity.

She wondered if they'd only met for a drink, before Henning handed Lewis the key to the study, or if they'd had dinner and talked for a while. She imagined the sound of the elevator rising, the civilized world's version of a man engine; maybe Victor had been too drunk to hear it, or maybe he'd thought Henning was returning early.

She wondered how long Lewis had watched Victor bleed before he threw him out the window, and she wondered what had been said.

Back on the porch steps, she sat and watched the hammock, willing it to move. She imagined Lewis's chest rising with each breath, the speckled cheekbone, the long-lidded sleeping eyes opening and looking at her and his lips moving to say *I wanted to see him fall.*

When the hammock finally swayed she walked down to the burned greenhouse. She carried a trowel and a sieve and her old dirty gloves, and pulled away a few larger charred pieces until she found what had been the trunk, and what had been Walton's notebooks. She dug through the ash, dumping it into the sieve, sorting out diamonds from the charred notebooks that had kept them safe. *Burn me, boil me*; a note to a daughter, a secret recipe to release the gems from the bindings.

In the last few months, she'd tried to leave Walton untouched, to take him in small doses so that he wouldn't shrink. She was afraid of forever losing the sweet, blistering sense of him alive and curious and wandering, all over the map in all sorts of ways; she didn't want him to be reduced to his end. But now she let him come again as she picked through the ash, saving some small bright wisps of fabric along with the stones: she saw him moving through the bright sunlight of Cape Town, his elegant, deceiving frame in crumpled linen, his mind shifting from whatever woman he'd spent the night with to the task at hand, the meeting with the bookbinder and the redemption of his partnership with a bad man. He would have been happy, hiding something, making a beautiful, touchable puzzle, a gift to his daughter to make up for introducing her to the man who'd almost ruined her life.

In the kitchen, Dulcy rinsed the diamonds, retrieved the ones from the green book's binding, still hidden under the sink, and dropped all of them in the brocade bag with the keys. She'd have to share them with Henning; it was only fair. She pulled out her own valise, and she made a list of things to retrieve from the hotel, and all the places they might go.

Then she went down to wake Lewis, to pack with him for another train.

ACKNOWLEDGMENTS

This is fiction; beyond being a woman who has sometimes wanted to run away, I'm not an expert about anything I describe, and while I did a great deal of research, I also put it away for the actual writing. Although my great-great-grandfather William Ludlow was a mining engineer from Cornwall whose notebooks edged me into the idea of this book, none of my characters are real, and I fictionalized my settings a bit, and I sometimes cheated on timing. There was an Elite Hotel in Livingston, Montana (now the Murray Hotel), but in 1905 the building was two stories shorter; the first transcontinental phone call wasn't made until 1915; and while many people have erred in judging the temperature of Yellowstone Park's waters, none to my knowledge did so due to an earthquake.

I owe thanks to many people, but I would especially like to mention Sabrina Crewe, Melissa Atkinson, and Maryanne Vollers for constructive and witty criticism; the people at Grove, for caring and helping; Dara Hyde and Dan Smetanka and the great humans of Counterpoint for turning this into a real book; and Steve, Will, and John Potenberg for their constant love and patience.

© Melanie Nashan

JAMIE HARRISON, who has lived in Montana with her family for almost thirty years, has worked as a caterer, a gardener, and an editor, and is the author of four previous novels.